LEAGUE
OF
GALLIZE
SHIFTERS

STALKING
HIS MATE

DIANNA
LOVE

STALKING HIS MATE
League of Gallize Shifters series

MATING A GRIZZLY is book three in a series of unusual shifters.

Having spent her life as a captive, Siofra escapes when her power surfaces to save her from an attack, which exposes her as a non-human. All she wants to do is find her brother who is also being hunted, then vanish to live free from shifters. That was the plan and it would have worked if a golden-eyed jaguar shifter hadn't stepped between her and a dangerous jackal, throwing a major kink in her escape when she falls for the sexy protector.

Rory didn't choose to be a jaguar shifter and is determined to not mate even though he faces death from the Gallize mating curse if he doesn't. The end may come sooner than he expects when his jaguar loses the ability to heal them, but that doesn't prevent Rory from racing in to save a young woman from a vicious predator. The moment Siofra is in his arms and his power reaches out to hers, he struggles against the primal pull of the one woman he's drawn to as a mate. Even if he didn't feel the need to end his bloodline, she hates shifters.

None of that will matter if Rory fails to stop the deadly Black River Pack from using Siofra in a grisly experiment when she's caught in a trap.

"GRAY WOLF MATE is a truly ground-breaking paranormal romance. Ms. Love is a writer who can conceive an innovative idea, and then cleverly bring it to life for readers to enjoy." Always Reviewing (League of Gallize Shifters book 1)

Note: All the League of Gallize Shifters books are stand-alone paranormal romances. For information on print preorder, visit AuthorDiannaLove.com.

DEDICATION

Thank you, Sherry Arnold,
for all your support through the years.

CHAPTER 1

Q

"WHAT DO YOU WANT, DYSON?" Siofra forced the question out as calmly as she could while her gaze darted to the warehouse exit door.

Too far away.

She'd never reach it before the jackal shifter caught her.

"I'm here to see you," Dyson replied, his sarcastic tone honed to a nasty edge.

She'd feared he would say that. "Give me a minute to finish."

Sweat poured down her face and soaked the T-shirt and bib overalls she wore. Big fans on each end of the metal building spun, but did little against the stifling August heat, even this late in the day. With Dyson standing so close, though, she perspired for a whole new reason. He'd been sniffing around her for the last two weeks, but she wanted nothing to do with him ... or any other shifter.

Why would *any* of the guards want her as a bed partner anyhow? She looked as drab and plain as she felt, plus they thought she was ... *off*. Who wouldn't be in her shoes? She'd been captured as a child and believed she was human ... only to find out differently.

That secret would die with her. She would never let the ...

She stopped short of thinking the name of her captors. They claimed to be able to hear her thoughts.

As a child, that had terrified her.

As an adult she had doubts but erred on the side of caution, because those people were definitely not human.

She'd been working her fingers to the bone in her current

misery camp. A sweatshop in the truest sense of the word. They'd stuck her in a crappy metal building with no air conditioning, somewhere in South Texas.

She'd found out that much about her location, but it didn't matter. No one was riding in on a white horse to save her.

She'd lived in camps like this since the night jackal shifters had shown up at her father's one-room apartment in Gary, Indiana, killing him and taking her.

At six years old, she'd been starving in Gary and freezing during the winter.

Compared to that, she'd at first thought getting fed and clothed was living a dream.

Once she had a full stomach, it became painfully clear she was not in paradise. She spent months expecting someone to rescue her.

Fifteen years as a captive had destroyed that hope.

"Your minute is up, bitch," Dyson bit out.

"Please. I have to finish this last romper," she said, turning the toddler outfit over to stitch a seam she'd already sewn once. She hadn't minded the last camp so much, because she'd been in charge of the small children. Older female captives had taught her reading, writing and more as she grew up. Later on, Siofra jumped at the chance to tutor the younger children. Sure, they were all captives, but the camp leaders didn't want to deal with idiots.

She didn't realize until later that an educated captive was more valuable for trading or selling when not kept for breeding.

She couldn't put this shifter off forever. "Your boss will be upset if I don't get done, Dyson."

"I don't give a fuck what you have left. They blew the whistle three minutes ago. You shoulda been done by now."

She'd heard the 7:30 PM signal for the end of her ten-hour sewing shift, but had stayed because she loved making children's clothing. It was the one bright break in her day. She hoped some child enjoyed the extra little flower and bug designs she added.

No sewing on Saturday, which sucked. Sewing, especially for children, beat being elbow-deep in washing clothes and cleaning the living quarters for animals like the one looming over her.

Tomorrow *was* Saturday, right?

Didn't matter.

What did matter was getting out of here and away from Dyson, who had a dangerous ego. If someone observed him from afar, he'd be considered attractive, with pale brown hair, thick-lashed eyes and straight teeth.

Up close, it was easier to see how all of that hid a monster and not just a jackal shifter.

She'd been lonely for years, but as much as she craved being with someone, it would not be any of the jackal shifters guarding this camp.

And never Dyson. She knew for sure she had not given him any encouragement, just the opposite. So why had he been coming on to her lately?

Most of the guards gave her a wide berth. They thought she might be possessed.

They might be right.

Her skin crawled every time Dyson flirted with her.

No flirting today.

Tension poured off him, mixing with the stifling heat to suffocate her more. She folded over a new seam to add one more row of stitches. Sweat trickled into her eyes.

Why wasn't Dyson out training with the others?

She'd once seen him snap and beat another guard to a pulp. Might be a good idea to talk to him and figure out what was going on while she did her best to drag out the time in hopes someone else would show up.

"What do you need me to do, Dyson?" she asked as if she cared. "As soon as I finish here, they want me at the kitchen." That would be her next six-hour shift of the day.

"That'll all wait," he said in a gravelly voice that sounded only half human. "I've got a half hour free and we're gonna fuck."

"What?" She jerked her head up.

He started unbuttoning his shirt.

"No." She pushed the chair back, scraping its wooden legs on the concrete floor. "I am not interested in having sex with you." She wasn't having sex with anyone, but definitely not a shifter.

She'd only had sex with one teenage boy, and that had been at a really low point when she'd been moved to a new work camp at sixteen. He'd been sweet to her and she'd been so lonely. He'd caught her during a hormone overload. She'd been happy for about two days.

The camp leader found out and the boy disappeared.

Dyson yanked his shirt off and tossed it.

His eyes switched between his natural brown and bright yellow. Not fully glowing, but close. Being a shifter meant nonhuman characteristics to begin with, but over the years she'd come to learn that glowing eyes were a sign of impending danger, particularly with Dyson.

She might be twenty-one years old, but she had little experience with men.

Dyson had bent over and started pulling off his boots.

Enough of this crap. "I don't understand, Dyson. I thought you had a girlfriend." Of course, Bernadette slept with half the guards.

His jaw muscles flexed and the crazy in his eyes kicked up another level. "You're wasting my half hour. Get. Naked. Now."

She glanced around, hoping the other two who normally stayed after would help her out, but ... they were gone.

Does my life not suck enough that I have to deal with this, too?

Baatar would fuss at her for staying after the end of a shift. She could hear him grumbling in that deep, soft voice of his. "Never be alone, *Sheef-rah.*" He was the only one who ever pronounced her name right, and the only man in the world she trusted. She thought of him as a brother, her sole family after years of having no one in her corner.

He said little about his past, just that he'd been brought here from China, but he didn't sound Chinese. His accent reminded her of a captive she'd met from Ukraine. Baatar had treated her as a younger sister from the day he arrived six months ago, the same day he stepped in to protect her the first time.

Also, he didn't see her as a freak, probably because he didn't fit in either.

She stood and started wringing her hands, trying to think of how to escape.

Baatar was doing some kind of training today, too far away to be of any help, which was probably why jerkface here chose this moment. Baatar despised all the guards but would think she was currently safe in a group of women.

Barefoot now, Dyson unzipped his pants.

She'd say he looked determined, but that would be too kind for the predatory gaze staring her down.

She could not overpower a shifter and definitely not this one, whose breath often smelled of a lime tea he drank. Jugo Loco juice, a stimulant they got from wolf shifters. The Black River wolf pack was a crazy bunch. They had chemists developing drugs to hype up a shifter, as if anyone needed that?

Backing up slowly, she searched for a weapon.

The only thing on the next table was a tape dispenser for sealing packages.

Death by tape gun, sure, that would do it.

Completely confident that she would do as he said, Dyson bent over again to shove his jeans down past his knees.

Her heart raced and the roar of blood rushed through her ears. She had one chance to escape and it was right this second.

She took off for the side door, exiting into the wooded area surrounding the building. Sweatshop camps were always deep in the woods to make it easy for shifters to run down captives.

Dyson's roar shook the building she'd just vacated.

She couldn't outrun him, but she was not going to stand there and allow him to rape her.

She'd hurt him somehow.

Crashing sounded behind her, which meant he was still in human form. He'd be so much quieter as a jackal running through these woods. Not shifting only meant he had no doubt he could take her down on two legs.

Panting hard, she made a mental note to take up running if she survived this. She'd rather find a place to read quietly than get sweaty exercising, but in hindsight, that had not been good planning on her part. She needed to be stronger for any hope of living to her next birthday.

She could hear him cursing.

No time left to second guess.

Stumbling to a stop, Siofra turned around and held her arms straight up in the air, as if calling to someone.

She had one play.

Making her voice as deep as she could, she shouted, "Spirits of the light, come to me now." That so wasn't happening, but the jackals all thought she was crazy, which she intended to play to the hilt right now.

Dyson burst into the small space where she'd chosen to stand her ground. "I will kill you, bitch, if you screw with me."

Odd threat considering he specifically said he *wanted* her to screw him.

What would help her sell crazy?

She moaned and swayed from side to side, waving her arms and lowering her lashes until she could just see Dyson. "Yes, I do need your help, spirits. No, please don't kill him," she said in a trance-like voice. "That would be wrong." She peeked at the shifter through half-closed eyes.

He frowned at her, but he wasn't charging forward.

"No, really," she begged, and moaned some more. "That would be such a ... brutal loss to his manhood. Just protect me with your loving arms."

Dyson leaned forward as her voice dropped to a whisper. Maybe he was buying it.

She started nodding. "I understand. I understand. If you feel you need to use force then do ... as you deem necessary. I will pray for his ... "

Unexpected cold air rushed over her heated skin.

Crap.

She peeked out to find someone else had joined them.

A young woman with curly brown hair, wearing a plain white blouse and long brown skirt right out of the Victorian era stood between Siofra and Dyson, wringing her hands.

The woman happened to also be translucent and floating above the ground.

No, no, no. This was the wrong time to be distracted by someone ethereal.

Dyson showed no sign of seeing the ghost.

Siofra wanted to only *pretend* she was dangerous to be around, not bring in spirits who generally got in the way and caused more trouble than help. She knew the pattern. They'd started showing up when she suffered through her first period.

Not the best memory of passing into womanhood.

That little distraction was all it took to snap Dyson out of his momentary hesitation.

He lunged at Siofra.

CHAPTER 2

SIOFRA DODGED SIDEWAYS BEFORE DYSON'S body hit her. He caught an arm around her, though, taking them both to the ground.

She pushed at him. Shoving a truck would be easier.

He yanked at the straps on her denim bibs, breaking the button clasps. She kicked her feet so hard her shoes flew off.

He ignored her, ripping the material and yanking on each side.

Her ghost woman moved around frantically, looking lost in the middle of all this.

Siofra couldn't spare attention for someone who was as much help as a snowball in a firefight. She shoved her knees up hard, trying to knock Dyson off balance.

Not happening.

She screamed at the top of her lungs. "*Helllppp!*" Maybe Baatar would—

Dyson slapped her across the face.

The world spun.

When her eyes focused, the ghost woman looked furious and slapped both hands at Dyson.

His head passed through her air slaps.

Dyson sat up, looked around and muttered, "What the fuck?"

Tears burned Siofra's eyes and her jaw felt knocked out of shape, but she deepened her voice and tried again. "It's a demon ghost and it's pissed at you."

He looked down at her. "You don't scare me, witch."

"I'm not a witch, asshole."

"Exactly. You're nothing but a freak."

She had never felt so powerless, which was hard to imagine after years of imprisonment and slave labor.

Another ghost appeared in her usual attire of jeans with a T-shirt that read *Live. Love. Laugh.*

Right. Great advice from someone Siofra had never seen laugh, plus the ghost needed to draw a circle around the word "live" with a line through it.

This spirit came to her from time to time, but never spoke. She'd been a pretty woman when she died, except for the sad look that never left her eyes. Her presence must have pushed the other frantic ninny ghost aside, because the first one slowly became invisible.

Sad Lady bent down and put her hands on Siofra's feet. A pressure pushed the soles of her feet down on the ground and buzzing started under her heels.

Was pinning her feet to the ground supposed to be helpful?

Major spirit fail.

Dyson's claws shot out from his fingers. He sliced across the middle of her overalls, ripping the front in two. He laughed, a creepy sound. "This is gonna be fun."

Tears poured from her eyes. She cried at the crappy life she'd been given and pleaded with the ghost in a thin voice, "Help me, please help me."

The woman in jeans faded and blinked out, but the curly-headed ghost was back, wringing her hands in between pointing at Siofra's feet.

So. Not. Helping!

Dyson slashed a claw across Siofra's chest once more, this time breaking skin. She yelled at the burning sensation.

His weight held her in place with the ease of a building sitting on her. She called out for help again and got a piece of her overalls shoved in her mouth.

The ghost frantically pointed at her feet.

Siofra silently screamed, *What?*

Dyson popped open the sides of her overalls and every muscle in her body tightened in fear. Panic exploded through her. Her body vibrated. She dug her fingers into his arms, trying to push him away. Her toes curled into the dirt from terror over what

Dyson was about to do.

A sizzle of energy vibrated against the balls of her feet, then moved up into her calves.

What was happening to her? She didn't want this monster to think being attacked turned her on.

Her ghost started floating away as if her job was done.

Damn ghosts always showing up at the worst time and never making any sense.

Siofra lunged up again, but Dyson slapped his massive hand on her stomach, holding her in place. He used his free hand to grab the waist of her overalls to pull them down.

No! She would not let him do this.

Siofra lunged up to push her thumbs into his eyes.

He was faster and jerked his head to the side, then gave her another wallop that sent stars through her gaze and knocked the rag from her mouth. But pausing to strike her had interrupted his attempt to get her pants down.

The buzz climbing her legs grew stronger, and the energy moved up higher.

Maybe she *was* a freak and crazy, just like everyone said, but no woman deserved this. She shouted, "Why, dammit? Why are you doing this? I've never given you reason to hurt me."

Lowering his face until his glowing eyes stared hard into hers, he said, "It's your fault they want to give Bernadette to the Black River pack, because she's beautiful and not crazy. All I have to do is get you pregnant and your ass is out of here in her place. I get my woman back and I won't have to look at you again. I tried to stomach doing it the nice way. You put me off too long and now I'm losing her in four days. You better test positive before that or you'll do this every day from here on out."

He thought to get Siofra pregnant? How could he not know about her?

She couldn't believe the stupidity of this.

Slapping at his hands, she shouted, "You idiot. You can't get me pregnant. They already told me I'm sterile." That word still sent her stomach tumbling when she thought about it. On one level she was grateful that she could not have a baby they would then take from her and sell, but in her dreams she lived as a free person and had a life with a family of her own.

Being a guard meant Dyson should have heard about her infertility. The camp doctor had put her through additional tests to confirm it.

"I've gotten plenty of you bitches pregnant for the bosses," Dyson bragged. "You're no different than the rest other than being a loony piece of ass." He shredded what was left of her T-shirt and moved his claw to rip a new opening all the way down the front of her pants.

Panic overrode all thought.

She grabbed his forearms and used them to yank her upper body off the ground. "*Noooo!*"

Power spread all at once up into her chest, flooding her arms and finally her fingers where she grasped his thick biceps.

Her burst of energy made contact with Dyson.

He went rigid, as if hit with a lightning strike. He bellowed in pain, then started shaking.

She couldn't open her fingers to release him. They were stuck to his body. Energy buzzed so loud in her ears she couldn't hear anything else.

He kept shuddering and his neck muscles stuck out unnaturally from strain. She feared they would snap and veins would burst.

She would never survive his retaliation, because shifters healed quickly and he'd be out for blood.

Finally the buzzing calmed. Her fingers felt like they would obey her mind now, but she was too shocked by the wild look frozen on Dyson's face to move a muscle.

A roar of fury reached her right before a massive boot kicked Dyson off of her. The shifter's body went airborne, slamming a tree and falling to the ground.

She dropped onto her back with her hands in the air and the tips of her fingers smoking.

That was new and not good.

"Are you okay, Siofra?" a deep voice asked in a panicked voice.

She could see his blurry face and hear his words, but her lips wouldn't work.

He dropped down to a knee and shook her hard. "Siofra, wake up. They will come soon."

Blinking, she sharpened her focus.

Taller and with way more muscle mass than Dyson, her camp brother had a savage look to him with his dark beard and hair askew. He'd been the first person to care about her in all these years.

She started shivering and shaking her head. "I think I ..."

"Calm down, Siofra. I am sorry to be rough, but guards are howling. They know Dyson is dead."

Dyson dead? How was he dead? *Did I do that?*

The guards would kill her.

"I don't hear them," she mumbled, still hearing the energy buzzing in her ears. Thankfully, she hadn't hurt Baatar.

He kept talking in a low, but urgent voice. "Yes, but I hear them. You must leave." He lifted her to her feet and yanked his shirt over his head to cover her.

"How can I get out of here?" she mumbled, not able to form a clear thought yet. Then she lifted her head. Even she could hear their howls now.

Panic hit her with a renewed punch.

Her mind snapped back to the moment. She argued in a string of confusion, "I don't understand. What happened? It's all woods around us. They'll catch me in no time."

Baatar dug through Dyson's clothes as he talked. "When they bring me in, I am not in deep sleep like they think. I watch whole way. There is road two miles on other side of river. Cross river, get to road and do not stop. Dark will fall soon. Find someone to help you, but be careful. Once guards know you are gone, they will send someone to highway to hunt you. I will keep them busy and give you good head start."

Leave without him? No. And he hadn't answered how the shifter could be dead. Shifters healed, always. Had Baatar somehow killed him while she was out of it? "Come with me, Baatar. You said we'd find a way out of here and live safe one day." Her hands trembled as she tied the ripped parts of her overalls around her waist to hold up what was left of her pants. Baatar somehow had her shoes on her feet, and in the next moment, her clothes were straightened enough for her to run.

"I wish for hat to cover your white hair, Siofra," Baatar grumbled, still getting her ready.

She'd figure out hiding her hair if she got out of here. "Come with me," she repeated. "Please."

His dark eyes held a longing for a second, but he shook his head. "Listen, baby girl. You cannot stay. This is best chance for you to escape. I will distract them plenty time for you to get away."

"What about you?"

"No worry. I *will* get out, too. If they do not catch you tonight, I am gone tomorrow. I can move faster alone." He grabbed her hand and shoved a wad of cash into it. "Use this to find way out of area fast, but save some for food. Do not wait for me or we will both be caught."

She stared at the money. "Where'd you get this?"

"Dyson's pants. He got paid two days ago. Did not leave camp to spend yet. Put somewhere safe."

She made two stabs at shoving the money in a pocket on her pants. If she kept shaking this bad, she'd never make it.

Baatar grabbed her shoulders, drawing her full attention to his gray eyes. "Stay away from shifters no matter what. Even females. Do not be so nice to them."

He meant when she'd cared for a female jackal's child when the woman lost her mate. Sometimes life got so confusing. She found male jackal shifters disgusting, but she couldn't so easily hate a woman and child who were not a threat to her.

"I know. I will." She shook her head. "I'm sorry I didn't listen to you and leave the building the minute I heard the whistle. This is all my fault."

"No! Not your fault that bastard attacked you, but be more careful starting now. You have to watch your own back until we find each other again. You know where I will go when I am free. You show up, leave the sign we talked about, then find place to wait. Do not get impatient."

"I won't. I'll wait." She had zero patience, but for Baatar she'd do her best so he was proud of her and they could reunite.

"Go now." He turned her toward the river, but her gaze fell on Dyson's body at the base of the tree as she swung around.

Baatar had not done that. What *had* happened? That power she'd felt ... that had killed a shifter? She hated those jackals even more for this. She'd never hurt anyone before.

Now, she was a killer.

"Isn't there a fence?" Yes, she wanted to escape, but this was all too much to process so quickly.

"There is fence before river, but you can climb over. No electricity, but sharp wire. Be careful. Jackals have no worry about captives getting over it. They are so sure they can track and outrun humans, they do not think about one running far enough to go over fence."

Baatar had struggled to hide that he wasn't entirely human, because he was abnormally strong and fast.

But so were the guards.

"They'll catch me," she worried aloud.

He shook his head. "They will be too busy chasing me. First I leave my scent all over this place and Dyson. Then I run in different directions, like zigzag. I am bigger prize because fools think they will gain more money for me."

Baatar gave her a hug that warmed her chilled heart. She'd never find a man as good as him to spend her life with. After her father handed her over without a fight, only to die in spite of that, and now Dyson tried to rape her, she had no use for men.

Escape and survival were her only goals. "Be careful, Baatar."

"I will. Keep head down and find hat soon. Do not show eyes either. Do whatever you must to stay alive and hide from these bastards."

Nodding, she turned to leave and stared at Dyson's rigid body again. "I just want you to know I didn't mean ... to kill him." And she still had no idea how she'd actually done it, but suspected her ethereal visitors had upped their game from being irritating to dangerous.

Baatar said, "Do not look at him or waste guilt over that prick. He did not deserve his life."

Howling rose in the distance, coming their way this time.

Baatar started wiping his scent all over Dyson's clothes. "No more time. You are strong. You can do this, Baby Girl. Go!"

She took off running, plenty of adrenaline still racing through her.

Behind her, it sounded like a pack of giants were breaking

down trees. Not looking back, she kept spinning her feet as fast as she could.

She would not waste this chance Baatar was affording her.

Please let him escape. Don't let them kill him.

He was the first person she'd trusted since being dragged away by strangers as a child.

Now, even Baatar would be gone.

Only until he escaped. She had to believe he would make it out.

He'd told her his plan to head northeast, somewhere cold enough to snow. He'd spoken of a place thousands of miles from here.

Where exactly was *here* besides being in South Texas?

Years of being a bookworm and reading everything she could in outdated magazines would help, but only if she found a map and figured out how to read it. It wasn't like her captors handed out maps to the camp slaves to keep them in the loop.

She worked her way through the woods, plowing through brambles that tore at her already wrecked clothes. It seemed forever before she found a fence with barbed wire strung tight along the top.

Finding a toehold, she lunged up.

Climbing with no experience was difficult to begin with, but then that whole lack-of-exercise issue reared its ugly head again. She struggled over the top, slicing her hands on the barbs and gritting her teeth to keep from making a sound.

Sweat drizzled down her forehead. If a shifter caught her blood scent, he'd be on her in a second. She flopped to the other side with minimal injuries.

The first taste of freedom took her breath.

Her heart thumped wildly at the idea of leaving these people forever.

Getting back to her feet, she checked her hands and ... the wounds were already healing. What. The. Heck? Now that she thought about it, she rubbed her fingers over what should still be a burning cut across her middle, but it felt fine and little blood stained Baatar's shirt.

Had the energy that killed Dyson somehow healed her as it ran through her body? She'd think on it later.

Keep moving. Do not stop. She silently repeated the words Baatar would be telling her right now.

The trees thinned out until she reached the river that supplied their water.

She took in the wide expanse of the fast-moving stream flowing around boulders and frothing where the current slammed up against immovable objects. She wore a pair of slip-on flats and had to be careful not to lose them like she had the one time she'd crossed a river when they'd moved on foot to a new work camp. That had been four years back. Or was it five?

No point keeping up with time passing when someone stole every minute of every day from you. One day turned into the next. Work, work and more work, with just enough food and sleep to keep the laborers strong enough to rinse and repeat. The only reason she knew she'd turned twenty-one had been the humiliating physical exam they gave women of childbearing age who they felt were ready to handle a pregnancy.

Choosing what looked to be the best entry point, she ran thirty feet up the bank to start jumping rocks until she had no choice but to drop into the water and wade across a pool that formed above a drop-off. Slogging through the thigh-deep water drained her energy along with her panic.

Finally on the other side, she dragged her soaked body out on the bank and looked back, expecting to see a jackal after her.

Were they all chasing Baatar?

Please be safe, brother.

She had to keep moving.

Like Baatar had pointed out, it would be dark soon. She had no idea exactly where the road would actually be, but she raced forward in what she hoped was the right direction.

Unlike natural jackals in the wild, the camp shifters weren't primarily nocturnal, but their eyesight was far superior to hers in the dark.

She had no idea if she had covered a mile or two miles, but she kept rushing on. The waning daylight told her it had been a while since she'd left Baatar. Every step away hurt her heart at leaving him, but she couldn't argue with his reasoning. When he escaped, he would be faster without her.

But that didn't ease her worry for him.

As the light dwindled to twilight, everything in the woods around her looked the same. Was she lost? She'd read that lost people often walked in circles.

What if she made a circle and returned to the camp?

She stumbled to her knees, caught her breath and pushed up fast ... only to face another ghost.

This one was an old white guy with a white beard and sad eyes buried in a field of wrinkles. He wore a flannel coat over dark work pants. Clearly, he hadn't died in Texas in August.

She swiped at the sweat about to run into her eyes.

He held a bucket in one hand.

With the other hand, he pointed to her right.

Unlike the last spirit, who never spoke, she heard this old man's voice in her head. *Take that path.*

That happened sometimes, but she'd never seen this old guy before now and some ghosts had been very unhelpful.

Should she trust him?

Exhausted, she muttered to no one in particular, "Screw it. Why question this ghost? Not like I know where I'm going."

She nodded a thank-you at the glowing farmer and raced away in the direction he'd pointed. Her legs pushed through weeds and bushes, slowing her progress. Please don't let her end up running straight to the entrance of Camp Misery, as she and Baatar called their prison.

But a half mile away, she reached a highway. A two-lane country road.

Which way now?

Where was that translucent farmer when she could use another map tip?

She felt a little tingle run up her body as she looked right, then left.

Okay then. Instincts were all she had to go on. She faced the center of the road and closed her eyes, then held her arms out to her sides. Her fingertips pointed in each direction the pavement ran. When her left hand tingled, she opened her eyes and headed that way.

Obviously there was good reason to question her sanity, but she'd lived moment to moment, only for getting through the next task, since six years old. She could stand here worrying about her choice and wasting precious time, then end up captured.

Or she could keep moving.

Darkness had blanketed her in the last few minutes. She'd made a hundred steps on the hard surface when the pretty female ghost in T-shirt and jeans appeared, but the ghost seemed to have a hard time holding her shape.

The spirit held a hand out, as if telling Siofra to stop or wait.

Really? Not the best advice for someone trying to escape.

Out of the sea of black, a little white dog came running up and slid past the ghost, who smiled and nodded.

Some camps had dogs and Siofra liked dogs, but she stood there, caught in confusion.

The little dog's tail wagged and it lifted a paw.

The spirit faded then came back just long enough to point at the dog.

What kind of message was that?

When the animal whined, Siofra squatted quickly to keep it quiet. The pooch jumped into her arms. "Hey, you. Do you have a message for me?" Yep, she was destined to wear a straightjacket. She whispered, "I wish I had time to play, but I'm a little busy trying to stay alive. You should head home." Stupid advice probably since she could see no sign of a house anywhere in this darkness. "You have to go. There are bad beasts in this area."

He licked her face.

She didn't want a jackal to kill him just to hurt her, and they might.

Maybe she could carry him with her in case she saw a house along the way. "Who do you belong to, buddy?"

Headlights came out of the darkness next as a car raced up to her and slammed on brakes so fast Siofra froze in place. If that vehicle held shifters, there was no point in running. They'd catch her in seconds.

Her heart pounded furiously. Baatar would say run anyway, but she couldn't seem to stand up, much less make her legs work.

The dog climbed completely into her lap and shook.

If the car had shifters, she'd help the dog the way Baatar had helped her. She'd take off running and drop the dog quickly in the dark along the way.

The shifters would track her and leave this little guy alone.

Of course, that was assuming she held more value to them than a lost dog.

When the driver door opened, an interior light shined over a young woman, giving Siofra a rush of relief. The woman had her hair twisted up in a bun on top of her head.

Dark eyes peered from her face. "Toto! There you are."

Siofra started to put the dog down so it could go to its owner.

"Oh, no. Don't you put that little bastard down. My mom will kill me if I lose him again." The woman came over and accepted the dog Siofra handed off. Then she gave Siofra a confused look. "What are you doing out here in the middle of nowhere, walking?"

Siofra knew an opening when she heard one. She dug around for an idea based on books she'd read and said, "I had a fight with my boyfriend. I said I wouldn't screw him so he dumped me out here."

The woman's mouth opened in a horrified O shape. "Men are stupid pigs."

"That is the truth."

Toto's keeper asked, "Where're you going?"

That would be harder to answer. "I just want to get back to ... town." She'd heard the shifters talk about going to town.

"You mean Columbus?" The dog kept trying to wiggle out of her hands.

"Yes." Siofra hoped Columbus had a bus station. Was that city even in Texas?

As Toto squirted free, Siofra grabbed him before he completed a nosedive to the ground, and pulled the wiggling fur ball up into her arms.

"You are driving me nuts, Toto," his keeper complained. "See if I let you out to pee again. You'll be tying your favorite part in a knot next time and holding it." The woman looked around and muttered, "What the heck. Someone gave me a ride once. I can do that for you. It's not far out of my way."

"Really?" Siofra asked, having no trouble sounding sincerely desperate. "Thank you so much."

"I'm Lisa."

"I'm Siofra. I really appreciate this."

"Eh, I figure you can't be an axe murderer, you don't even have an axe. Besides, I took two years of karate and you're going to have your hands full holding that little bastard."

Siofra smiled at the odd young woman, happy to find a kindred crazy soul.

She only hoped the jackals couldn't track her in a car.

But what about Baatar?

Would he get away from the ... *Cadells*?

Was she far enough away now that they couldn't hear her thoughts? Was that threat even true? She released a breath of relief at allowing herself to finally think the name of the horrible people who had enslaved her for so long. Now her mind was as free as her body *if* the jackals didn't find her.

CHAPTER 3

Two days later, eastern Ohio

"WELCOME TO OUR FUCKED-UP SUNDAY," Rory muttered and glanced at skies getting darker by the minute even though it was only half past seven. If not for a storm approaching, they'd have another hour until sunset, but at least the rain would cool things. He and the other two Gallize shifters on this team could track during inclement weather.

That wasn't the problem.

None of them could fix the FUBAR they'd just discovered in an abandoned brick plant below this ridge. They were thirty-five miles west of Pittsburgh, Pennsylvania, in a rural section of eastern Ohio.

"Copy that," Justin Labeau whispered in agreement. The bear shifter led today's operation, which had begun as an intelligence-gathering mission. Like Rory and Vic, Justin remained in his human form, but could move his big body with agility that a human his size would envy.

Cutting his dark-brown gaze at Rory, Justin pointed out, "Good thing I brought three of us to do this."

"Yeah, yeah." Rory would give the bear his due, because Rory had asked what the hell they needed three for on this type of operation. Justin had originally wanted four, which Rory had argued against as well. He'd been wrong as hell.

They could use four now.

"Boss wants the new guy brought up to speed, but nobody saw this coming. It may still be a drop point for Jugo Loco, too." Justin shook his head as he turned back to face the scene. Bounty hunters tracked both humans and shifters, but the bunch they were watching today was known for running distribution routes for the Black River pack. Where Rory's team expected illegal product being guarded until trucks showed up, instead there were ten cages holding women and children.

Rory eyed the bounty hunter shifters, also in human form, moving around the dirt lot once used for brick production. Two shifters had the distinctive face tattoo of the Crazy Eights hunters. That part of their intel had been correct. The others might be short-term hires. Trees bordered the tall ridge all the way around to a gate wide enough for a big truck to enter.

At least those weren't humans in the cages.

Humans would be dead or gone by now if the Black River pack was behind this operation. That ruthless organization of rogue wolf shifters kept only prisoners of value.

Humans were food.

Miserable cannibals probably believed they were technically in the right since humans were not shifters.

When shifters came out publicly to humans eight years ago, the Black River pack took full advantage of the chaos that erupted, expanding their territory internationally. They were still headquartered in South America, where they harvested plants for a hallucinogenic tea known as Jugo Loco, but today their network spread through other countries, including the US.

Evidently, experimenting on shifters and distributing the dangerous tea wasn't enough.

No, that bunch also trafficked female shifters.

These bounty hunters were thought to be meeting with the Black River wolf pack about Jugo Loco. That might still happen, but nothing in the intel had mentioned women and children.

As if Justin had heard Rory's thoughts, which he couldn't in human form, he said, "I don't know what the hell they're up to down there, but those guards wouldn't be standing around if their captives were staying here for long. They're expecting someone today, but the question is, how soon? This could turn out okay if we have enough time to bring in backup. If not, this may fuck up our deal with Scarlett."

Rory lifted his binoculars and scanned again, then muttered, "I don't envy the snitch who gave Scarlett Sullivan faulty information. From what Tess said, Scarlett does not tolerate bad intel."

"Tess also said she doesn't work with someone twice if they let her down," Justin growled out a sigh. "This sucks. Scarlett could be a great resource in areas that we don't have contacts. If we don't bring the intel she's expecting in return, she probably won't give us anything again." He looked over at Rory. "Tess said Scarlett's a loner ... and a shifter. Think she might be a cat?"

Rory had wondered the same thing. "I heard that about her, too. Don't know, but a cat would fit. Bet Cole knows."

"He's not going to give up anything Tess gave him in confidence unless a crisis comes up. At that point, Tess would tell us herself now that she's on the team." Justin returned to watching the guards below.

"Based on how Scarlett runs her own network, she could be a lioness," Rory mused.

"That would be different," Justin said. He blew out a long breath and grumbled, "Come on, Vic. I'm ready to find out what's going on down there."

Rory had just murmured his agreement when Ferrell, the jaguar he shared a body with, sent him an image of holding a lion's head down with one massive paw.

Arrogant prick.

Speaking to his jaguar in his mind, Rory said, *That's a lion. We're talking about a female. A lioness. One day, you're gonna meet a predator who'll kick our asses just because you're overconfident, Ferrell.*

Superior, Ferrell corrected telepathically. Smug attitude front and center.

Rory's jaguar didn't talk to him the way some of his Gallize teammates claimed theirs did. Ferrell rarely spoke and only one word when he did.

From what Justin said, his bear kept up a running commentary on everything and had a wicked sense of humor. Those two got along like two halves of one apple.

Gray Wolf started out as Cole's adversary and had been tough for Cole to manage over the past seven years, but they'd discovered how to get along. Finding Tess, Cole's new mate, had settled Gray

Wolf's ass down. Cole and his animal had never been as close as they were now.

Rory had nothing like that.

His jaguar could be a major dick at the worst time. Oh, he could control the beast, for now.

Ferrell tested Rory's limits on a regular basis. Over the past few months, things had become worse. He and his jaguar had some serious disconnect happening. Rory had been slower and slower to heal any significant wound even after shifting, which normally accelerated his healing.

Was his sly-ass jaguar gaming him by holding back power at those times?

Ferrell would act like he agreed sometimes when Rory knew he didn't, especially on one topic. Mating. When the time came, Rory would have the last say on that.

A Gallize had approximately ten years, from the point he first met his animal, to take a mate. That sounded simple enough, but if he failed to find a mate capable of accepting the power shared during bonding, his animal would begin going mad.

That would force their Guardian to put down the dangerous shifter.

The whole complicated thing had started long ago when a witch known as Mother Cadellus placed a curse on the Gallize.

Still, nothing Rory had to be concerned about for another three years.

When the curse began affecting him, he'd submit to the Guardian. His mind was made up.

Mate, Ferrell snarled, interrupting Rory's thoughts.

Rory sent back, *No, Ferrell. We will not mate.*

His beast pounded at him to be released.

Rory grunted in discomfort.

Justin turned to him. "What?"

"Fucking gas, man. Where's Vic? I'm tired of squatting behind a damn bush."

Before Justin could reply, Rory heard two clicks on his comm unit, which indicated Vic was on his way up the hill to report. He'd been sent down to eavesdrop on the shifters. Rory had picked up wolf scents earlier when he'd gotten downwind of the two with face tattoos. He'd smelled hyena, too, and maybe another kind. Bounty hunter outfits utilized shifters who were not aligned with a pack. That left out the Black River Pack wolves actually being part of a group like this one. Those wolves weren't allowed the choice to leave the pack.

Justin lifted his field glasses and scoped another look at the cages covered with camo netting. He'd been the first one to spot a small face peeking out from the corner of one cage. All of them were ready to rip up some shifters for caging those women and children.

Vic eased up to them, silent as a tiny mouse moving through blades of grass. But he was no mouse. The new guy shifted into a wolf. Rory didn't think even Justin knew what kind of wolf Vic hid inside.

The Guardian would know, but he shared information only when he considered it important to the team or the mission.

Tall, at just over six feet, Vic's loose T-shirt and jeans gave him a lanky appearance, but he had rough-cut muscle. Dark brown hair cut short on the sides and thick on top did nothing to round the square head. He'd come back from overseas duty with a hollow look in his blue-gray eyes, but the guy showed up ready to do his part and moved with damn good stealth.

Just the fact that Rory knew nothing about Vic's wolf raised his curiosity antenna.

When the new guy moved close enough, Justin asked, "We good to wait on the backup I called in?"

"I don't think so. They've got the first of two transports showing up in thirty-seven minutes. The road those vehicles will be traveling in on is downwind and guarded at the entrance two miles up."

"Fuck," Justin growled low.

Backup was on the way, but thirty-seven minutes might cut it too close or bring in the cavalry just as the trucks for these captives arrived. The bounty hunters would kill the captives to prevent anyone from testifying against them.

The new guy wasn't through dumping bad news. "They got nine women and four children, all shifters just as we thought."

Rory asked, "Nine? What's in the last cage?"

"Nothing as far as I can tell," Vic replied. "And I don't think those captives are being sold for breeding."

Nodding, Rory cursed to himself. If the Black River pack was behind this, as they suspected, those kidnapped shifters were all headed to bad places. Once the pack had what they needed for experiments in their labs, or for breeding, they shoveled the rest off as slaves.

Some even went to the Cadells, who were the Gallize shifters' number one enemies and followers of Mother Cadellus.

Vic's grim expression didn't let up. "Even if we wait for someone to arrive so we can track them, we can't get in place to follow without shifters sent ahead seeing or smelling us on their exit route. Plus, if we sit back and let them separate those prisoners to ship out, we'll likely never see some of them again."

"Copy that." Justin stretched his neck one way then the other. The bear shifter was ready for action. "We need to contain that site before anyone shows up."

Rory reminded him, "If we go busting in there, we'll lose any hope of intel."

Justin flexed his jaw. "Agreed, so this is what we're going to do. One of us will insert covertly around the east side and hide in the trees. Once that one is in place, the other two go in hot in a frontal assault. When all hell breaks loose, the two at the front take down every guard except one. We let that shifter think he's escaped. Logic says he runs to the woods to get out of the open. With the way this ridge blocks most options for escape, I'm thinking he'll take the tire track path going into the woods behind the cages. When he does, our early insert follows him."

No one said anything at first.

Rory had calculated the risk and thought out loud. "Two can handle those six guards below, if that's all the shifters, but there could be more. If that happens, this plan has every reason to not work." Inserting into enemy territory without enough intel or backup was not the best option, but some operations just had to be made up on the fly.

Still squatting next to him, Justin murmured, "Always the glass-half-full-of-poison guy."

That bear shifter couldn't get through a day without pissing off someone, most often Rory, as of late.

Ignoring Justin's jab, Rory explained patiently, "I'm not saying it won't work, only that I can come up with at least three ways it will go to shit in minutes."

Justin said, "You two do your part and I'll do mine."

That meant Justin intended to be the one inserting, which could put Justin at the highest risk of getting killed if more than one ran into the woods. Also, whoever took off after the runner might be led right into another pack of shifters. Rory and his teammates could each handle more than one *if* these shifters weren't juicing on Jugo Loco.

True to its name, a shifter using the drug might fight like an insane berserker.

Rory interjected, "If I take lead, that'll free you up to direct the attack."

Justin glared at him. "Why? A minute ago you were telling me this has zero chance of succeeding."

"I didn't say zero chance, only that it had holes." Rory should take the lead to insert covertly for one simple reason. Like Cole, Justin had a mate to go home to, which Rory would never have. Before Justin and Cole found mates, none of their group thought they had a chance at surviving the mating curse. Bonding with a powerful Gallize shifter would kill a human and even some non-Gallize shifters.

Their best option was a Gallize female. Those women weren't originally intended to be shifters, according to what Rory had learned from their Guardian, but recent information suggested that some *could* be.

More than that, a Gallize female possessed an equal amount of power so she could handle bonding with a Gallize shifter.

Finding a polka-dot unicorn would be simpler.

Just as well. Rory was the last of his bloodline. If these guys lost him today, they'd miss him as he would his brothers-in-arms, but losing him would be the better choice.

"You haven't given me a good reason to let you take the lead," Justin pressed, throat muscles bunching with tension as he waited.

"It's simple, bear. I'm the best choice. I have better stealth than either of you and I'm faster."

Justin's gaze settled on him in a hard way, calling bullshit as clearly as his next words. "Is this because I'm mated, cat?"

"Vic's not mated." Rory almost smiled at countering Justin's argument so smoothly without having to outright lie.

That bear would smell a lie.

Vic shrugged. "He can have lead. I got no death wish."

Rory growled softly at the unknown wolf, because Vic had just given credence to Justin's suspicions.

Rory dropped his voice to a deep tone. "I'm doing my job and protecting our team leader, but if you've changed your mind about leading, let us know."

Shaking his head and muttering a string of curses, Justin said, "You're such a dick. Okay, you insert and get in position inside the tree line behind that second building. You have twelve minutes from the point we split up." Nodding toward the trees, Justin said, "Get past the tire tracks over there. Vic and I will break down the front door. We're all going dark until I send two clicks. That's the signal we're going in."

Moving around to rise to his feet behind a wide tree, Rory stretched limbs tight from all that squatting. "Sounds like a plan, oh bear leader."

Glaring up at Rory, Justin said, "I can't wait to see the woman that'll put up with your surly ass."

Justin would have to wait a long time and even then he'd end up disappointed.

Rory enjoyed an occasional tangle with a woman who wanted no more than he did. The proverbial one-night stand. Everyone left satisfied. Sexually, at least. He often walked away with a deeper sense of loneliness that he should be used to by now.

Cohabitation had once been in his plans, but that was no longer in his future.

Even so, some mornings he hated climbing out of a cold bed.

He made his way around the far side of the hill bordering the back lot of the brick plant, which spread over eighty acres. The empty office building stood far away, close to the river. A wolf that decided to run would have to choose a direction to take along that riverbank. Content that he knew what he would do, Rory quickly eased around piles of sand and forgotten equipment until he slipped into the woods.

Moving with stealth afforded him by his cat, he paused when he sucked in the strong scents of fur and terror.

The cages were lined up and covered with netting tossed loosely over them, hiding the captives from sight overhead. The wolves should have spread out their guards and prevented someone like Rory from infiltrating.

Overconfidence and arrogance had led to many fatal mistakes in the field.

Weaving his way deeper into the forest, Rory caught the smell of jackal and fresh blood. Closing his eyes, he listened for a sound, because that hadn't come from the direction of the cages, but further out in the woods.

His mind filled with an image of a jackal body ripped into ten pieces and scattered over a bloody landscape.

That damn Ferrell considered himself a freakin' Rembrandt of horror. His beast preferred painting gory scenes to get his message across rather than trying to communicate with words. Prick.

When the sharp smell of fresh blood hit Rory again, his jaguar growled over and over. Ferrell wanted out now.

Not yet, you crazy bastard.

The jaguar slammed his insides hard enough to make Rory's claws flick out. Damn beast.

Seizing control, Rory withdrew his claws and started moving again, if for no other reason than to settle Ferrell down. The jaguar wasn't much for being still, except when stalking prey.

Rory hated to be right.

An unexpected jackal could screw up everything.

Staying downwind of the guards and the cages, he followed the scent that drifted through the trees and grew stronger the deeper he went.

A whimpering sound barely reached him.

He'd made another two hundred feet when he spied a break in the woods. Moving closer, he discovered two picnic tables under a canopy of large oaks. Probably once used by workers for lunch breaks.

Two males blocked his view of someone they had prone on top of a picnic table. He'd found the source of the jackal stench. Bare feet belonging to what he guessed was a woman or a large child kicked, and a sound squeaked out as one shifter bent over his prey.

Those fools had their backs to Rory. He knew how to move around and keep them from scenting him easily, but these two were just plain stupid to trust the shifters out front to cover their asses.

Neither guard wore a shirt. One had on shorts and boots, and stood with his arms folded over his chest, observing what his bald buddy was doing.

Tattoos covered Baldy's head and ran down the middle of his back, stopping at the band of his jeans. Some weird design that made no sense to Rory.

"Please don't," a female voice ordered in a frightened voice.

Stretching his neck, Rory could see the squirming form of her lower body in torn jeans. White hair flashed in a gap between the men.

The white hair didn't make sense. She didn't sound old and her feet belonged to someone young. Also, Rory couldn't smell another shifter present besides the jackals.

Were those shifters about to feed on a prisoner?

Or was one of them threatening to shoot her full of some drug?

Her voice jumped up a notch with her panic. "P-please don't do this."

Baldy had a voice that sounded like he should shift into a pit bull. "I warned you once to shut the fuck up unless you're ready to come clean. We get paid for fertile shifters. That kid you were hugging is not yours. Are you related to them?"

"No. I met them on a bus yesterday."

"Not having a kid with you is one mark against you. I don't smell any animal. That's two marks against you. If you're not a shifter, you're not worth the time it took for those wolves to drag your ass here. If you don't prove to me you're something worth selling, I'll drag that boy over here to get you to talk."

"No. Don't hurt that child. Do what you will to me, but please don't hurt that little boy."

Rory admired this terrified woman who put a stranger's child before her own safety. A Gallize warrior would face anything to protect an innocent, but what average person would face being slashed by jackals to protect someone else, and a shifter at that?

Rory checked his watch. Due to making good time, he had over four minutes until Justin and Vic would wreak havoc. A lot could happen in that much time.

Busting in to break up those jackals now would screw the plan. But Rory would not stand down while a shifter mauled or raped anyone, definitely not a defenseless female.

He moved closer to get a better look and cast another glance at his slow-ass watch. Three minutes, fifty-two seconds.

If he jumped too soon, he'd put Justin and Vic in danger by alerting the guards and destroying the element of surprise.

If he waited too long, that woman might die or end up ripped apart by those claws extended from Baldy's fingers. The middle claw had dried blood on it, which meant the bastard had already hurt her.

Ferrell gave Rory the image of his jaguar playing with a tattooed bald head like it was a soccer ball.

Rory had reached the path he expected the escaping shifter to take. If he killed these two, and the shifter on the run did come this way, he'd end up having to kill the runner, too, once again screwing the original plan.

A new image of two headless jackals wandering around in their human forms filled Rory's mind. He shook off the vision, but he was trembling with the need to tear into those shifters for harming that female. Any sound of fighting would bring the other guards here, which would be yet another spectacularly bad idea.

Now his annoying jaguar created a picture of multiple headless canine stick bodies with tails, all dripping blood.

Crazy beast thought he could take on all the shifters. If even one was jacked up on Jugo Loco, it turned a winnable battle into possible defeat. Shifters on that shit were hard to kill.

Ferrell snorted a laugh.

Baldy kept a beefy arm holding the woman down. Was she a shifter? If not, why would the wolves have kept her?

It took Rory's extra-sharp hearing to catch her pitiful, "Touch me ... and you die."

One minute she's terrified and the next she threatens these two?

Baldy slapped her.

Shit! Rory grabbed his head to keep himself from shifting. His fucking watch moved like molasses.

Three minutes, eight seconds.

CHAPTER 4

BAATAR IS SO GOING TO chew my ass over this.

Siofra stared into the dead eyes of the vicious jackal shifter holding her down on the wooden table like she was a picnic lunch he planned to devour. He and the ugly buddy beside him acted weird. Their pupils were dilated.

Were they on drugs?

Her first Sunday of freedom sucked.

Two days ago, she'd thought her luck was changing the minute Toto's keeper gave Siofra a car ride from the side of the road. But that luck had run out yesterday.

She hadn't done anything wrong, just unknowingly sat beside shifters—a female lynx shifter and her cub—on the bus they'd taken out of Columbus, Texas. She didn't hold it against the woman and her son for being shifters.

Siofra wouldn't have known what they were if the little boy hadn't started changing while he slept. The woman had sent a panicked look to Siofra as if she would out them.

Siofra had a moment of indecision, because Baatar's constant warnings echoed in her head ... telling her that any shifter was a threat.

But she saw only a frightened woman trying to protect her child. Siofra had smiled and whispered, "Just wake him up and calm him down." After that, they were bus buddies. The woman whispered what she was and how she'd been moving slowly across the country to find family who would protect them.

Siofra couldn't treat that woman and child any differently than the children and female captives she'd cared for over the years.

Male shifters were definitely not to be trusted any more than a Cadell, but Siofra had trouble hating anyone.

She'd never been a hater at heart.

On that bus ride, she'd imagined finding a place to settle with Baatar where she could find a job taking care of young children.

Now she couldn't see her future.

Siofra didn't blame the lynx shifter for getting caught. It was just a matter of Siofra being in the wrong place at the wrong time. Story of her life, apparently. She'd been holding the sleeping boy for his exhausted mom as the three of them took a stroll around a restaurant where the bus had stopped last night. She'd been more than ready to stretch her legs after hours upon hours of sitting.

The bounty hunters jumped them the minute they stepped out of sight of the restaurant windows. She was dragged into a van and whisked away in a matter of seconds.

Baatar would have yelled at her, but given the same situation, she knew in her heart he would have been nice to the mom and her cub, too. That's what a good man would do.

Baatar would not, however, be staring up at a crazy shifter with no hope of getting away.

She had a lecture coming from her camp brother, which she'd welcome if she could find a way out of this. And if he ever escaped.

The only positive was that neither of these two recognized her white hair. They weren't from the Cadells.

"Touch you and I'll die?" The bald shifter laughed in her face. "You think you can threaten me, bitch?" he gritted out with a mouthful of bad breath.

Not really, but she was desperate for any way to keep him from putting his hands on that little boy. She'd been trying to rally her energy and hoped the threat would cause it to show up or make these two think twice about being around her.

"Time for you to shift, bitch, if you don't want to be our next meal."

His disgusting buddy nodded in agreement.

Fighting to keep her voice as calm as she could, Siofra said, "I-I don't know what ... "

Pissed, he sliced a claw across her stomach and burned a new hot path through her skin.

She arched with the pain and opened her mouth to scream.

He slapped his hand over her mouth. She clamped her teeth down hard, breaking skin and tasting his nasty blood before he snatched his hand away.

"Shit! Bitch bit me!"

She sucked in what was left of her scream so she wouldn't have to bite him again, but her stomach hurt so much. Had he infected her with his shifter blood?

Could he turn her because she bit him?

Please, no. Anything but a jackal.

He slashed a claw down her arm. She keened at the pain.

The second guard was smaller and had a bad case of the shakes, but he laughed. "Just cut her open and force her to shift, Vern. If she doesn't, we use her to feed the group."

Tears streamed from her eyes. Her skin burned where he'd clawed her and she couldn't draw a deep breath.

She'd sold crazy before. Could she do it again? She had nothing else for defense. She warned him again, "I have bad energy inside me. If you hurt me, it will show up and you'll die."

An empty threat this time, when she felt no weird power tingling in her body and no ghost coming to get in the way.

"You're crazy, you know that?"

Score. But hey, she must be if even a stranger realized it.

Vern lifted his claw-tipped fingers once again. "I'm going to open you up. If gutting you doesn't make you change, you ain't a shifter."

He smacked a hand over her mouth to muffle her scream again.

As Vern's other hand came down to strike, his shaky sidekick slammed into him, knocking Vern to the side.

Still braced for horrible pain and death, it took a second for her to realize she was free of Vern's grasp. Adrenaline had to be the only reason she could twist around and scramble off the table in spite of her bleeding wounds.

Cupping her middle, she stumbled to the nearest tree and turned to look behind her at the sound of fists hitting bodies.

A man was attacking the jackal shifters.

She had to be hallucinating. No man had ever come to her rescue except Baatar.

This guy had a beefed-up body and stood as tall as balding Vern, but those jackals were hyped up on something. Probably Jugo Loco.

That man had no hope to defeat them.

Her savior turned his head her way for a second. Fierce golden eyes met her gaze and a buzz of energy raced through her. The moment passed just as quickly. Returning to the battle, he knocked the bald one off his feet and now fought the shaky sidekick with a series of strikes that looked like something impressive from an action movie. His movements were a blur of quick, accurate hits, where the jackals' were off-balance and sloppy.

Vern came up from the ground looking furious and out for blood. He swiped a clawed hand at the new guy, slashing his neck and ripping open his shoulder.

Based on strength and speed alone, Golden Eyes had to be a shifter, which meant he'd heal fast, but at the moment he fought injured.

Vern took advantage of hurting the new guy and punched him off his feet. She clenched her hands, wanting to help him. She should be running, but guilt would rip her apart. This man had stepped into danger and allowed her to get away.

Her brain kept screaming, "Go now!" She should, but she couldn't just turn and run, leaving him to face two shifters strung out on drugs.

Not after he'd saved her from being gutted.

Baatar would not be happy with her, but this was one of those moments that defined a person. Like helping a lynx shifter and her child.

Siofra could not live with herself if she left this man to die. Anyone who stood between her and danger was worth fighting to save.

Terror swamped her at stepping in.

What could she do to help?

Golden Eyes was back on his feet, but Vern slugged the guy's damaged shoulder. Her savior sucked in a deep breath.

She fisted her hands, wanting to shove that punch back at Baldy.

All at once, the buzz of energy she'd felt two days ago returned. It built with intensity and flowed through her bare feet, then up her legs. It spread throughout her core and all the way to her fingers.

She clutched her middle as the energy ignited a fire in her gut. At the same time, the pain in her stomach subsided and her wound began to heal.

How was that happening?

Siofra had little experience with freedom most people took for granted, and she'd spent her life without much hope for a better tomorrow. From this point forward, she would follow her new, personal Rule Number One.

Don't waste time questioning any good luck that falls your way like small dogs running up to you in the dark, golden-eyed strangers who appear out of nowhere to save you, or weird energy that manifests itself whenever it wants.

Especially if said energy gets your butt out of danger.

What had Baatar told her? *You are strong. You can do this, Baby Girl.*

Of course, he'd also told her to stay away from shifters.

Details, details.

She couldn't stay away from all shifters. That was becoming painfully obvious. She had to find a way to help the others escape before she got out of here, but maybe the man fighting the jackals was here to save them.

She raced forward, heading for the jittery jackal, who had just gotten to his feet after being knocked on his ass.

He'd smirked the whole time his friend slashed her skin.

He must have sensed her coming or heard her footsteps, because he tried to whip around.

She lunged forward at the last second and grabbed the exposed skin at his waist, hanging on for dear life as he staggered. He jerked back and forth, trying to shake her off. The creep smelled nasty, like he'd rolled in crap. She dug her fingertips into his back and felt energy shoot out of her fingers.

His arm flew around to backhand her, but before his hand could connect, he tensed, then froze in that position and shuddered hard.

Just like Dyson.

Foam came out of his mouth.

That hadn't happened with Dyson.

She let go and backed up. Her hands trembled and she lifted them, staring at what had apparently become weapons. If he died, that would make two people she'd killed.

Loud cursing and the sound of heavy fists hitting bodies dragged her attention from her hands.

What about Vern? He was bigger than either Dyson or the one she'd just put down. Vern continued blasting hits at the new guy, whose shoulder hadn't even begun to heal. He would die if she didn't do something.

But what if she killed *another* person?

What if she stood around debating her moral dilemma and the guy who saved her from these jackals got shredded?

She could still feel the energy circulating through her core.

Pushing her conscience to the side to face later, she started for the bald guy. This time, she'd try to limit her attack to just grab, shock, and let go real fast.

Just as she reached for his arm, the jackal went flying backwards twenty feet, sliding to a stop on his back.

What the heck? She stared at the body.

Fingers touched her arm gently. A deep voice warned, "Don't get too close. He's still dangerous, just knocked out."

She jerked her head around to the broad chest of Golden Eyes, but kept her gaze down even though it was dark. Her mismatched eyes were as identifiable a feature as her white hair. She'd hidden her eyes with a pair of bent sunglasses she'd found in a bus station garbage can and fixed. They'd ended up smashed when the wolves kidnapped her.

Thunder rumbled overhead, but she paid it no mind.

A sizzle of energy slid down her arm and hummed where this man's hand touched her skin, as if her energy gave him a little hello.

She stared at that spot, expecting to see something.

A red glow. A blue glow. Any glow.

Why was that buzz happening? Was she doing it … or him? Was it the same energy that had killed Dyson? Would it hurt this man too? She started to step away, but all at once, her teeth chattered and she couldn't stop the shaking that racked her body.

"Hold on." He pulled her to him. "You're going through shock, but you're safe. I won't let them hurt you again."

She should be backing up and running.

But she couldn't. It felt so good for him to touch her.

For years, she'd longed for a man to hold her in a way that made her feel cherished, wanted, cared for and ... loved. That would probably never happen, but freedom was supposed to mean a new life where she could feel like the women she read about in magazines and books.

The other bounty hunters were just beyond the trees. She'd heard rumors whispered by newcomers in the camps, about laws that had been passed making it illegal for shifters to hunt and sell other shifters. Maybe those rumors were true, because this man acted as if he were here to save the caged women and children. He probably had more people with him. If so, she could sneak out once the bad guys were taken down. She should be counting her lucky stars and heading the opposite direction.

But being held in this man's arms hampered any thought of breaking free to run. Just a few seconds more.

She needed this right now, this minute, and couldn't make herself let go any more than someone dying of thirst could turn away a drink of water. If the world exploded into a fireball on her next breath, she'd have this to hold onto as her last memory.

He rubbed her back and she just stood there like a content idiot, soaking up the comfort she had so rarely received. Baatar hugged her sometimes, but it was more like getting a pat on the head from a big brother.

This man had her up against his warm body and wrapped in his powerful arms, which felt *nothing* like sibling reassurance. He murmured soothing words that swirled around in her chest and latched onto her heart.

She could stay here forever.

What? No, not forever. She had to keep moving. And she would in just a moment. One tiny minute couldn't make that much difference, could it?

He spoke close to her ear in a reprimanding tone, "That was a crazy move to jump on a shifter. I can't believe you did that."

At his censure, she pushed away.

He immediately opened his arms, which she appreciated. Sort

of. She'd liked being held, but she had to make sure the others were being rescued, then get running again.

Plus, he'd just criticized her.

"Really?" She narrowed her eyes into thin slits, which helped hide her mismatched gaze while countering his look of censure with one of her own. "I saved you and you're going to lecture me?"

"No, I wasn't." He took a step back and shoved a hand across his mussed, dark-brown hair, which only made him look rugged and hot. He grumbled, "I was trying to say thank you, dammit."

"Thank you, dammit? Nice."

His golden gaze locked on her with a disgruntled expression. "Just thank you."

"You're welcome." She might sound more appreciative if he hadn't bitten out the words. Just when she had the upper hand in this exchange, she noticed his shoulder wound and felt like a jerk for sniping at him. But he had her off-kilter and she hated to feel out of balance around a man.

Had something just made a scratchy electronic noise?

When he lifted his hand to his ear, he grimaced. That shoulder still wasn't healing. Why not?

Dropping his hand, he said, "Time to find a place for you—"

Lightning crackled through the sky, interrupting him and warning that the summer storm would unload soon.

Still focused on his awful injury, she reached for the jagged skin torn from his shoulder. "You're bleeding badly."

"It'll be fine, but you need to ... " he started to say, then he paused and became motionless at the same moment her energy pulsed between her hand and his shoulder.

What shocked her even more was how she felt *his* energy surge to meet hers. The same energy that had killed one ... maybe two people. Okay what was going on?

But this had been like two energy puppies making friends instead of hers acting like a rabid dog.

His shoulder appeared to be healing. Had her unpredictable energy done that or had his healing ability finally kicked in?

The combined hum from whatever they were both generating rushed over her skin.

She snatched her hand away and stepped back. He was a shifter. What had his energy been doing to hers?

He shook off his momentary confusion and asked, "What's wrong? You're looking at me now like I grew three heads."

She whispered, "You're a shifter." And she'd been touching him, had allowed him to comfort her.

Baatar would be shouting like a madman if he stood here now.

Golden Eyes returned to talking in a soothing voice. "Yes, I'm a shifter, but I won't hurt you. I just need you to stay calm and hide until we finish dealing with these *bad* shifters. I expect another one to come this way soon and I have to be ready for him." He'd emphasized bad as if to separate himself from the entire population of dangerous shifters.

When she didn't speak, he urged, "Work with me and we'll get you returned to your people."

She took a step back as a raindrop hit her head. "Actually, I don't have any family. I'm good. I'll just mosey on."

Not very far, though, until she could determine that all those in cages had been saved.

Now he looked pissed. But that was normal for a male shifter, right?

He said, "Don't run. You can't outrun me, plus I'd like to talk to you."

"Why?"

"I just want to ask you something, dammit."

"What? Ask me now." She had to keep him talking. Maybe the shifter he was waiting for would show up soon to take his attention. That would allow her to sneak around to see what was happening with the women and children. If she got caught again and died, it would be with a clear conscience.

More drops began to tap against the leaves and ground.

"When you ... " His gaze ripped past her. "*Move!*"

Wheeling around, she barely had time to dive to the side before Baldy ran her over. When she scrambled to her feet and turned, Golden Eyes had hit Vern straight on, knocking him to the ground. They rolled around, pounding each other until they separated and got up to make another run at each other.

She continued backing toward the woods behind her.

Lightning-quick blows landed with dull thuds until Golden Eyes kicked the jackal in the gut, knocking him back and pinning him to the ground with his body. He slammed a rock-crushing fist at the jackal's jaw.

The shifter's arms flopped to the ground. He groaned.

Not dead.

Her heart rate doubled. She should have been deep in the woods by now, maybe even to a highway. Not staring at the most beautiful gaze she'd ever seen and trying to figure out how to save the others. Maybe she could zap the rest of the guards.

Not unless she could do it all at once, and that was assuming her energy would show up when she needed it.

Rain drizzled, enough now to drench her hair and clothes.

Without moving his gaze from her, Golden Eyes muttered, "Stop. I told you. We're here to help."

"You can't help me." She'd made the mistake of making one shifter friend along the way and had ended up captured by association.

Baatar expected her to be smarter than that. She was making too many mistakes, like getting cozy with a male shifter and wasting precious time trying to find a way to save strangers. Baatar had accused her of having an oversized heart, and not in a good way. He kept telling her that caring for strangers would one day put her in deep trouble.

She didn't want to tell him he'd been right about getting in trouble.

The jackal laid out on the ground took a drunken swing at her savior. Golden Eyes slapped his hand away then popped Vern one last time, knocking him out.

She took two more steps back.

Those gold eyes lifted to hers once more and this time that gaze pleaded with her. "Wait for a few minutes. We *can* help you. We'll take you to a sanctuary."

He meant lock her up with a bunch of shifters. Shaking her head and looking away, she said, "You're safe. I can't stay."

His face fell with an incredulous expression. "I'm safe?" Then his head jerked around to look in the direction where the cages were being guarded.

Now that they weren't talking, she could hear the sounds of fighting going on back there. A rescue team?

She asked, "Are those your people I hear fighting?"

He turned back to her. "Yes."

"Can they save everyone in the cages?"

"Yes. We can save all of you."

Now that she knew someone would save those women and their children, she felt a huge weight lift off her shoulders.

When he spoke this time, it was an order and came out with a load of power. "Don't move."

The power rushed over her and past. She stuck her chin in the air. "Your magic will not work on me. For once, do the right thing and let me go."

"Magic? I don't have any magic." He pushed up from the co-matose bald shifter and kept talking. "What about you and that energy? Are you a witch or a healer?"

"Neither. Stay away from me. My power kills." Swinging around, she was gone, letting his curse fade behind her.

He had a shifter's speed to catch her.

But by the time two minutes had passed with no sign of him, she took a deep breath of relief. Maybe one more decent man like Baatar lived in this world.

Too bad Golden Eyes was a shifter and she'd never see him again to find out what he'd wanted to ask her.

That made her sad, and okay *that* might be foolish thinking, but she couldn't change the fact that he'd given her a moment of comfort like she'd never experienced before.

Right now, she had to get out of these woods while she had a chance.

CHAPTER 5

R ORY'S MOUTH FELL OPEN AS the nymph ran off.
The damn jackal beneath him started shifting.

He'd been trying to keep one of these shifters alive to provide intel for Scarlett. She'd given them what they'd all believed would be a Jugo Loco distribution meeting in exchange for the team handing her the name of the person running these bounty hunters.

If he could take this jackal back alive, they could wring the truth out of him and fulfill their part of the deal Tess made on behalf of the Guardian.

This shifter had been ready to gut that woman and in another few seconds, he'd be changed into a jackal.

Rory reached for the bald head that had contorted into an elongated snout with fangs. The jackal slashed his claws, trying to gut Rory. He missed but filleted an arm. Fucker. Rory trapped the shifting upper body between his legs and twisted the half-jackal head hard until the neck snapped.

Bastard ripped a new wound on his other arm.

Pushing off the jackal's body, Rory stood and stared at the empty spot where the woman had been.

A moment ago, his shoulder had been no more healed than his new arm wounds, but with one touch of the nymph's hand his shoulder had begun mending.

That sensation had dropped to a trickle as soon as she backed away.

He'd struggled not to grab her back into his embrace. Yeah, that would win him Asshole Of The Year award. He'd never forced a woman to be with him, but ... that fearless female drew him like a human magnet.

Of course, she wasn't exactly human, now was she?

Staring at her that first time had pulled him toward her.

He couldn't call up the color of her eyes. Why not? He was good with details like that during any operation.

Holding her had stirred parts of him to life that had no place on a mission.

Not a witch or a healer, according to her.

A nymph healer, maybe.

What else could she be with that shoulder-length white hair glowing around her head, barefoot and clothes half on? He'd gotten a look at her stomach when she'd first dropped off the table and the slashed wound had been bleeding.

But as she'd turned to run just now, her ripped shirt exposed the same spot on her stomach, covered in unblemished creamy skin.

Not even a scar.

My power kills. Those words echoed in his mind. Everything about her had been a contradiction. She'd killed a jackal, then healed Rory, then warned him to stay away from her or ... what? Her power would kill him?

She'd damn sure taken down that other jackal. With her bare hands no less.

What the hell was she?

He'd wanted to chase her. So had his cat, but Rory had to be here now and his beast couldn't be trusted not to go rushing after the nymph.

Something about the way she averted her gaze bugged him.

She'd been around shifters. Maybe she normally kept her eyes down around the alphas and was just being careful.

He felt the skin on his shoulder moving and looked down to see the wound continuing to heal. Relief washed over him. About damn time. His healing had been getting slower and slower lately. The last thing he needed was the Guardian noticing.

The noise of Justin and Vic fighting the bounty hunters out front quieted down.

Shit, if things had gone as planned, that meant one of the other shifters, probably a wolf, should be on the run. If he came this way, he'd see the dead guards. Rory hoped the escaping wolf would be too invested in running to pay attention, but who knew?

This direction made the most sense based on the recon Rory had been able to do when they first arrived, but he had no guarantee the runner would head this direction for sure. That was the thing about a busted op. You had to rely on *possible* outcomes.

If Rory shifted into his jaguar, he could communicate with Justin and Vic telepathically, but only if they had also shifted into their animals.

As a Gallize, they avoided shifting unless there was no other option.

Rory moved around to find a hiding spot and wait for the runner.

It didn't take long.

But now he had a new issue.

If the guard racing into the dead jackal scene was the expected runner, he'd shifted into a brown wolf.

Ferrell growled softly, his happy sound, because he knew they had to shift to keep pace.

The wolf skidded to a stop and took in the bloody scene, then lifted his nose and turned his head until he faced the thicket Rory hid behind.

Calling up the change, Rory groaned as his clothes shredded so Ferrell could take his place.

With Ferrell loose, Rory fought to hold his beast back. Ferrell would never stand down with a predator coming for them.

When the wolf lowered his head and stared hard at the thicket, his eyes glowed yellow, with tiny pupils. Too tiny for the fading light.

That one could be on the Black River pack's crazy juice.

Rory's jaguar sent him a new visual of a wolf laying on his back and exposing his belly.

Sure. That wolf would just roll over and give up.

Listen to me, Ferrell, Rory said telepathically. *The only experience you have fighting a shifter jacked up on Jugo Loco was that jackal, and he was a dud. Let the wolf come to us and make the first mistake.*

Ferrell answered by bunching his muscles for an attack.

I thought you weren't ready to die, Rory muttered silently to the crazy cat.

As the wolf crept forward cautiously, Rory doubled down on his control to keep Ferrell from leaping first. He called out telepathically to Justin, hoping this wolf meant his teammates had changed as well. Rory said, *The runner ain't runnin'. He stopped where I had to take out two jackals. His eyes are crazed like he's whacked out on BRP juice and he's scented my jaguar. We're gonna tangle any second.*

Justin sent back, *Don't engage. They had two more guards hidden. It may not be Jugo Loco. Not sure what they're on. We're still hung up out here. Abort the plan to track. If he's a big-ass red wolf, get away from that one now. He almost killed Vic before we shifted. Should be one bastard left fighting Vic. Let me get that dealt with and ...* Silence filled the pause then Justin said, *Ah, hell, we're missing two wolves. Get the fuck out ...*

At that moment, Rory locked Justin out mentally as a second wolf with a red coat the color of Georgia mud came crashing onto the scene.

CHAPTER 6

a

FOR ANY HOPE OF GETTING out of this fight in one piece, Rory had to ignore Justin and Vic, everything except the two wolves heading toward his jaguar.

Where the first wolf had the whacked-out, glowing eyes of a rabid shifter on drugs, this second one looked downright alien with black empty orbs for eyes. That monster wolf stood another head taller than the runner and had the misshapen body of a shifter on mega-steroids. Beneath the rust-colored coat, his muscles bulged in an unnatural way and his shoulders expanded so much he had a deep valley between them. His head was too big for his body size, but he could probably cut a Rottweiler in half with one bite of those jaws.

Human steroids hadn't altered that shifter's body.

Rory would bet that wolf had been pumped up with some unholy drug the Black River pack had cooked in their labs.

A demonic growl rumbled from Ferrell.

Two juiced up wolves against one crazy, injured jaguar.

What Rory's beast lacked in intelligence, he made up for with arrogance.

Well, Ferrell would take down at least one and Rory never planned past the moment in which he lived for a good reason.

Time was not something he dwelled on.

When it came to fighting, Rory and Ferrell were always on the same page. He gave the jaguar his head.

With a roar of fury, Ferrell burst from the thicket with claws out and jaws open, but he didn't go straight at the wolves. Instead, he dove to the side and rolled, coming up on all fours, then turning to meet the enemy.

Not expecting that move, the massive wolf ran over the smaller one in his rush to attack Ferrell. Saliva dripped from the wolf's snarling lips. No sane thought going on there. Just a locomotive load of power determined to kill a cat.

Ferrell didn't budge until the last second.

When the wolf dove to make his attack, Ferrell flipped to the side, vacating that spot in a microsecond. Rory's cat twisted in a brilliant move to push up on all four paws and spring onto the wolf's back just as the wolf tried to stop and turn.

Ferrell locked his jaws on the wolf's neck, but he only got a third of the bulky mass. Jerking and twisting, the wolf snapped his teeth, trying to latch onto Ferrell's leg. His jaguar dug his front claws deep into the wolf's shoulders, pulling hard to rip muscle. He bit the wolf's neck again, going for a better grip, but nothing slowed down the monster they rode.

Teeth snapped hard against Ferrell's back leg and Rory shuddered at the pain the second wolf was inflicting.

Ferrell reached around with a claw and ripped at the big wolf's throat, yanking to tear it apart.

The second wolf shook his head back and forth, ripping Ferrell's leg the same way.

Rory told Ferrell, *Let go of this one and stop the other one from tearing our leg apart.*

His jaguar snarled something that could have been the word *no.* Fucker.

Slashing sharp claws across the big wolf's neck again, Ferrell's paw came away with bloody muscle and veins this time.

The steroid wolf folded to his front knees.

Now Ferrell swung around, dragging the second wolf with his torn hind leg. His jaguar lunged to catch the wolf's hindquarter with his teeth and claws, shredding fast as a revved-up sewing machine.

That forced the wolf to howl and whine, jerking to get away from Ferrell. Rory's jaguar had once again proven himself in battle. He let the jaguar finish off the wolf.

One thing they agreed on was no playing with an enemy. If attacked, kill the opponent in the fastest way possible.

A massive grizzly bear and a wolf that looked like a giant fox crashed through the forest as Ferrell finished off his kill.

Then Ferrell wobbled two steps and collapsed on one side.

No longer in the middle of battle, Rory opened his mind to hear Justin yelling at the top of his telepathic voice. *Answer me, Rory!*

I hear you.

Justin's grizzly and Vic's wolf—*a maned wolf?*—padded up to Rory's jaguar. The grizzly took one look around and brought his gaze back to Ferrell.

Panting through the pain, Rory said to his jaguar, *You did it, you beast. We live to fight another day.*

For that, he got the image of Ferrell sleeping in the middle of Rory's bed, which he might just let the cat do this time.

Sucking up his courage, Rory called up the shift back to human form. That really pissed off his mangled leg. His foot flopped at the wrong angle.

Energy flowed around him as Justin and Vic returned to their human forms, too. Justin took one look at Rory's leg. "Fuck, that's ... we can't fix that right now."

"I know." Rory couldn't say much until he got the damn thing healing and that wouldn't happen quickly. "What about ... captives?"

"Right before Vic and I inserted, I sent word of what we were doing and for the helicopter on the way to come in hot rather than setting down a click away. I had a feeling something was off and feared they might hurt the captives before we could take all of them down."

Rory gritted out, "That's why you're the leader."

Justin didn't respond to that, instead saying, "We'll lose whoever was coming to pick up those in the cages, because the first transport should have been arriving by now and would have been scared off, but we saved the women and children."

From all the blood on Justin and Vic, they looked mauled from head to toe. Good thing Justin had gone with his instincts for the sake of the captives. With the chopper on site, no one had to carry Rory out of here.

"What can I do for you?" Vic asked, his gaze on Rory's leg.

"I'm not a medic like you, but I can follow instructions."

Rory started directing Vic on how to wrap up his leg until he got home to rest and heal. He sure hoped this would get better soon. They all had fast healing, but with the problems Rory had been experiencing, this level of damage could take days to heal instead of hours.

When his healing had stalled over the past months, he hadn't been sure it wasn't Ferrell fucking with him, but regardless of what was going on, he wasn't going to give Justin a new reason to jaw at him. The last two injuries had been simpler wounds and he'd been able to hide his sluggish return to solid health.

Not now.

What about that healer nymph? Where was she when he needed her?

Maybe he had imagined the whole thing. She'd said she wasn't a healer. Could be that his animal pushed more energy to the wound when it sensed a potential threat from her power.

He'd like to think that, but Ferrell did only what Ferrell wanted and lately had been stingy with giving aid.

It would take a damn magician to heal sooner than two weeks. He had a real concern that the damage to his leg could be severe enough that he might not make it all the way back to fully healed even then.

He and his Gallize teammates had something better than a magician.

They had a three-hundred-year-old sea eagle shifter they called the Guardian, but that didn't mean Rory had any desire to point out his healing issues to the boss.

Now that the ringing in his ears had died down, he heard women and children wailing in the distance. "Are the captives okay?"

"Yes," Justin said, then explained, "I left them in the cages and they're pissed, but if I let them out you know most of them will take off. I tried to tell them someone was coming to deliver them to a sanctuary. That really set off two of them, screaming at me that they were not living on a reservation."

"I know. I rescued a woman from those two jackals and told her we were here to help her, but she took off while I fought that bald bastard. We need to find her." Why had he said that? She'd clearly wanted to run.

But knowing she was out there alone twisted his gut in ways he'd never felt before.

Justin looked around and came back to him. "By the time I can cut Vic loose to hunt her, she'll be gone. Can't save everyone."

The urge to crawl after that woman and make sure she was safe ate at Rory in spite of the pain riding his body. He didn't like the idea of letting her go. Not being able to heal pissed him off. He had to fix this shit.

As soon as he could hobble, he was coming back to track her and find a way to convince his nymph to let him help her.

Whomp, whomp, whomp announced the helicopter's arrival.

"That's Hawk comin' in," Vic muttered as he tied off the bandage he'd put around what was left of Rory's leg.

When Vic went to meet the helicopter, Justin squatted down next to Rory. "I'm gonna say this now while no one else is around."

"What?" That came out nasty, but Rory's hackles went up at Justin's tone.

"You should talk to the Guardian about whatever is wrong." Justin held up his hand. "Don't waste time bullshitting me. I know something is up with you. I've noticed issues from time to time over the last couple months since Cole and I found mates, but I've tried to leave you alone."

"Noticed what?"

"You never make anything easy, do you?"

"You're the one who started this," Rory snapped back. His leg hurt like a mother and the rest of his body felt like he'd been beaten with a spiked log. Couldn't Justin find someone else to rag on?

Brown eyes bearing down on him, Justin said, "Fine. You've got a fucking death wish or you've got some skewed reasoning about being point man in every mission. Not that the rest of us don't appreciate you diving in to take the first bullets, but that's not how we work."

"You could just say thank you instead of being a dick," Rory said, but the levity was lost on Justin.

"Unless you want to be laid up for a while, you need to call the Guardian about fixing your leg. You've been hiding wounds for some reason. I'm guessing they aren't healing the way they should.

While he's working on your leg, you'll have the perfect opportunity to straighten out whatever the hell is going on in your head. If you don't, you're off the team."

"Don't threaten me, Justin." Rory clenched his teeth against a wave of pain from moving around. "I'm going home to heal. I'll let you know if I need the Guardian."

Ferrell sent Rory a video image of the Gallize headquarters destroyed worse than a tornado hitting the building.

He sighed. If the Guardian took Rory out of the field, his jaguar would last maybe three days before he forced the change while Rory was sleeping.

It had happened once overseas, eight months ago when Rory had been badly wounded and passed out for more than a day from exhaustion. The shift had helped him heal faster, but his jaguar had gone tearing through the jungle looking for something to kill.

Not to eat, just to kill.

Rory regained consciousness right after shifting, but he couldn't grab control of Ferrell while the jaguar was on a rampage. When Ferrell finally slowed down, and before he'd harmed anything, Rory seized control. He'd been able to keep that from the Guardian and his team, but back home in the states he couldn't hide something so glaring if it happened again.

Truth was, he *wouldn't* hide not being able to manage his jaguar. If Ferrell pulled that trick again, they wouldn't be waiting on a mating curse to submit to the Guardian.

Justin shook his head. "It's not a threat, asshole. That's a promise. I'm trying to keep you alive. If you're suffering from the mating curse, say so. We'll figure out something."

"It's three years too early for me to have the curse and you know I'm not lying when I say I'm not affected."

"Fine. Then get your head out of your ass if you want to stay on the team. I'm not standing by watching a brother of mine walk into hellfire because his head is screwed up, or risking that whatever is going on with you won't put someone else in danger." Justin stood and started giving directions via his comm unit.

"When have I ever put any of our team in danger?"

Growling softly, Justin sighed heavily. "Never and I know you never would, but something is going on. I'm just saying if you can't figure it out, talk to the boss."

Rory held his tongue when he wanted to lash out, but Justin was only doing what Rory would do in his shoes. The problem was that no one could save Rory.

Without a mate, he'd eventually fall victim to the curse, and the Guardian would put him down.

Rory didn't see any of that as a problem.

There would be no avoiding the curse, because Rory refused to consider a mate.

There would be no more monsters like him.

CHAPTER 7

Monday morning, downtown Pittsburgh, Pennsylvania

THE SOUND OF SOMETHING SMALL moving around nearby pierced the veil of sleep Siofra had stolen for a few hours. Was it friend or foe? Considering a flea could knock her over in her current physical state, any critter was suspect.

She cocked an eye open to see dirt and gravel scattered over the surface of the parking deck where she'd found a corner to hide. Nasty grit dug into her cheek where her face pressed against the ground.

The first hint of daylight cast a soft glow over the space. She'd never seen a parking deck in person before, only in pictures, but she appreciated the massive structure for a whole different reason than those who parked here every day for work. For her, it had been shelter.

Baatar had always said her ability to sense things around her was unusual for someone who wasn't a shifter, but then he had gifts as well and wasn't a shifter either.

She'd never told him she occasionally had unnatural help.

She'd needed one person to not look at her as though she were a freak.

Baatar might think she was a bubble off, but he wouldn't say it and he'd always had her back.

No more, though. Not until they found each other again. They *had* to find each other, and not just for her sake. Baatar needed her to watch his back now, too. His bad emotional episodes were coming more often.

She spied the noisemaker sneaking her way. Moving on thin legs, a grungy-brown rat hunted a meal just before dawn. Or maybe it had been up for hours and was making one last pass before heading back to its safe place.

Lucky bastard. She'd never had a safe place.

Pittsburgh might be heaven for the rat, but this wasn't her last stop or she'd consider following the critter home to see what safe looked like.

It waddled closer and paused, lifting its head and sniffing through a pointy nose. Then it strayed to the side as if ignoring her.

Innocent enough in appearance, even with those sharp teeth, but she'd learned never to assume an animal was simply an animal. Some creatures shifted into men, or women, who would kill you for pure entertainment.

Some animals walked on two legs all the time.

She uncurled her fisted hand from where it rested close to her face and stretched her fingers flat to touch the parking deck surface. Would the strange energy that saved her from being raped by a shifter show up again? She'd escaped the bounty hunters yesterday, but she couldn't take much credit for that.

She'd seen golden eyes, coming and going throughout her brief sleep.

Was the man who owned that gaze okay? Had his shoulder finished healing?

Was he dead from another attack?

Energy tingled in her fingers and hands.

She fisted her hands then slowly opened them again, fearing the deadly energy as much as she feared it not showing up if she needed to defend herself again.

But she didn't want to kill anyone else. She'd never wanted to kill *anybody*. She blinked back sudden tears born of exhaustion as much as guilt.

Dyson might have deserved to die, but she didn't need death on her conscience. She wanted no part of being judge, jury and executioner for anyone.

That crazy shifter had intended to stick a baby in her, and he'd died for that even after she told him the truth.

She'd had no idea she was infertile until after the third time she'd suffered a bout of debilitating nausea and unexpected bleeding. That's when another captive, one Siofra had nursed back to health, took a huge risk to divulge a secret the camp managers would kill her for sharing with other captives.

The camp doctor had been drugging her when she came in for what he called standard tests. He'd put her under, then while she was asleep, he'd perform an in vitro procedure to insert a fertilized egg in her.

A shifter's egg.

Then he'd have her returned to her sleeping quarters. She'd wake up feeling miserable. In less than forty-eight hours, she'd bleed heavily and they'd rush her back to the doctor, who then sedated her again.

She'd wake up afterwards and ask what was wrong.

The doctor would shrug and say she was having female problems, as if those two words encompassed any medical issue for a woman.

She'd always harbored a tiny bit of hope that she'd one day live free, especially once Baatar came along and they whispered about it. But she hadn't truly believed it would happen.

Now she had a chance at freedom, but would never have children. That hurt on a primal level that she had to stop thinking about or it would cripple her.

Dyson must have known about her infertility and still he'd tried to rape her.

His vile act had cost him.

But had it cost Baatar, too? Her heart squeezed with worry over her adopted brother more than anything. He believed the Cadells wouldn't harm him and risk losing money they could make when they sold him, but she didn't have that faith.

Mr. Rat's nails scratched the rough surface when he angled around and crept closer.

What was that vermin after? Did he think she was dead and fair game as a meal? She probably smelled worse than a two-day-old corpse. She'd been wearing the same clothes for days with no shower.

Lifting her hand with the palm out, she ordered, "Leave and live, or stay and die."

Powerful words coming from a woman with no weapon, less than twenty dollars in her pocket and not even a tingle of energy in her fingers now.

The rat took another couple of steps closer, pausing an arm's length away. Close enough for her to see his whiskers twitch and dark eyes flick back and forth.

Not that she wanted to harm any animal, but she wondered where her blasted energy had gone. She had no real idea what would trigger it again, other than terror.

That had definitely worked. Too well.

She'd had no control either time when the energy had surfaced in a blast of heat and power.

She muttered at the rat, "Please go. Don't be stupid."

Pulling her hands close to her body to push herself up, she paused. Why wasn't that rat scurrying off? Energy or no energy, most creatures that size would run.

Suspicion bloomed in her mind.

What if the Cadell leader had sent this rat?

Siofra had grown up hearing stories about Mother Cadellus, a witch revered by all the Cadells Siofra had been shunted between. That witch supposedly used necromancy to see through the eyes of a dead animal and speak through its mouth.

Siofra's skin crawled at the idea of this being a dead rat moving around, and narrowed her gaze to evaluate the small critter.

It showed no sign of having been reanimated. Not that she was familiar with those things or had ever witnessed such an act, but she'd seen dead animals. This one sure looked healthy and alive.

Sitting back on its butt, the rat gave her a curious look.

That didn't seem normal.

Siofra waited to hear a woman's voice spill from its mouth, but that didn't happen.

Finally, it dropped to all four skinny legs and waddled off toward the nearest dark shadow.

"Thank you," Siofra muttered. "One battle won today and no one died." She slowly reached her feet and bit her lip to keep from crying out. Her legs had gone through hell just getting here. Please tell her the mission for homeless people would not be far.

She'd walked all night and into early morning to reach this city.

After that, she was never going to chide herself again about not exercising. That was why she'd slept like the dead for a few hours.

Her feet and legs were hurting, but they'd just have to suck it up and deal with the pain. That, she could handle, but her body wouldn't go much farther without real food. She put her hand on the wall next to her when a wave of dizziness hit her.

It passed, but her body had a limit. She needed to feed it, and soon.

Wiping the sleep out of her eyes, she kept an eye on her surroundings while taking stock of what she still possessed. Baggy trousers and a T-shirt she'd found digging through a clothing donation container near the edge of the city. Those clothes had been meant for the needy and she could be their poster child at the moment. She'd found sneakers a size too large, plus a dishtowel she used as a scarf to cover her hair.

Back at the city where she'd caught a bus in Texas and had been able to buy a few things, she'd slipped a pair of scissors into a thrift store dressing room and attacked the white hair that had fallen to her waist for years.

Now the wavy locks barely reached her shoulders in a hairstyle more destitute waif than chic.

Retying the scarf around her head, she moved to the edge of the parking deck where she had a great view of the Ohio River.

She'd seen the sign early this morning as she walked through this part of the city. That river would account for the cool breeze wafting across this level. Four levels below, two vehicles entered the parking garage. She had to leave now while this place was relatively empty.

Her stomach growled, reminding her again that she'd eaten nothing but peanut butter crackers during the long hours it had taken to walk over thirty miles from where she'd escaped in Ohio.

The shifters who'd captured her before Golden Eyes arrived hadn't bothered to search her pockets, so her last twenty dollars was still there from when she'd gotten away. But she couldn't spend money she needed for food as she traveled further.

The lynx shifter had been more than happy to share lots of information with Siofra before they were captured, like how to find a mission for the homeless when she needed a decent meal.

Siofra had made plenty of notes on a scrap piece of paper during their long ride.

Freedom should feel exciting and wonderful, but she was still on the run. The Cadells never stopped hunting anyone who escaped.

Pulling the tail of her T-shirt up, she did her best to clean her face until she found a bathroom.

Once she ate a decent meal, she'd be revived enough to make it further.

She gathered what few items she possessed and shoved them in the flowery tote bag she'd found at the same donation box, and headed for the stairwell. When she reached street level and started toward the busiest direction, unnaturally cool air brushed her skin.

A presence formed next to her.

Siofra closed her eyes, wishing for peace at least until she found a way out of this city, but this spirit stood so close that hair lifted on her arms and the air chilled even more.

Could she first get a cup of coffee and food?

"What?" Siofra asked, opening her eyes to find the filmy image of a woman in her late twenties with ebony skin. She wore contemporary clothing of jeans and a frilly blouse. She had dark braided hair, grayish eyes and a nice smile. Nothing had changed from the last two times Siofra had met her.

She'd started calling the ghost Abigail, because the name seemed to fit.

The ghost floated backward, remaining ahead of Siofra as she walked.

"What can I do for you, Abigail?" Siofra asked, not expecting a reply. No one walked near her at the moment. Over the years since she'd first seen spirits, some had spoken to her, some tried to communicate with hand signals and some just stared until they got on her nerves. Why hitting puberty had opened a door to the dead, she had no idea.

She'd never had a spirit harm her or anyone else. Not until the one showed up when Dyson attacked her. Had that spirit given Siofra the deadly power?

That was a scary thought.

After a few seconds, a shimmering Abigail shook her head

slowly from side to side.

What could that mean?

"I have to find food," Siofra explained, glancing around to be sure no one noticed her. "I need you to move, please."

Being on the run meant not drawing attention, a concept lost on ghosts.

She could walk through Abigail, but the one time she'd tried that with a spirit, something in her body had short-circuited her brain and she'd blacked out.

She'd regained consciousness flat on her back.

This was not the time to lose touch with the world.

Abigail had gotten her into trouble the last time they'd met, while Siofra was on kitchen duty.

Siofra took a side step, hoping to slip past, but Abigail floated over and shook her head again.

Siofra got tough. "I asked you nicely to move. If you don't do it, I'll walk through you and you'll explode into a million bits of light."

That was such a lie.

Frowning at Siofra, the spirit must have believed her. She floated to the side and held an arm out with an irritated look on her face as if Siofra was being unreasonable. Siofra started forward, then glanced over one more time to find the ghost had vanished.

If she weren't so freaking tired, she'd have just crossed the street to see if taking a different sidewalk would have made the ghost happy, but Siofra had a limited amount of energy. Nothing was stopping her from reaching food.

Ghosts had been helpful as she escaped, but they had also caused her problems with their erratic behavior in the past.

What was she supposed to do? Sit here all day waiting for a positive sign from a ghost? Not the wisest move when she had no identification and only enough money to buy a handful of snacks to hold her over when she walked between cities with shelters.

The one thing she couldn't do was draw the interest of a cop. Worst place possible for her to be was in jail, because one of the Cadell groups would eventually find her if she stopped moving.

If that happened, she'd end up locked in a cage, *if* she survived their brutal punishment.

Or worse than that. The Cadells would sell her to the Black River pack. She shuddered over the stories she'd heard about what they did to females in their labs. Those miserable bounty hunters in Ohio had laughed and talked about waiting to sell the female shifters and their children to that pack.

But her golden-eyed white knight had shown up to save them.

She swallowed at the memory. Why did she miss him? He was a shifter after all, a male shifter at that.

Because he was so incredibly nice and protective, her heart argued in his defense.

And he had a strange energy, too. She would tuck that memory of meeting him into a special place for someone who couldn't be lumped in with all other male shifters. Someone who had given her a moment of peace she craved to feel again.

Shaking off the memory, she put her mind to finding food.

Foot traffic picked up as daylight peeked around buildings.

When she saw a college-age woman waving a sign that offered a sandwich special at the deli behind her, Siofra smiled.

She'd found an information source.

Walking up to the pretty young woman, Siofra waited to be noticed. The smell of food coming from the shop almost took her to her knees.

"Want a Reuben on rye, tall drink and chips for only five bucks?" the young woman asked.

"Thanks, but I can't afford that," Siofra said, then rushed ahead with what she did need. "I'm looking for the mission."

"What mission?"

Siofra licked her dry lips and said, "Wherever they feed the homeless?"

That's when the woman took a step back and gave Siofra a full inspection.

A new female ghost shoved her face between them. Siofra swatted with her hand as if flies had attacked her and muttered, "Stop it. I'm starving." She was also lightheaded and getting dangerously close to passing out if she didn't eat very soon.

Now the sandwich-sign woman changed her expression from concern for a hungry person to fear of a crazy woman talking to invisible people. *Argh.*

Siofra leaned to one side, past new ghost lady, to see the sandwich woman pointing to her left and saying, "There's a soup kitchen that way."

The ghost wore a striped blue dress with puffy short sleeves, white apron, sneakers, and her nametag read Thelma. She shook her head fervently.

Clamping her teeth, Siofra tried to talk without moving her lips. "Get out of here."

She must have spoken louder than she intended.

The young woman with the deli sign snapped, "Hey, I'm working. I belong here, so don't be telling me to do anything."

"Sorry. I wasn't saying that to you," Siofra mumbled and tried to get past the blasted ghost, who now swayed in whatever direction Siofra took.

Everything spun in Siofra's vision. She had to reach the soup kitchen.

"You need to move on," the woman said as she backed toward the door to the restaurant, clearly going for help.

She had no idea how much Siofra wanted to move on and get to the food, but *Thelma* wouldn't butt out of the way.

Slowly, Siofra circled Thelma, who looked even more demented than she'd just acted. Amazingly, Thelma remained floating in one spot. Maybe she'd reached the end of her territory. In one of the conversations Siofra had with a male ghost who regularly came to her at camp, but only in a specific spot, she'd asked whether he could leave that location.

Instead of answering the question, that ghost had looked surprised. In Siofra's mind, she'd heard the question, *Why would I do that?*

At the next large intersection, Siofra fell into step with a loose group of people dressed too casually to be office workers. They were happy and chatting. Probably enjoying a day off or on vacation, something Siofra had read about normal people doing.

Would she ever feel normal?

When the light changed, she looked across the street to see the soup kitchen. *Yes!*

Hurrying forward now with renewed energy at the thought of eating, she wiggled her way through the slowpokes meandering along.

A half block before she reached the kitchen, an ethereal being ahead of Siofra rushed back and forth through people walking on the sidewalk.

One man sneezed and rubbed his arms as if chilled.

Another blurry spirit came at Siofra from the street side this time. Both filmy beings rushed around her then, in and out of the crowd.

Keeping her head down, Siofra stepped one way, then the other, trying to outmaneuver these ghosts. Had her presence in this city somehow pissed off the local ghosts?

People were starting to complain about being bumped and rubbing their arms as if chilled when the temperature had to be in the eighties already.

Thelma appeared in front of Siofra again and held her arms out to each side, making it clear Siofra would have to walk through her.

Evidently Thelma had no territorial restraints.

Siofra could see the place for food. Why was Thelma blocking her way? Was there a threat? She didn't see anything except indigent people entering the building. Besides, if Siofra did not reach that soup kitchen, then she might as well lie down and die right here. She had nowhere else to go for help and without food she was in danger of passing out.

Still, confusion and fear had her backing up. She bumped into someone. She jumped forward and spun around to find a middle-aged woman in a dress suit glaring at her.

Lifting a hand in apology, Siofra mumbled, "Sorry. My mistake."

Behind the woman, two more spirits joined the translucent circus in progress.

After the woman stalked past her, Siofra swung back around and hissed, "Stop it."

Thelma had a disgruntled look on her face, but remained planted in the middle of the sidewalk.

Stand here until she passed out or barge ahead and try to reach the food?

Screw it. Siofra was so close to being faint from hunger she could hardly think. Maybe now that her new energy had surfaced, she could use it in a good way and move through the waitress spirit.

She started forward and Thelma crossed her arms.

The other ghosts began flying faster and now emitted sounds of wailing and moaning.

Siofra looked around to see if anyone else heard it. Nope.

The noise climbed to a deafening level in her head.

She covered her ears, but that did nothing. She panicked and ran ahead, blasting through a wave of cold air. Not enough for her to black out, thankfully, but the frigid blast rocked her body.

Everything blurred and that hideous noise got worse.

She waved her hands, batting at the wraiths. "Stop it."

"What's your problem?" a guy yelled. "I'm on freaking crutches." He pushed her to the side as he passed.

Siofra stumbled and nearly fell. Was Thelma behind this fiasco? Why?

Horns honked. People were shouting and someone shoved her in another direction. Siofra couldn't make it all stop. Her vision whirled and blurred. She backpedaled and stepped off a short drop.

The sound of cars crashing filled the air.

Caught in the turbulence of ghosts and the world spinning around her, Siofra took off running with her hands over her ears, screaming, "Stop it. Make them leave me alone!"

Someone shouted, "*Look out! Stop!*"

More icy cold blasted her face and skin. Her body felt as if it separated from her mind. Dead faces flew at her from all directions.

She swatted wildly, trying to knock the ghosts away, and slapped herself in the process.

Tires squealed.

Something hit Siofra in the back. She went flying forward, landing on hard pavement.

Finally, everything was quiet and dark. She gave in and shut her eyes.

CHAPTER 8

α

Monday afternoon, Spartanburg, South Carolina

RORY CLAMPED HIS HANDS AROUND each side of the gurney holding his body as Cole Cavanaugh pulled the wrapping off the mangled mess that had once been a healthy leg.

Shit, he wanted to throw up.

Twenty hours and it hadn't even started healing.

His claws kept shooting out the tips of his fingers and his toes, then he'd force them out of sight again. He couldn't blame that on Ferrell. Trying to shift happened to any of them when they were heavily wounded, because they healed faster in animal form.

But whatever had been off with Ferrell for a while was getting worse, which was saying something. His jaguar had never seemed normal.

Sucking in a hard gulp of air, Rory released it in a hiss.

Cole hesitated for a second, then finished unwrapping the leg. "Sorry, buddy. This sucks, but that wound smells bad already. Have you healed at all since yesterday?"

"Not much," Rory mumbled, fighting to keep his stomach from erupting. Even his shoulder that had begun healing after the nymph touched it had slowed in mending.

Any other time, his smaller wounds would be closed up by now, even with him in human form. Blood would have stopped oozing from even significant wounds. But not the leg.

Ferrell had gone entirely silent. Not even any gory pictures. That was another thing that didn't happen. When Rory was wounded, his jaguar would slam around, howling in pain until they shifted and healed.

Never a quiet moment with that beast injured, so why now?

Giving Rory's leg a long look, Cole cocked an eyebrow at him. "Why aren't you healing?"

"Hell if I know. Probably got some of that juiced-up blood on me and it's screwing with my metabolism." That excuse sounded pretty good even though it made zero sense medically, even for a shifter.

"Huh?" Cole cocked his head like his wolf did sometimes. "Why'd you wait until late today to come in? Why didn't you come in last night for the Guardian to work on you?"

Rory wouldn't be here now if a special meeting hadn't been called. Justin had asked if Rory wanted to pass. Not a chance.

Giving a shake of his head for effect, Rory said, "Thought shifting and sleeping would get it going, but—"

The door to the infirmary room where they'd parked Rory opened, saving him from more small talk when their boss walked in. Thankfully, the Guardian was a man of few words. He expected his team to grasp the importance of any topic quickly without his having to repeat himself.

Cole stepped back. "Hello, sir."

"Cole." The Guardian looked up the length of Rory's body from his feet to his face. "You've looked better, Rory."

"Yes, sir."

"Why haven't you healed?"

Had to be an echo in this place. Smarting off at the boss would not be a wise move, though. "Have no idea, sir." That was the truth. It confused Rory as much as it did anyone else.

The Guardian stood for a long moment with a thoughtful expression, which made the toughest Gallize shifter squirm when those eagle eyes focused on him. Supposedly, if a shifter lived as long as the Guardian had, eventually the animal became so enmeshed with the human that they shared the animal's eyes even in human form.

That certainly appeared to be true of the eagle shifter.

Moving his head as if he'd finished with his thoughts, the Guardian said, "Cole, I believe your mate and Ms. Sullivan should arrive soon, correct?"

"Yes, sir. Tess should be here by five."

"Very good. A half hour should be enough time for us. Would you go ahead of us to meet them in case we run a bit late?"

"Yes, sir." Cole exited, closing the door softly behind him.

Addressing Rory, the Guardian said, "I wish this would not be painful, but—"

"I remember what you had to do for me after that shifter shoved a titanium rebar spear through my chest." The bastard had worked for a Cadell and had paid for his part in capturing Rory and Cole's mate when the Guardian showed up.

Any time titanium entered a shifter's body, the tissue and muscle took longer to repair.

Rory still had nightmares about that healing.

Nodding solemnly, the Guardian said, "Very well. The sooner we get started, the faster this will be behind you."

Rory drew up all the backbone he could muster to keep from screaming when the first wave of healing power struck his raw legs. He blacked out during the process and was just coming back when the Guardian said, "Your leg will be strong enough to bear your weight in another hour, but you'll need more time to completely heal."

"How much time?" Blinking sweat out of his eyes, Rory pushed up on his elbows. He felt as if his body had been twisted in six directions, but his leg only throbbed with dull pain at the moment. Far better than that limb had felt before.

The head of the mechanical bed lifted until the pillow met his back.

"I wish I could say for sure. Based on your lack of healing before you came in, it could take two or more days."

Not good news. Rory gave in and leaned back as the Guardian pressed a key on the control pad to push him all the way to a sitting position.

Clearing his raspy throat, he said, "Thank you, sir."

"For putting you into so much pain you passed out?" Dark eyebrows lifted over those eagle eyes.

Had the Guardian made a joke?

"That does sound screwed up, sir, but it beats a week or more of being off my feet while the tendons and muscles mend." More like, it beat having a leg rot and fall off, but he did not want to have that conversation with the Guardian. Rory would figure out his problem and fix it.

After two knocks, the door opened and the smell of roast beef filled the room as a young man on their service staff placed a bed tray across Rory's legs and uncovered the plate. Rare beef had been piled next to three servings of broccoli and a special power shake. Ironically, as one of the team medics, Rory had created this menu as a meal for anyone on the team who was healing.

With a nod from the Guardian, the young man left as quietly as he'd entered.

A heavy silence followed as Rory wolfed down everything he could get his hands on. He wasted no time on manners. Any shifter, especially his boss, would understand his need to feed an injured body.

When he wiped his mouth on the linen napkin and leaned back, he turned to his boss to hear what the Guardian had been waiting to say.

With that quiet resolve that clung to him like a second skin, the Guardian asked, "Are you sure you have no idea why your body has not even started to heal after so many hours?"

Damn. Guess this conversation was going to happen anyhow.

Looking up to meet that intimidating gaze, Rory told the truth. "I don't have a freakin' clue, sir. I remember all of the battle and nothing stands out as exceptionally different that happened." Nothing except a wood nymph who had shaken him with that haunted look.

Something about her had called to him ... what?

No, hell no. She had not called to him. He just felt protective over a female with bounty hunters after her.

Was she safe on the run?

"Justin's report indicated you volunteered to take the lead to insert yesterday," the Guardian said, clearly moving on from Rory's problem with healing.

Justin wouldn't have come right out and said anything, but he could be clever when writing a report to get his message across. Asshole.

"Yes, sir," Rory replied. He'd learned a long time ago that saying less could be more.

"That makes four times you've volunteered to take point since Cole survived the Cadell attack and bonded with Tess."

"Five, actually, if we're going to count." Rory would own this right up front to hopefully get his boss to see that he had been the best choice each time.

Walking to the side of the room and pausing to stare at nothing, his boss said, "You are correct about the total number of times. I was pointing out only the times where Cole, Justin or both were on a mission with you."

Rory kept his mouth shut. This conversation was not headed in a good direction. No reason to pick up a shovel and help bury his own ass.

Turning back to Rory, the Guardian leveled him with a concerned look. "I can recall only one previous time when one of my Gallize shifters began losing the ability to heal himself."

"Really?" Rory asked with genuine interest. Maybe it was just something that happened from time to time and the Guardian could fix it. "Did you figure out what caused his problem?"

"Yes. He was doing it to himself."

"Uh, I don't understand, sir."

Speaking with measured words, the Guardian said, "Due to his frame of mind, he was killing his animal."

What? Rory sputtered, "You think I'm *killing* my animal? Is that even truly possible?"

"I don't think you're doing it intentionally, but I do think that may be what is happening. To answer your second question, yes, it is possible, but it would terminate the human side as well. We are not immortals, but beings that fall between those and humans."

Monsters. Rory kept that label to himself, too. He might not be happy about what he'd become, but he respected the Guardian and his Gallize brethren. He would not push his personal beliefs on them.

Cole and Justin were ecstatic over having found mates. Rory couldn't be happier for them, but he didn't want to continue his bloodline.

The Guardian spoke with a soft tone at a steady pace, which indicated he was imparting significant information. "It took me a while to realize the lion shifter whose animal was dying had never embraced his new life as a Gallize shifter."

"Hmm. I've embraced the hell out of mine, both here and overseas."

"You did gain control of your jaguar and you've certainly performed well in difficult situations, but that's not what I'm talking about. Every Gallize goes through a transformation to fully accept his animal and become one in purpose and in being."

Rory's neck heated as the Guardian circled closer and closer to what he'd kept secret for so long. He'd made peace with his situation and accepted that his life would not be a long one, but that didn't mean he was ready to submit to death. Not for another three years.

Listening to the Guardian made him realize something he hadn't thought much about.

Given a choice, Rory would continue living.

The mating curse determined how long an unmated Gallize could live, but he'd never given thought to dying sooner ... or staying longer. He thought his future had been predetermined.

Was he killing his jaguar?

Ferrell snarled low, coming back around now that Rory had begun healing, but his animal had never been withdrawn before, especially when they were injured.

Thinking back on the problems Cole had experienced with his wolf, Rory asked, "I never saw Cole have any issues with healing and we all know he didn't like his animal one bit at first."

"That's true, but that's why Sammy came in to give Cole one last chance to make it as a Gallize shifter. While working with Sammy, who was no easy taskmaster, Cole gained control *and* accepted his wolf as part of his being. Those two eventually found a middle ground to work as a team. Had he not, he would never have lived long enough to meet his mate again, because he would have suffered the same fate as the lion shifter."

Swallowing, Rory asked, "What happened to that shifter, sir?"

"This occurred in 1782. He kept his problem well hidden for eight years, until the day he was badly injured in a bloody knife fight with a human. His body tried to shift, but managed only a partial change."

Rory grimaced at the mere thought of getting stuck.

The Guardian continued, "Once I was alerted, I tried everything I knew to save him, but he languished in that half state for weeks. Had he been entirely human, he would have died in a day. Had his animal not been so close to death, he'd have shifted and healed in a day. Instead, he died in the most inhumane way."

"Why didn't you end it?" Rory might regret his angry tone later, but at the moment he couldn't.

How could the Guardian allow one of his to suffer that way?

"I would have," the Guardian replied. "But he made me wait until his brother could be located and brought to him. He had things he needed to say before he died. His brother had been a missionary for many years and back then communication was slow. I went myself to find the man, because no one else could fly across oceans in the eighteenth century. Still, it was difficult due to little information beyond a letter my shifter had received a year earlier. I did find his brother and put him to sleep to fly him back."

Shit, that had to be a brutal trip even for the Guardian, to carry a full- grown man over the ocean.

"Once the lion shifter and his brother spoke for an hour, he asked his brother to wait outside and called me in. He said he regretted killing his animal and not because he was dying as well, but because his animal had been there for him and had saved him many times in spite of his not wanting his animal. He asked me to put his animal out of misery. I fulfilled his request."

"Sorry, sir. I shouldn't have questioned you," Rory mumbled, more than a little embarrassed to have sounded so accusatory.

"Accepted. I am concerned about you, Rory. You're a fine man and an excellent Gallize shifter, but your recent interest in volunteering to take every point and being slow to heal is troublesome."

Coming from this man, troublesome was the equivalent of crisis level.

"I hear what you're saying, sir, and I admit I've had moments of ... confusion. I don't have a death wish for me or my jaguar, if that's what you're thinking."

Ferrell sent Rory the image of his human nose sticking out a foot from his face.

Nothing like your animal calling you out as a liar.

But Rory really did not see himself as having a death wish. He had never wanted to be a shifter and had fought an internal struggle for years to accept what he was but ... he needed to move this conversation to a different topic until he had time to think on it more. "I admit that I feel it's important to protect Justin and Cole. What if they're the only ones to find mates?"

The Guardian's expression didn't change at the switch in topics, but Rory sensed that his boss knew he needed some space and therefore answered the question. "That would be disappointing, to say the least, but the health and well being of every Gallize shifter under my protection is my sole purpose for being here. I will do all within my power to guide and heal all of you, but I can't save anyone who doesn't want to save himself."

Rory dropped his head into his hands and closed his eyes to stop the onslaught of guilt. Had he been slowly killing his animal?

Ending up with Rory had not been Ferrell's fault.

Ferrell sent Rory an image of his jaguar laid over on his side, not breathing, and with his eyes staring straight ahead, empty in death.

A large hole had been dug next to the jaguar's body.

Cut it out, drama queen. I'm trying to think and figure out how to fix us.

He got a rumbling snarl inside for that and a picture of Rory lying by the hole with his jaguar staring at him with a smile.

Ah, the asshole was back. That was better.

Rory had to cure this problem with his jaguar, but that would not change his position on mating. As a young man, he'd assumed he'd settle down and have a family, but that was before he knew he was a shifter.

No descendant of his would have to face his life and future.

One more image flashed in his mind of Rory in human form striding toward a blood-filled ocean full of piranhas.

He snapped his eyes open and sat up straight, then sent a silent message to Ferrell. *If you don't want to die, stop giving me reasons to take you with me into that ocean.*

CHAPTER 9

RORY USED A CANE TO hobble into a meeting room on the street level of their Spartanburg headquarters at five minutes to six. The Guardian and Cole were seated at the other end of the table and Justin had a spot near the door.

He looked around the new space which had no windows, so no need for blinds against the late-day sun. How had the Guardian found a building this close to downtown with multiple below-ground levels?

His boss had been around a very long time and held property in many states. And countries.

The Guardian might have known about this place from years back, because the building had the sturdy feel of one built fifty or more years ago. Cole and Justin had originally set up a location in this area as a temporary headquarters, but then Cole had mated with Tess, who ran the southeastern division of SCIS, short for Shifter Criminal Investigation Services. At that point, the boss decided to give them a permanent home for operations in this region.

Taking a seat on the far side of the long conference table, Rory stretched his achy leg out to the side.

Cole spoke to everyone. "Tess met with Scarlett. She's on her way here to tell us if we've lost that resource or not. Tess will be here soon, too."

Justin had been scrolling through something on his tablet, but closed it and leaned back, scowling. The bear shifter said, "You'd think she'd be more of a team player than to pull back because we didn't get a name."

"Not really," Cole replied. "As Tess put it, the good news is that Scarlett is completely detached from SCIS. Not a team player at all. She takes on the investigations she wants and has zero loyalty to anyone. She's only interested in her goal of protecting innocent shifters from attacks and preventing Jugo Loco distribution."

Justin shrugged. "I don't see any way we could have had a different outcome."

Cole admitted, "We all know you and the guys did a hell of a job with a screwed-up op, but we've got to smooth this over. Based on what Tess says, Scarlett has contacts in areas we just don't have in spite of our extensive network."

The Guardian asked, "Do you still believe we can trust this woman at this point if she feels we breached our agreement?"

"We'll know as soon as we hear from Tess."

Rory had nothing to add. He hadn't made the deal. He was just a cog in the machinery.

Cole added, "I haven't met Scarlett in person either so I don't know what to expect, but I would think she'd be glad for the rescue effort."

The Guardian maintained the normal unemotional expression Rory had seen many times when the team worked through an issue.

The boss asked, "Do you believe Ms. Sullivan can find the tiger?"

No one answered until Cole said, "Maybe, but do you want to tell her about the Gallize right now?"

"No. Not unless that information is pertinent to locating him."

Ever since Justin's mate, Eli, had a vision about a Gallize tiger shifter in the northeast area of the country, the Guardian had been intent on locating him.

The only tiger shifter it could be, according to their boss, was one that should be dead. The Guardian had tracked all of the Gallize shifters for three hundred years. How he did it, Rory had no idea. Gallize shifters were male descendants of five boys gifted with the ability to shift into animals. A long, long time ago, a Gallizenae druidess blessed those five original babies while they were still in utero.

Blessed? Rory had *her* to blame for the mess he was in.

Ferrell growled low, but was behaving for the most part now that the leg wound was improving.

The same druidess had gifted five female babies with powers of their own, though not the ability to shift. A female Guardian tasked with watching over the female Gallize went missing two hundred years ago. Without her, locating a Gallize female today had more to do with luck than skill.

Tess and Eli were thought to be Gallize descendants, but Eli happened to also be born into a shifter family. She changed into a grolar, part grizzly and part polar bear, which had nothing to do with being a Gallize.

When the door opened next, a striking woman with a head of black hair and an air of confident control walked in on spike heels. Tess wore a navy skirt suit and white silk blouse like a Manhattan businesswoman with the backbone of a Navy SEAL.

When Rory had ended up captured with her, he'd been present to witness that strength in action. She'd been the only person capable of saving Cole as the wolf shifter fell victim to the mating curse.

Cole died and Tess brought him back.

That had been an unbelievable feat and a powerful example of the strength of Gallize bonding.

Cole's business demeanor softened as soon as he laid eyes on his mate. He stood up and gifted her with a smile of welcome as she walked around the table to stand with him. She matched his smile and sent it around the room as a hello to everyone.

Tess announced, "Scarlett said she shouldn't have to meet with you after you didn't get the name of the person running the bounty hunters ... "

Justin said, "Are you kidding me?"

Cole snarled, "Give her a chance to finish."

Tess continued, "Scarlett didn't want to come here today, but she wants to thank you in person for saving the captives."

Looking chagrined, Justin said, "Sorry."

All was forgiven, because Cole's mate smiled again and added, "I'm only willing to accept your apology if you give Scarlett a chance without blowing up at her. I don't know if she'll continue to work with us or not." When her eyes moved to Rory, she said,

"Sorry about what happened to your leg."

"Thanks, but I'm good." He nodded at the Guardian. "He used his double-whammy healing." That had been the first time he'd made full eye contact with her. He asked, "What's up with your eye color?"

She blushed. "Uhm, I think, uh ... "

The Guardian zeroed in on her as soon as Rory asked the question. Their boss broke out a rare smile and said, "Congratulations. I'm extremely pleased at this news."

Cole put his arm around her. "Thank you."

Rory asked, "What news?"

Tess found her voice. "We're expecting. We guessed that my eyes changing from blue to lavender had to do with the baby."

Watching the happy couple, Rory envied Cole for the life he had ahead of him and the woman who would share that life, but the moment passed. He reminded himself that he did not want what they had.

He ignored how, for the first time, that reminder had a hollow and insincere feel.

Ferrell gave a deep groan and said one word with deep longing. *Mate.*

Rory didn't acknowledge Ferrell. Instead, he said, "Way to go, you two. Congratulations."

"Thanks."

Justin groaned. "Eli wants one, too."

Tess laughed. "Then get busy."

"I have been, when I get a chance to be home."

The Guardian angled his head in the odd way he did sometimes. "You've been working very hard, Justin. We have new personnel back from overseas. You should take some time off."

"Thank you, sir, but we have a lot going on in the southeast. While our guys are all top notch, I know how they need time to adjust when they come back to the States. I'll ask for time soon." Grinning at Tess, Justin said, "The good news is you'll have a babysitter any time you need it. Happy for both of you. Bet you catch hell at work for that eye color, though," he teased.

She waved it off. "I'm telling everyone it's contacts and a new look I'm trying out." Tess snapped around at the Guardian. "Speaking of eyes, Scarlett will be here soon. Do you plan to stay for this meeting, sir?"

"I do."

"Well, uhm, she might notice your eyes." Her cheeks flushed with embarrassment as if she'd criticized his eyes.

The Guardian took no offense. "I realize that and appreciate your concern, Tess, but I plan to be more involved as we slowly reveal the Gallize presence on a limited basis. I trust your judgment on allowing Scarlett to meet my shifters and I have no problem with her seeing my eyes, but for now I would prefer to not tell her about the Gallize. One step at a time."

Nodding, Tess said, "Got it. And, yes, I do trust her. She maintains autonomy from all as an independent contractor for SCIS."

Rory had a love-hate attitude about SCIS, which captured criminal shifters and sometimes shifters they just tagged as criminals. Not everyone in SCIS had a moral code like Tess. She enforced an iron rule about treating everyone fairly, regardless of whether they were human or not.

The door opened and Hawk said, "Scarlett Sullivan is here." He backed away as a woman entered. She had brunette hair braided in some complicated style that left some woven strands falling past her shoulders—how'd women do that stuff?—and eyes a deep forest green. At first, her expression had been hard and irritated, but with one inhale and slow look around the room, those eyes revealed a hint of concern.

He couldn't blame her.

She hid a cat of some type. He was certain of that now. But she'd just walked into a room filled with apex predators. Her cat felt powerful, but her hind sense had to be warning her to back out slowly and vanish.

The Guardian stood and stepped forward. "Very nice to meet you in person, Ms. Sullivan. Tess speaks highly of you and your skills. You're welcome here and I guarantee your safety."

Scarlett raised her gaze to the Guardian. The quick lift of her eyebrows was the only indication she'd noticed either his eyes or the power that rushed out with his vow of safety.

"Nice to meet you," Scarlett said with more professional tone than sincerity. Her gaze moved to Tess, who gave Scarlett an encouraging look and nodded as if to say, "He *is* the baddest predator in the room."

Being the only other cat shifter present, Rory decided to break the ice. "Thanks for your intel. You were spot-on about the bounty hunters. They just didn't have Jugo Loco."

"Good." That drew her attention to Rory. She inhaled in his direction. When he canted his head at her in a nod of acknowledgement, she simply said, "Yes, I'm a cat."

The Guardian remained patient as they all waited to see if she'd stay. He suggested, "Would you like to sit down? We'd appreciate a moment of your time."

Turning to the Guardian, Scarlett said, "I accept your assurance of safety, because Tess would not walk me into a trap, but I do have one question. What the hell is this? A meeting of ... alphas?"

A rumble of quiet laughter circled the room and even the Guardian smiled.

Justin cleared his throat and said, "You're close. We're not alphas of any group or clan, but *he* is the one we consider our alpha." Justin nodded at the Guardian. "Any more than that, he'll have to share."

Tess stepped around Cole and took a seat on Rory's side of the table. Scarlett walked around and sat between Tess and Rory."

Once she was settled, the Guardian explained, "These are unusual shifters. Every one is as powerful as an alpha who can draw on a pack's power, possibly stronger. Just as you have secrets, we do as well. We will share what we can when it's necessary, but we would prefer to show mutual respect by agreeing that any question may be asked, but that doesn't mean every question will be answered."

Scarlett lifted her chin. "I'm good with that." Propping an elbow on the table, she said, "Now that introductions are out of the way, thank you for saving the females and their children, but what happened yesterday?"

Rory could feel tension roll off Justin and figured he'd help his buddy out by answering first. "We showed up expecting to find pallets of Jugo Loco. We discovered the captives and called for backup to safely extract them. At that point, we believed we still had a shot at gaining the intel we originally planned to deliver.

Then we found out someone was expected to arrive soon to take part of the group before our additional people would arrive. If we'd allowed them to separate the captives, we couldn't have saved all of them. We had to shift our entire plan from an intel gathering operation to a rescue mission on the spot."

Justin picked up the thread, saying, "We still had a plan to get your intel, which was to allow one of the bounty hunters to go free and track him."

Frowning now, Scarlett asked, "That didn't work?"

Justin's tension had settled. "Two of us could have taken down the six shifters guarding the cages, but when Vic and I went down there, two more were hiding and they were jacked up on Jugo Loco. One wolf was a behemoth. So oversized he had to be amped up with some kind of steroid drug for shifters."

"Shit," Scarlett cursed softly.

"Exactly," Justin said. "At the same time we were fighting those six, Rory had taken the lead to insert into the woods so he could track the runner. Instead, he ended up facing the steroid wolf shifter and his sidekick at the same time. He almost lost his leg in that fight."

Rory didn't correct Justin's edited version, which didn't mention the two jackals he'd told Justin about during the debriefing. That was unnecessary information at this meeting.

Scarlett turned to Rory. "Sorry about your leg."

He nodded in reply.

Then addressing the room, she said, "Saving those shifters is absolutely more important than any intel—"

Justin leaned back. "Good."

"—but I still want what I expected from our agreement."

Justin sent a glare to Cole, which Rory read as, "*What's with this ballbuster?*"

Cole lifted a hand, silently asking Justin to be patient.

As normal, the Guardian listened to everyone before he gave his thoughts on any situation. "You have a valid point, Ms. Sullivan, but you're concerned only with this one time."

"You can call me Scarlett and what are you talking about? We've had only *one* deal."

"I would like to propose that with a little patience and cooperation on both sides, that you would gain far more than a single name by forming a working association. If you were to agree to consider an ongoing relationship with our organization, you would be able to ask for aid when needed in exchange for sharing intel with my people as well."

Leaning back, Scarlett lifted a finger to poke her cheek. "I get the feeling you probably have an impressive intelligence network."

"Yes, we do."

"Then what could you possibly want from me?"

Standing with one hand in the pocket of his suit pants, in something Rory had come to think of as a practiced, human-like move to appear relaxed, the Guardian replied, "My people have worked on large scale operations for a long time, which often involved conflicts between countries. The ultimate goals have been peace and the protection of innocents." He extended his free hand to encompass the people around the table. "These teams here are now tasked with more complex situations. We're finding our network is not as effective at the ground level, where you seem to be deeply enmeshed in the everyday shifter world."

She tapped her cheek, as she seemed to ponder his words. "When you say innocents, are you talking about humans only?"

"Absolutely not. We will always protect preternatural beings, just as we did on this last mission."

"Maybe not a Power Baron," Justin muttered.

The Guardian merely lifted an eyebrow and Justin fell quiet.

"I get what you're saying," Scarlett said. "If I agree to this, is there any limitation on what I can ask for?"

The Guardian qualified, "Only if it is outside my ability to grant your request or would put my people in an unreasonable level of danger."

Rory wanted to chuckle. He couldn't recall anyone every saying a mission was too dangerous, but the Guardian would never send his people in when there was no hope for survival.

Sitting forward, Scarlett dropped her hand to the table. "I'm willing to give this a try."

Giving her as pleasant a look as someone with ancient eagle eyes could, the Guardian said, "Thank you. We shall also give it a try."

Scarlett smirked at the counter to her comment. "Back to the bounty hunters."

Justin groaned.

She snarled.

Tess told Justin, "Don't forget your apology."

Scarlett asked, "What apology?"

Waving her hand for Scarlett to continue, Tess said, "It's a personal thing. Go ahead with what you were saying."

"I do want to find the person running the bounty hunter groups. They're dealing Jugo Loco, but as you saw, they're also trafficking innocent shifters who only want to live in peace. I went to the Friends Of Shifters shelter to check on the captives you brought in."

Cole interjected, "I didn't think they'd allow anyone inside the FOS shelters without getting clearance, which normally takes a few days and a lot of red tape."

"That's true. As one of the founding members, I helped craft that waiting period, but I have constant access."

Rory grew respect for Scarlett in that moment. There were groups of humans who actively targeted anyone who helped shifters. Scarlett had just shown a return of trust for meeting the Guardian and his shifters by revealing her strong association with FOS.

Tess asked, "Are they okay?"

"Yes," Scarlett said with a heavy sigh. "The children are still terrified and the women are wary, but some asked me to tell the team that they're sorry for yelling at you for not releasing them from the cages. They didn't know who you were."

Running a hand over his tawny hair, Justin said, "Tell 'em it's fine. We get yelled at from time to time." He smiled, the earlier tension abated.

Scarlett paused then said, "But one is missing."

Rory did his best not to react. He forced his breathing to stay calm or every shifter in the room would focus on him. His damn jaguar brought up the image of the nymph waving goodbye and running into the woods.

That was a first. No gory or insulting image.

Justin's forehead scrunched up. "Who?"

Rory wouldn't look at Justin. He'd told him about the female he'd saved from the jackals, so Justin was fishing for what Scarlett knew.

"Said her name was Jane, but the shifter didn't believe that. This woman is not a shifter." Scarlett drummed her fingers on the table. "I hate to start off our new association by burning a request for a nonshifter, but this woman helped a shifter female and her son. Because of being with them, she got caught in the bounty hunters' dragnet. They said two jackal guards took the woman away and never returned."

The Guardian asked, "What exactly are you requesting?"

"I'd like you to find her and bring her back safely," Scarlett said without hesitation. "I don't want to leave her to all the predators who might be after her once they catch her scent at the site where you killed the bounty hunters. Once she's safe, I'd also like a chance to question her to see if she has any additional information on the bounty hunters."

After a moment of silence when no one dared speak before the boss, the Guardian said, "She clearly escaped. Do you have any idea where she might have been heading?"

"I have more than that. I know where she is right now."

Rory sat forward before he realized he'd moved. She knew what happened to his nymph? "Where is she?"

Scarlett stared at him. "You saw her, didn't you?"

"I attacked two jackals who had a woman pinned down. She ran and I had two wolves on me next." He kept it vague, because Scarlett didn't need to know he'd held the woman. Prickly as Scarlett was, she might get her hackles up over that. He said, "Between getting the place locked down and caring for the captives, plus my leg dangling loose, we had no one to go after her. You say you found her?"

Scarlett took a moment and said, "Yes. I found out an hour ago that a woman fitting her description was arrested in Pittsburgh, Pennsylvania, then sent to a hospital."

"Was she injured?" Rory prodded. He could feel eyes on him due to his immediate interest, but he didn't care. He had a burning drive to find her again. He'd worry about why later.

"Yes and no," Scarlett hedged. "She stepped in front of a

slow-moving car that knocked her out. She wasn't physically harmed, but bystanders claimed she was acting strangely and waving her hands wildly at something no one else could see. They thought she was off her rocker and sent her to a mental hospital. Pennsylvania has a provision for sending someone to be observed for a limited time."

That woman hadn't seemed the least bit crazy when Rory spoke to her.

The Guardian announced, "We will help you locate this woman and bring her back, but I also have a request."

"Fair enough. What is it?"

"I'm looking for a tiger shifter on his own in this country. Before you ask why, I am concerned about his health."

Scarlett said, "Those are fairly rare. You have any idea where *he* is?"

"We have some possible places to start looking, which I'll share, but for now I'd like you to put it out on your network and see if anything pops up."

"I can do that," Scarlett agreed.

Rory's heart thumped harder and harder. He'd spent the long, miserable night thinking about his nymph and how his body had healed right after she touched him. Now he could find her.

Justin asked, "What does this woman look like?"

Rory caught himself before he blurted out the answer.

Scarlett said, "I have a sketch I'll send Tess. She's in her twenties, average height and size, has white hair to her shoulders. One brown eye and one blue."

Shit. Rory never saw her eyes.

With her power, she might be a Gallize female.

He had no business going after a woman he had no intention of mating, not when one of his Gallize brothers needed a mate.

But damn, just the idea of anyone else touching her had his jaguar rumbling and his gut in knots. What the hell was wrong with him?

He only needed to find out why her touch had healed him.

This punched-in-the-gut sensation didn't feel like that was the only reason, but he would not stand in the way of a Gallize getting a mate.

They thought she was crazy, but she'd just been ... sweet. And brave. And scared.

The Guardian walked over and extended his hand to Scarlett. "Thank you for your alliance. We'll form a team immediately to locate this woman."

Scarlett stood and shook his hand. "You're welcome. I hope this turns out to be a good thing for all of us. I'll see what I can shake out on any tiger shifter and let Tess know what I find."

Tess said, "I'll walk out with you."

Once those two left, the Guardian announced, "Cole and Justin, I want to see you in the conference room."

Rory struggled to stand, which started his leg throbbing after sitting for so long. "Sir, I'd like to join that meeting."

"No." With that final word, Cole, Justin and the Guardian walked out.

Ferrell sent Rory an image of the woman who had haunted his dreams last night. Again, she smiled and took off into the woods, but this time she ran into the wide-open jaws of some monster with blood dripping from its fangs.

Rory leaned on his cane and looked down at his aching leg. Could he shift and heal it faster? Would it even heal any more on its own?

Asking to be put on this team might push his boss to lock Rory away in Wyoming until he remembered who ran this operation. Any shifter with a lick of good sense could see there was no changing the Guardian's mind.

"Shit," Rory muttered and hobbled forward.

No one ever accused him of having good sense.

CHAPTER 10

SIOFRA GRABBED HER HEAD. IT felt twice its normal size, just like her thick tongue. She licked her dry lips and blinked, trying to get her eyes to focus, but there wasn't much light. Her body registered being in a prone position, on a mattress no more comfortable than the one she'd slept on in the camps.

No, please don't be a camp bed.

Squinting, she lifted her head and saw blank walls in the semi-darkness. Not really blank. One wall, an arm's length away, had a single word carved into it with a sharp object.

Help! The letters were jagged as if created in panic.

Her skin pebbled with a chill that started in her chest. Not the camp, but where was she?

Was it still Monday?

Was she still in Pittsburgh?

Ambient light filtered through a glass panel on a very sturdy looking steel door. As her eyes adjusted, that small window allowed her enough light to see the room better.

She struggled to sit up. Her arms shook and were weak as noodles.

Sliding her legs over the side of the single bed, she clutched the edge as she eased her way to a sitting position.

What time was it?

Better yet, what day was it?

A paper cup of water had been placed on the floor.

If they wanted to kill her, they could have done it while she was passed out. Why poison her?

She suffered a moment of dizziness when she leaned over and

lifted the water. It sloshed in her trembling hand. She sipped the refreshing liquid even though it was warm.

Another wave of dizziness hit her and she nearly dropped the cup. Lying down again seemed like a good idea.

She'd barely eased back onto the mattress when a noise in the hallway reached her. She let the cup fall to the floor and became perfectly still. Would that be someone coming to see her? What had she done to end up here?

She lowered her eyelids until she could peek while appearing asleep.

The flick of the lock sounded, then the door opened and two men stepped in, pulling the door shut softly.

Both wore lab coats above dark trousers, but nothing about those two fit her idea of hospital personnel.

One stood over six feet tall, had olive skin, dark eyes and thick black hair combed straight back. He had the frightening face of mobsters, but he didn't look Italian. He seemed more Latin. A scar split his eyebrow, giving her hope he was not a shifter even though she'd seen some with scars, but every speck of her intuition said she needed to run.

His badge identified him as Dr. Rabinowitz.

Oh, sure, and she was the queen of England.

Shorter by an inch, his partner had similar Latin features except for the blond hair spiking out of dark roots across his head. He wore a diamond earring in one ear and a sneer she bet had been there since birth. He'd stolen the ID badge of Dr. Wexler.

While pseudo Wexler watched the window on the door, Rabinowitz wannabe approached Siofra. "I know you are awake."

She'd like to say she moved fast as a ninja to leap away from him, but an honest person would say she resembled a frightened crab with arthritic legs.

He stopped as she squeezed herself as tightly as she could into the corner. His words had a Latin accent. "You are hard woman to find."

"Who are you?" she asked.

"Is not important."

"Are you shifters?"

From over by the door, the Wexler one laughed. "Hell, no."

This was bad, but maybe not Black River pack bad since they weren't shifters, if they had told the truth.

The Cadells could have sent them.

Either way, these men were not here for her benefit.

Under her breath, Siofra murmured, "I need help. Please, spirits of light, show yourself now if you're nearby."

A glimmer of energy began forming next to her bed.

Pretend Rabinowitz stared at Siofra with suspicion.

A young female ghost in an oversized hospital gown that drooped off one shoulder appeared. Her frizzy hair jutted out in all directions as if she'd never been introduced to a brush. She was missing all but three teeth and paused in licking the bottom of a boot to grin at Siofra.

When her lips moved, a childlike voice spoke in Siofra's mind. *Pickles and hotdogs for lunch. Can't be late.*

Siofra's shoulders sagged with defeat.

What had she expected? The spirit of a Special Forces operative to be walking these halls, who would tell her how to knock these guys out and get past the hospital staff?

If only.

Phony Rabinowitz muttered, "Do not start shit with me. I heard you were crazy and talked to spirits. If you had not caused a scene near the homeless mission, we wouldn't have had to come here for you."

Crap, that's why the ghosts had been trying to stop her.

He pulled his hand from his jacket and tossed dust at her.

Sparkles flickered in front her eyes. She tried to jerk back, but she had nowhere to go in the corner. The dust remained suspended in the air surrounding her face.

With no idea that had been coming, she inhaled in reaction, sucking the dust in.

Lights swirled around her. The spirit floated in and out of focus, lips still moving.

Siofra couldn't hear the woman. She also couldn't control her arms or legs. She crumpled to her side, hitting the bed in a heap, vaguely aware of being picked up and tossed over a shoulder.

The man carrying her moved forward and the floor blurred past.

The door opened.

Someone shouted, then she heard the fake Wexler doctor tell his sidekick that he had this.

The big guy carrying her slowed. A flash brightened everything for a second, then dimmed. The guy toting her picked up speed again. He stepped over two men in white pants and shirts.

Well, hell. Would she end up back with the Cadells after all?

Baatar would be so disappointed and that hurt even more.

Her vision blurred then returned to focus. What had been in that dust?

Warm air blew up her hospital gown and she blinked to sort out the dark surroundings. Dim illumination from streetlights touched the sidewalk, grass and then the pavement. Then the sound of a car door being opened sounded loud to her ears.

He dumped her limp body inside ... a van. Not a car.

She had to get out of here, but her body would not obey her mind. She couldn't make even her toe twitch.

One of them asked, "Think we should shackle her?"

"Sure. Better to play it extra safe so we don't lose her. They said she had some freaky power, so no telling what she might try to do when that dust wears off."

The Wexler wannabe leaned into the rear of the van, still as surly looking as he'd been in her room. He pulled her limp body around and yanked her arm up.

"Ouch." That's what she thought she said, but it came out as a garbled groan.

When he reached over her body to yank her other arm up, she saw the inside of his wrist where he had a tattoo of a snarling wolf.

She'd been kidnapped by magic users aligned with a Black River pack. She screamed in her head, rocking back and forth all alone in the cargo area.

How had *they* found her? How would they even know?

The Cadells had told them.

The ride seemed to take forever, though in truth she had no concept of time. She didn't waste her energy trying to fight the shackles. When the van finally stopped, it was even darker here than outside the hospital she'd been in.

Spike opened the rear doors and removed her shackles, leaning close to give her a warning. "That's not the only magic my buddy and I use. Don't push me to pull out something vicious."

Point taken. She nodded.

Two shifters, because she recognized the unnatural look in their eyes, dragged her from the van and over to where someone hit her full blast with cold water. She tried to hunch into herself, but the wolves held her arms in their immovable grip.

When the brutal bath ended, the last of the dust was out of her system. They walked her through the compound. Where was she? The only building looked to be a large wooden house, not tall, but spread out. Lights blazed inside.

She tried to take in everything, remembering what Baatar had taught her about escaping any situation if she ever got out of the work camp and got caught.

First, she had to be aware of all possible exits.

She could only find one and it was the way she'd entered.

As doors opened ahead of her, the two shifters walked her into a room where a man stood behind a desk. He wore fatigues and had a heavy brown beard to match his dark-brown hair. When he glanced up, she stared into the glowing yellow eyes of his wolf.

Her heart thumped out of control and she knew from living around jackals that every shifter in this area could hear her heart rate.

Their boss cocked his head and smiled. "You should be very afraid. I am Hector. You put me through a lot of trouble to locate you. The Cadells said if I found you, they would trade you for Baatar."

She was too stunned to think. Hector, as in Mad Dog Hector? Everyone in the camps had heard the horrible stories about this animal. He was the crazy wolf shifter who cut pieces off a body to see how long he could keep someone alive without all their parts.

The guard on her right backhanded her.

She fell to the floor and grabbed her throbbing face. He could have killed her if he'd hit her harder, but she couldn't drag up appreciation for being hit with only half his strength.

The other guard jerked her back to her knees.

Hector said, "That is your only warning to lower your gaze and show respect."

She looked at the rough wood floor that needed to be swept and nodded, unable to get a word out. If she needed to act subservient to bide her time, she would. She'd bitten her tongue. Blood trickled from her lip and the jaw she cupped was already swelling.

Hector said, "Give her water."

After a series of footsteps, a guard handed her a cup of water. She rinsed her mouth out and spit back into the cup, turning it pink with her blood.

But now she could talk. "I'd like to—"

A guard grabbed a wad of her hair and twisted her head back with a claw at her throat.

She dropped the cup and fisted her hands. "Please let me—"

"Why should anyone listen to your pleas?" Hector asked with amusement in his words. "You have made many angry. First, the Cadells are furious that you killed a jackal."

"No, I—"

"Shut. Up."

The guard holding her hair twisted it tighter.

She kept her lips closed, but tears burned her eyes. *Don't interrupt the insane man while he's speaking from his private podium.*

Hector continued his oration, which had to be for the benefit of the ten shifters standing around the room. "You think I care if you kill a jackal? The jackal pack he belonged to may want your blood, but me? I would reward you with an extra meal for killing one. The Cadells are not so happy with your deceit."

What deceit? Her confusion must have shown in her face.

Hector explained, "Your power. You never showed any signs of your power before killing that guard. If you had, they would have sold you to me for a pretty penny, but once you escaped you became fair game for everyone. Then there are the humans. You caused a wreck in the middle of Pittsburgh. Everyone will want to sue you for the damage. You should thank me for saving you those problems."

Damage did not sound like deaths. For that, she was thankful, but not for this miserable scum capturing her.

"Now we come to your greatest crime."

What could possibly top all of that in his eyes?

"You helped Baatar escape. We have been in negotiations for

over a year on that one. The Cadells kept holding out until now. We had just reached an agreement when you two escaped."

Baatar? He got away? *He got away!*

She had to get out of here and find him.

He had plenty of muscle and speed to outmaneuver anyone, but he'd kept his mental and physical issues to himself until he'd had one around Siofra. His troublesome episodes had gotten worse in recent weeks. With her help, he'd kept his sporadic loss of control hidden from the Cadells, but he needed someone to protect him when he lost touch with reality.

They were a pair, for sure, but he was hers to watch over.

She had an idea, but first she had to convince Hector to trust her.

With her hair pulled back so tightly, she could only squeak out, "I can help you."

Hector snapped his fingers and the guard freed her.

Siofra lowered her chin and stared hard at Hector's boots so she could keep an eye on his face in her peripheral vision. "Cadells are never going to give you Baatar. Not for me. Not for ten of me unless you pay them a ton of money as well. But *I* can find Baatar, save you all that money."

"Why would you?" Hector's eyes turned black with suspicion.

"I want to find him as much as you do. I had no idea he had also escaped, but it's perfect timing to blame it all on me. If I help you find him, I want a blood oath you will allow me to walk free." These wolves would never let her leave or give her a true blood oath. She just needed to make them think she believed the deal would work.

Hector didn't appear to be sold yet. She had to be careful. Shifters could smell a lie. She pushed her gaze lower to the floor. "I've spent years as a Cadell captive only to have a jackal try to rape me to make me pregnant even after they determined I'm infertile." Maybe knowing she couldn't be used as a breeder would keep lowering her value to them.

He studied her a moment. "I still do not see the reason you would betray Baatar?"

"Who is he to me?" she sneered, keeping her eyes averted, which was good because her face might give her away. "What would you do if someone killed the person you love?" she asked.

Baatar had done no such thing, but this wolf should not be able to find a lie in that.

"I would gut him."

She shrugged. "I can't do that. I'm not a killer." Smiling hurt, but she had to look the part of some evil crazy person when she lifted her gaze. "Handing him over to the Black River pack would be far worse."

If she could cross her fingers, she would.

CHAPTER 11

Southwestern corner of West Virginia

RORY RUBBED HIS CALF TO ease the ache still stinging there. He had a killer headache from lack of sleep and a foul mood that matched his jaguar's usual nasty attitude. Ferrell liked the dark. He wanted out to run through these woods. It had been a long Monday and it wasn't over yet. Rory could not get his jaguar to be quiet while there was nothing to do but wait.

The team had arrived around nine. Had to be ten by now and they still didn't know if they'd located the woman they'd been sent to retrieve.

He intended to find a soft bed and crash out for days once this was done, but not until he knew for sure his little white-haired nymph was safe.

Ferrell snarled again. *Mate.*

His jaguar was losing its ever-lovin' mind.

Justin and Cole, also in human form, sat a few feet away.

If the compound they observed tucked deep in this forest turned out to be a Black River pack location, their rule to not shift might change. Little air moved, but it was actually cooler tonight in this corner of West Virginia than it had been in Spartanburg.

He owed Justin for this, especially after cursing the bear under his breath when the Guardian refused to allow Rory to go on this mission.

In fact, when Rory pushed his way into the meeting, the boss had warned he was seriously considering putting Rory into a static state so he could finish healing.

At the idea of being put into the equivalent of a medically induced coma by the powerful eagle shifter, Rory's jaguar had almost pushed out of him.

Justin must have realized Rory had a problem at that moment. He'd smoothly bumped the topic away from Rory's health. "Why do you want to go on this mission?"

"It's more that you need me to be there. That young woman has power unlike anything I've ever encountered. She killed a jackal just by putting her hands on it, but she claims to have no control over the power. Even so, she didn't harm me. I think she trusts me after I pulled those jackals off of her."

"Powerful *and* unmatched eyes?" the Guardian asked with sudden interest. "Why didn't you mention that before now?"

"To be honest, I didn't know about her eyes until Scarlett told us. The woman kept her eyes averted and I was focused on calming her down to convince her to hide while I cleared the bodies before the runner showed up. As for her power, it strikes me as off-the-charts." Rory asked his boss, "Do you think she might be a Gallize female?"

"Possibly, but mismatched eyes are just one marker and not an absolute indication, even when matched with power."

Cole joined in, asking, "If she's so dangerous and you're still healing, why would you want to go with us? You would never take a teammate who couldn't stand up or fight at a hundred percent."

The Guardian's intense gaze locked on Rory as he also waited for the answer.

"The jackals I pulled off of her were trying to get her to shift, because she'd been caught with the other shifters. She was hurt at first, but during a skirmish when she stepped close to one that wasn't dead, I pulled her back. I think she was still in shock, but she allowed me to hold her to calm her down." He'd never forget the feeling of that no matter how long he lived.

"Oh?" That's all Justin said and Rory heard ten questions right behind it. Damn bear.

Rory hurried to push past Justin's curious tone and explained, "That's why I don't think she'll allow anyone else close to her, especially a shifter. When she got her wits about her, she backed off fast. I told her we would help her and she said we *couldn't* help her, that shifters are all dangerous. She seemed sincerely confused about her power. I think she could be a risk if someone else approached her until we know what we're dealing with, but she'll talk to me. I believe that."

After his appeal and pointing out that the woman could harm someone even accidentally, the Guardian agreed to allow Rory to go with the team under one condition. If he had not healed by the time he returned, the Guardian would expect him to accept being put into stasis for a week or two.

Nope, nope, nope. That was not on Rory's wish list.

He understood the Guardian was worried about him and had only Rory's best interest at heart, but his jaguar would snap.

Ferrell sent him an image of fetching a dead eagle and returning it to Rory like a Labrador would on a pheasant hunt.

If the Guardian ever picked up one of those images, he might deal with Ferrell himself. The Guardian could speak to them mind to mind, but Rory had never known his boss to just enter a mind unexpectedly.

"How you doin'?" Justin asked without turning his head from where he studied the house through binoculars. The place was lit up like they were having a party.

Rory pulled his hand from where he'd been massaging his calf and said, "I'm fine."

Cole snorted. "I smelled that lie from over here." He spoke softly because of his comm unit, which all five of them wore tonight. But since Rory waited with Justin and Cole, he had removed his ear bud for the moment.

Until they confirmed this was indeed a Black River pack location and the pack had the white-haired woman, they could only sit and wait. A second team had been put on ready in case new reports came in about someone else who might have her.

Scarlett stood by her intel and claimed they'd find the woman here. To her credit, she'd been sending information nonstop once she discovered his nymph had been captured.

He did a mental headshake. He had to stop even thinking that moniker for their target package. She was not *his* in any way, shape or form.

Leaning back against the base of a tree, Justin asked, "What do you think, Rory? Could she be a Gallize?"

"I have no idea, but Cole didn't know Tess was a Gallize until we all watched her bring him back to life."

"She's fucking amazing," Cole said in a voice loaded with admiration.

Rory asked, "How'd you know when you met Eli that she was your mate, Justin?"

The bear shifter scoffed. "Shit, I was clueless about Eli at first, but my bear knew she was our mate, which opened my eyes to the possibility. I did realize she was an alpha bear capable of handling the power in our bond. She's got plenty of her own. Once I realized that and my bear wanted her as much as I did, it didn't really matter if she was a Gallize."

Considering his two mated friends, Rory asked, "What about now?"

"Huh?" They both turned to him.

"Can you tell other Gallize shifters how they might recognize a mate?"

Justin continued his surveillance while he answered. "That's a good question. We should be analyzing this for the others, especially if the woman we're hunting is a Gallize."

Cole said, "Tess hid her power for years because she feared it would make her an outcast, but once I felt her energy it ... shit, this will sound stupid, but—"

"But what?" Rory pushed.

"I think my mate's power called to mine ... or my animal and my power recognized hers."

Justin lowered the glasses a fraction. "Not stupid. I think you're onto it. I feel the same thing with Eli. It's as if our energy is in sync when we're together and misses each other's power when we're apart." He chuckled. "Now I sound loony."

Rory didn't comment when he'd normally agree about Justin being loony just to poke at his friend. He was too busy recalling how the nymph's energy had buzzed up to where they touched and ... she'd healed him. Or maybe her power had performed the actual healing.

Had his power recognized hers and that's why he healed?

No way.

She might be a Gallize female, but she was not *his* mate, just a healer. His healer. He had no business feeling proprietary about her, but bottom line? He didn't like the idea of her power calling to another Gallize shifter.

Add him to the loony list.

Rory's jaguar sent him a new image of the nymph walking with her hand on Ferrell's back. He silently warned, *Don't even start that shit, Ferrell.*

He got a snort in return. How much trouble would it be to just say one word?

Ferrell growled, *Mate.*

No. Pick another word, Rory countered.

He received nothing but silence this time.

Rory told his beast, *You could be working on fixing my leg.*

He got a picture of a jaguar limping along on three legs. Damn drama queen.

"Shit, something's going down," Justin murmured.

Twisting around, Rory shoved the comm unit back into place and snapped into mission mode. "Got the audio, Cole?"

"Yep." The wolf shifter held a small electronic listening device that resembled a miniature bullhorn, which would pick up audio from three hundred feet away.

In this case, they were half that distance. Even with shifter hearing, they could miss something significant without the electronics.

Cole informed the team he was linking all the comm units into the feed so everyone would know what was being said.

When the audio picked up, one of the wolves was telling two others, "Everybody is looking for that bitch. She's gotta go as soon as the boss finishes with her."

A second wolf snickered. "He should turn her over to us. We haven't had a group plaything in two weeks. 'Bout time for a new one."

Rory's body vibrated. They could be talking about any female, but his gut said they were discussing his nymph. His jaguar raged to get out and go after those wolves. Rory locked his control down to maintain his position until Justin signaled any action.

Kill wolves.

Shit, his jaguar said two words. When had that ever happened?

Never.

Another wolf shifter walked out of the building and kept his voice down as he said, "Boss is almost through with her."

The one who wanted a gangbang said, "He giving her to us?"

"As soon as he gets all he needs first."

Rory cut his comm mic and told Justin, "Time to go get her."

Cole said, "We don't have confirmed identi—"

"It's her, dammit. I know it."

Cole and Justin swung their heads at Rory with matching frowns. Justin said, "What the fuck? We just forget the plan and dive into this shit?"

This was going to get him busted big time with the Guardian, but his body was about to explode into a maniac jaguar determined to protect the nymph.

Fighting the panic to go after her, Rory said, "If one of you told me you knew in a way you couldn't explain that you were right about something, I'd believe you. I'm telling you right now, they have our target. If you aren't willing to go in, then at least agree to let me insert."

Justin cursed silently but in a vicious tone. When he looked back at Rory, he said, "Stop putting me in the position of trying to be fair when it comes to you."

"I understand and that's why if you'll let me go now, I'll be the one to tell the Guardian what I did. Not you. That isn't fair. I'm responsible for what I do. I don't want to screw this mission, but I have to get in there. If we wait, they may take her out another door, then we'll be too late to stop the group rape."

Cole and Justin cringed at that statement. Gallize shifters were the most honorable men Rory had ever known and they'd do anything to protect a woman, human or shifter, but they were hesitating.

Rory's claws shot out, drawing Justin's worried look to his hands.

Shit, his jaguar was raging to get free.

Shifting without a valid reason on this mission would be the one thing the Guardian would not let pass.

CHAPTER 12

FROM WHERE SHE KNELT ON the hard floor, Siofra held her breath as Hector walked around his desk and put a hip on the front of it. She peeked up to find him staring hard at her. Lowering her gaze again, she considered what to say next.

She couldn't outright lie, not with all these Black River pack shifters standing close, but she'd learned by age ten how to do a damn good two-step around the truth just to survive.

She did not have shifter-level heightened senses, but the smell of fur overwhelmed her even with them all in human form.

Hector asked, "You would help us hunt down this man the Cadells tell me you were friends with?"

"Yes. I don't see him as a friend." That was true only because she considered Baatar a brother, so much more than a friend. But she'd had to sound confident even if her heart hurt just saying those words.

She was in a compound deep in the woods in the middle of nowhere. Convincing Hector she told the truth was her only way out of here and she had slim hope of that.

"That is not what I hear, *chica*. They tell me you two were close. That Baatar sometimes protected you."

She huffed a dry laugh. "Of course he did. First of all, he liked me. I'm very likable," she quipped.

Hector said nothing, so she added, "Baatar is a wise planner. He said he'd help me escape. He needed me to help him understand things that confused him here."

"What things?" Hector demanded.

"He wasn't born here and hasn't had a lot of time to acclimate to this country. He needed a guide." Also the truth. While Baatar was very intelligent and resourceful, everyday things and slang terminology sometimes tripped him up. She added, "I knew all the guards and their schedules where he'd only arrived in the camp six months ago."

Not slowing down, she shrugged. "He made it clear he would help me escape and I took him up on his offer. Why wouldn't I? The Cadells were probably planning to sell me to your pack to be used like a guinea pig. Baatar orchestrated my escape. He told me exactly how to get out of the camp and find a highway. I didn't even know there was a highway. That was key in making it out of their territory."

No one could question that. Every bit of it came from reality. Some wolves she could peek at studied her with confusion, but no one appeared ready to condemn her words if their alpha did not.

Hector said nothing for a while. She could feel him staring at her, probably in a dilemma.

He asked, "You would deceive him after he helped you escape?"

She had never thought of herself as a siren, but she tried for a sly smile. Giving another lift to her shoulder as if to dismiss the importance of her giving up Baatar, she said, "I'm a woman. We don't see things like that as deceit so much as ... creative thinking." She bluffed, hoping she sounded like a cold bitch willing to use a man to get whatever she wanted.

Baatar would roll his eyes at her if he stood here.

Low growling started and someone muttered, "*Puta.*"

Mission accomplished.

Hector lifted a hand and the room quieted at once. Stepping around to the front of his desk, he paced back and forth, muttering to himself until he paused. "Do you know the price of lying to me?"

"No, but I can probably figure it out," she muttered, sure her imagination was up to par after having lived around jackals.

Hector's sick smile came through in his words. "I promise you that you have no idea. If you lie to me and even if you escaped—which is impossible while surrounded by shifters—I would send teams everywhere to find you, even if it took years. They would bring you back to face the consequences."

Okay, so she had no imagination equal to that of a monster who probably tortured kittens to relax.

"Why would I lie to you?" she asked, trying to lock down a deal. "I met Baatar six months ago. Why would I put my life on the line for someone I've known almost no time when I've known others in the Cadell camps for years? I'll be very clear. Baatar said he was the greater prize than I am, which is true. He was treated better than even the shifters who guarded us. He will do whatever it takes to remain free. It seems only fair that I do whatever I must for my freedom."

"How will you do this?"

Her heart flipped with hope. "Give me two of your shifters and I will lead them to Baatar. Once we find him, you let me go. No tricks or double cross. You give me a day head start before you tell anyone, like the Cadells, and no one will ever hear from me again."

"You would accept my word for this?" he asked, amused again.

It took so little to entertain a lunatic.

Still talking to the floor, which actually made this easier, she said, "Of course not. I would require you to announce the terms of our agreement to your men with me standing next to you and to give me a blood oath. Your men won't follow someone whose word counts for nothing." She could sense the smiles in the room. Those guys would only be disappointed in Hector if he *did* keep his word to a captive female.

But it was the best bargaining chip she could come up with when her pockets were empty.

Baatar would be proud of her if she pulled this off. He'd laugh about all the things she'd done to get this pack to lead her to him. He'd said if they were ever free, there was only one thing she should *never* mention around strangers.

All she needed was a chance to get close to Baatar. He always told her not to worry about anything except staying alive and sticking to the plan.

Hector acted as if he considered her proposition. "I believe we can do this, but I need to make some arrangements first. My men will show you to a private room where you will be given food and time to rest."

Not the answer she'd been hoping to get immediately, but he sounded as if he just might give her a chance to find Baatar. She'd also avoided being sent to one of their labs, at least for now.

Nodding at the shifter next to her, Hector said, "Take her ... what is your name?"

"Siofra." She could have lied, but he had to know her name and wanted to test her.

"Take Siofra to her room."

The guard hooked a hand under her arm and lifted her like a twig. When she pulled away, he released her, allowing her to turn and walk at his side.

She took being treated better than when she'd arrived as a positive sign, too. This might just work.

She enjoyed only a brief moment of relief, because now they headed for the exit into the scary darkness, and she trusted none of these guards.

Three steps outside the front door, chaos erupted on the side of the building with men shouting and wolves howling.

Someone ran by her guard and spewed orders at him in Spanish.

They must have decided she was not a threat, because both of them tore off in that direction. She could hear Hector bellowing orders in Spanish inside the building.

Moving cautiously, she sidestepped until she reached the edge of the building and stepped into a black void. No windows on this side where light could spill out to illuminate her way along this narrow strip of ground that had been cleared.

She kept her hand on the wall of the building and continued moving, not at all sure where she was going since she'd been brought here hidden inside a van.

But the road they'd traveled on had been smooth until the last half mile. She could run that far without too much trouble.

She'd escaped once by finding a highway. She could do it again.

What crappy timing for some rival group to attack this place when she had Hector convinced to let her take a pair of shifters to track down Baatar. She knew her brother well. He'd outwit the two wolf shifters, take them down and free her.

Now, she was back to starting over again.

She just hoped Baatar would wait for her before he gave up hope of her finding him and disappeared permanently. She also hoped he was not suffering bad physical and emotional problems without her around to watch his back.

Another possibility dawned on her.

Could the attackers be a faction of the Cadells coming to take her back so they could sell her after all?

That would be her freaking luck.

Whoever it was, she needed them to keep the wolves busy until she reached the road. If she couldn't flag down a car fast enough, a shifter from one of the groups would catch up to her quickly.

She hesitated.

If she ran, she couldn't return to face Hector.

He'd never believe her again.

Better to take her chance at freedom and finding Baatar on her own than place her hope for the future on Hector honoring his word.

At the back corner of the building she paused before stepping away from the building where lights were on, which would make her visible to anybody.

Easing around the corner, she saw a man fighting with a guard. When the light hit his face, she recognized him and those flashing gold eyes.

What was *he* doing here?

He fought hard, but he limped around on a bad leg. Why wasn't he shifting? He'd heal and be stronger to fight.

She looked to her right where a path with two rutted lanes led into the woods. That could be the way to the highway or maybe … where they'd parked a vehicle.

With keys in the ignition.

There was her fantasy imagination. She'd never been behind the wheel of an automobile, but might as well wish big.

A grunt of pain jerked her head back to the fight.

The guard had knocked Golden Eyes down and had his foot crushing the injured leg.

That turned her stomach.

The guard shouted to someone else who came walking over, grinning. He held a syringe.

Oh, no. They were going to inject the shifter on the ground, the one who had saved her from jackals. The wolves wouldn't kill a shifter they could knock out and take captive.

Baatar was going to kill her himself if he ever found out about the decisions she'd made, but she couldn't walk away from this.

Baatar would tell her it was shifter-on-shifter, so who cared?

She did, dammit.

When the second guard stepped around the first one to inject Golden Eyes, the wolves had their backs to her. She had her opening.

She rubbed her hands together, hoping for her rogue energy.

Nothing but sweaty palms. *Damn!*

Go to Plan B.

As the guard bent down to stab the syringe, she ran at top speed and plowed into the standing guard. It all happened so fast. She hit the first one, he knocked into the second guard and she landed on top of both of them.

A claw swiped her side. She cried out, but a hand gripped her arm and pulled her off those two.

"What the *fuck* are you doing *again?*" Golden Eyes yelled at her.

She yanked her arm away. "*That is it!* I will never save your sorry ass again, you ungrateful jerk!"

He shoved her behind him and faced the two guards, but another man showed up and growled loud like a bear. He lifted those two wolf shifters by their necks and slammed their heads together.

Looked as if Golden Eyes and his buddy had everything under control.

She started easing backwards and bumped into someone who grabbed her arms. Shit.

"You lose something, guys?" the one who had her in his grasp asked.

Golden Eyes turned to her with a look of disbelief. "Were you going to run again?"

"What do you think? You didn't need me with all your shifter friends," she shot back.

Golden Eyes grabbed his head. "Have you not realized how dangerous it is out here alone? If you are this determined to get yourself killed, then it shouldn't take long."

She gave him a pissy look. "Well, thanks for the encouragement, Mr. Doom and Gloom."

The one that had growled like a bear, now spewed a breath trying to stop laughing as he mumbled, "She's got your number."

"Stuff it, bear," Golden Eyes said, confirming her guess. She snatched her arms from the loose hold of the guy behind her.

The bear spoke softly as if talking to someone not here, but she didn't think he was communicating with ghosts. Golden Eyes had been wearing a communication device when he rescued her from the bounty hunters, so the whole bunch probably wore them.

Golden Eyes stalked over to her.

A muffled boom shook the ground, stopping him in his tracks for only a moment before he continued to her.

She took a step back and hit that wall of muscle behind her again. The man grunted and moved away. Lifting her nose to her grouchy white-knight shifter who kept turning up like an unwanted houseguest, she said, "Who the hell are you and your friends?"

"We're part of a domestic counterintelligence group. We protect humans and shifters from the Black River pack. We were told you might be here, and if so, we had to extract you before they harmed you."

"What agency?" She pinned him with a fierce look, then realized she was showing her eyes and immediately dropped her gaze.

"None you'd know and why are you hiding your eyes?" he asked. "I already know they don't match."

She was suddenly tired of being asked, pushed and ordered. Lifting her gaze to his face, she said, "Fine. It no longer matters anyhow. You've pretty much screwed any chance I had of getting free."

"We're here to save you, dammit," he said through clenched teeth.

"Maybe I didn't want you saving me ... dammit."

The bear shifter came over and said, "We're clearing out."

Golden Eyes asked, "Did we get the leader?"

"No. He and some of his guards fled through a tunnel booby-trapped with C-4 to implode the path. None of ours were hurt, but we can't follow them."

"Got it." Golden Eyes turned back to her. "Let's go."

"No."

"Shit. What now?"

She slapped her hands on her hips. "You expect me to go with you and I don't even know who you are?"

"I told you, we're ... " He took a couple of deep breaths and said, "I'm Rory. What do I call you?"

His change of tone from snarling to something nicer surprised her and softened her irritation. She said, "Siofra."

The guy she'd bumped into said, "Sheer-uh?"

"No. Sheef-rah," she said, exaggerating it for him. Then she asked, "How did you know to look here for me?"

Golden Eyes answered, capturing her attention again. "After we saved the shifters you were captured with, the same person who had sent us after the bounty hunters found out you were in a hospital and wanted you picked up. By the time we got there, our contact learned you'd been kidnapped. Between that original resource and our ability to track almost anything, we ended up here. We have specific instructions to rescue you and deliver you to headquarters." He paused with a thoughtful look.

Headquarters? Where was that? She asked, "Are you accusing me of a crime?"

"No."

"But you're not going to let me go free, are you?"

"We have orders to bring you in, but it's for your own safety."

She was supposed to be happy about that? She didn't even know these people.

Some new concern entered those golden eyes. He said, "Wait. You just said maybe you didn't want to be saved. You *were* a captive, right?"

Oh, crap. She'd said that in the heat of the moment, because she couldn't seem to keep her thoughts straight around this guy. She *had* been a captive at first, but at the end she'd been negotiating to work with Hector's shifters.

Admitting that would probably land her in jail.

She had to be careful how she replied to get around this shifter who would smell her lie, but she also had to avoid being locked up at all costs or she'd never find Baatar. "Those wolf shifters sent two magic users to the hospital to grab me, then they brought me here and these shifters threatened me."

Golden Eyes and his friends said nothing.

This was going downhill fast. "I-I want a lawyer."

"You're not getting one," Rory said with absolute certainty. "We're taking you in, then you're talking to our boss before you go anywhere else."

"Is he a shifter ... like you?"

"No."

Thank goodness. She felt her chest relax until Rory added, "He's a far more powerful shifter than any of us."

She'd thought Hector was her greatest threat ... until now.

CHAPTER 13

R ORY RODE IN THE BACK of the van with ... Siofra.
Was that even her real name?

It hadn't smelled like a lie when he heard it, but she hid secrets for sure. From the terrified look and obvious exhaustion, he could understand her not spilling her guts to strangers.

Vic drove the van that bumped along the dirt road as they left the Black River Pack compound. The whole van stank of wolf. Once Vic delivered them to a private airport in the area, Hawk would pick up Rory and this unusual female, then fly them to headquarters.

Hawk should arrive by eleven, as Rory had explained to Siofra.

After Cole shared Hawk's ETA in military time back at the compound, the nymph asked why they were talking in code.

The Guardian wanted her returned immediately and had specified that Rory be the one to escort her.

By the time he'd herded the despondent woman to the van left behind by the wolf pack, the rest of the team had scoured the building for all the electronics and any bit of intel they could glean.

Most of that was piled back here with him.

And her.

Rory had argued against binding her wrists, while at the same time making it clear there was no question she'd leap out of a moving vehicle to escape.

Justin had given him a look of death and demanded, "If you don't want to secure her physically, then what the hell do we do with her, genius?"

Cole stepped between them and suggested Rory ride in the back as her guard since the boss wanted him to return with her.

Even Ferrell voted in favor of riding with her.

His agitated jaguar had been sending him a flurry of bloody images since Rory had failed to shift when the wolf shifters attacked him.

Agreeing to ride with Siofra calmed Ferrell and allowed Rory the chance he'd been waiting for to get some answers.

Now he just needed to convince this frightened woman to talk during the short ride to the airport.

She'd been staring him down with those beautiful eyes, and the bruise on her cheek and jaw had him wanting to rip a wolf apart. She still wore a damp hospital gown, but he'd given her a blanket to wrap up in and a bottle of water she currently squeezed into an hourglass shape.

He'd had Vic flip on the rear interior light. Rory didn't need it with his keen shifter eyesight, but the dim yellow lamp allowed Siofra to not be entirely in the dark.

A thousand questions rolled around in his head, but the top one was about her energy. During the few seconds he'd touched her when he pulled her off the wolf shifter she'd bowled over, he'd felt a jolt of that energy bleed into him through his hands and feed down to his leg. Again.

His damaged limb had stopped aching and started healing a tiny bit in that one moment.

He desperately wanted to find out if she had the power to heal his leg, or maybe even the issue with his animal.

But he couldn't very well take her into custody then ask her to heal him. She wasn't under arrest, but she was right about not being able to walk away. In her shoes, he wouldn't be happy either. For now, what he could do was find out what the hell was going on with her and what the Black River pack wanted with her before they got separated.

Actually, this conversation had to happen before they reached the local airport where they'd be flown to Spartanburg.

Rory would not hold any truth against Justin when he filed his report. Just like he'd told his friend, Rory would take full responsibility for pushing the extraction plan timeline. That move would have screwed them all if the woman had not been on site when they entered the compound.

She had been, just as Rory had known with his sixth sense, but the Guardian had no tolerance for lack of discipline on a mission.

If the team switched directions halfway through every mission just because someone had a feeling, people would die.

He wasn't sure what he'd say to his boss, but he'd felt pulled to go in immediately to save her.

Would she talk to him? "How're you doing, Siofra?"

She grumbled, "I'd be better if I was free." She glanced over at him. "Why do you always yell at me?"

The question threw him a curve, forcing a defensive reply. "I don't." Any of his teammates would have called him on that lie.

"Yes, you do," she countered. "And you do it whenever I'm helping. You have no right to be angry with me."

He couldn't argue that point. He did feel bad about yelling at her, but she kept racing into battles where claws ruled. "Okay, you're right, but I wasn't angry with you."

The wary expression on her face questioned his words.

He explained, "I'm sorry it sounded that way. I admit I was furious, but not at you. I kept seeing you jump into battles between shifters and you weren't a shifter. That makes me crazy every time I think about it."

"Why?" Her soft question pushed him to talk when he hated trying to explain himself.

But he didn't want her to think he hadn't appreciated her selfless act. He said, "I don't like seeing you hurt. I don't want you sliced up by razor-sharp claws or killed by a shifter fist to the head. Hell, your face is swollen and turning color from someone hitting you. I bet a wolf did that, right?" Just thinking about it had his insides torn up and Ferrell growling.

She touched her cheek. "I failed to lower my eyes when I spoke to their alpha. One of the guards backhanded me to fix my attitude." She gave a sad smile. "Didn't work. "

"Which wolf?"

She dropped her hand. "Why?"

"Because I will find him one day. When I do, he won't harm another woman ever again."

Sitting back, she studied Rory for a long time until finally saying, "That's nice."

The fury inside him that had been bubbling since they climbed into the cargo area subsided a little.

Using his medic's bedside manner voice in an attempt to keep her hackles down, he asked, "How'd you come to be caught with the shifters the bounty hunters had in cages?"

"Why?"

Adversarial little thing. "I'm trying to understand how you eventually ended up captured by a division of the Black River pack."

"Men."

"Men? I need a little more."

She chewed on the side of her lip, looking like she was doing all she could to keep from screaming at him. With a glance to the side, she whispered as if speaking to a different person. "Not now."

If she thought he hadn't seen her lips move or heard those words above the noise of the diesel engine, she was wrong. Who had she been talking to? Asking about that would only sidetrack her attempt to communicate.

Brushing her white hair off her face in a tired motion, she leaned back with her arms crossed. "Men, as in men are the bane of my life. They live for the sole purpose of destroying any chance I have for happiness. They always want, want, want *something* from me. No one ever gives a damn about what I want."

That was a mouthful for her, but it hit him in the heart.

What life had this woman led before now? She sounded like she'd had a relationship go bad and she spoke as if all men had conspired to destroy her life.

Giving him a pointed look, she said, "Just like you and your buddies. I appreciate you coming to save me, but the only thing I've asked you for—*twice*—is to let me go."

She had him there.

But what could he do? He was obeying orders. More than that, he had this burning need to protect her, even if that meant protecting her from herself. She had a determined streak that said to hell with risk.

"Where'd you grow up?" he asked, trying again.

"A slave under a man's thumb."

Had she been a captive before? Undeterred by her distant attitude, he kept pushing. "Where were you before you met up with the female shifter and her son on that bus?" He had the route the long-distance bus had taken from Texas, but she could have switched buses.

"Texas."

Truth. "Where were you living in Texas?"

"Somewhere in South Texas. I caught a bus in Columbus."

"Are you running from someone?"

She rubbed her forehead and looked away, debate playing out in her expression. She didn't answer, instead slashing her unusual gaze back at him when she asked, "How'd you hurt your leg?"

He got that she wanted a break from questions, and that was fine. She'd answered a few. He'd learned from being a jaguar shifter that patience paid off when pursuing a prey, especially one as nervous and untrusting as this one.

She lifted her eyebrows as if to challenge him for not replying. He swallowed a chuckle.

That she could be surrounded by monsters and hold her own was downright sexy. She might be nervous, but she had plenty of fight in her.

He explained, "During our first meeting, after you ran off, I got attacked by two jacked-up wolf shifters. One shredded my leg to the bone."

She sat up and tiny lines formed at the bridge of her nose. "Were you shifted?"

"Yes. I won the fight, but my leg came out on the short end in that one."

Easing back against the wall of the van as it bumped onto a smoother road and jostled them, Siofra said, "That was a day or two back." She stopped as if trying to determine the day, then shook it off. "Have you shifted to heal?"

She seemed fairly clued in about shifters, which was another piece of her makeup that churned his curiosity. But he hadn't planned to share as much as he had. He tried to make it sound standard, which was not the case.

Shrugging, he said, "I shifted, but this just happens to be a slow recovery." Admitting that raised his dread at seeing the Guardian, because Rory's leg had not healed any further. It would take only one look for the Guardian to make good on sending him to Wyoming or putting Rory into an unconscious stasis.

Thinking about injuries, Rory asked, "How's the wound where that jackal cut you with his claw?"

Moving her hand to her stomach, she said, "Fine. Getting better."

"Lie. I saw your midriff when you ran from the bounty hunters. Your skin had healed completely in minutes. Your bruises from where they hit you tonight are already fading, and your arm is almost healed where that wolf clawed you."

She gave him a flat stare. "Why ask me when you know the answer?"

Yep, she was skittish and not ready to trust him, especially after that trick question. He admitted, "To see if you'd tell me the truth and find out if ... you're a healer."

She turned to stare at the electronics and files piled between them and the wall separating the cargo area from the driver. She wouldn't look at him for a while.

He waited as patiently as Ferrell stalking dinner.

When she finally turned to face him again, she sounded despondent. "I told you I'm not a healer. I have no idea where this power came from, but it's not safe."

To her credit, she kept warning him about her power, but he hadn't sensed any threat when they'd touched. Just the opposite.

He leaned forward, propping one hand on his knee and dropping his other one to gently squeeze the aching leg. "I don't know that it's dangerous to everyone. It didn't harm me." He debated on how much to say, but ... he was in deep water with the Guardian, his jaguar could be dying and he was staring at the one person who might be able to help him.

His jaguar had calmed around her for some reason, too.

Rory might be making a mistake, but he took a leap of faith and told her, "In fact, your touch healed a wound I received during our first encounter."

Her mouth fell open, an honest reaction. She snapped her lips closed and asked, "How ... I don't ... how do you know my energy healed your wound?"

"If you'll recall, you saw my shoulder get ripped open and I hadn't shifted. When your fingers touched my damaged shoulder, I felt your power rush into me and start mending it. The minute you pulled away, my shoulder healing slowed, and it stopped completely the next day."

Her eyes widened with surprise. "Really? What about now?"

He shrugged. "It's getting there."

Talking to her about this went against every belief he had to never admit a weakness to anyone, but he'd carried his secrets for the longest time.

Where had that gotten him?

The Guardian believed he was killing his animal.

Rory had no idea if he was doing the right thing by telling a stranger, but he could feel his life force dwindling. He'd ignored it for too long.

She had no reason to trust him, but she had once. If she would again, he had a feeling he could find his way out of the mess he and his jaguar were in.

Could a nymph repair him beyond what his Guardian had accomplished?

She chewed on her lip again, but this time she seemed to be considering something and said, "I felt your power, too. It was ... huge, strong. I've seen jackal shifters heal fast and I never got the sense that they were as powerful as you."

There was a new snippet of information.

Where had she been around jackal shifters to observe them?

She was starting to give him tiny bits of truth, which he interpreted as tiny steps toward trusting. His instincts said this was huge for a woman on the run, and that he needed to move ahead carefully.

He let the topic of jackal shifters be for now and answered her. "I am more powerful than most shifters when entirely healthy, but there is no absolute rule for any shifter." That sounded better than admitting he and his jaguar couldn't fix this problem. "My boss is a powerful healer. He worked on my leg and it's on the mend."

Lie, Ferrell sniped at him.

Now his jaguar wanted to use words?

Mate heal.

Rory sent back, *I'm trying to fix whatever is wrong with us, but she is not our mate.*

His jaguar remained quiet, and felt withdrawn. Not a good sign.

Ferrell didn't even send him a bloody image. That was actually a bad sign. Was his animal giving up on them? What the hell had Rory done to fuck this up so badly?

Siofra's gaze dropped to the leg he'd been rubbing. He lifted his hand away, a kneejerk reaction to anyone noticing him in a weakened state.

Ridiculous action, considering he'd already admitted the wound was not healed.

She stood up with her hand on the back door and leaned over to keep from hitting the roof. The hospital gown hung on her like a sack.

He went on immediate alert.

Was she about to jump, thinking he wouldn't go after her with a damaged leg? If so, she was very mistaken.

No, she squatted down and leaned forward on her knees, then reached out to touch his leg. She paused at the last second, staring at his black fatigues, and looked up with big eyes. "Can I see it?"

His heart thundered in his chest.

He wanted her to touch him in the worst way and not just to heal his leg. That was just plain strange. He shook off the crazy thought and focused again.

She was still waiting for his answer.

"Sure. You can see it, but I warn you it's not a pretty sight." He pulled up the pants leg until he revealed the hideous collage of raw muscle, bones and skin trying to regenerate.

She cringed, but to her credit she didn't throw up.

He wouldn't take any drugs to dull the throbbing out of fear it would slow his healing even more. Based on what the Guardian had done, his leg should have mended more by now.

The sadness in her eyes touched him in a way that few things did. He didn't want her pity, though. He'd closed off his emotions years ago to survive being a Gallize shifter after losing his brother and ultimately his family.

She barely spoke. "You really think I can heal this? I'd like to do that for you, but I'm not sure I know how."

No one got through to him, really deep inside him, but the genuine concern in her voice woke his heart with a jolt.

He admitted, "I don't know, but I'm willing to try ... if you are."

She reached out again, but pulled back.

His heart dove to his feet. "You don't have to," he said, letting her off the hook.

"It's not that I don't want to, but I have no control over this power. Sometimes it doesn't show up at all and other times it's been ... deadly. I don't want to hurt anyone, especially you."

The truth poured through her heartfelt words.

His jaguar hummed. Rory's pulse skyrocketed when she said "especially you." "When you say deadly, do you mean that jackal you killed with your hands?"

"It was an accident!" she said in a pleading voice as if she needed someone to believe her. Her face crumbled. "They were both accidents."

"Both?" he asked softly.

She covered her mouth and her eyes welled with tears. When she spoke, her words were thick with emotion. She shook her head slowly as she stared straight ahead, lost in some memory, but kept talking as if on autoplay. "I ... I didn't even know I could do it, but the first one ... he was ... a jackal ... bigger, stronger ... " She cupped her throat, a movement of fear, and kept staring with unfocused eyes. "I tried to get away, but he had me down and ... " Pausing, she swallowed a choking sound. " ... he ripped my clothes and ... I could feel energy in my feet, then my legs and ... then he tore my pants and I panicked." Her voice went up to that of a child in distress. "I don't know. I grabbed his arms and ... the power just ... shocked his body and he ... " Tears ran down her face, but she was too locked in her nightmare to realize anything but the horror she relived.

She moaned in terror.

Shit. He reached down and picked her up under her arms, lifting her across his lap. He pulled her close and held her against his chest, rocking her. "Shh. It's okay. Sounds like he deserved whatever he got." He kept her that way, holding her safely while she bawled her eyes out.

This woman was no killer.

She was a survivor in a world of preternatural monsters, a whole different level of predators from human ones.

Rory had no idea what her power was all about, but he was damned glad it showed up in time to zap that piece-of-shit jackal.

At least he hoped she'd stopped him before he raped her.

When her sobbing finally slowed down, she was sniffling and hiccupping at the same time. If it hadn't been such a dire situation that had brought on this moment, he'd smile over how adorable she was when she had her claws pulled back and allowed him to hold her.

She felt good in his arms.

Too good.

He should put her on the bench next to him.

Not fucking happening.

He paused at noticing his jaguar was still silent, but not withdrawn this time. No, this was different.

Ferrell seemed ... peaceful.

Was she healing his animal without any idea what she was doing?

When she wiped the back of her hand across her nose, then on her hospital gown, he did chuckle.

She lifted her swollen eyes to him. "What?"

"Nothing."

"What?" she repeated.

He should have figured out by now she was persistent, if nothing else. "I like how comfortable you are right now. You're pretty and sweet. A winning combination."

She looked at the hand she'd just wiped on her gown and rolled her eyes. "Not my best moment, but the only shower I've had was getting hosed down by the wolves so this rag is as good as a tissue."

He should have killed all the wolves.

"Whoa," she said, putting her hand on his chest. "What's wrong? You're squeezing the breath out of me."

"Sorry. Just ... I don't like hearing about one more person abusing you."

She cocked her head, giving him a deep look. "Why? You don't even know me."

"I don't have to know a woman to not want her misused."

"Thank you," she whispered. She touched his cheek and her energy hummed against him.

"You're welcome. Did you stop that jackal before he ... "

"Did the deed?" she finished. "Yes, but I still don't know how it happened. I have no idea how I killed the bounty hunter jackal who was attacking you, either, but ... I was trying to stop him from hurting you."

Did she think he was going to hold that against her? "I'm glad you did. Thank you for putting yourself at risk again, but I don't want you hurt."

"You're welcome," she whispered. Letting out a deep sigh, she said, "Sorry for crying all over you. That's been coming for a while, but I'm recovered from my pity party. I want to take another look at your leg."

She thought crying over almost being raped and killing two men unintentionally was having a pity party. Damn, had no one cut this woman any slack?

He helped her to her feet and waited as she knelt again.

When she positioned herself in front of his leg and wiped her face on her gown again, Rory lifted the pants leg once more.

"That's awful," she said as if to herself.

"I've had worse," he admitted, but failed to add that it had been a long time ago when he was learning to control his jaguar.

"Ready for me to try to touch you?"

He put a finger under her chin and lifted so she would face him. "Only if you want to try this. I don't want you to do anything you don't choose to do. Before you do, I need you to know that I still have to deliver you to our boss, because we made an agreement with the woman who sent us to rescue you. She protects shifters and is taking care of all those women and children we saved from the bounty hunters. She's the one who was adamant about finding you."

"What are you saying?"

"Whether your touch fixes any of my leg or not, I can't just let you go. To be completely honest, I would have a difficult time knowing you were out there alone and being hunted, but I have orders to take you in. No one will hurt you there. We all want to help you, but I won't let you do this and not know everything."

"Are you trying to talk me out of testing my energy to heal you?" she asked, with a twinkle in her unusual eyes.

"No. Maybe, hell I don't know." He dropped his hand from her chin. "I've never had to ask anyone outside of our group for anything. I just don't want to be one more man taking advantage of you."

She listened quietly and some understanding dawned in her face. She murmured, "Not like the others."

He asked, "What?"

Brushing away whatever she'd realized, she nodded. "I understand what you're saying. Thanks for being honest with me, but I still want to try if you're sure you want to be my guinea pig." She gave him a crooked smile.

His heart did a double backflip. He was in far more danger from that smile than he was from her energy.

"I'm willing. I know you have concerns about your power, Siofra, but you can't hurt me. I'm hard to kill."

She flinched at the last word and he regretted going that far, but he didn't talk to women a lot. He could make them happy as hell in bed, but not with his words.

Talking always got him in trouble.

He'd pointed out all the potential negatives, so he gave her the positive. "Your power has already touched me and didn't harm me those times."

"There is that, but I don't even know if it will show up again," she murmured.

"I understand." After all this woman had been through, he was amazed and humbled that she was willing to try to heal his leg even knowing he would still deliver her to his boss.

She focused all her attention on his leg as if she were a surgeon. When she reached out this time, she carefully placed three fingers along the damaged calf.

Heat and energy flooded his leg, shooting up into his body. The muscles and tendons tightened as if cinched down with a ratchet. The pain was excruciating. Far worse than what the Guardian had put him through.

Ferrell howled and banged, fighting to get out. That energy was flooding him.

Rory gripped the edge of the bench and banged his head back, moaning.

Siofra's voice came to him from a distance. "I'm sorry, I'm sorry. I'm not touching you. Rory, please don't die. I'm sorry."

Shit, he'd gladly die right now. His leg felt as if claws were ripping it apart again and his head wanted to explode. His eyes rolled so far up in his head, everything went dark.

His last thought was to ask her not to escape, but the words never made it to his lips.

CHAPTER 14

SIOFRA WATCHED IN HORROR AS Rory shuddered, like Dyson had.

No! This can't be happening again.

The van stopped and the driver's door slammed. They were going to kill her the minute they saw Rory. She pleaded, "Rory, please don't die. Please."

Maybe they should kill her and keep her from hurting anyone else. Rory had not been hurting her.

He'd been kind and nice.

How could she do this to him?

The rear door opened and the man Rory had called Vic stood there with his jaw dropped. "What's wrong with him?"

Her teeth were chattering so hard she couldn't talk. "He ... he ..."

Rory stopped shuddering at that second and slumped, not moving.

Vic reached in to touch Rory's throat. Then he shook Rory. "Wake up, man." Vic slapped his face. Still no response. "Shit. What happened?"

She was too caught in her panic to think clearly and blurted out, "I don't know." She had no idea what went wrong. She'd wanted to do something good for Rory. Why had her power turned on him?

Until those words left her lips, Vic had been giving her a concerned look equal to the one he gave Rory. "How can you not know? You were back here with him."

"I was trying to help him."

"Help? What the fuck did you do?"

"I don't know," she shouted as tears ran down her face. "I just touched his leg ... "

"Rory was conscious when I closed this door, now he's not. I can't smell a lie, but he's out cold and all I'm hearing is you touched him. What are you?"

She flinched as if he'd struck her. *What are you?*

A monster?

Vic spoke into his comm unit. "*Justin!* I just found Rory unconscious. This bitch used some power on him and his pulse is thready."

She couldn't argue, because she had used her power.

"Got it," Vic said, then looked at her. "Put your hands where I can see them. Make one wrong move and I'll cut them both off before you take another breath."

She slowly put her hands out, not taking her eyes off of Rory. He was still breathing, but it was shallow breaths.

Please don't let that man die. Not that one.

Vic whipped a pair of metal cuffs on her wrists then yanked her out of the van. She looked around, desperate for help on any front.

The only person who had come to her aid was unconscious. Her fault.

They'd parked close to what looked like one of those corporate-style helicopters she'd seen in magazines, the type that could hold a group. The rotors still turned slowly.

A young man jumped out and hurried over, yelling, "Justin told me Rory's in bad shape. I'm ready to power up the minute we get him on board."

Vic yanked her around by the cuffs and told the other guy, "Secure her in the cabin. I'll bring Rory then we're out of here. She looks meek, but she did something to him with her power, so be careful around her."

"Hell, Justin warned me, too. He interrogated one of the wolf shifters who said she's working with the Black River pack," the pilot said.

She didn't think Vic could look any more dangerous than when he'd discovered Rory, but he proved her wrong when he leaned close to her and said, "You hurt Hawk or any more of my brothers and you'll wish you'd died yesterday."

Her heart sank at the anger boiling around her.

She glanced at Rory's pale face and closed eyes. He would help her. She knew it in her heart. He wouldn't blame her for what happened, but ... she blamed herself. She'd known her power was deadly even if she hadn't hurt him the first time they touched.

She was never touching anyone again.

She moved away from Vic and said, "I did not intentionally hurt Rory. It was an accident. Don't touch my hands, because I will not be held responsible for anyone else getting hurt."

"Fair enough." Vic reached into the cargo hold and pulled out a towel holding some electronic drives. He shook those loose and whipped the towel open, then wrapped them around her hands and used a looped zip tie to secure it.

The pilot started to reach for her arm and pulled back. "Are you like touching a lightning rod?"

"No. I just ... my hands carry energy. I think."

He reached around to his back pocket, pulled on a black pair of gloves, then cupped her arm and led her to the helicopter where he helped her up the steps.

When Hawk had her seated, he pulled a harness over her and clipped it into place.

She doubted that was to keep her safe, but more to prevent her from getting up and moving around. Hawk was taking no chances around her. She'd never felt more of a pariah than right now.

Vic called to Hawk, who dashed out of the helicopter. Then the two of them carried Rory in and draped him over a seat across from her.

She leaned forward, whispering, "Rory—"

Vic stepped in front of her, which forced her to sit back so she could look up at his angry face. He said, "Don't touch him, don't talk to him, don't even fucking think his name."

Why had her power hurt the one man who looked at her as if she were special? She wished she could rip this energy from her body.

Hawk dove into the pilot's seat and flipped levers. The rotors powered up, spinning faster.

She'd never ridden in a helicopter and didn't want to now.

Heights made her sick because of a bad memory with a jackal. She tried to keep her mind on Rory.

What if he died?

Her chest seized at that thought. Energy rushed through her body like an electrical wave. If she could trade places with him, she would.

She had a frightening thought of him lying cold in a coffin and ... the force inside her strengthened and expanded. It was fiery, burning her from the inside out. Was the energy going to kill her now?

Would she explode and destroy the helicopter.

No! No more deaths! What had caused this reaction?

She'd been thinking about Rory dying.

Stop thinking about that, she ordered mentally. Think of anything nice or more people will die.

She grasped for the first idea and conjured an image of Rory happy and walking alongside her ... at the beach. Yeah, the beach was calm, right? Not that she'd ever been to one, but the pictures in travel ads had looked inviting.

Her energy slowed. It didn't go away, but neither did it continue to press against every inch of her body.

Since that worked, she leaned back and closed her eyes. She was on the ground, sand actually, at the beach. She envisioned Rory splashing in the water like a kid, which did not fit the stern man lying across from her.

She opened her eyes to check on him. He was so pale and barely breathing.

Outside the window, she saw only clouds.

Her stomach roiled and her palms dampened.

The panic raising her blood pressure and causing nausea agitated her energy.

Crap. Okay, she closed her eyes. Where had she been with her mind-over-panic control? Rory had been yelling at her to join him in the water or he'd toss her in.

Her heart bashed against her insides, reminding her she was not on the ground.

Focus, she ordered herself. Now was not the time for a panic attack. Back to Rory and the beach. She smiled at him, but shook her head that she didn't want to get wet. He took a step toward her.

Squealing, she ran as hard as she could, but he caught her at the waist and swung her around, laughing out loud. She marveled at his rich sound of joy.

Then he lowered her to the sand and turned her to face him.

He was no longer laughing. His eyes flashed golden and he cupped her face as he lowered his head, taking her lips on a fantasy vacation. The man could kiss. This wasn't just a kiss, though. It was a devouring. She ran her hands up his chest and hooked his neck, pulling him closer.

His hands had a few ideas of their own and were taking her bikini top off.

She owned a bikini?

He yanked the whip of material away and oh, yes, her breasts begged for him to touch her.

She rubbed up against his chest, teasing him, but torturing herself. "Please ... "

"Please what?" a rough voice snapped.

She blinked her eyes open and found Vic's snarling face staring at her as if she'd lost her mind.

What had she said ... or done?

Her body was on fire, but she couldn't blame it on the energy that had receded. No, her little fantasy trip with Rory had left her hot and bothered. Her hands were clenched. She relaxed her fingers as much as she could with the towel wrapped around them.

She almost thanked Vic for containing her hands so she hadn't unconsciously given herself relief. That was the sexiest mental breakdown she could ever recall.

Giving Vic a little thrill would have been the freaking dog turd cherry on this shitty day.

Her breathing hadn't quite steadied.

Shifters could smell a woman's arousal. Had Vic realized what she'd been thinking? If so, he didn't show any sign of it, still scowling every time he looked at her. He'd reach over and check Rory's pulse from time to time, but other than that he was quiet as a stone.

Why had thinking about Rory dying upset her energy?

Why had thinking about him being happy made it back off?

This power inside her just hit a whole new level of weird. The only positive thing at the moment was no spirit riding beside her as they flew through the air.

She asked, "Can I have some water?"

"No. You'll survive. Can't say the same about Rory."

She slumped in her seat and avoided the window. The helicopter was steady, but her stomach didn't care. She wanted out, but not up in the air.

She clasped her clammy hands and put all her attention on Rory, studying his chiseled face. He was all harsh lines and rough edges. Was there a softer, fun side of him like she'd imagined?

What made *him* happy?

Her breathing slowed down as thinking about him calmed her fears.

Rory had held her when no one had ever held her. Stolen moments with the teenage boy hadn't allowed time for cuddling. Baatar was a wonderful man, but he got uncomfortable if she cried, like when a child she cared about had been taken from the camp. Where was that child now?

Good news for Baatar was that she didn't melt down often. She'd sure felt like a water bucket over the past twenty-four hours, but damn, she was not cut out to kill people.

Not even if they deserved it as Baatar and Rory had said.

No more tears. Time to buck up and find a way out of this mess, but not until she knew for sure Rory would survive.

The trip took hours, but she had no idea how many. She didn't have a watch and had refused to do anything but think about Rory. She'd created one long running story about the two of them and by the time the chopper landed, she didn't want to leave it.

As the rotors slowed, she got her nerve back to look out the window. They'd landed on top of a building, but not a tall one. Maybe two stories. Lights burned across a city. What time would it be? Three in the morning or later?

Where had they taken her?

Four large men dressed in dark fatigues and T-shirts similar in style to what Vic and Hawk wore greeted the helicopter. Another man stood behind them with his head turned toward the helicopter, but she couldn't see his face.

She blinked to clear her vision and still couldn't make out his face. Was he doing something to shield his face?

Forgetting about him, she watched as men came aboard with medical equipment. These wouldn't be standard doctors who worked on humans or Vic would have taken Rory to a hospital before flying out.

Shifters avoided hospitals, from what she'd learned over years around the jackals.

Humans could not help them.

In less than a minute, Rory disappeared behind all that muscle as they carried him off and placed him on a stretcher. She could see only because she extended her neck to the point the harness cut into her.

One of the men wheeled Rory's motionless body away, slowing only when they reached the man standing by himself. His face still would not come into focus.

Every man out there behaved as if that faceless guy was some kind of god.

He had to be their leader. The powerful healer Rory mentioned. Her heart jumped with hope that his leader would bring Rory back to them.

After the man finished looking over Rory, he nodded at Vic and said something. All of the team except for the pilot entered an access door and disappeared from the roof.

Their leader headed for the helicopter.

Oh shit.

Her heart dropped to her feet. What would he do to her? Vic had surely told him she had harmed one of his men. Rory said he and his team had been sent to bring her back safely, right?

Nothing about the way that man walked toward the helicopter gave her a sense of comfort.

Hawk didn't turn to look at her. He now maintained a rigid position compared to his casual manner while flying here. As their leader reached the steps to the cabin, Hawk jumped up and stood in the doorway, looking down the steps. "Hello, sir."

"Hawk."

"Would you like me to stay?"

"Yes. Please wait nearby."

"Yes, sir." Hawk stepped back as his boss entered, then dashed out of the helicopter.

Their leader had seemed big on the tarmac. In here, she felt the oxygen pushed out as his presence took up every cubic inch, especially since she could now see his face clearly.

When he moved to take the seat across from her, that blasted energy in her chest swirled but didn't charge forward, thankfully.

He lifted his gaze to her and her heart wanted to just quit.

He had the eyes of an ... eagle? Was he an eagle shifter? She'd seen plenty of shifter eyes glow and begin to change to their animal's eyes, but his pair seemed to be permanently fixed.

That couldn't be good. Not for her.

When he spoke, he had a refined baritone that belonged to a much older man than the one who appeared to be in his forties.

On the other hand, his mature voice matched the ancient eyes. He said, "As I understand it, you are the woman we were asked to locate, rescue from kidnappers and bring safely to Spartanburg."

So she was in Spartanburg? She had some memory of that city being in one of the Carolinas, but she couldn't say for sure. "So I've been told, but I don't know anyone here."

Any other time, she might have smarted off just from being so weary, but she had enough survival sense to realize she faced a serious threat.

At his silence, she clarified, "I don't know you, your men or who asked you to come get me."

"I understand. The problem is that while guarding you, Rory has become seriously harmed. I could not rouse him."

She heard the unspoken part where this man had the kind of power that should have brought Rory awake. Crap.

He asked, "What did you do to him?"

How to answer his question and not put her butt in deeper trouble with the only person in her corner unconscious?

When she'd tried to explain what happened with Vic, her words only incriminated her further. If she admitted she had been trying to heal Rory with her powers, she could be put to death for use of a deadly power on another person if Rory didn't make it. She'd heard that talked about in the camps after humans passed the law.

Baatar would be losing his mind if he knew she was in this

much trouble for helping a shifter.

Rory was the only one who could get her out of this mess. For now, she kept it simple and said, "I honestly can't tell you what happened, but I had no intention of harming Rory."

"Part of that is true and part is not."

But she had told the truth. She really did not know why her power turned on Rory.

Desperate for any friendly face, Siofra said, "I don't know who knew about me being captured, so could I please talk to that person?"

Eagle man sat so still she started wondering if he had petrified.

When he did move, he turned his head oddly, as a bird would, which startled her so much she jerked. She hadn't actually jumped only because she remained strapped into the seat.

Movement outside the window drew her attention. Vic walked back to the helicopter and Hawk strode out to meet him.

"You will speak to the person who sent us," eagle man said, whipping her head back to him.

"I hear a but at the end of that." She'd tried to keep her tongue in her head, but she was tired and wanted to find out what happened to Rory.

"But not until Rory recovers."

Lots and lots of scary warning in that statement.

He said, "You will be held in our building until I've determined whether Rory will survive."

"I want nothing more than for Rory to be healthy and awake." Find a lie in that, eagle man. "How long are you holding me?"

"Not long."

She could almost hear the tick, tick, tick as time wound down until this man decided he had waited long enough. As threats went, that one scared the hell out of her.

How did she manage to find a worse situation no matter where she landed?

Baatar would tell her because she refused to put herself first and kept jumping in to help people.

She couldn't change who she was and only regretted harming Rory. She did not regret agreeing to try to fix his leg.

Her first goal was still to get free and find Baatar. Now that she knew he had escaped, she knew where her brother would be headed. But she needed Rory to open his eyes first and let her know he was fine. She needed that more than anything right now.

None of that would happen while she was trussed up in this seat. She asked eagle man, "If I promise to keep my hands to myself, can I have the cuffs removed?"

"Not until you are contained in the building where I can prevent you from harming anyone else."

She didn't want to touch anyone.

Eagle man had made that statement as if he had zero doubt he could stop any power, even hers.

She didn't know if she should question his mental state for making that comment without having had any experience with her energy or be terrified that this man was so powerful he didn't need to know what she could do.

He didn't change his quiet tone when he said, "Vic?"

That shifter was up the steps and in the cabin faster than any jackal shifter she'd been around could move.

Who were these people?

"Sir?" Vic stood at ready and he had a wad of black material in his grasp.

"Now that I've met her, you and Hawk deliver her to the holding center."

"Yes, sir."

When eagle man stood up, Vic asked, "Did you receive the report about her working with the Black River pack?"

"Not true," she muttered.

Vic had a dismissive glint in his eyes. "Our people interrogated him. There is no lying to us."

"Then he's misstating what happened." Argue with that truth.

Vic's boss turned to her. "Again, you speak the truth, but not all of it. Lying by omission is still lying."

What did these people think? That she should just open up like they were all friends?

Sure, Rory and his buddies appeared to be the good guys, but she had zero reason to trust this eagle. Getting flown to some unknown location and locked up in a "holding center" did not give her a warm and fuzzy feeling. She'd told this man all she could short of admitting she'd experimented with an unknown power in an attempt to heal Rory.

Without Rory's testimony, she faced death for that.

Eagle man said, "For your sake, I hope you can explain yourself in a way that clears your actions. If not, and especially if Rory does not recover, you will not have to worry about running from anyone ever again." With that, he left.

Continuing his scary guard gig, Vic walked in and shoved a black bag over her head.

She squeaked at the unexpected action and grumbled, "I don't even know where Spartanburg is."

Vic said, "Let's keep it that way."

At least she was done flying, but she'd never felt so vulnerable. The sound of her harness unsnapping came next, then his hand hooked her arm, pulling her to her feet.

She walked through balmy early morning air to eight steps descending into cooler air conditioning.

Her hospital gown had dried, but it did little to keep her warm. Her teeth chattering might be a delayed reaction to all that had happened as much as to the chilly air.

They stopped and a whoosh sound followed, then he moved her two steps ahead where the sound happened again and the movement felt as if she descended.

An elevator?

Must be, but it kept going and going when she would have thought they'd reached the street level by now.

Her mind kept returning to Rory. He had to get better. Not just to save her hide, but because he mattered to her in a way she couldn't explain. Whenever that man touched her, her world shifted a little more toward center.

Her energy had seemed to really like Rory's energy, which made what happened even stranger. Every time she got around him, he left her feeling better about herself. That she deserved to be treated as a person who mattered. Maybe even that he cared.

He would live.

He would open his eyes and smile at her again.

He would tell her this would all work out.

The elevator stopped and the doors made a soft noise again. Vic led her down a long hall that smelled clean. Were her feet leaving dirty footprints on the cool floor? Felt like tile.

When he stopped, she didn't hear a lock being opened by a key, but the next thing she knew he'd walked her forward and pulled the bag off her head.

Four white walls. One single bed, nicer than her camp cot, though. Clean sheets, a pillow and a light blanket. A water bottle and a snack bar.

Vic tossed the black bag on his shoulder while he unwrapped her hands and removed the cuffs.

She rubbed feeling back into her wrists. "Can you tell me how Rory is doing?"

"No." Backing out of the door to keep her in sight, he closed it and she heard something click this time.

What kind of security did this bunch have?

The kind that had her stuck deep underground in a room with no doorknob, no windows, and no hope of breaking out.

She would have human rights if this strange power had not manifested. Now she was subject to the preternatural rules and had no idea what all of them were.

Would eagle man give her a chance to convince them she was not part of the Black River pack?

Maybe, but there was no way to do that without admitting she'd been making a deal to work with Hector's shifters when Rory and his people showed up.

She put her chances at getting out of this about the same as convincing that eagle to shift and give her a ride.

CHAPTER 15

SIOFRA SAT CROSS-LEGGED ON THE bed with the blanket wrapped around her shoulders. She would kill for something to read, anything to keep her from obsessing every second over Rory and her future.

Something on Spartanburg would be nice so she'd have a better idea where they'd taken her and how far it was from meeting Baatar.

She'd been here for hours. When Vic had delivered a sandwich to her and didn't look happy to be doing it, she managed to see his watch. Based on that time, it had to now be around two or three in the afternoon. But what afternoon?

She counted her days of freedom, rolling her eyes at considering this freedom, and came up with Tuesday. It seemed as if she'd been on the run for weeks instead of only a few nights and days.

Things were definitely rocking along now with her new life.

She had no shoes, no money, no ... anything. And they thought she had tried to kill Rory, the only man to step between her and danger since Baatar.

A man who had risked his life for her ... a nobody.

Her heart whimpered. *Please don't die, Rory.*

The door opened unexpectedly again and Vic stood there. He had no food in hand.

Her heart tried to climb her throat. Had Rory died?

Vic said, "Get up. The boss wants to see you."

"What about Rory?"

When he said nothing, she snapped, "I just want to know if he's still alive, dammit."

Maybe the break in her voice got through. Vic said, "Still breathing. Still unconscious."

What had it been? Twelve hours?

She dumped the blanket, stood and straightened her shoulders. She would not face him as a beaten woman, but someone who deserved to be heard in spite of the hospital gown.

She walked alongside Vic down a hallway and around a corner, then down another hallway until he directed her to enter a large room with a big table in the middle. Five chairs had been placed along each side with only one chair at each end.

The two men who had seemed to be Rory's friends during the battle at the Black River Pack compound stood on either side of where eagle man sat at the end. She'd heard Rory call the bear shifter Justin, and the other one Cole, but she'd gotten no indication of Cole's animal.

Vic led her to the closest end where he had her sit opposite eagle man. Oh, joy.

The lights had been dimmed just enough to give plenty of illumination without blinding someone, probably because shifters had sensitive eyesight.

Justin, the bear shifter, stood with his thick arms crossed and his brow furrowed. Not too happy to see her, that's for sure.

Cole studied her through gray-blue eyes, and had his thumbs hooked in the front pockets of his jeans. He'd been the calmer one when Rory and the bear got into a disagreement, but he was no happier with her right now either.

Eagle man said, "Rory is still unconscious. We'll get to that in a moment. You will explain first why you claim the Black River pack wolf shifter was lying. He claims he was present when you offered his boss, Hector, a deal to work together."

Put that way, it did sound bad.

Before she said a thing about Hector, she wanted to establish that she had saved Rory during the fight at the Black River Pack compound. "I would first like to point out that your men heard Rory yell at me for jumping in to attack two wolf shifters who had him pinned down last night."

Eagle man said, "Point taken and we know you are telling the truth about that incident, but we do not know your motivation for any action last night. Back to Hector."

She swallowed and took her best shot. "I had a problem in Pittsburgh and got disoriented. I lost track of where I was and stepped in front of a vehicle that wrecked, but I don't think anyone was hurt. It was absolutely an accident, but I woke up in a hospital."

"A mental hospital," the bear corrected.

"That may be true. It's not like anyone told me what was going on. When I woke up from whatever drug they gave me, I was groggy, then I heard someone coming into my room. I was locked behind a steel door."

The bear asked, "They didn't put you in a straightjacket?"

Boy, he hated her. She managed to not snap at him, but just barely. "Anyhow, I didn't want to go with the two men who came into my room, but they used magic dust on me. I figured out then that they were magic users, but not who they were with until I saw a tattoo on the wrist of one."

"Describe it," the bear ordered.

She gave them details of a vicious wolf design with his fangs showing as he snarled. She said, "They took me to that compound your team raided, hosed me down and delivered me to Hector. He wanted to know where a ... friend of mine was—"

The eagle man raised his hand off the table. "Stop. Friend is a lie. Who is it?"

She did not want to put one more person on Baatar's trail.

"Do I have to remind you that this is your one chance to prove your innocence?" he asked.

"Nope. Heard you just fine. Before you call me a liar again, this person was originally a friend, but I think of him as a brother now, more than just a friend."

She got a nod of approval so she continued. "He must have escaped after I did—"

"From where?" blue-eyed Cole on the left asked.

Damn. She was talking herself into a hole. If she'd had a chance to clean up and compose herself, she wouldn't be so rattled. That's exactly why they did this now and with her looking as rough as she had upon arrival, and still wearing a ragged-looking hospital gown.

She explained, "I was captured as a child and I've lived in different places over the years, being shuttled from one work camp to another. Six months ago, my friend was brought in. He stepped in a couple of times when the jackals were harassing me. We got to know each other and he helped me escape after one of the guards tried to rape me."

She paused to let them realize she was not being called out for a lie, confirming her words. Clearing her raspy throat, she said, "I helped a female lynx shifter I met on a bus from Texas to Pittsburgh, which is how I ended up captured the first time."

Cole walked around the room and poured a glass of water, which he set in front of her.

"Thank you." She grabbed the glass as he returned to his original position.

"Why Pittsburgh?" the bear shifter asked.

"That was all the money I had to get me as far as I could go once I found a bus station. While on the bus, the woman's little boy started to shift while he was sleeping and she was scared I'd turn them in, which I would never do."

Justin asked, "Why not? You aren't a shifter."

"Because I don't screw over an innocent person just because they are different from me," she snapped, tired of having her good intentions questioned. She continued, "No one else saw the boy start to shift. Once his mother realized I was not a threat, we became casual friends. Then bounty hunters looking for shifters grabbed us. They thought I was a shifter, too. Your people found us. Rory showed up in the woods as a jackal guard was clawing me to make me shift. He fought them. There were two. I helped take down one. He *will* confirm that."

"If he lives," eagle man said.

"He will."

"How do you know?"

"He told me he was hard to kill. I believed him ... and still do," she said without thinking about it.

That drew some odd looks from the two men standing.

The eagle man lifted a finger, indicating for her to continue. She took a deep breath and said, "I was telling you how Hector wanted to find my friend. I did offer Hector a deal, but ... " She raised her hand. "I was trying to trick him into letting me lead two of his wolves to find my friend."

"You lied to him," the bear shifter pointed out.

She gave him a look of duh. "Of course I lied to him. I'm not going to betray a man I think of as a brother."

Now they looked disgusted with her. Crap. She couldn't read minds. "What's wrong now? I'm telling you the truth."

Blue eyes said, "You just admitted to being clever enough to convince a shifter you weren't lying."

She dropped her head to the table.

They had no reason to believe her even though they knew her words were true. "I quit," she mumbled against the polished surface. "I've tried and tried. You all win. Every man, except Rory and my brother, has screwed me coming and going. I'm tired. Just kill me and be done with it."

The table surface was cool. She could sleep right here.

"You're not finished," eagle man said.

Sighing loud enough for shifters outside the room to hear, she pushed herself up and propped her crossed arms on the surface so she'd stay upright. She hadn't slept at all, and she wouldn't. Not until she knew Rory would live. "What?"

Their boss asked, "Who was your mother?"

Talk about a left hook in the conversation. "I have no idea. I only knew my dad. Before he was killed and I was captured, he told me she abandoned us. Now you know as much as I do about her."

The two men standing looked at their boss, who nodded. Were they checking to see that everyone believed her?

Their boss said, "Tell me about your power."

What could she tell them? That it was deadly and erratic? How would that help her with what they believed she did to Rory? "Would you tell me how Rory is doing first? Please?"

Justin scowled, but his boss answered, "They tell me he's resting and stable."

"Thank goodness," she murmured.

"But it has been twelve hours," eagle man said, letting her know this meeting had more purpose than just asking questions.

She'd reached her deadline for Rory to recover.

Her mouth went dry. For now, she'd keep everyone talking

as long as she could. It was her only hope. "As for my energy, it showed up when the jackal tried to rape me in the Texas camp." She'd noticed little odd things before that, but nothing specific. She hadn't so much as lit up a lightning bug before Dyson. "I panicked at one point during the attack and ... this energy just rushed up my arms as I grabbed him and ... " She stopped.

"Finish."

Crap, how much worse could it get at this point?

She probably shouldn't put that question out to the universe with the way her life kept running head first into Disaster City.

Taking a deep breath, she launched back into her explanation and hoped for the best. "When I grabbed the jackal to push him, my energy sort of exploded inside me. He acted as if a bolt of lightning had hit him. He arched hard then just shook and fell down on me. My friend ... brother ... showed up because he heard me screaming. He told me to run and how to find the road, then said he'd draw the jackals away. They would follow him, because he was far more valuable than I was."

"Why?"

That eagle guy didn't waste a lot of words.

She would tell what she could about Baatar, but she would not talk about the one thing he had asked her to keep secret if she escaped. She cared for Rory, maybe even as much as she cared for Baatar, which she honestly didn't understand since it had happened so quickly, but she owed her brother her loyalty. "I don't know the whole story about why they brought him in, but every captive was subject to being bred or sold to the Black River pack. Evidently there was something special about him and they planned to sell him."

The bear asked, "Are you saying you were kidnapped to be used as a breeder?"

"Maybe. I never knew their full intentions. They captured me when I was six, after all. Regardless, that didn't work out so well once they determined I'm ... sterile." Her throat wanted to close up every time she said that word.

Eagle man asked, "What about your friend? Was he a shifter?"

"Oh, hell no! He can't stand shifters." She grimaced and smacked her hand over her mouth. What was she thinking? Okay, her hand cut her words off before she could add that neither of them liked shifters, but the action also told them she hadn't meant to say that. Yeah, not the brightest thing to admit in front of this bunch.

Besides, she'd decided that she only disliked male shifters.

Where did that leave Rory?

He wasn't a shifter, not to her.

Just a man who had to live or ... she'd never be the same again.

Cole said, "You say you were captured at six? By whom?"

"The Cadells." She'd barely spoken those two words when so much power rolled through the room she felt it push against her.

Eagle man stood and boomed, "*You're from the Cadells?*"

Cole's hands curled into fists and the bear shifter started growling.

They were looking at her as if *she* claimed being part of the Cadells.

"Hold it!" she shouted right back, then stood to make a point. She was done being looked down upon by everyone and treated like yesterday's garbage. "I'm not from them or representing them. I. Was. A. Captive!" She smacked her hand on the table. "Just like I am now. The Cadells capturing me doesn't mean I like them any more than I like you, because I am a captive. Again."

"Can we believe her, boss?" blue eyes asked.

For the first time since meeting him, the eagle man had a moment of hesitation.

Her hope of surviving this just dropped to subterranean level.

The door blasted open and everyone turned to find Rory standing there. His hair stood straight up and he was still on the pale side, but his eyes burned with fury.

Oh shit, oh shit. She started saying, "I am so sorry, Rory."

He came straight at her as everyone yelled at him to stop.

CHAPTER 16

R ORY STILL FOUGHT DIZZINESS AS he stepped into the conference room, but he was not going to let this interrogation go down without him. He strode over and pulled Siofra into his arms. "Are you okay?"

She wilted against him. "Yeah, I'll live ... now. I'm so glad you're alive."

"Rory?" the Guardian called out, sounding curious more than angry.

He grudgingly released Siofra and stepped back to face his boss. "Yes, sir."

"How are you?"

"Pretty damn good."

"What about her attacking you with her power?" Justin asked, full of condemnation.

The Guardian stared hard as if trying to determine if Rory was entirely lucid.

Hell, he was way better than lucid, but the fear he'd felt rolling off Siofra when he opened the door now made sense. "What time is it?"

"Around four," the Guardian answered.

"AM or PM?"

"PM on Tuesday," Justin clarified.

Siofra had been under the microscope for twelve hours? He asked her, "Didn't you tell them what you did?"

"I told them I didn't mean to hurt you."

Rory frowned at her. "Why didn't you tell them you were trying to heal my leg?"

"I haven't had this power long and feared they'd think I had been *experimenting* on you, which ... I sort of was." Her voice fell off at the end.

"Is that true?" Justin asked, still stern but sounding more confused than anything now.

Rory swung back to face Justin, Cole and the Guardian. "Yes, but she is not at fault. When I first met her back where we found the bounty hunters, I grabbed her arm to keep her from getting too close to one of them. I told you I felt her power, but only for an instant. Even so, in that nanosecond, healing began immediately in my shoulder where the jackal had ripped it open. So, while we were on the way to the airport from the Black River Pack compound tonight ... wait, this is Tuesday so that would be last night. Anyhow, I asked her about her energy, told her how it had affected my shoulder and she offered to try to heal my leg."

The Guardian asked, "How much had your leg healed at that point after your meeting with me?"

Damn, he hated to answer that question, but he wouldn't shy away from his boss. "To be honest, sir, not any improvement."

Cole had been staring at Rory with shock. "You *showed* her your damaged leg and let her use unstable power on you?"

"I did," Rory said. "I know that's stupid for any shifter in most situations, but the boss will understand why."

The Guardian's voice came into Rory's head with a question. *You thought she could heal your animal?*

Rory nodded and his boss said nothing else, letting it go for now.

Clearly not on team Siofra, Justin grumbled, "But she almost killed you."

"No, she didn't," Rory argued. "First of all, I told her I took full responsibility for whatever happened. And second ... " He propped his foot up on the table and lifted his pants leg to show his perfectly healed leg. His recovery had surpassed even what his boss had done. Maybe what his boss *could* do.

The Guardian's normally stoic expression lit with surprise and it took a lot to shock a shifter who had lived for over three hundred years.

Siofra squealed and clasped her hands, jumping around. "It

worked!"

Rory smiled at her. "Yes, it did. Thank you."

Cole asked, "What went wrong to knock you out for so long?"

Inhaling deeply, Rory explained, "She has so much power you can't imagine. She hasn't been trained in how to use it. That's no different than us having no control over our animals." Now that he knew she was safe, he asked, "So what's going on here?"

Before anyone else could reply, Siofra jumped in, giving her version. "They thought I tried to kill you and that I was in league with the Black River pack."

Rory swept a look across Justin, Cole and his Guardian. "What do you think now?"

The Guardian replied, "That we still have a lot of questions, but—"

"Wait a damn minute," she shouted, cutting him off. "I've been grilled nonstop by everyone and I'm done. He's safe. I did heal him. End of statement."

Rory winced at her blasting the Guardian.

Justin and Cole were cringing like they expected thunder to roll through the room at any minute.

Releasing a stream of air that came out as a weary sigh, the Guardian said, "If you had permitted me to finish, I was about to say that all questions can wait until you've been allowed to shower, eat and enjoy a night's sleep. You appear tired and I would think ready to exchange that gown for clean clothes. I have informed the person who requested your rescue that you are safe. She would like to speak with you first."

"Oh." She looked properly chastised. "Sorry. Guess I do need that shower and some sleep." Running a shaky hand over her hair, Siofra said, "Sure, I'll talk to her."

Nodding his acceptance of her apology, the boss said, "We have hotel rooms available upon our request. I'll have someone procure you clothing and incidentals for the evening while you speak with Ms. Sullivan. I'll send a guard for security tonight. You'll be perfectly—"

"Rory," Siofra said, cutting the boss off again.

Justin and Cole cringed again at her impertinence.

"—safe," the Guardian finished, then added in a firm voice,

"No. Rory needs to recover completely from being hit with your power. Justin will assign someone."

With one look at the panic on her face, Rory gave up trying to be patient and not piss off his boss any more than Siofra had managed. "Sir, I'd like to speak."

The Guardian stood there, saying nothing.

Rory silently pleaded for a tiny break. Maybe the Guardian heard him, because his boss said, "What is it?"

"I was pretty wiped out over the past four days with little rest, but I slept so hard after she, uh, healed me, that it's like I caught up on a week of sleep at one time. I haven't felt this rested in a while. I don't mind handling her security tonight."

Justin rubbed his eyes and mumbled, "Taking the lead again, cat?"

Rory snarled, "Can it, bear, or do you not want to go home to be with your mate and get busy on that cub?"

Justin dropped his hand and glared back at Rory. "You know what? That one is all yours, asshole, *if* the boss is good with it."

The Guardian's assessing gaze went from Rory to Siofra and back to Rory. Something happened during that moment to make him agree. "You may guard her tonight."

She let out a loud sound of relief and told his boss, "Thank you."

"You're welcome," the Guardian said with his usual graciousness. "Thank you for healing him, but do not experiment again on anyone. I specifically do not want you touching any of my people—or them touching you—until we better understand your power. Is that clear?"

"Yes, and I wholeheartedly agree. I don't want to hurt anyone."

"Good."

"I am tired, dirty and hungry, but when will I be released?"

As the Guardian headed for the door, he turned and said, "I wish to know everything about your time with the Cadells before making that decision."

She hesitated, then nodded. "Sure thing."

Cadells? While Cole, Justin and the Guardian left the room, Rory stared at Siofra. The second the door closed, he asked, "What's this crap about you being with the Cadells?"

"They captured me when I was six. That's who I escaped from in Texas. Can the rest wait until tomorrow so I don't have to say it all twice?"

The Cadells were the oldest and most dangerous enemy of the Gallize. Rory was torn between wanting to hug her and the desire to demand answers about that group, because that was tough intel to get.

But if the boss did not keep her to answer his questions tonight, he must have thought those inquiries could wait, and so could Rory's.

She looked like a weathered ragdoll with dirty white yarn for hair. If he hadn't known she'd been dragged through some hellish situations over the past twenty-four hours, Rory would rather keep her in a room in this secure building.

A hotel would be nicer.

He'd started to mention to his boss that she was a definite flight risk, but changed his mind. The Guardian had granted his wish to stay with her tonight. That made it Rory's job to ensure she didn't flee.

Justin's glare weighed on Rory's conscience. His friend had wanted to argue, but instead he'd tamped down his frustration over Rory jumping in to be the lead yet again and let it go.

Rory owed the bear better than to put Justin in a position of struggling to be his friend and also do the right thing. That grizzly shifter might have a point about problems with Rory's mindset, but now was not the time to admit it openly or to hash that out. Rory fully expected to face the Guardian's music very soon.

For now, he had bigger things on his mind, like keeping Siofra from running tonight. She'd do it, especially after getting hit with the third degree here.

On the other hand, if she was as exhausted as she looked, she might be glad for one night of peace in a safe place.

She turned those strangely beautiful eyes on him and said, "I am dying to get out of this stupid gown and get a quick shower."

He had an image of her naked with water crashing over all those lush curves and running down between her legs. Shit, he couldn't breathe. He might never get that image out of his head.

"Rory? What's wrong?"

Everything. "Nothing. Tonight you can stand in a nice hot shower until you wrinkle."

She stared at him as if that sounded foreign.

The door opened and Hawk caught Rory's attention. "Ready for Scarlett?"

"Yep. Send her in."

Scarlett stepped past Hawk, who closed the door behind her. Rory watched the anger climb through Scarlett's expression as she took in Siofra's bruised jaw, ratty hospital gown and pale skin.

Scarlett asked, "What happened to her?"

"The Black River pack interrogated her," Rory replied. He turned to Siofra. "This is Scarlett Sullivan, who sent us after you. And this is Siofra," he finished, turning back to the woman in jeans and a blue silk shirt, with braids pulled back into a ponytail.

Siofra addressed Scarlett. "Thank you, but why did you send them?"

Stepping closer, Scarlett explained. "I give aid to shifters, especially females and their children. The one you helped on the bus ride told me everything about how you helped her." Indicating Rory, she added, "I have a working relationship with these people and asked them to rescue you."

"Are you a shifter?" Siofra asked.

Showing only a momentary surprise at that question, Scarlett said, "Yes."

"This is all so strange," Siofra wondered aloud.

Rory said, "No kidding. You've had a hell of a couple days."

"That's not what I meant." Siofra moved her gaze from Scarlett to Rory. "I've spent my life around jackal shifters, which colored my opinion of *all* shifters, especially males. I understand that there are good and bad people in the world, but honestly ... until I met that woman on the bus, I never expected to find a good shifter."

Smiling, Scarlett said, "There are more than you can imagine, but unfortunately there are also plenty of monsters." Glancing at Rory, Scarlett asked, "I'd like a moment *alone* with Siofra."

He did not want to leave Siofra alone, but he had no argument. It wasn't as if Scarlett meant her harm. Even if she did, Scarlett wouldn't live past the first strike.

He looked at Siofra and offered, "I'll step out."

"But ... " Siofra turned her body, practically blocking his exit.

She didn't want him to leave her either?

Ferrell rumbled softly in appreciation.

What was she doing to his jaguar? Rory told her, "I'll be just down the hall making arrangements for tonight and for things you'll need."

Giving him a puny smile, Siofra said, "Okay. Thanks."

As he closed the door behind his exit, he heard Scarlett say, "First, here's my card. Call it any time you need anything."

Out of respect, he left the women to their private conversation. As dense as he was, he understood that a woman would share things with another woman before she'd talk to a man.

He went to find Hawk first and asked the pilot to speak with housekeeping, which managed rooms kept below ground for any of their people. He had Hawk request clothes to fit a five-foot-four woman of average size and personal incidentals for a young female. That allowed Rory time to find a computer to request a room through their central booking.

But he discovered a room reservation already in place.

Guess the boss had a specific hotel in mind.

He gave the women eight minutes, which felt like a lifetime, but was stretching his patience.

Rory knocked as he opened the conference room door.

Scarlett looked up with a narrow-eyed scowl. "What?"

Did she really think that would put him off? "Time for Siofra to go. She's hungry and tired."

When Scarlett glanced at Rory's nymph, apparently even she could see the longing in Siofra's face and said, "We'll talk more later."

Siofra clutched a card in her hand. "Okay, and thank you."

For a ball buster, Scarlett could be pretty nice to a woman in trouble.

Rory walked over as soon as they were alone. "Ready to go and ... eat?" Yes, he wanted to feed her, but he'd almost suggested a shower, as if priority one was getting her naked under a blast of water.

Only in his overheated mind.

She'd been without amenities for days, and getting hosed off with cold water did not count as truly clean. He could just see them blasting water at her like a dog in the yard, drenching her hospital gown, leaving her exposed to their scrutiny.

Great. Now he imagined the thin material plastered against her wet body, revealing her sweet secrets.

"Hmm," she mumbled, looking into his eyes for so long he worried she'd seen his visual of her.

His dick sure as hell took in the view.

Her gaze sharpened and she pulled back. "Yeah, I'm ready to go. Not like I have to find my purse or anything," she quipped, unable to hide her embarrassment over having nothing to her name.

Here he'd been lusting after her and she was trying to get through one more day of being captured and interrogated.

She took a step back and looked down at her feet. "Does anyone have a pair of sandals I could borrow so I don't have to walk into a public place barefoot?"

"Got you covered. Housekeeping put together clothes and incidentals while you were talking to Scarlett."

"Oh? They have my size?"

He explained, "We keep a lot of things on hand. I said you were five-four and average size."

"Ha. Average?"

A grin tugged at his lips even though he tried to speak with a straight face. "You mean I should have said you've got the body of a goddess with perfect breasts and awesome curves?"

She stared at him, speechless for the first time since he'd met her.

Shit, what the hell was he doing talking to her like a woman he was thinking about taking home that night?

Rory backtracked. "Uh, that was not professional. Sorry for—"

She put her fingers on his lips. "If you take that back, I will hit you with enough voltage to light up this building." Then she ruined the threat by adding, "Of course, I'd first have to figure out where that energy is in me and how to bring it to the surface."

Oh, the energy was there. He felt the buzz in her finger on his lips. He smiled. She was something else.

A tap on the door announced her clothes had arrived. He thanked the staff and handed her a tote bag and pointed to the door to a private bathroom for this conference space. "You can change in there."

She snatched the bag and disappeared for ten minutes, but there was no shower, just a powder room set up for meeting convenience. Rory could have taken her to a shower in this building, but Siofra had been so stressed when he found her that he wanted her to be able to enjoy a shower away from all this, where she might actually relax.

His jaguar had Rory growling and anxious.

Neither of them liked her out of reach. Ferrell sent Rory the image of an empty bathroom.

Rory silently explained, *The only way she could get out of there is if she could teleport.*

Ferrell grumbled and bumped him gently, but calmed down.

Rory had never seen his animal act like this, anxious about someone. Ferrell was worried about Siofra. That was a dead-end street of thought and Rory tired of explaining to his jaguar that they couldn't keep her.

The door opened and, well, hell.

She must have found a brush in that tote. She had her white hair pulled back from her face and hidden beneath a gray ball cap that had been washed a few times and touted an Irish beer. The workout clothes they'd included fit her snugly, showing off her fine assets, and she had sandals on her feet.

That camouflaged her just fine if she didn't meet anyone's eyes, which she seemed to do naturally.

Better than all that, she was smiling.

At him.

Something inside his chest cracked and he feared it might be the hard case around his heart.

He'd deliver her to the hotel, secure her room and get her showered ... there was that visual of water rushing across her body again.

Wrong direction, brain.

He would only stand guard to protect her *while* she showered. Right.

No mixing it up with a woman who deserved to be someone else's mate, who his boss had just forbidden the team—including

Rory—from touching.

What if he had to touch her to protect her?

Okay, yeah, he could do that as long as it was for a purely pro-fessional reason. Besides, even though his team and boss didn't understand, Rory knew he could handle her power.

The only trouble he had was prying the image of her naked body glistening with water drops out of his mind. That visual had imprinted permanently on his brain, an image he couldn't blame on his jaguar this time.

Shouldn't be a problem to keep her contained since he wouldn't be able to sleep tonight. Not unless he could reprogram his head to delete the lust fogging his mind.

He could do his duty *if* she lost that great big smile.

He kept waiting on her to turn down the wattage. Nope. She walked over, still beaming like sunshine.

At him.

He was in trouble.

CHAPTER 17

SIOFRA KEPT HER GAZE AVERTED from the hotel staff as Rory handled the details and took the key card from the manager. People were coming and going in everything from casual clothing to business dress, so she shouldn't worry about how she looked.

They were near downtown Spartanburg, which was in South Carolina, according to what Rory had told her. He'd also told her that the heavy traffic had been from rush hour.

She'd never been in a rush hour. She'd only read about these things, or seen them in the carefully selected library of movies she was allowed to watch. She'd also never been inside any place this luxurious, much less spent a night in a hotel. Everything smelled so clean, but not as if a harsh cleaner had been used like in the dormitories where she'd slept every night in the past.

This was more like fairies had sprinkled fresh flowers into the air.

She'd expected everyone to stare at her, but after putting on the workout clothing and shoes, and hiding her unusual white hair, she didn't stand out.

Rory declined any help with luggage, carrying her tote and a small duffle bag to the elevators.

When they left his headquarters, he'd asked her to just close her eyes rather than cover her head with a bag again.

She'd appreciated that thoughtfulness. She hadn't opened her eyes, even once, as a show of her trustworthiness.

He'd explained that it wasn't as if they were trying to hide the building, but that they didn't want her to know any more about the lower levels than necessary.

She could understand their security measures, but she still struggled with being locked up and interrogated. That seemed to be a fallback choice when it came to men.

What was it about the Cadells that had set off eagle man?

Rory led her into an elevator everyone had just exited and zoomed them to the fourteenth floor.

She didn't know what to expect after walking down the carpeted hallway, but she never would have dreamed the gorgeous room revealed when Rory opened the door.

He stepped aside, waiting for her to cross the threshold.

She paused, trying to take in this moment. She'd lived with nothing for so long. She'd slept on floors and ratty cots, sometimes wearing clothes until they shredded from age and wear.

This was too much. She needed smaller steps before walking into a place like this where she didn't belong.

He asked, "Something wrong?"

"Uh, no." She entered and stepped carefully into a space with a sofa and chairs. She needed a shower, now, so she would not get anything dirty.

Once she got past the shock that this would be her own little playhouse for the night, she looked around. "Where's the bed?"

Maybe that beautiful sofa opened into a bed. She'd seen pictures of convertible sofas.

"There's a bed in the next room." He gave her an odd look. "Have you ever spent the night in a hotel?"

She flashed back on her life in one work camp after another and would have laughed if it hadn't been so sad.

Shaking her head, she said, "No."

He surprised her by taking it in stride and explaining, "Then you're going to love this one. It's a suite, which means you get a living room and a bedroom. You must have made some impression on my boss to be given an upgrade like this."

He was trying to make her feel comfortable and not like a clueless fool. Her heart sighed at the way he treated her.

She said, "Oh, I made an impression all right. Your boss wanted to hang me until you showed up."

"Huh." Rory scratched his jaw. "Then this might be an apology."

"Pfft. Would that man apologize to anyone?"

"You'd be surprised. He's powerful and tough, but he's the most fair and decent person I've ever met besides my teammates."

She tried to match the admiration in his voice to the man who had threatened that she might not see tomorrow. "Think we're talking about two different people."

Rory stepped over and placed his bag on the floor by the sofa and hers on the coffee table. "I didn't say he wasn't vicious when crossed, but he has our backs no matter what happens and is generally a stuffy gentleman."

"Must be nice to have so many people to depend on," she murmured to herself.

Returning to where she stood, Rory said, "It is. I'm sorry you didn't have someone like him watching over you."

She'd had no one until Baatar ... and now, apparently, Rory. Thinking that way was dangerous. It led to wanting something she could never have.

Baatar would be yelling at her for even talking to Rory.

She didn't care. She'd been alone for years and Rory couldn't be put into the category with bad shifters. He was nothing like the jackals she despised.

Her mind might have a hard time accepting Rory's kindness when Baatar's words kept hounding her, but her heart recognized sincerity.

Rory had been staring at her just as she'd been staring at him, but he seemed to snap out of whatever had held him still so long. He asked, "Do you want to clean up and go out to get something to eat or do you want me to order room service?"

"Go *out* to eat? Where?"

"Anywhere you want. What kind of food would you like?"

She hadn't eaten in a restaurant since she was six and that had been only in places with the entire menu available twenty-four hours a day.

She wasn't a heathen. She'd been taught table manners, but the idea of eating in a restaurant both excited and intimidated her.

Then the reality of her situation slammed into her moment of happiness. "What if someone like the Cadells or Black River pack recognizes me?"

"Hide your hair under the hat, but your eyes ... " His frowned a second, then snapped his fingers. "Get a shower. I have the perfect place to go where you'll be fine."

"Really?"

"Really." He grinned and her heart noticed.

Rory probably got all the women he wanted with that smile.

What woman wouldn't want a man who treated them well and had a protective streak a mile wide? He'd make a considerate and caring husband some day. He did have a grumpy side, but all he'd have to do is smile to own a woman's heart.

She frowned, thinking about women throwing themselves at him and Rory owning their hearts.

His irritated face returned. "What's wrong now?"

She would not admit she hadn't liked the idea of him making another woman's heart flutter or ... those women sleeping with him. That was too insane for even her to understand.

Instead she blurted out, "I don't have any makeup."

His eyes twinkled and that might be more dangerous to her heart than his smile. He stepped over and ran a finger down the side of her face, raising chills on her arms. "When you're pretty, and you are, you don't need any."

This man had to be too good to be true.

No one had ever made her feel pretty, but he'd done it twice already. At the building, he told her she had the body of a goddess and now he said she didn't need makeup.

He'd also stopped talking as if he'd said too much.

If he only knew how he'd raised her self-esteem with so few words. She wanted to see him happy again. She lifted her hand and ran her fingers lightly over his face, but couldn't find words to speak.

Rory closed his eyes as if her touch soothed him.

She brushed her fingers over his lips. So fast she didn't see him move, he caught her wrist and held her hand there, sucking her fingers.

His eyes opened and her favorite golden gaze held hers as he kissed her fingers, then he lowered his head, bringing those lips to hers.

Energy sparked, but it wasn't painful. She shut her eyes to absorb everything she felt more powerfully. His mouth moved tenderly over hers and she wanted more. His fingers drove through her hair, cupping her head in a careful way. His other hand covered her back and eased her to him.

Oh, yes. Being closer improved everything, except the kiss. She didn't think it was possible to improve perfection.

She'd been kissed only a few times by one boy.

She'd never been kissed by a master.

Heat and energy filled the space between them. Hers, his, she had no idea where one ended and the next one started. He smelled like the outdoors and a warm summer night.

He never pushed for more, but she couldn't say the same for herself. Her body complained about Rory not touching her everywhere.

When he broke away, he said, "I can't be doing this." Sounded as if he were talking to himself and not her.

Don't stop yet. If he did, her world would go right back to the crapfest it had been before he'd given her a little mental holiday. She gripped his shoulders and pulled up to kiss him again.

He caught her head in both hands, returning the kiss and not so gently this time. Yes, that's what she wanted. His mouth plundered and she welcomed him. Time drifted, but not slowly enough when Rory once again ended the kiss.

When he did, he set her backwards a little, on her feet but away from him.

She feared looking into his eyes to find he was angry for her not listening to him the first time.

But his golden eyes still glowed with a hunger that took her breath. He said, "My boss would have my head for this."

He didn't sound the least bit sorry, and that tickled her beyond belief.

She cocked an eyebrow at him. "I liked it." Would he deny that he had?

"I did, too, but I can't be doing that again."

Disappointment washed away her joy. She would not allow him to see her hurt. Rory was being good to her. She couldn't ask more of a man than that, could she?

He said, "You get showered and dressed so we can go eat."

She'd completely forgotten about the meal. "Give me a few minutes and I'll be ready."

"Take all the time you want."

"No way. I'm excited to eat in a restaurant, but I'll warn you, there's only one more set of clothes in that bag and it's not fancy. Just jeans and a blouse."

"That'll be perfect. I'm not much for fancy." He walked past her and opened a door, revealing the bedroom. Pointing to another door inside that room, he said, "That's the bathroom."

There he went again, making it easy for her to find things that should be obvious for normal people, so she didn't feel like an idiot.

She snatched up the tote and hurried into the room he'd indicated, which was not like any bathroom she'd ever been in. This was a bathing room for royalty.

Closing the door, she poured everything from the bag onto the marble counter that stretched eight feet wide.

Sorting out the supplies they'd included, she grabbed what she needed to shower. She'd have stayed an hour in that hot shower if her stomach hadn't growled.

Not true.

She'd have made her stomach wait, but not Rory.

He was taking her to a restaurant.

She didn't care what they served. She'd eat anything that didn't bite her back.

When she had her hair dried and her teeth brushed, she took a moment to consider the finished look. Meh. She hated to hide her hair under the hat again, but wouldn't risk getting recognized or putting Rory in danger.

Backing away from the mirror, she gave herself thumbs-up for at least looking human again.

Then lost her grin.

She wasn't human. She didn't know what she was other than a ghost magnet, and since Dyson had attacked her, an unexpected lightning rod.

Way to kill her happy mood.

Shaking it off, she straightened the bathroom and walked out to the living room.

Rory had his mobile phone at his ear, but took one look at her and quickly ended the call. The hungry expression that filled his face gave her ego a helium injection. Some instinct she could not name whispered that the man had more on his mind than dinner.

Why did that thrill her when he was a shifter?

When he looked at her that way, she forgot all she was supposed to not like about shifters.

All she saw was a man in a body cut with muscle, a sincere person who had shown her more kindness than anyone except Baatar, and a man who had trusted her touch.

A sexy man with a smile that turned her insides upside down.

She didn't see a bad shifter or even *just* a shifter when she looked at Rory. Maybe she should, and had every reason to based on the life she'd been forced to lead, but living free of the Cadells was making her reassess how she looked at others.

Her breasts didn't give a fig what he was either. Must be that weird energy humming to life that woke up the girls. They ached, wanting to be against him.

This could be the most perfect night of her life. She had a fabulous hotel room to sleep in and a sexy-as-hell man taking her to dinner, almost like what she envisioned a date to be.

But the night would not end well.

Much as her body wanted to find out what hid behind Rory's heated gaze and spend the night sleeping hard on a real bed, she couldn't risk falling asleep.

Baatar needed her and Rory's boss had not committed to a time for releasing her.

If she relaxed too much, she might miss her chance to escape.

CHAPTER 18

RORY CHECKED THEIR SURROUNDINGS, THEN helped Siofra out of the cab in an older part of Spartanburg where he knew the owner of a restaurant. He cupped her arm and kept her between him and the buildings while they walked along, enjoying a ten-degree drop in temps since the sun had gone down. Perfect for an early evening stroll. Not bad humidity, either, for August in the south, but that wouldn't last.

He'd like to take her somewhere fancier than the Italian restaurant he had in mind, but he didn't want her to feel out of place.

The one thing he understood about women was to not walk them into an uncomfortable setting. That would normally mean to inform them ahead of time of all details so they could prepare with everything from hair to clothes to makeup.

He'd learned that lesson as an awkward teenage boy.

Siofra needed no dolling up. She had a special flair all her own and outshined any woman in the room just by smiling. He loved her smile.

But that smile would be as recognizable as her hair and eyes. For that reason, he didn't want her out in the open much.

This short walk was to give her a moment to feel normal.

She'd never eaten in a restaurant or spent the night in a hotel.

She said the Cadells had captured her when she was young and she'd only recently escaped from them.

What kind of hell had she been through, living with them?

This whole night could be a first and he liked being the one to share firsts with her. He could tell that just walking down this sidewalk like a normal person was special for her.

His heart clenched at the life of imprisonment she'd lived. She was clearly educated and knew the basics she needed for functioning in life, but she probably had little experience with things most people took in stride.

He now understood why she had not been quick to tell the truth. He wouldn't have trusted anyone after living in captivity since childhood.

She could have tonight to be herself. Tomorrow would take care of itself.

He would watch over her and dare anyone to interfere or try to harm her. No one should know that she was in Spartanburg, but in the preternatural world you had to expect the unexpected.

Especially if the Cadells were involved.

At the next entrance, he led her into a building and took a roundabout way to reach the rear of the structure, then out and across a short parking lot to a steel door where he pushed a buzzer.

He'd kept up a constant scan of their surroundings the entire time. No one had followed.

When she took a half step away, he snagged her arm and towed her back between him and the door.

She stiffened. "What's wrong?"

"Nothing. I just don't want you out of my reach."

He expected her to snipe at him, but she looked up as if he'd just given her a gift.

Before he could ask her what she was thinking, the door opened and a deep voice said, "Yes?"

Rory brought on a country twang. "Do you know how to make those little round spaghettis?"

His friend snorted, opened the door wider and said, "Get in before I turn you into a stew."

Hustling her inside, Rory said, "Siofra, meet Domenico."

"Nice to meet you." She sounded shy. Cute.

The Italian chef made a half bow, then straightened and said, "It will be my pleasure to serve you in spite of the company you keep."

She laughed, a tinkling sound that warmed Rory's cold heart.

Domenico led them through the kitchen where cooks were busy preparing food and grousing at each other. They followed the chef through a narrow, dark walkway for ten steps.

He paused and turned to wave an arm to the left. "As you re-quested, my friend."

Rory gave him a pat on the shoulder. "I really appreciate this."

"Good. Enjoy. Marcia will bring you everything."

Rory showed Siofra to a booth separated from the rest of the patrons by sheer privacy curtains. That allowed her to see out, but no one could see her. It was the closest he could give her to being in a restaurant without being exposed.

 He'd called Domenico and explained he had a nervous guest who had not dined out much, and that he was protecting her. Rory had done a favor for Domenico a year ago and the chef had been waiting on the chance to repay him ever since.

Rory didn't date many women who wanted dinner, only des-sert.

Sharing a meal with a woman like Siofra felt like a first for him, too. In fact, he hadn't felt this way since back when he'd gone to his prom.

Siofra was sitting so carefully, as if she'd make a wrong move and embarrass him, that watching her snagged at his heart.

He could imagine her worry over choosing from a menu so he leaned over close and said, "This guy is great, but he won't let me order. Says he knows what we need. Hope you like everything."

She let out a pent-up breath. "I'm sure I'll love it. Just the smells in here are amazing." Then she finally relaxed.

What did you talk about with a woman who had led a life like hers? He didn't want her to feel like he was interrogating her, but the ability to chitchat had not been a requirement for his job. If it had been, he'd have needed remedial courses.

She had asked him to wait until tomorrow to hear about living with the Cadells.

He'd intended to respect that, but he wanted to learn more about her. "Would you tell me about the Cadells, Siofra?"

Her face paled and she stared at the tablecloth.

Well, he'd fucked that one up.

He sucked.

Ferrell sent Rory an image of Siofra dumping a bowl of spa-ghetti on his head. Hard to argue with his jaguar.

"They came to our apartment. My father was terrified of them. He handed me over." She paused and swallowed hard. "They still killed him and took me as slave labor," she started slowly. "We were in Indiana in a city called Gary. At least, that's what I remember, but it's been so long and I've had no one to talk to about it, so I might have some things wrong. I'm guessing they had some run-in with my father." She lifted her shoulders, sounding unsure what else she could say.

He put his hand over hers. "Sorry, I didn't mean to bring that up after you asked me to wait. I just ... it was bugging me. We don't get a lot of information on the Cadells. Hearing you'd been with them was ... bizarre."

"It's okay. At least you didn't act as if I was with them voluntarily like your boss did."

"He's protective of his people." The Guardian had probably wigged out the minute he heard the word Cadell from the lips of someone who had knocked Rory off his feet with her power. Rory hadn't heard much of that conversation and Siofra had a way of dodging answers that had more than likely ruffled the Guardian's feathers.

"Eh, your boss made up for it with the hotel room." She seemed to brush off the insult easily, but he could tell she was tired of being persecuted for things out of her control.

After that first dumb question, he wasn't sure what to say next. He might as well be that skinny teenager on his first date again, terrified of saying the wrong thing.

Siofra lifted her gaze to him and her eyes sparked with challenge. "Payback time. Tell me who *you* are, Rory."

When she looked at him like that, he wanted to give up all of his secrets, but he had enough self-discipline to not make that mistake.

If he wanted her to talk, this was his opening. He didn't share things about his family, but then again no one had asked about them in many years. "I grew up in Virginia. I was the oldest of three boys."

"Are your brothers married?"

"No."

"Where do they live?"

His heart hurt the minute she said the word "brother." "One is backpacking across Europe and the other one, uh, died."

"Oh, no. I'm sorry."

"Me, too." He had to move off that topic. "As for me, I went into the service, was trained for Special Forces, and ended up here."

That so wasn't the way it happened, but he couldn't just lay out his history to her or share about the Guardian calling up his jaguar when he turned twenty-one.

"Are all of your family shifters?"

"No. Just me."

She angled her head at that. "How ... I've never heard of a shifter coming from two human parents." She shook her head. "On the other hand, I only know what I've learned around jackal shifter guards."

And this was just one reason he avoided talking about his family and never with a woman, but those women generally weren't interested in him using his mouth to talk.

His brain kept separating all other women from ... Siofra.

He gave her the best answer he could about being a shifter born of human parents. "There's a lot about shifters we don't know and it will be decades before enough information is shared that we have a better understanding of the species." Saying that made him feel like a bug to be studied, but he'd spoken the truth.

"What's the deal with your boss?"

"What do you mean?"

"Does he run the organization you work for or does someone else pull the strings, and why do his eyes look like an eagle when he's in human form? I'm guessing he must be some sort of eagle shifter."

At one time, the Guardian would not have shown his face to outsiders, but he'd told the Gallize shifters that he would have to risk personal exposure to better serve them as a leader in this new era.

Once Rory figured out what had happened after Siofra's power had knocked him out, he realized the boss had done what he always did when it came to protecting his Gallize. Whatever it took. He'd exposed his face to a stranger, someone who had been with Cadells, to find out what had happened to Rory.

That was humbling and admirable, but Rory still couldn't tell Siofra too much. "Our boss does head up our organization. He's the top of the shifter food chain for us. He's a little older than most shifters you've met and that has something to do with his eyes."

"What's his name?"

He hedged by saying, "We just call him sir."

Rory had no idea how he was going to get off this topic, but Marcia saved him by showing up with two glasses of red wine. Rory had no background in wine but knew whatever Domenico sent would be good.

Siofra watched her glass of wine with wide eyes that turned worried.

Marcia said she'd be right back with food and disappeared.

Rory asked, "Do you not like wine? I'll get you something else."

"I don't know that I won't like it." She stopped talking and started fidgeting. "I'm just concerned about whether I can handle it."

He put his hand over her cold one, drawing her attention to him. "You can have anything you want. Don't hesitate to just say no."

"I'm learning to use that word," she muttered.

He hurt for what she'd endured around people she feared telling "no."

When Marcia returned carrying a tray loaded with piles of plates, Rory waited as she covered the table with food. She shredded cheese over a couple of the dishes and asked if they needed anything else at the moment.

Rory told her to tell Domenico the wine was wonderful, but to please bring his guest a soft drink.

The minute she left, Siofra started apologizing. "I didn't mean to be difficult. I really appreciate the dinner and—"

"Hush," he ordered in a gentle voice. "It's not an inconvenience. I should have asked, because I knew wine was coming."

Marcia returned quickly, placing everything Rory had asked for in front of Siofra, who hesitated only a minute then dove into the food.

As they ate and shared dishes between them, she relaxed and

Rory enjoyed the kind of evening he never had. Siofra wasn't like the other women who would be sliding their hands all over him, teasing him with what was to come.

She made him happy just by being here.

She acted as if this meal meant more than diamonds and silk. He'd never considered a meal anything other than trying to show a courtesy before he got down to business with a woman.

He hadn't been after a relationship with those females any more than the women had wanted one with him.

But this meal? He liked just taking his time and enjoying the way Siofra smiled from time to time and occasionally teased him as if they'd known each other much longer.

Little by little, she opened up about her jobs at the camps. While it sounded like a miserable existence, her eyes lit up when she talked about caring for the children and making them special outfits. He could see her being a strong mother, willing to stand up to protect her family.

The idea of her having a family made him happy.

The thought that she'd share it with another man, not so much.

She started to reach for a serving dish and paused with a light-hearted look. "Are you going to eat the rest of that lasagna or am I going to have to arm wrestle you for it?"

Little moments like that told him she was beginning to trust him more. He busted up laughing at her.

She grinned. "What?"

"It's yours."

"Good thing. I wouldn't win arm wrestling with you so I'd have to pull the poor-me girl card."

He bet she'd never really pulled that card in her life. He said, "You don't know what's coming for dessert. You may need your girl card for that."

She scraped the last of the lasagna onto her plate, not the least bit self-conscious about eating so much.

He loved it.

He also loved this meal. Domenico had outdone himself.

"Eh, I don't care about dessert," she said. "I know as a shifter you can clear this table and still be hungry, so you can have everything else. I just want this."

"You have pretty good knowledge of shifters."

She paused and he had a moment of regret until she said, "One of the jobs I worked in the Cadell camps was in the kitchen. We always had jackal shifters. Took a lot to feed them."

Another small nugget from her. To keep the evening light, Rory noted how she'd piled her plate. "You like lasagna, huh?"

"Honestly, I've never had it before. It's now my new favorite food of all time."

His jaguar purred at sharing another first with her.

She cut her eyes at him and angled her head in a thoughtful way. "What's your favorite food?"

"Never thought about it. I just eat a lot."

"Oh, come on. You have to have a favorite."

For years, he'd avoided liking anything enough to miss it if he could never have it again. But he'd had a family at one time, and her sweet tone sent his mind back to a time when he was growing up. "Cherry cobbler."

"What's that?"

"It's made with crust and cherries and ... hell, I don't know. It's like a cherry pie mixed up and dumped in a loaf pan. Give me a plate of that when it's warm with a scoop of ice cream and that's the closest to heaven I'll ever get."

She forked another piece of lasagna into her mouth and chewed with a dreamy look on her face. Then she wiped her lips with the napkin and said, "You eat cobbler a lot?"

"No. Haven't had it in five years."

Her fork stalled in midmotion. She turned to him. "Why not? You're a free person and I know you must have money to afford it."

How could he tell her that he only wanted the homemade cobbler his mom used to make for his birthday, and those days had stopped happening when he went into the military.

Actually, that was wrong.

It stopped when she didn't hear from him during the longest year of his life after he first became a shifter. He'd been experiencing crazy physical problems until the moment a black ops team of shifters snatched him. By the time they delivered him to the Guardian, he was losing his mind and ready to attack anything.

The Guardian called up Rory's jaguar.

He spent the first month just trying to accept that he was not human and the rest of the time getting his ass kicked as he learned to handle his animal. Gaining control took many more months, then he entered a special division of the military.

Rory went home one time, had an argument with his baby brother, and left. His brother, curious about shifters when they came out, later died while at a meeting of shifters. His mother blamed Rory, but not because he was a shifter. She had no idea about that.

She blamed him for not being there for the brother who idolized Rory.

That was the end of any family visits and cherry cobblers.

"Rory? You were going to tell me why you haven't had your favorite dessert in five years."

"Someone in my family used to make it. I haven't been around them for a long time. To be honest, I'm not up for talking about my family tonight."

Siofra flashed a suspicious glance at him, but let it go and finished eating. She even managed to scarf down a full helping of cannoli when Marcia served them dessert.

Domenico came out of the kitchen, looking like the Italian chef he was from curly black hair and big brown eyes to his thick belly. Sweat drizzled from beneath his white cap. He worked hard creating great food over hot fires.

"It is good, yes?" Domenico's thick black eyebrows lifted in expectation.

Before Rory could answer, Siofra said, "That was the most amazing meal I have ever eaten and that dessert deserves awards."

The chef didn't need to know that was her first time in a restaurant, because the food had seriously rocked.

Rory chuckled, "I can't say it any better than she did. Thanks for this. It was perfect."

Domenico made another half bow. "It has been my pleasure. I will have something new for your next visit."

Her face fell a little, but she kept her smile in place. "I can't wait."

Funny thing was that Rory had the same moment of disappointment he felt certain Siofra had suffered. When would the two of them ever do this again?

Never.

He hustled her outside where streetlights glowed now that dark had pushed away any sign of sunset. He glanced around to check for threats, but he felt so good about dinner that he decided to take her for a stroll before taking a cab to the hotel.

A soft evening breeze added to the peaceful feeling until Ferrell went on alert, growling that a threat was nearby.

Rory had kept a keen eye out for anyone following or paying attention to them. He'd seen no one.

His jaguar sent the image of a giant rat with fangs.

That's when Rory noticed a rat keeping pace with them about five feet behind. The rodent was hardly visible in the dark as it ran from shadow to shadow.

That continued for the next block.

What the hell?

Evil. One word from Ferrell and Rory went on high alert.

Magic was afoot.

Siofra had been chatting happily. "I think being a chef would be amazing, but ... it's probably because I'd have food around all the time." She snorted at that and added, "Still, I'd love to learn how to cook more than basic food in large quantities."

After a few more steps, she stopped talking about food and asked, "What's wrong?"

Rory whispered, "Maybe nothing. Just keeping an eye out."

The next time he looked over his shoulder, the rat continued to move at a steady pace, like a little robot.

Siofra followed his gaze and had a tiny jerk reaction. "What the ... "

"Wait until we can talk," he said to keep her from saying anything else around this rat. He also didn't want to be distracted around a possible threat.

The strangest part was that he couldn't scent the rat.

Not that he wanted to smell that stinking creature, but everything about it seemed bizarre.

When he pulled Siofra into a hard right turn at the next corner, she yelped.

That damn rat stayed with them.

"Sorry, Siofra, but I think we have unexpected company," he explained in a whisper, keeping her close. "Be ready to jump when I tell you."

Based on what little he knew about her, Siofra's normal reaction would be to snap at him about jumping when he said, but she seemed to grasp the gravity of his concern. "I'm ready."

Looking over his shoulder, he waited until an available cab approached and waved a hand. He picked up his pace, forcing her to jog until they reached the cab as it pulled to the curb. He opened the door, rushed her in and slammed the door behind him.

Fucking rat scurried over and sat up a few feet from the curb, staring at him like they knew each other.

Rory gave the driver an address and the cab sped away while the rat sat frozen in that spot.

What the hell was that about?

Riding back to the hotel would have been a short jaunt, but Rory wanted to first determine if they were being tracked. He changed their final destination a few times. Then Rory instructed the driver to take them to Cleveland Park.

Siofra's eyebrows went up when they finally stopped, but she didn't question it.

He paid the driver and helped Siofra out while he scanned around them. "Let's walk off our dinner then we'll go back, okay?"

"Sounds good."

He could smell her fear, but she kept her chin up and acted as if this was exactly what they'd planned. He would have taken her to the hotel if he knew for sure they weren't followed. If someone was using magic with animals, he wanted a chance to see if it happened more than once and believed himself capable of protecting her from a rat.

If it happened again, he'd have to change tonight's plans.

After a short stroll, he located a bench with plenty of light near a playground and said, "We'll sit a bit."

"Sure."

Her answers were getting shorter and sounding more panicked. When she sat next to him, he eased closer to her and put his arm around her shoulder. Sixty feet away, a man watched his little boy climb around on the activity structures.

A couple walked their dog along the jogging path.

Siofra's body had become rigid. She whispered, "What's going on?"

"Not sure yet, but you're safe with me. I just want a moment out here in the open where I can determine whether someone is following us."

"You mean the ... rat?"

Sure, it sounded crazy, but he said, "Yes."

She didn't say another thing for the next few minutes, just sat very still. What was going through that mind?

Pigeons generally flew only during the day unless lights were on near trees, which was why it didn't surprise him to see just a few land nearby, peck around and fly off.

A gray one made two laps around their bench and arced down, landing with stiff motions about fifteen feet away.

Siofra gasped. "Oh, shit."

Did she know what was going on? He warned, "If you know something, don't hold back or you'll get us both killed."

She looked around at him for the longest moment and finally said, "Okay, I'm not sure, but here's what I think. When I was with the ... "

Her words fell off as the pigeon headed over to them. It didn't bob its head as it walked. Once it reached the light, Rory could see dark, empty holes for eyes. Fuck.

He knew of only one thing that might be.

Siofra's mouth was open and terror flooded her gaze.

When the pigeon stood below them, it looked at Siofra and opened its beak. "You must go home, Siofra."

CHAPTER 19

T HIS PARK WOULD BE A nice place to visit before sunset next time, but with her insane life there would likely be no next time.

Siofra stared in shock at the bird looking up at her with dead eyes and tried to find her voice. Was this Mother Cadellus of the stories she'd heard for so many years, the scary witch of her nightmares?

She cringed under the weight of Rory's confused stare, but appreciated having him with her to face this. She'd been having a wonderful evening with Rory and had hoped the rodent following them from the restaurant had been just like the one on the parking deck where she'd slept ... a harmless natural creature.

But when Rory had asked, she feared putting him in danger more than looking crazy to him. She'd been telling him this might be related to Mother Cadellus when the pigeon walked up and spoke, shocking her into silence.

Rory asked, "Do you know who this is, Siofra?"

"Possibly." She cleared her throat and asked the bird, "Are you, uh ... "

"Yes. I am Mother Cadellus."

Rory cursed and demanded, "What's this all about?"

The pigeon turned its black gaze on Rory. "Who are you and what business is it of yours?"

"I'm her bodyguard, because people have been trying to kill her," Rory said, sounding like hired help.

Siofra didn't want to tell this bird, or Mother Cadellus, anything about Rory either. Instead she argued, "I don't consider a place I was held captive and had a man forced on me as home."

Swinging the black eyes back to Siofra, the pigeon said, "They were trying to give you value. Everyone must carry a load in this world."

Rory's grip on her shoulder tightened, but he was staying out of this, probably to keep Mother Cadellus talking.

Siofra should have taken a moment to think through her next words, but she was too pissed to think straight. A taste of freedom would do that to someone who'd lived her life.

She leaned forward and snapped, "Carry a load? I was held prisoner from the time I was a child. I had no family. I've lived in camps from one location to another with no—"

"*Shh!*" Rory hushed her as a couple strolled by.

Turning to the couple, the bird began moving around and pecking at the ground in a normal manner.

As soon as the couple walked out of hearing range, Siofra finished her tirade. "I was dragged everywhere and made to live with nothing and no hope for ever having a life. They put me through hideous experiments without my consent then a guard came to rape me to get me pregnant. That is *not* a life or a home."

Appearing to ignore Siofra, the bird kept walking around.

Had Mother Cadellus been thinking and needed to keep the bird moving while she was distracted?

Returning to its original spot, the pigeon said, "You will understand more later, but for now you must come back and help us locate Baatar."

Siofra froze.

Rory asked, "Who?"

This sent the bird's empty stare to Rory again. "Shut up until I give you instructions."

"Dream on, birdie."

Cocking its head to one side, then the other, the pigeon said, "You are clearly not human. What are you?"

Rory shrugged. "I don't answer questions put to me by rodents on the ground or in the air."

Oh, shit. Siofra didn't want Mother Cadellus focusing on Rory. She had no idea what kind of power this woman wielded. Before he could open his mouth and make it worse, Siofra asked Mother Cadellus, "Why should I help you find Baatar? He didn't deserve to be captured any more than I did?"

Turning back to her, the possessed bird said, "You are part of a large family that takes care of each other. Baatar is not of our family. He has a purpose and has caused our family tremendous grief by running away, just as you have. It is your responsibility to find him so that he may serve his purpose."

Siofra had never held a conversation with a truly insane person, but she'd know crazy when she heard it even if the mouthpiece didn't belong to a dead bird.

She would help no one capture or hurt Baatar.

Leaning forward, Siofra waited as a young guy and his dog jogged near them, but he took a turn that sent him running in the opposite direction. When he was far enough away, she spoke softly to the bird.

"I will *not* help you find him and I will *not* go back to be abused again."

Making a clicking sound at the back of its throat, which would seem unnatural had the bird been alive, it said, "That is unfortunate. If you had done this the easy way, our people would have brought Baatar back and shown him how he could be of great value. He would have been treated well."

Siofra recalled when Baatar told her to run, he claimed they would not hurt him. He was the greater prize.

Of course, anything would be a prize above her, but why was he so important? She asked, "What do you plan to do with him?"

"You are not at a level to know these things."

Stupid twit. Siofra said, "Then you won't find Baatar. He's vanished by now and not even I can find him."

"That is unfortunate. I will be forced to recover the investment we've made in him since he was a child another way."

Baatar had been captured as a child, too? "Oh, really? How will you do that?" Siofra asked, equally curious and worried, but trying to sound unimpressed.

"There's only one group who can locate Baatar quickly and that's the Black River pack."

Scoffing, Siofra said, "I just saw one of their divisions and they didn't have a clue how to find him."

"That's because they don't have my help. Once I negotiate a

compensation for the money and time we've spent, I'll make a deal to join forces with them to track down Baatar, but I would rather have him back in the fold on his own."

Siofra's heart drummed like a metronome wound too tightly. Could this bitch and that wolf pack find Baatar?

The woman's cold voice poured from the dead pigeon once more. "Just remember that you are responsible for what happens to him. He would have been treated very well had he returned to us first. That wolf pack will not take such good care of him. And you *will* return to where you belong, but you will not enjoy life as much this time. Do not think this bodyguard can protect you."

With that, the pigeon shuddered once and fell over, now a stiff corpse.

Rory had to lean on his training as a sniper to sit as still as possible while that bitch bird spewed vile garbage and threats at Siofra.

The minute the pigeon returned to its dead state, he let out a long breath. "Okay, we need to talk. So you *know* the person who manipulated that bird?"

"No, not exactly. I grew up hearing about Mother Cadellus using dead animals to do her bidding, but ... I thought it was folklore. I've never witnessed *that* before today. I thought she was more myth than anything." Siofra grabbed her head. "This is awful. I have to find Baatar."

An expected surge of fury rushed through him and Ferrell roared to get out.

What the hell was going on?

He could come up with only one explanation. Jealousy. He'd *never* reacted to a woman talking about another man. Still, neither he nor his animal wanted another man around Siofra.

He asked Ferrell to settle down so he could help Siofra and damn if his jaguar didn't quiet immediately.

Turning her to meet his gaze, Rory held her face in his hands. "Who is Baatar?"

"Someone important to me. He was brought into my camp six months ago. He told me they'd captured him a long time ago, but he never said they'd taken him as a child, too."

"What do you mean by important?" Rory asked, struggling not to growl and wanting to kick himself for having this reaction. He had never reacted this way to any woman.

That had clearly just changed and he didn't like this feeling one bit.

Siofra stopped fidgeting with her hands and squinted her eyes, studying him. "Why are you asking me that?"

What was he supposed to do? Ask if this guy was someone she'd been involved with—or still was—and humiliate himself?

"Were you two an item?" popped out of his mouth all on its own. Evidently he had no trouble embarrassing himself when it came to Siofra.

"What?" She pulled back in horror. "No. Eww. Baatar is like a brother to me."

"Good." Rory released a breath, at peace over that answer.

Ferrell rumbled a peaceful purr.

Siofra sat up and crossed her arms. "Why?"

Shit, he did not want to get into this conversation. So he hijacked the topic. "What do you think they'll do with Baatar?"

With just that little incentive, Siofra forgot about her last question. "If you mean the Cadells, I have no idea what they have in mind. He said they brought him here from China, but he does not look Asian or speak Chinese. He hasn't told me his entire story yet. We avoided speaking much in the camps, keeping our conversation about escaping."

She was clearly scared for her friend. Rory kept silent so she'd continue talking.

"Baatar has been my only true friend, someone I adopted as a brother. He's watched over me like I'm his little sister. When he found me with the jackal shifter who tried to rape me, Baatar pushed me to run right then. I didn't want to run without him, because we'd been talking about how we would escape together, but said he'd keep the jackal shifters busy so I could get away. He believed they would not harm him or come after me because he was more important to the Cadells. That was the only reason I finally ran."

Rory tried to put this all together. "Sounds odd for the Cadells to work with anyone to get a captive back."

"Mother Cadellus said they spent a lot of money on Baatar and the Cadells probably don't want to screw up their deal with the Black River pack."

She was telling the truth. While she had her guard down, Rory wanted all he could get. "What makes Baatar a prize?"

"The Cadells can't figure out Baatar." She sighed heavily. "He's a big guy with some kind of power, but he can't make it manifest in any useful way. He's just abnormally strong and fast." She shook her head at some hidden thought. "He has bad moments where he walks around banging his head and chest, talking to himself. It's getting worse. I watched his back in the camp and he watched mine. Now he has no one."

Rory wasn't seeing the prize aspect of this guy Baatar. Sounded like a nutcase, but in fairness to someone born with a power they had no clue how to manage or use, Baatar was okay in Rory's book because he had protected Siofra. The Black River pack lived for getting their hands on shifters, but they would get really excited about someone with untapped power.

Wait until the Guardian heard about the dead critters and Mother Cadellus.

Hell, Rory had suspected it might be that witch when he'd seen the dead pigeon eyes, but he'd only heard snippets about the crazy witch who cursed the Gallize shifters. He'd been told to always be on the lookout for any strange situation with a dead animal. He'd never encountered any, which was why it had taken a moment to realize he'd been in the presence of true evil.

Then a new thought hit him. If Siofra knew so much about the Cadells, could she know about the Gallize?

He doubted it. When she asked about him having two human parents, she'd sounded sincerely dumbfounded and let the topic drop as soon as he brushed it off. Also, she hadn't seemed particularly frightened or wary of the Gallize shifters, as a Cadell would be, just shifters in general.

She grabbed Rory's hand. "Now you can understand why Baatar needs me. I'm begging you. Please let me go now. I have to find Baatar and help him before these people get their hands on him."

Oh, hell no. She was not leaving his sight. "I can't do that, Siofra. My boss allowed you a break from questioning, because he expects me to deliver you in the morning to talk to him."

She snatched her hand back. "I'm worried about a man's life and all that matters is me talking to your boss?"

"No, I want you to be safe first."

"Then help me find Baatar."

In that moment, he wanted to throw duty to the wind and be the man she needed, but he could just see the Guardian's face if he agreed. Rory was already hanging by a thread and one more wrong move would break it.

His boss expected all of the Gallize to put duty first and Rory couldn't face himself in the mirror if he let down the Guardian and his team.

He tried to reason with Siofra. "I understand what you're saying, but I can't just go off on my own." Her disappointment hit him so hard it physically hurt. "Let me talk to my boss in the morning and see what we can do." He intended to contact Justin tonight, who would decide if this called for an emergency meeting.

If Mother Cadellus was after one of the Gallize, Rory would drag everyone in, but this was just some guy Siofra knew. Once the boss talked to her tomorrow, Rory would lobby to help her find her brother even though it could push the Guardian over the edge. He'd do that for her.

Siofra jumped up. "That bitch and the wolf pack may have Baatar by tomorrow."

Rory glanced around as he stood.

Two people who had been laughing as they strolled now paused to stare at them.

He cupped Siofra's arm and pleaded, "Don't do this here. Please. We need to go."

She yanked her arm back. "I have done nothing to deserve being held against my will. In fact, I helped you with those bounty hunters, then saved your leg. I need you to let me go."

This sucked so much. He did owe her and one thing he didn't want to do was die owing anyone, not for something that important. He might be three years from facing death by mating curse, but his animal still didn't feel right.

He might not have three more years.

Herding her to the curb, Rory hailed another cab.

The minute she got inside the car, she said, "Call your boss."

That would be a double hell no until he ran this past Justin. The driver had some Middle Eastern music turned up and wouldn't hear them, so Rory asked, "Why?"

"If he wants answers on the Cadells, he'll have to meet me *now* to get them, or he gets nothing. This deal is good for one hour."

He didn't know if she had anything worth disturbing the Guardian for unnecessarily, but he could see no way around making that call.

Not when he couldn't guarantee she'd answer anyone's questions tomorrow.

He didn't want to push her after all she'd been through and he doubted he could at this point. She was clearly terrified for Baatar, someone she considered a brother. Apparently her duty to him topped everything else in her world.

His animal wanted Siofra as their mate and Rory had crossed a line in the hotel. One he shouldn't have crossed. Hell, he was fighting possessive thoughts that he had no right to think.

Rory had to do the right thing and hand Siofra off to someone else before he couldn't walk away.

But he would allow only someone he trusted to take over guarding her, which had to be Justin or Cole. Neither of those two would make a move on her. They were happily mated.

Rory now understood the magnetic pull of a potential mate and the idea of not seeing her again hurt worse than any wound he'd suffered. Hurt as bad as losing his brother.

He couldn't understand that, because he wasn't trying to mate her, but he wanted her just the same.

CHAPTER 20

C OOL AIR CIRCULATED THROUGH THE conference room
on the street level in their Spartanburg headquarters, but nothing matched the icy shoulder Siofra turned on Rory.

He could deal with being in deep shit with the boss and his
team, but he hated having this gulf of silence between him and
his nymph. He leaned against the wall to the side of where Siofra
sat at the end of the table, stewing. That wasn't as bad as the hurt
filling her eyes.

He'd let her down, but he had no way around it. He couldn't
just turn her loose.

Twenty minutes ago, Rory had called the Guardian to share
his Mother Cadellus encounter and explain that Siofra needed to
speak with him immediately.

There had been a long silence before his boss said he was on
the way. From where, Rory had no idea. Being a sea eagle who
lived on the East Coast, up in Baltimore, the Guardian flew in his
animal form at night.

Calling Justin had resulted in a loud earful of cursing, but Justin
ran the team Rory had been assigned to, which meant he had to
be kept in the loop. It wasn't as if Justin wouldn't drop everything
to come to the aid of a team member, but he hadn't understood
the panic to meet now.

Rory didn't blame him. They were all jumping out their col-
lective asses for some guy named Baatar. The Mother Cadellus
encounter could have been reported in the morning since it involved no one on their teams.

Justin stomped through the open doorway into the conference

room with a cup of coffee and growled.

He cast a vicious look at Rory and pulled a chair out on the opposite side of the table from where Rory stood.

After Siofra made her initial demand, she'd stopped talking to Rory and hadn't said a word since entering the building.

In the next moment, the Guardian entered and looked as put together as he had hours ago and any other time Rory met with the powerful shifter. His boss paused, then took a position to Siofra's right, leaving Justin on the Guardian's right.

Why hadn't his boss gone to the power position at the head of the table? This seemed almost congenial.

"Hello again, Siofra," the Guardian said in the cultured tone of a time gone by. Yet his dialogue often included current terms and phrases, showing how he morphed with each era he lived.

"Sir." She swallowed and fidgeted with her hands. Where was the fierce woman from less than an hour ago?

The Guardian asked, "What happened tonight?"

Siofra explained about the rat and pigeon, and repeated that she'd never had that happen before. Her words would ring true to Justin and the Guardian even if Rory had not been standing nearby to naysay anything he heard as an outright lie.

Damn, he loved hearing her voice again. He was going to miss her, miss being with her.

And that right there was why he had to back away.

He had to suck it up and let someone else on the team take his spot ... as long as it was Justin or Cole.

No one else was allowed near her.

Ferrell snarled, sending Rory an image of Siofra with a fence around her and the jaguar stalking the perimeter.

He groaned silently at his screwed-up thinking when it came to this woman. The minute he handed her off, he had no more say. He fell back on the mantra he'd been repeating to himself since her ultimatum in the cab.

Siofra was just a woman.

She would be gone after tonight.

If she stayed around, he'd end up in her bed.

The minute Rory had started that mental chant, Ferrell started sending him a volley of gory images of Siofra dying hideous deaths.

When Rory ignored him, Ferrell sent an image of Rory in a coffin.

"Rory?" the Guardian called out.

"Sir?" He stood away from the wall, wishing he'd been paying attention.

"I asked if you had anything else to add to what Siofra told us."

"No, sir. I've obviously never met this Mother Cadellus before, but if all the stories we've heard are true then it fits that she used a dead pigeon to specifically contact Siofra."

Siofra flashed Rory an annoyed glance.

That could be considered communicating, he mused silently.

Sitting back, the Guardian addressed Siofra. "As I understand it, you wish to answer our questions about the Cadells now, is that correct?"

"Not really," she said with more confidence this time and sat back with her arms crossed.

Rory's mouth dropped open, then he snapped, "Are you kidding me?"

Without looking at him, she turned a tired voice to him. "What?"

"You said this was what you wanted to do and the only way you'd share what you knew about the Cadells was if our boss came in tonight."

She turned fully to face him and said, "No, that's not correct. I said 'If he wants answers on the Cadells, he'll have to meet me *now* to get them.'"

"Same difference," Rory argued.

"It might be the same if I had intended to share all I know right now, but that's not the case." She cut back around, now having to look directly into intense eagle eyes, which had darkened in a bad way.

Sensing the Guardian's irritation, now Rory had the urge to pull her to him and talk her way out of this mess, but she bulldozed ahead. "I *will* make good on my offer and I'll gladly tell you everything I know about the camps they kept me in, how they operate, and the people involved. I may not know their names and specific location details, but I'm good with faces."

When she paused, the Guardian took his time before asking, "What is the catch?"

"I have to save the man I consider a brother. The man who helped me escape. He escaped after I did, but he doesn't speak good English when he gets flustered and he has problems with his power."

Justin took a slug of coffee, put the cup down, and asked, "What kind of power? What is he?"

Rory waited to see what she'd say.

Siofra said, "I don't know how to describe what he is, because he doesn't seem to know. He has moments where he can't control his body and he talks to himself. He said he'd lived in the mountains of China for a long time before being brought here six months ago."

"Is this Baatar Chinese?" Justin asked.

"I don't think so," she said, concentrating hard on her answer. "He doesn't have their facial features and he's huge. He has an odd accent. I don't know what it is, but not Chinese." She clasped her hands in front of her and said, "All he wants is to be free to find peace. Like I said, he has more strength than a human his size, but one time he had a seizure of some sort and passed out. I thought he'd died. He needs someone to be there when those moments get bad. I have no allegiance to the Cadells. If you help me find Baatar and promise to help him, I agree to spend two days answering any questions you have on them. But ... only if I can go free after that as well."

Rory's heart and his jaguar screamed no.

Not because he didn't want for her to find her friend or to live free, but because he didn't want her to leave at all. He wanted her where he could keep her safe from Cadells and any other threat.

If the Black River pack or Cadells got their hands on Siofra again, she would die. He knew it.

But the longer he stayed around her, the more difficult it was to fight his animal who wanted her as their mate and to stick to his own conviction of never mating.

What was his option, then? Ask Justin or Cole to go with Siofra?

What if something happened to one of them and they didn't

make it back? From what Rory had been told, Gallize mate for life. That would leave either Tess or Eli a widow with no hope of a mate for the rest of either woman's life.

Tess was pregnant.

Just because he felt this insane need to put his neck out there to keep Siofra safe didn't mean he should risk his friends' lives or that of any other Gallize shifter.

Justin pissed him off on a daily basis lately, but he and Cole always had Rory's back and he had theirs.

Silence blanketed the room as they all waited on the Guardian's decision. He sat forward, leaning one arm on the table when he spoke to Siofra.

"I will agree to this if you can find Baatar in one week."

Her face fell. "One week? That's not enough."

Not losing his temper, the Guardian explained, "My shifters stay very busy dealing with closing down Jugo Loco operations, protecting humans and innocent shifters, plus aiding in the protection of national security here as well as in other countries. Even if it takes months of planning, when we send a team in, they handle most operations in twenty-four to forty-eight hours. A week is extremely generous."

She brightened and her voice filled with relief. "Oh, no problem. I don't want an entire team. I can't take more than one person with me anyhow. Baatar would be wary if more than one accompanied me. He trusts no shifters and would believe I was being used for a trap. No team. Just one, please."

The Guardian sat quietly then said, "You may have one, but your deadline is still going to be seven days."

Rory mentally thanked his boss, because he needed a deadline. He'd decided he couldn't dump this on Cole or Justin. He'd have to do his duty *and* keep his hands to himself, which should be simple with Siofra pissed at him.

She sat up. "Okay, then I agree, but I want to leave immediately."

Rory drew in air to argue that this could wait for them to leave in the morning.

The Guardian said, "You may leave as soon as you and our shifter are ready. Justin will assign someone to take Rory's place.

That shifter will have what he needs, plus he'll arrange for whatever you need, then you can leave."

"What?" Rory said on a blast of exhale.

His boss looked up sharply. "Is there a problem?"

Rory hated saying the words that came to mind, because it would not go well, but that didn't stop him. "I'm here now and ready to roll. I know everything there is about this situation, so we could leave immediately." There went his chance to wait until morning.

Justin addressed Siofra. "You two seem to be at odds right now. Sure you wouldn't prefer someone else?"

"You mean like you, bear?" Rory asked with a sarcastic cut. He was trying to protect the son of a bitch. "Tired of being home already?"

"You're a piece of work lately, you know that?" Justin muttered.

Siofra stewed quietly, but said, "If he'll leave tonight, I'll go with ... *him*. I only need his expertise and muscle. Anyone would be fine."

Rory glared at her.

She must have felt it. She turned and glared right back.

He got it. She was still angry he wouldn't let her take off on her own back at the park. She had a point about them having no reason to hold her when she'd committed no crime beyond trying to survive.

In her shoes, he'd be out of patience.

Justin grinned for the first time since coming in the room. "If our boss has no objections ... " Justin paused and looked to the Guardian who gave a curt nod before the bear finished saying, "Then good hunting, cat."

Rory couldn't make up his mind if he was relieved or not. Justin's short tone and the Guardian's grim expression didn't bode well for his future.

Ferrell had no trouble. He growled softly like he did when he got his way.

The Guardian stood. "I'd like to see you for a moment, Rory. Justin, would you make arrangements for transportation and whatever Siofra needs?"

"Yes, sir."

Rory followed the Guardian out with one last look at Justin, who he'd expected to be smirking. That wasn't the case. His friend met his gaze with one of disappointment.

He didn't have time to ask Justin what the hell that was all about when the Guardian couldn't be happy with Rory. His boss had to have noticed the tension between him and Siofra.

Just what Rory lived for, a road trip with a pissed-off female.

Ferrell sent him the image of a happy jaguar riding in a convertible with Siofra driving.

Bastard.

Rory fully expected to catch hell for getting involved with a woman he was supposed to be guarding. What if the Guardian had only agreed out there to end the meeting so he could tell Rory in private that Justin was going with Siofra after all?

The Guardian had the ability to make any decision he chose when it came to his Gallize shifters. But that decision would be a problem.

Rory couldn't stand aside and let her go with someone else. He had serious concerns about keeping Ferrell contained if that happened.

He had his argument ready, even though odds were against him winning an argument with the boss.

As soon as they were alone, the Guardian turned to him with a rigid composure that never seemed to hiccup. "You're still killing your jaguar. I think I know why."

CHAPTER 21

RORY SWALLOWED HARD, SEARCHING FOR anything to say. Why would the Guardian say he was still killing his jaguar? Things weren't fixed yet, but he was managing. With nothing better to use as an argument, he blurted out, "My leg has healed perfectly."

"I saw that and what Siofra did was impressive, but you haven't healed your jaguar. I can feel your power waning."

That was not what Rory expected to hear. "I understand, sir, but I will fix this and get better."

"Even if you can, which I am having serious doubts about, you're volunteering yet again."

"Yes, sir."

"I may still send someone else," the Guardian said, and not in a threatening manner. He simply stated his position.

Rory met this problem head on. "Who else would you send?"

"We have others, including four of our team who have returned from overseas. We need them here and they need time away from that environment."

"I don't think this woman will trust anyone else."

"Oh? She doesn't seem particularly happy with you right now. Why do you think she trusts you at all at the moment?"

Rory reminded himself to never play verbal chess with this eagle shifter. "She's angry with me because I wouldn't let her take off right after talking to Mother Cadellus. My duty required I keep her safe and bring her to you, which I did." He considered sharing everything and realized he was not doing his duty by holding back anything he'd learned. "Also, we have to be careful dealing with her around the Cadells. Mother Cadellus didn't realize I was a Gallize, but that was probably due to not meeting me in person."

"It was," the Guardian confirmed. He asked, "Does Siofra know you are a Gallize or that we exist?"

"No, sir, not that I can determine. The Cadells basically treated her as a slave, maybe worse. I'm slowly getting pieces of her story. She opened up some at dinner." Now that Rory thought about it, his ability to gather intel, once she was speaking to him again, might work in their favor.

"We can't expose anything around Siofra," the Guardian warned. "Even if she does give us intel on the Cadells, she's hiding something and I think it's about her brother."

"You caught that, too, huh?"

"Yes."

"I agree that she's holding back information due to a sense of loyalty to this guy, but I'll find out what's going on, sir."

"You still haven't told me why you volunteered for yet another mission," the Guardian pointed out, not letting it go.

Rory didn't have the kind of ego that pushed him to brag, but neither would he sugarcoat the truth. "I'm the best choice, plus I'll work on her to uncover everything I can on the Cadells while hunting this Baatar."

Crossing his arms, the Guardian stood in an obstinate pose with his feet apart and his expression firm. "Why are you the best choice?"

Don't lose patience with the Guardian. Rory wiped that from his mind before his thoughts pushed out unintentionally.

But, damn, why should he have to constantly explain himself when he'd just done it in the conference room? "I'm thinking you want the team from overseas to have some decompression time once they come home, which leaves that group out, sir. Everyone else I know about here and abroad are all assigned, which leaves me, Justin, Cole, Vic and Adrian. Vic is doing great, but he hasn't gotten comfortable here yet and we all know why Adrian can't do this."

Rory, Cole and Justin had lobbied to prevent the Guardian from putting Adrian and his wolf down even when Adrian stood there asking for it. Their friend had suffered extreme abuse for a shifter while captured overseas. By the time they found Adrian and extracted him, his wolf had started going mad.

But he was showing improvement in Wyoming in a special area where he could roam all he wanted.

The Guardian sighed. "I can't leave Adrian there forever, but you're correct. He's not ready to be among humans yet."

Seeing victory within his grasp, Rory nodded. "Right. Justin and Cole are mated. I'm not. I see this as simple math since Siofra will only agree to one person accompanying her." After laying out his argument, Rory felt a level of confidence over making a valid point.

After a long minute of remaining very quiet, the Guardian said, "More and more, I'm hearing you use the reasoning of not being mated as your decision for volunteering."

Lifting a shoulder in dismissal, Rory said, "I'm being logical. Why risk a Gallize shifter who is mated when finding a Gallize female is so rare for any of them?"

"Them?" the Guardian said pointedly. "What about you? Don't you want a mate?"

Damn. The Guardian should have been a cat. The man was seriously sly.

Rory might as well be straight with his boss, because trying to outmaneuver the Guardian was an impossible task.

But as Rory thought through his answer, he realized something annoying. The Guardian realized the truth. "Why ask me a question you already know the answer to, sir?"

Funny how Siofra had asked Rory the same question not long ago.

Sounding more thoughtful than irritated, the Guardian said, "I suppose I do and that bothers me. I shall be more direct. *Why* do you not want a mate?"

Rory scratched his forehead. He would have denied it if asked in passing by anyone else.

Taking a deep breath, he told his boss, "Let's just say that I have my reasons."

"I'd like to hear them."

Rory should have expected this conversation at some point. The Guardian knew all of them better than they knew themselves.

All but Rory. He knew himself and his future like no one else.

"I don't think I should mate, sir, because I don't want to procreate." No other man would have to suffer through this. "I don't think ... " Rory caught himself before he said something potentially insulting.

"It's fine," the Guardian said. "I want you to speak the truth."

If Rory got it out all at once, like ripping a bandage, maybe it wouldn't feel so bad. "There shouldn't be another one like me." He quickly added, "I respect you and my Gallize brothers, but I ... I feel that I should be a man or an animal, not both. I don't think being a shifter is natural."

"You are correct."

Rory had been preparing to have his head taken off, not hear his boss agree. "Sir?"

The Guardian explained in a compassionate voice, "We are not natural beings, not when compared to humans. We are supernatural and here as a result of the Gallizenae druidess who wanted children in spite of her destiny of remaining a virgin. She would only gift mothers pure of heart who carried a baby boy worthy of her gifts. That makes you very special."

Rory had delved into the history of the Gallize in the early days of being a shifter. He'd had a tough time wrapping his head around a powerful druidess with the ability to shape shift, who would never have her own children but still wanted to leave her mark on the world.

His boss said, "From all I've learned over my three centuries in this world, the goddess must have known that one day shifters of all kinds would be discovered and her Gallize descendants would be the true guardians of this world."

It sounded so much better when his boss talked about that than when Rory dwelled on what he was when alone in his head. He admitted, "I have thought about her reasons, too. I do believe you and my teammates belong here, and definitely with mates, but ... I don't."

When the Guardian said nothing right away, Rory added, "I can't see wasting a mate on me when I don't believe in who I am or that I should be here." Plus, if he hadn't been born a shifter, his brother would still be alive. As a human, Rory could have been around for Tyler and listened to his brother when Tyler wanted to talk about shifters.

Rory had been too angry and embarrassed. He'd argued with Tyler, telling him not to get involved with animals. Rory had left early from leave and returned to his overseas duties or he'd have been with Tyler when his baby brother attended a shifter meeting where he died.

"Could something else be influencing your beliefs?" the Guardian asked.

Rory asked, "Are you hearing my thoughts, sir?"

"No. I would not intentionally do so."

"Sorry, I do know that." But if a Gallize shifter projected strongly enough, the Guardian might catch the words by accident.

Reminding himself to keep his thoughts calm, Rory made one thing clear. "Regardless of how I feel about mating, I'm committed to doing my duty until I sense signs of the mating curse. At that point, I'll continue to do my duty to all of you and deliver myself to you. I've shared none of those thoughts with my teammates. I don't want them to ever doubt my abilities or sincerity when it comes to depending on me in a critical situation, because they come first. Can you now see why I'm the best one to send with Siofra?"

"I can't say I agree with your reasoning for being the best one to send—"

Ah, crap. *Here it comes. He's pulling me off this task.*

"—but I will not stop you from going," the Guardian finished. "I'm torn over allowing it, but I believe your leg is healed. Cole and Justin are to join me to hunt for the tiger. Justin's mate had a vision that the tiger shifter is in serious emotional trouble, which is understandable." He paused a moment. "I want you to understand one thing, Rory. No matter how much power Siofra has, even if she's a Gallize, she can't heal your jaguar."

"You think she's a Gallize, sir?"

"I honestly can't say. She has significant power, though ... I sensed a Cadell influence when I first met her. I couldn't be positive, which has never happened when I encountered one of them."

"You think Siofra is one of *them*?"

"I understand it is hard for you to accept, but that does not diminish my concern."

Rory had forgotten that she might be a Gallize. Either that or he intentionally blocked the thought, because he couldn't imagine seeing her with another man, even someone she called a brother.

But a Cadell? She'd definitely been telling the truth about how they'd treated her and her disdain for the Cadells. Still, she had power.

Was she a Gallize? Rory asked, "Not that I plan to do this, sir, but wouldn't bonding with a Gallize female heal something like my jaguar issue? I'm more curious for someone else who might face what I'm going through."

"I believe the fracture between you and your jaguar is being caused by the fact that your animal realizes it's living a hopeless existence. Your jaguar knows you have no plans to mate and that means every day is one step closer to dying long before its time. Siofra can't heal that. I can't heal it."

Well, shit. That sounded pretty fucking final.

The Guardian's voice held warmth when he said, "Only you can stop the slow death of your jaguar, which isn't that slow after all. You're not healing at all on your own. If you don't fix this with your animal, you're not going to wake up one day. I'm sorry, Rory, but I don't think that day is far off."

CHAPTER 22

SIOFRA TAPPED HER FINGER ON the passenger door of the sport utility, which was larger than her personal living space at the last Cadell camp.

She hadn't told Rory the entire truth about Baatar. Baatar had asked her to never speak of some things to anyone, especially a stranger, once they escaped. She had told Rory and his people as much as she could and as much as they needed to know.

Now she had to come clean about why they were driving toward Virginia. Life would be so much simpler if she could just say what she thought and tell all she knew.

Rory had secrets and hadn't given her all the truth either.

He and his people were not normal shifters, like the jackals and wolves she'd been around. They seemed to be decent and considerate, even if eagle man had scared a year off her life during their first meeting.

What would Baatar think if she told him there were decent shifters in this world?

He'd think they tricked her with magic, but the only magic she'd found with them was when Rory touched her. He woke her up inside and turned her emotions into a chaotic mess.

She liked that mess.

Her energy seemed to strengthen when he was near. Why?

Nothing like that happened around eagle guy or the other shifters on Rory's team, but when he left the conference room to talk with his boss, her energy had seemed ... distressed.

Yep, she would be certifiable if she ever shared that with anyone. Even Baatar would wonder.

For the hundredth time she looked over at Rory, whose jaw hadn't relaxed since leaving Spartanburg. His profile looked like a man trying to grind bricks with his back teeth.

"What?" he asked without taking his eyes off the road.

"Are you going to stay mad at me the entire trip?"

"Maybe."

"Why?"

He frowned as if not sure then said, "You were pissed at me first, at the park and through the entire meeting. Have you changed your mind?" He waved a hand at her. "Never mind. It's better if we just do what we have to do and get this done."

Grouchy guy. "I was upset when you wouldn't let me go when I asked you at the park. I'm terrified over what these people will do to Baatar just as I would be if they were after ... "

"After who?"

"You."

His rigid jaw relaxed and he swallowed, but said nothing.

"Also, I wanted to leave right away last night and we didn't get rolling until five this morning," she reminded him, justifying her earlier irritation even more. It was Wednesday already. She had to get to Baatar. She muttered, "But I don't hold grudges. I'm over it. You're the one still angry with me. It's going to be a long trip."

"Not really. We'll be in Richmond in two more hours, leaving us plenty of daylight to get started. You need to tell me how you're going to find him there, but I know that city well."

She closed her eyes, regretting having to do things this way and said, "We aren't stopping in Richmond."

When she felt his gaze on her, she opened her eyes, expecting a murderous look in his, but she was wrong.

He might not be happy, but he didn't look like he wanted to kill her. Yet.

Keeping an eye on the traffic, he shook his head and muttered something to himself. "I had a feeling Richmond was not the truth. You've grown up around shifters and know we can tell a lie by scent and other small things so you tiptoe around the truth. But I'm not a jackal or a Black River pack wolf to be played with words. If you don't give me the truth right now, we're heading back."

"Please don't," she begged. If they turned back, eagle man might not let her leave again.

"It's in your hands, Siofra. Convince me or we're turning around."

"Right, okay." She had to tell him what was going to happen. "Richmond *is* part of the direction, but we're headed further up the coast. Baatar gave me instructions for when we escaped in case we got separated, which clearly happened when I left the camp."

"Start with the actual city we're looking for," he said, more reserved than actually angry.

She said, "Portland, Maine."

"Are you fucking kidding me?" he yelled.

So much for reserved. "What's wrong with Portland?"

"For one thing, we could have *flown* there by now and rented a car to drive around."

Exactly what she'd have expected to happen. "That's why I said Richmond when you showed me a map. I didn't want to fly."

"Why not?" he asked with exasperation and confusion. "You're the one with a damn deadline."

"I don't like being off the ground."

"You just flew in a damn chopper," he ground out.

She raked a hand over her hair, wishing today would get easier. "I did not want to be on that helicopter and struggled to make that trip, but I was strapped into a harness with my wrists bound. Not like I had a choice."

That quieted him. "What did you do to get through it?"

Did he feel bad about that flight? She was not about to tell him she had Rory fantasies. "I closed my eyes, talked to myself in my mind and created images, anything to keep from freaking out."

He drove for a bit, not turning around yet. "Why are you scared of heights?"

Since he seemed willing to hear her out, she'd share the truth on this fear. "I was tricked into climbing a tree once on a dare when I was a kid. In my enthusiasm to prove I was tough, I climbed over sixty feet up then I looked down to gloat. I panicked instead and clung to the tree. After two hours, they sent a shifter up to get me. Those jackals were creepy. I hated for them to touch me and had to ride down on his back. I do have a deadline, but I also believe I can locate Baatar soon after arriving if he's there."

"Why did you bristle at the boss giving you a seven-day dead-line?"

"Because I have no way of knowing when he'll get there for sure."

He huffed out a breath and said, "Okay, fine. We drive, but I've been up for over a day and it's gotta be at least fourteen or fifteen hours to Maine, not counting fuel and food breaks. That means we're stopping somewhere to sleep and I don't want an earful about your deadline."

"Fair enough."

After a few minutes of quiet, he cut his eyes at her and asked, "What's wrong now?"

"You're mad again."

"Not mad again."

"Oh. Okay." She curled to her left, hoping to finally talk again. Until he said, "Never stopped being pissed."

She sat back hard and crossed her arms, muttering, "Stupid men run everything. Stupid shifters always have the last say. Stupid Cadells got me in this mess. Stupid ... "

"Lies," he filled in.

"Huh?"

He said, "Lies are stupid. They cause problems you don't need and alienate the people who can help you."

She steamed for a bit and finally admitted, "Sorry. You have tried to help me, but ... I don't know who to trust. Baatar told me to give up nothing and never trust a shifter. I've given up more than I should already and I've trusted ... you."

"He had a point. I have yet to meet a jackal shifter who deserved anyone's trust."

"True, but they weren't the worst ones." She relaxed now that he was speaking to her.

"Oh, which ones are the really bad ones?" he asked and sounded sincere.

"The Gallize. Those are the monsters."

He did a double take at her, drove for a moment without talking, then said, "Have you met one?"

"No."

"Then how do you know they're so awful?"

"The Cadells taught us from an early age that Gallize were dangerous shifters who could wipe out an entire camp. They come in the night and kill everyone, even the children. I have always cared for the children in the camps since I was eight years old and slept many nights worried they'd all die before daylight. Except this last camp. I hated that there were no kids."

He whispered, "Shit."

"Exactly," she agreed, glad he understood. "You are the first good shifter I've ever met," she added, before he thought she lumped him in with the Gallize.

Rory forced his fingers to loosen from the grip he had on the steering wheel, before it disintegrated under his hands.

Siofra knew about Gallize shifters.

Correction. She knew what Cadells had told her about the Gallize, which was tainted information at best.

This confirmed one thing. She had no idea he and his group were Gallize. She'd acted as though they were just shifters.

He believed her when she gave him a final destination. Now he needed more. "What will happen in Portland?"

She dawdled with an outdoors magazine she'd picked up at his headquarters building. She'd been reading it as Justin made calls to fulfill the list of clothes and incidentals she'd drafted. Once every-thing had been gathered, it was stowed in a small suitcase. Rory had his bag picked up from the hotel.

She put the magazine down and explained, "Once we arrive, I have to go to a specific grocery store to leave a message on a bulletin board. Then I just check back every day until I find the message he leaves for a rendezvous point."

Now he understood the gravity of a one-week deadline. She had to be worried that either Baatar might not be there yet and wouldn't see the message until after seven days, or he was already there and might have to leave before they posted anything.

Rory still had to sleep, but he just needed four hours and he'd be ready to roll again.

He realized one more variable she hadn't addressed. He didn't want to add to her worries, but he had to know what was coming. She wouldn't just volunteer her thoughts.

He asked, "What happens in a week if you don't get a message?"

She sat so still while engrossed in reading that she might not have heard him. The magazine fell from her slack grip and she turned huge eyes to him. "He'll be there. I have to believe he will, because your boss won't send anyone again and I won't have the money to come back right away. I just need to get my message posted."

Nodding, Rory prepared himself for a long-ass drive. They'd left just after five this morning and he wanted to make a chunk of this now.

Ten hours later, he pulled off the interstate for the last time since leaving Spartanburg. Siofra had been trying to stay awake to keep him company, but her head kept nodding then she'd jerk upright. She'd fall over if someone sneezed at her.

They were west of New York and the only sign he'd seen for a place to stay had been a motor lodge. The one-story buildings had recently been painted a happy yellow, which covered up the shabbiness.

He'd rather spend the night here than in a busy area with more people.

After grabbing the key, he parked in front of the end unit he'd requested. Siofra did as he asked and waited in the car until he had their bags in hand.

He said, "Let's go."

She jumped out and ran over to the door to use the key he'd given her. The sign had called these cottages, which he'd rolled his eyes at, but they weren't bad. Bed looked decent. It had a small kitchenette and cozy look overall.

Dropping the bags inside the door, he checked the bathroom. Smelled clean and no one could fit through the window over the tub.

When he turned around, she had face-planted on the bed. Actually, in the middle of the bed and fully clothed.

He pulled her sneakers and socks off. Tugged the waistband

to make sure she had on underwear. Yes. He pulled off the jeans someone had found for her. She could sleep in the T-shirt.

But she could not hog the bed.

Sliding his hands under her, he slowly rolled her to him and lifted.

She curled up against him and mumbled something unintelligible. Then she smiled.

Energy hummed between them and his dick must have thought it was time to rise and shine. Damn thing.

Hell, this was going to be a long trip. Carrying her to the far side of the bed, he laid her down and covered her.

Searching the small area, he found a place to put the room key and his vehicle key behind the refrigerator. He'd like to say he trusted her to not take off on her own, but he didn't.

By the time he had the door secured to his liking and all of his clothes off except his boxer shorts, he could have slept on a bed of nails.

Thankfully, the mattress proved to be a bit softer. He'd get decent rest, but he never slept hard on an operation. He had his phone set to wake him. If she went to the bathroom or opened the exterior door, he'd know it.

Ferrell would know it.

His jaguar had been a happy clam during the drive, because they had Siofra close the entire time. That would be a problem in a week or less. His jaguar was becoming more possessive by the day. Was it a natural desire for her as a mate or did Ferrell believe her power could save them?

He'd fought the truth since meeting her. Siofra made him want to mate ... with her. There. The harder he avoided admitting that to himself, the more it wore on him. Maybe now he could let it go. He had some honor left.

He'd failed his brother. He'd failed his parents. He was currently failing his jaguar.

He would not fail Siofra. Even if he had a change of heart about mating, he wouldn't do it to save himself and Ferrell. That would be unfair to a mate and feel dishonest, as if mating was about an ulterior motive.

Not love.

Rory would worry about all of that tomorrow.

He drifted off and slept long enough that he had reached that half-awake state when he felt something warm rub across his up-and-ready dick. On his next inhale, he smelled Siofra's scent ... and her arousal.

Fuck. He had to get out of this bed.

She rolled over and wrapped an arm around his neck, curling in close to him as if she'd sensed his need to run. She was muttering something and rubbing her breasts against his chest.

She ran her hand down her shirt and ... oh, hell. Was she getting herself off?

If he didn't get out of this bed right now, he'd lose his mind and his blue balls would never return to a natural color.

She hugged even closer with one arm, keeping a tight hold around his neck.

"Siofra?" he whispered. "Hey, wake up."

She rubbed those luscious breasts over his chest again and even through her T-shirt, he could feel the hard nubs. His dick throbbed. He didn't know what she was dreaming, but he sure as hell hoped he starred in it.

"Siofra," he tried again.

Her hand between her legs started moving and his voice turned desperate. "Siofra!"

"Whuu?"

"Wake up."

"No."

He tried to move and she begged, "Please, don't leave me."

"Then stop."

She mumbled, "Stop what?" But her hand between her legs ceased to move and damn if she didn't moan.

Reaching up to his neck, he tried to pull her arm loose. She held on tighter.

"Are you awake, Siofra?"

She answered on a sigh. "Maybe."

The little demon. "What are you doing?"

Her eyelids finally fluttered until she looked at him. "Don't you want me, Rory?"

He'd thought his dick couldn't get any harder, but when she

purred his name, it nearly exploded. He had to be careful how he answered that question. "Look, I can't hide the fact that I'm turned on, but I can't take advantage of you like that."

She let out a heavy sigh. "I don't have much experience, so I'm sure I'm going about this wrong, but … I have never had the freedom to do anything in my life. I got involved with a boy in the camp in my teens and … he disappeared. You're not a boy. You're a man who knows what you're doing and I'm an adult. I … want to be with you and I'm hoping you don't think bad of me for it, but I like you. A lot."

She was killing him. Killing. Him. "I don't think anything bad. In fact, I admire you for the survivor you are and, to be honest, I'm damned flattered. But as much as I want you, and I do, you wouldn't be happy with yourself in the morning." Damn, but he'd like to give her what she wanted, but he had to be able to face himself in the morning.

"I will only be unhappy if you say no," she said, so quietly he could barely here her over the pounding of his heart. She brushed her fingers over his chest and gave him the sweetest look he'd ever seen on a grown woman. "I just want to feel like a woman. Like a real woman who gets to make her own choices." She shrugged. "I was hoping you'd be, uh, interested, but … if not …"

Oh, hell yes. He could hardly think with the scent of her arousal in the air. "I'm definitely interested," he admitted.

"Really?"

Hearing the surprise in her voice hurt. He said, "Really. I don't know what is going on between us, but I've felt a pull toward you I've had to fight every step of the way."

"Then, uh, does that mean you will, uh … " Her smile wobbled with longing.

"Oh, baby. I want to, but I am not going to be another man who took advantage of you."

Her face fell, then her eyes lit with understanding. "You mean that jackal shifter who attacked me? He didn't even want to do it with me," she admitted.

Easing her to the side so he could bend his elbow and prop his head, he said, "That doesn't make sense."

"It didn't to me either at first until he said the Cadells were going to sell off his girlfriend because she was fertile and I wasn't. He was determined to put a baby in me so they'd sell me to the Black River pack instead."

Rory cursed. "That bastard. You said he didn't ... rape you before you zapped him, right?" He hadn't meant to ask that and bring up a bad memory, but it just came out.

"No. When I panicked, my power sort of electrocuted him before he could do anything."

"Fucker deserved to die."

"You told me that in the van."

"Worth repeating."

She smiled with lazy happiness. His gaze drifted to where her tits pushed to get out of that T-shirt.

"Does that look mean, you uh, want to ... " she murmured, blushing.

He closed his eyes. "We can't do this. You'll regret it later. I can't live with that."

She said, "Want to know what's hard to live with?"

"Yes."

"That attack. I've been trying to wipe the memory of that jackal from my mind since it happened. I kept thinking I never want a man to touch me again, but evidently I do. I want you to touch me. I want to feel alive and free, because it may not last long. I want a good memory to replace that ugly one."

His heart thumped the more he listened. She'd said men had always been in control. They'd want, want, want and never considered what she wanted.

Blood rushed through his body, going nowhere near the head where he needed it so he could figure out what to do.

His body knew what to do, but the head on his shoulders had to deal with the fallout.

She cupped his cheek. "You think too much, Rory. Why don't you let go once in a while and just feel?" She took his free hand and laid it on her breast. His fingers had been itching to touch her.

His hand refused to leave her, so he massaged her breast and her moan went straight to his groin.

When he played with the hard nub, she reached down between her legs.

He lifted the edge of the T-shirt above her breasts and his mouth went dry. "You're so pretty."

She paused her hand and said, "A breast man, huh?"

"Well, I am for yours, but you'd be pretty if you didn't have any at all. That's just a bonus."

Was he going to do this?

Lifting up, she kissed him and of all the things she could have done to draw a yes out of him, her kiss broke through his wall of determination.

CHAPTER 23

SIOFRA SUCKED RORY'S LIP AND held his head so he wouldn't pull back. She kissed his cheek where his five o'clock shadow had a good start on a beard.

You're so pretty.

She would hear those words forever, because she planned to keep his husky words close to her heart. Rory could be grouchy, a hard ass, secretive, and impossible to read at times, but this right here was truth.

His hands reached for her in a hungry way. His touch had the crazy mix of being magic and masculine. Not a young boy like her first time. This was a man who knew what to do with a needy woman.

His fault she was so damn needy right now.

She'd been dreaming of him making love to her and it never quite happened. In her dream, he'd get her hot and wet, just like in that hotel room when he kissed her, then he'd vanish.

Not now.

He was right here. She placed her hand over the front of his boxer shorts and confirmed what he'd been toting around behind the zipper. She'd wrestled with her attraction to him since that kiss, asking herself what she was doing kissing a shifter.

But this man had been created good and honorable. Even his people seemed like decent shifters. She had little experience with romantic relationships, but she'd met a lot of men during the years of her camp life.

She knew mean, abusive and evil.

Rory was none of those.

He was ...

He pushed her panties off and hijacked her thoughts when his fingers feathered across her sensitive folds. Oh, yes, she wanted to stay right here in this moment forever. How could this man be so gruff and rough at times then incredibly gentle when he touched her? He twisted up her core and had that crazy energy singing inside her.

"You're so wet and sexy," he whispered as he dipped inside her with one, then two fingers.

"More," she demanded.

"Not until you're ready, baby."

She caught the rhythm of his fingers and moved to ride his hand. How much more ready could she be? She whined, "Don't stop."

"Not a chance, baby." He dropped his head to suck on her breast. His tongue played with the tip and she arched up to him.

He pulled his fingers out of her and stroked her with a perfect touch at the same moment he nipped her breast.

Pain and pleasure tore through her and she let go. She called out his name, begged him and gripped his arms to hold on. He wouldn't let her down off that ride. She kept coming until she'd given up everything and fell back, weak.

"Stop," she pleaded, laughing.

He laughed, too. "You said don't."

She spoke between breaths. "I ... had an ... ambitious plan."

"Did you get what you wanted?" His voice was deep and husky.

She knew right then that he'd remembered her anger over men only getting what they wanted, never caring about her. This man would always put a woman first.

Of all the things she'd ever wanted, that right there topped the list.

When she could move, she reached over and curled her fingers around his dick.

He hissed, "Careful, baby. I've been on the edge for hours."

Really? That stroked her ego. She suggested, "Then let's take the edge off."

"I want to, more than you know."

Her heart sank. He was stopping now? She wasn't done by a

long shot. "Why?" She couldn't keep the heartbroken sound from her voice.

Brushing his fingers over her face, he said, "Don't even think I don't want you. I do. But I didn't actually plan on this so I am not, uh, prepared."

What was he talking about? The light bulb went off. She asked, "You mean you don't have condoms?"

"Nope."

"I already told you. I'm infertile." She'd never been glad to say that, but if it meant having a special night with Rory, then at least something good would come of her pain. "I'm clean, too. They had us checked all the time in the camp and I haven't been with anyone in five years ... since I was sixteen."

A battle of indecision warred in his face, making her feel encouraged, because he was close to agreeing.

"There's no guarantee that you won't get pregnant," he said, sounding disappointed. "I won't risk that."

She put her palm to his cheek, longing to tell him how much she wanted a baby if she lived free to raise it. But that wouldn't happen so she gave him the truth. "There *is* a guarantee against me getting pregnant." Admitting it this time did make her sad. "For months now, every time they called me into the clinic, I'd end up being put under without being told what was going to happen. Each time, I'd wake up in my room, not feeling good. Three to ten days later, I'd start bleeding profusely. They finally admitted they'd put a fertilized egg in me each time and my body rejected it." A tear slid down the side of her nose and she sniffled. "I can't get pregnant, but I can have ... this. I want this."

He licked his lips, but not in a hungry way. He was thinking. Then he kissed her tears away and said, "I can't change what I am and I have no plans to ever take a mate."

Giving him a smile, she said, "I can't change what I am and this isn't about mating. I just need something good to happen in my life for the first time ever. Something I can hold onto when times get dark again, because with my luck the sunshine will eventually go away."

"Not if I can help it. We'll find your friend and then I'll figure a way to keep you both safe."

She took a deep, shuddering breath, wanting to believe him, believe in him. If only life was that simple, but she couldn't set herself up to hope that much and face disappointment again. For now, she was on the day-by-day plan.

Today's plan was simple. She had a chance for a moment of happiness and refused to let it go. "Thank you, but it doesn't change my mind. The one gift you can offer me right now is to not stop."

He nodded, but it seemed to be to some silent conversation he was having with himself. "Then I want this to be the best."

She liked the sound of that and could be honest enough with herself to admit it intimidated her, too. What if she turned out to be terrible at this? Would he then regret it?

He didn't give her a chance to dwell long on doubts, because he lifted her T-shirt all the way off and shed his boxer shorts.

She would have had good reason to feel intimidated by his size, but she wanted to put her hands on him even more now.

His mouth covered her breast and his tongue flicked crazy fast. She clenched her legs when a new spike of heat coiled down there.

He played with her other nipple, matching the motions of his tongue. She cried out and tried to reach past him, but his big body prevented any hope of gaining release on her own.

She couldn't take this forever. "Please ... "

Moving his hips up, he rubbed the head of his dick through her folds and a sizzle of energy raced between her breasts and her groin.

Begging hadn't worked. She teetered along a feverish edge of need, ready to take the fall. The next time Rory brushed his cock over her wet folds, she opened her legs and lifted up.

He must have only needed that sign to slide inside her slowly, pulling out then pushing in further.

"More," she hissed, unwilling to wait.

He growled softly and pushed all the way home then stayed there and lifted up on his arms.

She was breathing hard, staring into brown eyes flecked with gold and full of hunger. "What?" she whispered.

"I need you more than I should right now." That sounded like a confession.

He kept winding himself around her heart. She admitted, "I

need you, too."

He dropped his head and kissed her, not moving his hips or any other part. His tongue pushed inside her mouth and made friends with hers, then he swept his lips over hers and kissed a path from her cheeks to her neck.

When he lifted up again, his eyes were golden and his power buzzed as if it was inside of her. Huh, maybe it was.

She had no time to think. He started moving, pushing his hips in and out as he held her gaze captive. She loved the feel of him. The harder he pushed, the more she dug her nails into his arms.

He didn't seem to mind.

In fact, his eyes lit with excitement.

She lifted her hips, bringing him deeper and climbing that razor edge again.

This time, he didn't leave her waiting.

Reaching between them, he went right to the core of her heat, stroking as he shoved inside, once, twice ... yeah, she split into thousands of pieces. Lost track of everything except the feel of riding that wave as he drove into her faster.

He shouted and filled her, still pumping until he slowed then stopped and dropped onto her.

"Umph." She laughed. "You weigh a ton."

"Liar."

She laughed some more. He had his arms blocking all of his weight, but she liked to tease him.

Time floated along until some annoying buzzer interrupted everything.

He grumbled, "Fucking alarm."

Her exact sentiments.

But she celebrated being free for now and having Rory close to feel. "How much time do we have? I want a shower."

"Half hour enough?"

"Sure."

Rory rolled half off of her, still dazed by that orgasm.

That had been ... rare. He couldn't remember it ever being that satisfying for him. Sure, he got a release during sex, but this had felt different.

Siofra gave him a shove, which wouldn't have moved him if he hadn't rolled all the way off on his own.

Still laughing, she pushed off of him and ran to the bathroom to start a shower.

He let her. Women were all different and some had to process what had happened immediately.

Would Siofra now think twice about what they'd done? Would she be hurt or distant? If she was, he had no one to blame but himself.

He really did suck, because he refused to feel any regret. He'd enjoyed every minute of loving her body.

Siofra yelled out, "I may be in here awhile. I'm achy and I'm as good as you at getting off."

Fuck, he was in.

He leaped from the bed, ripped the curtain to the side.

She stood under the shower with her head thrown back as water rushed over her body.

Yep, that's all it took. His dick saw that as a second wake-up call.

Rory eased in and joined her under the cascading water.

She smiled and brought her head up. "Hey you."

He leaned down and kissed her. "You are so sexy." The longer he kissed her, the hotter things got in spite of the cool water she had running.

Wrapping her arms around his neck, she whispered, "I want you."

He lifted her up and slid her down on his cock, water splashing all over them.

She latched onto his shoulders and lifted up, then dropped down. He cupped her hips to hold her still or this would be too fast.

"Hold on, babe." He wanted to be sure she got what she needed no matter what. Moving a hand to stroke her, she moaned and tightened her legs around him. He gritted his teeth to hold back his release as he brought hers on. She clenched him so hard he felt chills from his own release waiting close by.

When she dropped her head to his shoulder she said, "You feel so good."

"Not as nice as being inside you." Clutching her hips, he began moving slowly until he was pounding into her.

She moaned and dug her fingers into his arms.

Game over.

He came hard again, heaving breath after breath. He finally leaned an arm against the shower wall as she slid down. The other arm held up a limp Siofra whose legs couldn't hold her.

She mumbled, "How much time left?"

"Not enough to go again, nymph."

"Nymph?" She leaned in and bit his nipple gently.

His dick answered with a thump and she laughed.

When had having a woman laugh during sex seem perfect? Never before now.

He wanted her, not just a sexual want, but ... her. This woman. One word said it all.

Mate.

Want warred with commitment. He'd made a commitment a long time ago to not mate, but things were confused in his head.

Not in his chest. His heart pounded away like it had been given an electrical shock to wake it.

She put her feet down and stood, a little wobbly, which only made him feel like a king.

"We've got to get going soon," he said, grabbing a bar of soap and lathering it all over her body.

"Seriously? You think *that* is going to make me want to put clothes on?" She gave him a comical look, part annoyed and part amused.

Where had this woman come from to connect all the dots to make him smile? He'd never smiled this much.

He ignored her squeals of delight when he touched a sensitive area and groans of complaint when he moved on.

Once they got on the road, he could do some thinking. He couldn't make any decisions with a lust-swamped mind. This could be the most important decision of his life and one he couldn't be wish-washy on.

Before he could consider a mate, he had to fix his jaguar.

Siofra couldn't have children, which was no deal breaker for him since he didn't want to continue his shifter bloodline. Not that his child would be a Gallize. It normally wasn't because it skipped a generation at least.

Could he have a mate after all?

Flipping her around to face the wall, he joked, "This side should get me in less trouble."

"Not if you get creative."

He chuckled until he saw a tattoo on her back. The design was of an eye with a pointy oval pupil that had a triangle in the middle. Two long lashes below curved up to form a Celtic braid design encompassing the eyelid.

Fuck. That was the mark of Cadell.

She'd said she wasn't one of them.

"Rory? Did your arm get tired?"

Washing the rest of her, he asked, "What's this tattoo?"

She grumbled, "Ugh. I hate that thing. They did that when they took me from my dad. I saw some of the other little girls at camp with the same mark. Those jerks said it meant we belonged to the Cadells. When I got older, they tried to tell me my dad did it before I was captured, but why would he? Such liars. I never see it and no one talks about it, so I try to ignore being branded like cattle."

Rory had never seen the tattoo in person, but he'd been taught about it as part of his training.

From what he'd learned, some Cadell fathers marked a first female child with the iconic tattoo. Everything about this design and her story fit.

Siofra hadn't lied about being a Cadell.

She had no idea she was actually one of them.

That explained the power.

His stomach sank.

She definitely wasn't a Gallize female.

CHAPTER 24

SIOFRA STOOD AT A BULLETIN board inside a grocery in Portland, Maine. They had arrived as the grocery store opened for business.

This was her one hope for finding Baatar.

She adjusted the handwritten index card advertising a missing forty-year-old truck with rusty body and bad seats. The email she included would go nowhere. Rory had checked that it belonged to no one.

Baatar would know that message and post a reply ... unless he'd failed to reach Portland by now. Based on what Hector of the Black River pack had said, Baatar had escaped after she had, as he'd intended.

That would have been Saturday morning and today was Thursday, which would have given him enough time, *if* he'd also had money in hand when he escaped.

Or he could be somewhere alone, suffering a seizure or mental breakdown with no one to watch over him.

After giving the thumbtack one more hard press, she stepped back with her heart thumping wildly.

Please let Baatar see this, even though it will mean disappointing Rory.

After those stolen hours with Rory in the little motel and the many miles they'd traveled, she'd begun facing a new problem. She didn't want to walk away from Rory. Yes, she would love to live free with Baatar, but she didn't want to give up Rory.

But if she stayed with Rory, Baatar would be captured.

Sure, Rory and his people meant well, but the memory of two magic users kidnapping her from a hospital room secured by a locked steel door remained vivid in her mind.

"Need anything from the store before we go?" Rory asked.

To know the future would be nice.

To have more time with Rory would be even better.

She drank in how hot he looked with his dark brown hair mussed by the wind and that sexy body hidden beneath a long-sleeved navy pullover he'd left loose over his jeans.

The weather had been refreshingly cool, which had to be why Baatar chose this place.

He said he wanted to live where it snowed.

She'd need more than the jeans and the knit pullover she wore to survive snow. Boots would be nice. For now, she enjoyed her sneakers. Not so much the cap.

She'd nearly forgotten what it was like to walk around with her hair loose.

"Siofra?" Rory said her name softly as if it was his secret name for her.

"I don't need anything. We should leave."

He walked at her side as they left.

She'd explained to Rory when they arrived that she had to wait until early morning to post a coded message. That meant she got another amazing night with him, because she could not return until tomorrow morning to see if Baatar had been there and left her a message.

Baatar had read about this area and this store in a magazine article on his flight from China.

His English was basic, but he'd understood enough to remember the details he'd shared with her.

The magic user delivering Baatar to the Cadell camp had warned he'd kill the entire airplane of innocents if Baatar made any attempt to escape. It would have been difficult to try since they had titanium cuffs on Baatar's wrists and documentation that showed him as an international fugitive being delivered to the United States.

Baatar had said the trip over made him sick constantly. His insides churned and twisted no matter how hard he worked to be calm.

Maybe his power caused him to react. Could that be behind

Siofra's issues when she'd flown in the helicopter?

Sunshine gave a sparkle to everything. She cupped her hand over her eyes and turned her face up to the warmth. After so many months in the heat of Texas, she embraced the weather up here.

"You said we have to wait until tomorrow morning to check for his message, right?" Rory asked.

She nodded. "He told me to be very careful in case anyone was tracking one or both of us. I can't alter our contact plan without putting him at risk."

"That means we have a day to burn. What do you want to do?" Rory asked as they strolled toward the old port.

"I don't care. As long as we stay in the area, but nowhere around this store, we're good."

"Let's kill a little time walking around, then I've got a place for lunch."

She'd come to realize Rory enjoyed showing her new things, like this morning when he took her to a diner called Betty's, which had been busy even very early. He clearly liked walking and the restaurant hadn't been far from their hotel. In fact, everything seemed close enough to reach on foot, so she hadn't minded leaving his sport utility parked.

Even along the way from Spartanburg to Portland, Rory had stopped at rest areas, showing her the beautiful settings where people could just stop to use a clean bathroom and stretch their legs while their kids and animals played.

Now he had something else in mind? She asked, "Where are we going for lunch?"

"It depends on whether you have a phobia about water," he said, angling them through a quaint shopping area.

She told him, "I don't have phobias."

"You don't fly."

"Phobia sounds like a disease. I just don't like to fly." She shrugged with a grin.

Instead of scowling, as he would have when they first met, he just chuckled and said, "Got it. So you're okay on a boat?"

She gave him a big smile. "I have always wanted to ride on a boat."

Once they took in the shops along the way to the docks, he

led her to where he bought two tickets for a ferry ride to Peaks Island. When he pointed out the island, she felt relief at being able to easily see it. Perfect. She'd remain close to Portland, yet go on a small adventure.

Since she was too excited to pay attention, he had to keep guiding her this way and that until they were standing at the front of the ferry when it departed the dock. Rory explained how Peak's Island was a small community. A five-mile race was held each year on a road that circled the island.

She'd been leaning back against his chest, standing between arms he braced on the rail. Her eyes were closed, letting her feel everything, like the cool wind that brushed her face. A nice breeze, but not strong enough to dislodge her cap.

She mused, "I would like to run a race one day. I'm not fast like Ba ... my brother, but I would train to do that."

"Really? Why?"

She opened her eyes to see they were almost to the island. "I read everything I could get my hands on and one magazine had a story about local road races. I know there are big competitions in different areas, but those local races sounded more like community fun than a brutal competition. I'm not a runner, but they had one-mile races for kids. I'd like to see that one day. I started teaching the children in one camp to run, only because I could keep up with them." She laughed. "I made up a race for a quarter mile and I sewed prizes for them. They enjoyed it."

He kissed her neck and she sighed.

Such a loving guy. Even when he got grumpy, she enjoyed him.

Rory said, "You'll be a great mother some day."

She tensed. "I will never be a mother of my own child, but if I ever get the chance to live a normal life and choose a job, I will care for children and maybe adopt some."

"But you'd like to have your own."

Her heart sighed. She admitted, "Yes, but I can love any child."

"They could be wrong about you," he said, so determined to make her happy even now. "If they are, I've screwed up big-time by not using a condom."

"Maybe, but I've proven them correct time and again." She refused to think about her inability to become pregnant when she was about to have another stolen moment. "We're here."

He backed up and let her head for the exit with him right behind her.

Once the handful of cars drove off, people departed with the group spreading out along the long dock leading to the island. She envied these humans, assuming most, if not all, were. Even if some shifters were secretly mixed in, they still had normal lives.

They had the freedom to come and go, to choose how to live.

A gust of wind lifted her hat.

She grabbed at it, but missed.

Rory lunged and caught it, then looked around at everyone before placing the cap on her head and tucking her hair out of sight. "No problem. No one was paying attention," he reassured her.

Her heart continued having a little cardio workout for a few more steps.

She noticed a number of couples holding hands and reached over to snag Rory's, weaving her fingers with his. He startled, then folded his hand around her smaller one.

That hint of a smile lifted the corner of his lips.

She enjoyed making him happy. He'd been giving her experiences she might never get the opportunity for again.

And he would be the reason she found Baatar if all this went as planned.

She'd have to talk to Baatar about shifters. He'd argue, but he was an intelligent man and he'd listen to her. In a perfect world, she'd find a way to keep Rory as hers to give joy to every day. But her world was far from perfect.

She would have to settle for making children happy if she had that opportunity. Any time she could put a smile on a child's face, her heart grew a little stronger and more content. She'd missed having kids at the last camp, but only for a fleeting moment, thrilled to see no children captive when she'd arrived.

He squeezed her hand gently. "Ready for lobster?"

Her stomach growled right on time. "Clearly, yes. How many can I have?"

"I'll buy as many as you can eat as long as you stop before you get sick."

"I won't get sick. I would never waste food or anything you did for me."

He paused at the entrance to a quaint restaurant humming with activity, and gave her one of his long looks before opening the door.

The meal turned out to be as amazing as everything else they'd done, plus she got him to talk of the things he'd enjoyed growing up.

"I couldn't play football, so I took up baseball," he said and chomped down on another bite of his pie.

"Why not football?" She stole a bite of his dessert and licked her lips after she ate it.

"Don't do that."

"Do what?"

"Lick your lips like that or we'll make a scene when I clear this table and bend you over it." He leaned close, saying, "That way I can push in deep and have both hands free to enjoy your lovely titties."

She fisted her hands to keep from rubbing her sensitive breasts that perked up with just that suggestion.

Rory's gaze dropped to them and he gave her a knowing smile. He inhaled deeply. "Ah, your unique perfume."

He was talking about her arousal.

She looked around the room nervously until he said, "There are no other shifters in here. Your sexy little secret is safe with me ... until I get you alone."

Narrowing her eyes at him, she warned, "You should be careful what you start and fail to finish. I'm a determined woman who may surprise you ... when we're not alone. I might decide to lick you up and down instead of getting the ice cream I'd had in mind."

He muttered a soft curse. "You win. Let's get out of here."

She laughed, but had a moment of disappointment when she thought their outing was over.

Silly woman. Her Rory was full of surprises. He suggested they walk around the lower part of the island and follow a loop that was just over two miles.

Now, he took her hand in his, giving her yet another gift she could hold dear forever. But every time he did something wonderful, her determination to leave with Baatar weakened.

She gave herself a stern talk. *You are a terrible sister to think of staying with Rory. Baatar needs you. Also, Rory does not want a mate. It's not like he'll keep you around once he is done here. Have fun, but don't forget why you're here.*

With that settled in her mind, she relaxed and soaked up every moment with Rory. Leaving him would hurt, but the longer she stayed, the harder it would be for both of them.

Her body had finally calmed down from his sexy whispers.

Then Rory murmured something sensual and teasing right next to her ear again. If he didn't stop it soon, she would come the minute he touched her.

She darted into a museum that had umbrella covers. What a clever idea to display unusual sleeves for umbrellas.

He entered right behind her and pulled his sunglasses off. The message in those deep brown and gold eyes said she could run, but he was faster.

They'd just left the museum area and were strolling along the coast highway when Rory became very still. He gently squeezed her hand and said, "Don't look around, but we're being followed."

Adrenaline wiped out all thoughts of sex. "Maybe it's Baatar and he saw me in town."

But that didn't make sense. Baatar would stick to the plan just to keep both of them safe.

Rory sighed. "Not unless he's a wolf shifter. Be ready to do exactly what I say when I say go."

CHAPTER 25

R ORY COULDN'T FIGURE OUT WHAT went wrong. There had been no shifters on the ferry. He'd walked the entire boat with Siofra under the guise of showing it to her so that he could be sure there were no unexpected riders.

She clamped her fingers in his hand hard and smelled of fear.

Turning toward her so he faced the coastline, he leaned down smiling and said, "When I point, be sure to look excited." He lifted his arm to indicate a flock of birds. She turned on a smile that wouldn't fool anyone up close, but would do, and nodded as if he'd shared something important.

He took that opportunity to scan behind them, but saw no one. Standing back up, he tugged her to the left when he saw an entrance to the wooded area. While the northern half of the island had more neighborhoods, the homes on this end tended to be scattered along the coast road, which left a large chunk of forest.

The predator following them stayed in the edge of the woods. He probably thought it gave him an advantage to remain hidden until he attacked or maybe he was just collecting intel for someone else.

Rory would bet on intel. Shifters in the northeast had been careful not to create problems. An incident on this island would be all over the news, which any local packs would not want.

If their tail belonged to the Black River pack, even better, because they didn't attack except as a pack and Rory had scented only one.

Either way, if he allowed this shifter to get off the island with information about a white-haired woman and a shifter, this wolf's pack might have an alert to find Siofra.

Rory would make the wolf meet him on Rory's terms. He gave Siofra's hand another squeeze and said in a calm voice, "We're going into the woods ... now."

He took a hard left and walked quickly toward the tree line while watching for any humans who might see them. They'd passed a few people outside, but being a Thursday, the tourists were sparse at this end of the island.

When he saw no humans nearby, Rory made his move as quickly as he could without pulling Siofra off her feet. He towed her through the woods until he found a lake, probably a pond, he recalled from a map of the island, which he'd taken a moment to review at the ferry office.

What hadn't been on the map was whether there were any suitable trees near the water, but the one he spied now was perfect.

Turning to her, he kept his voice barely audible. "See that tree just ahead? I'll hoist you up, then you climb as far as you can."

Her eyes got big and she started shaking her head. "I told you ..."

He kissed her to silence her words. Yes, she'd explained how she was terrified of heights and particularly of being up in a tree, but she was tough.

"I don't like asking you to do this, baby, but you made it through that helicopter ride. You can do this."

She jumped into his arms, clinging to him.

Ah, hell, he already hated himself for asking her to climb the tree. Kissing her firmly, he eased her back down and said, "Listen, Siofra. I know this scares you, but don't look down. You trust me, right?"

"Y-yes."

"I'll come for you and I'll keep you safe, but I need you out of the way while I deal with this shifter. We can't leave the island until I find out who he is and what he wants."

"Let me stay with you. I'll help," she pleaded.

"You're going to be a terrific help. He'll follow your scent to this tree and I'll step in as soon as he shows up. Please, hurry and get up there."

Backing away, she wrung her hands and stared up at the limbs going up, up, up and looked lost, but being the little badass she was, she turned and put her hands on the trunk.

She grumbled, "Hurry up, before I change my mind."

Rory gave her a boost to the first limb. She pulled herself up and carefully got to her feet, then climbed another level up and glanced down, moaning.

He waved for her to keep moving. "Don't stop. Don't look down."

Without replying, she turned her head to face upward and nervously worked her way higher.

Damn, he was proud of her.

Ferrell sent him a picture of ripping a wolf to pieces.

Rory muttered, "We don't know who he is yet."

That pissed Ferrell off. His cat had been so happy and content, Rory hadn't even thought about him, but the jaguar battered his insides now.

Rory hissed at the pain and silently warned, *Stop it, dammit, or you'll get Siofra killed.*

Never had his cat behaved so quickly.

Ferrell demanded, *Protect.*

That had been the most selfless word Ferrell had ever given him while agitated. Usually, his jaguar wanted to maim and murder, which was all about making Ferrell happy.

Rory took a couple of breaths to get past the internal pummeling the damn cat had given him and said, *Yes. We will protect her if you work with me.*

Ferrell calmed, but grudgingly.

With one last glance up to see that Siofra had reached the highest point she could safely climb, Rory cursed himself one more time for asking her to face a personal fear. He had no other choice with no one to help but an island full of humans.

Neither could he shift to fight where a human might see him. It would only cause chaos. The only exception to that rule was if a Gallize shifter needed his animal to survive.

He headed toward the center of the island where the backside of the road loop he'd been walking with Siofra would have returned them to the docks.

When he reached a spot he felt would be far enough away to

draw the wolf in, Rory would then backtrack to catch the shifter as he sniffed at the tree.

Hopefully, the wolf would believe Rory had left Siofra alone so that he could move faster without her.

Never happen.

Rory rushed along the bank of the water until he disappeared into the woods. He ran fifty strides and did a wide U-turn to double back when his boot plunged into a hole covered by branches. The forward motion of running threw all his weight against his leg and snapped his ankle.

"Fuck." He fell forward on his hands and yanked his leg. Pushing himself up, he clamped his teeth against the pain of grinding bone on bone and twisted his leg. He pulled the foot out with the boot still on it, then hurried to stand up.

He took a step and his ankle turned to the side in a sickening shift.

Ferrell roared, *Mate!*

Rory couldn't hop fast enough to reach Siofra in time, but Ferrell could on three legs. With no other choice, Rory jerked his shirt over his head and shed his clothes.

Every second he wasted left Siofra in danger.

He called up his jaguar and the hard shift pushed his attention away from the miserable ankle. When his jaguar stood in his place, his animal had to hold his rear leg up and let the paw dangle.

But Ferrell didn't hesitate to go after Siofra.

Rory reminded him, *If you take control and start killing, we'll lose Siofra.*

Mate, was all Ferrell said, but that was enough to let Rory know his jaguar understood they had to work together. He might feel bad about leaning on the way Ferrell felt about Siofra to control his animal, but his jaguar was privy to Rory's thoughts.

They both had her best interest at heart.

When the tree came into view, that fucking wolf shifter had started climbing in his human form.

How Ferrell ran as hard as he did on three legs amazed even Rory, but the adrenaline rush overshadowed any pain. That joint would have healed by now if his jaguar was not suffering from damage Rory had caused. Rory had to figure out how to fix them, and soon.

Ferrell roared a deep sound from his chest.

The wolf shifter, wearing only shorts, had just reached the first limb and jerked around at the sound. He could go up, but he'd be at a serious disadvantage once Ferrell started climbing.

Rory couldn't hear Siofra. She wasn't making a sound. He hoped she would hold on and not panic.

Taking his only choice, the wolf shifter leaped to the ground, bursting into his wolf form on the way down. He hit and rolled, coming up on his feet and snarling. Saliva dripped from his jaws.

Ferrell would be on him in seconds. He said, *Kill.*

Rory argued, *Not yet. Let's find out if there are more looking for Siofra.*

Kill.

Guess using Siofra as a control word would go only so far.

The wolf didn't wait for the battle to reach him. He ran forward hard and jumped at Ferrell with claws out and fangs ready to rip into skin.

Rory's jaguar went up on one leg, which threw him off balance. When the wolf hit him, Ferrell went over sideways, clawing and biting at the wolf.

But his jaguar was on the bottom. Bad place to be in this fight.

The wolf knew it, too. He attacked viciously, trying to get to Ferrell's throat. Rory's jaguar clamped down on the wolf's muzzle and held on. For a minute, wolf claws slashed and fought, but Ferrell closed his mighty jaws harder until Rory heard bone crack.

He told his jaguar, *You've won. The wolf is down. Let me change back so I can question him.*

Ferrell growled and shook the wolf's head.

Dammit, Ferrell. Let go of his head. He's done.

His jaguar breathed hard a couple times then opened his jaws and shoved the wolf off of him.

Shifting back was going to suck big time. Ferrell had won, but his sides and neck were ripped up, plus the busted back leg. But in spite of all that, Ferrell relinquished control and allowed the slow, painful shift to happen.

Dying had to be easier than this.

Ferrell actually whimpered once, and he had never made a

sound of pain.

When Rory lay on the ground breathing hard and smelling of fresh blood, he rolled over to his knees. Two strides away, the wolf was returning to human form.

Rory winced at the mangled head. Would that shifter be able to talk?

Struggling to his feet, Rory hopped over to the now human-looking shifter and dropped to his knees. He checked the man's pulse, which he could barely feel. Blood leaked from multiple holes in his neck where Ferrell's sharp teeth had made deep punctures, but one rip had blood pouring.

Ferrell had hit one of the carotid arteries.

Shit.

He asked the guy, "Who are you? Who sent you?"

The shifter's mouth tried to work, but one side of his jaw had been broken. Still, Rory heard what sounded like, "Fuck you."

"Not me, asshole," Rory said, then snapped the wolf's neck, leaving dead blue eyes staring up at the sky.

Searching the shifter's body, Rory found a Black River Pack tattoo.

This guy couldn't have known he was going to bring Siofra here, so he had to have been tracking Rory through the city. If that was the case, he might have only been a patrol watching for any unknown shifters in his area.

Rory mentally searched the ferry trip.

People had been out in kayaks and boats, traveling between the mainland and the island. This shifter could have followed the ferry and gotten onto the island unnoticed until now.

"Rory?" a pitiful voice called out.

Hell, he had to get Siofra out of that tree. Hopping all the way to the tree, he looked up. "You okay, baby?"

"No. I just watched your jaguar almost get killed." She hugged the tree like it was her best friend.

"Nah, he can handle a wolf if it's not jacked up on drugs."

"Why was he limping? And why are you hopping?"

"I'll tell you when I get you down."

"How are you going to help me when you can't even walk?"

He didn't have an answer for that.

CHAPTER 26

SIOFRA HEAVED ONE HARD BREATH after another. If she didn't calm down, she'd have a full-blown panic attack and fall. That wasn't going to help Rory, who was bleeding everywhere.

Some might belong to the wolf shifter, but she'd seen that wolf rip into the jaguar. Rory was hurt worse than his hobbling gave away.

"Give me a minute to shift and see if Ferrell can climb," Rory offered.

Ferrell was his jaguar's name? She couldn't do that to Rory or his animal. She called down, "No."

He thunked his head against the trunk, mumbled something grouchy then looked up at her again. "I'm too tired to argue right now, baby."

"Then don't. I can do this."

Panic registered in his face. "Oh, hell, no. You'll fall and break every bone in your body."

She didn't need any help with being terrified. "Shut up, dammit. You're not helping."

"Just give me a minute and I'll get you."

He intended to climb up here with a bad foot and other injuries? *Suck it up and get out of this tree, Siofra.* She yelled, "You want to help? Catch me if I fall."

That brought out heavy cursing, but she'd already started down, hunting the next limb. Anger fueled her movements, which kept her thinking about clobbering Rory instead of what she was doing. Going up had been an effort, because she'd had to pull herself up to the second branch, but descending meant she'd have to lower herself to dangle as she found that last big branch.

Then she'd have to figure out how to drop to the ground.

Her hands shook every time she reached for a new hold.

Rory had stopped cursing and was encouraging her. "You're doing great. That's right, keep finding your footing and get a good grip before you move."

She was sucking air as hard as she could, but feeling pretty proud of herself with every few feet lower she reached. She eased her body down to sit on the limb she'd have to dangle from to reach the last thick one.

Looking over her shoulder, all her confidence fled.

She lunged to grab the trunk again. Her heart slammed her chest over and over. She couldn't do this.

"How you doing, baby?" Rory called up softly.

"Good." Not.

"Stand up on that limb to get both feet in place then ease down until you're sitting with both legs on one side."

Was he insane?

She did not want to do that. She'd just wait for him to heal. That sounded like a great idea until she recalled how his leg had not healed a day after being injured by the bounty hunters.

He might need her to heal him now.

Every time she'd faced an adversity in the past, she'd tell herself the same thing she said now, "Time to grow a pair of lady balls, Siofra, and put on a pair of big girl panties that can hold them."

Rory made a coughing sound.

"Are you laughing at me?" she warned.

"Never."

She heard the smile in his voice and dropped her forehead against the tree.

"Sit there, baby, and I'll come get you."

"No." What was the worst that could happen?

Break her neck.

She shouldn't give herself pep talks. She wasn't good at it.

More cursing from below.

Pushing up slowly, like molasses-in-the-winter slow, she finally got to her feet and figured out how to sit with both legs on one side of the branch.

With him giving her calm instructions, she reached over to her right and grabbed the branch, thankful when she didn't fall off.

She moved her hands to the same side and held her breath as she rolled to her stomach, then dropped down. The strength in her arms had to come from an adrenaline rush, because she was no workout enthusiast. She dangled, waiting to feel the limb.

Her sneaker covered feet found the wide branch and she carefully shifted her weight to her legs, then used the trunk to make the same move again.

When she dangled twelve feet above the ground, her damp palms started slipping.

Rory said, "It's okay, baby. I'll catch you."

How could he do that?

Did it matter, because ... her hands slipped.

He caught her and fell backwards, grunting with the effort, but he'd kept her safe to the ground.

She scrambled off of him and turned. "You're bleeding everywhere."

"I know."

"Can your jaguar heal you?"

"I'm not sure, but I have to try or we won't get out of here. The jaguar won't hurt you."

"Do it," she ordered. She hadn't even thought about his jaguar attacking her, but Rory had sounded sure his animal wouldn't and she trusted him.

"Yes, ma'am."

"Very funny. Hurry up."

"Can't do it fast again," he said, struggling to breathe. His chest moved up and down, but his exhales sounded ragged. He ordered, "Turn your back."

"Why?"

"Won't be pretty."

"I don't care."

"Just ... do it, please."

She turned around only to get him moving, but as she thought about it, she had to watch his back while he was vulnerable.

The sounds behind her were horrifying. He groaned once, but that was the only sound he made with his voice. The rest were bones snapping.

When it got quiet, she looked around slowly.

His massive jaguar tried to sit up and growl. The wounds hadn't made sense on Rory, but now she could see their natural position from the battle.

Those wounds weren't healing even a little.

She said, "Hi, uh, Ferrell. I want to help you heal if I can." She started rubbing her palms across each other, building up heat like the day in the van with Rory. Energy pulsed inside of her, but was it healing energy or the killing kind? What if she hit Ferrell with so much power she knocked him out for twelve hours like she had Rory?

Ferrell rolled up on his chest with his front legs stretched out and his hind legs flopped to the side. The paw on his bad one lay at the wrong angle.

He stared at her with faith she had to make good on.

Stepping over to him, she couldn't get over how huge his head was and his body spread out forever. That wolf never had a chance even with the jaguar injured.

Should she try to pet him first?

What if her energy shocked him? Would he bite her?

That would only happen once. She'd have no head after that.

Kneeling down so she could get close to his wounds, she froze when he moved his head toward her.

Growling softly, Ferrell put his chin on her shoulder. His head was heavy, but she could handle the weight.

Tears pooled in her eyes and chills ran across her arms at such a sign of his complete trust. She'd never felt anything so humbling and empowering at the same time.

"Okay, I'm going to try something and it might have a little buzz or shock to it," she said, hoping she wasn't being a crappy bedside doctor like the ones who had lied to her before they hurt her.

Carefully reaching for a gash on his shoulder, she used just one finger. Energy hummed at the tip and she could feel his energy rush to meet hers.

Ferrell made a strange sound, but not angry. Just confused.

She added another finger and watched as the wound began to

heal, leaving dried blood. Going from place to place with careful touches, she wanted to shout with joy as jagged rips began mending, first the underlying muscle, then the ones in his coat began closing and blood stopped oozing out of him.

Shaking from the fear of hurting him, she said, "I need to see your chest." Would he know what she meant?

He pulled away and rolled over, exposing his underside.

The worst gash was just under his front right leg and sliced halfway down. Feeling a little bold, she spread both hands to cover the entire wound and energy sparked when she touched him.

His head came up and he gave a sharp growl.

She didn't move until he laid back and his tail started swishing back and forth.

Guess that had been his version of a jaguar "ouch." The last thing she did was cup his bad ankle in both hands and closed her eyes as warm energy flooded her hands.

In just a moment, she could feel the bone moving into place, so she let go as it healed.

Sitting back hard, she stared at her hands. Had she really just done all that?

Ferrell jumped up, growling and stretching.

She laughed, pretty pleased with herself over healing him.

He rushed to the pond, diving in and splashing about as he cleaned off dried blood. He played a few minutes, then seemed to heave a big sigh before he climbed out and shook off.

Had Rory asked him to get back to business?

How did that work with those two?

When Ferrell looked over at the dead guy, she did, too.

Her stomach tried to send her lunch back up. She held her breath and stared in the opposite direction.

But the sound of movement pulled her back. Ferrell was dragging the shifter into the woods, where he started digging with super speed. When he had the shifter in the hole, he covered the body with dirt, then bit a fallen branch he used to move back and forth over the shallow grave.

Done with that, he ran back to the water, rinsed his paws and legs quickly then came over to her.

As she watched, the jaguar began changing and in the next

moment, after a much faster shift, Rory knelt on the ground. He got up and walked over to her, not the least bothered about being naked.

She started to get up, but didn't move fast enough. He hooked her under her arms and lifted her to him as if she were a twig and not a substantial female.

"You are the most amazing woman this world will ever see and gorgeous on top of that." He brought her to him until their lips met. He gave her a powerful kiss that sent her heart cartwheeling.

When the kiss ended, she had her legs around him and he had her wrapped up tight.

He swallowed and said, "I don't want to let you go, but I have to get you back to the hotel where I can keep you safe. I don't know what's more incredible. You scaling that tree then coming down on your own or healing a wounded jaguar."

She kissed his face and his lips again, then pulling back she said, "You told me Ferrell wouldn't hurt me."

"He won't. Ever."

"Why'd you name him Ferrell?"

Rory's cheeks had a pink tinge. Was he … *embarrassed*? He admitted, "I could hardly manage him at first, so I kept saying my feral jaguar. Eventually, the guys would ask how feral was doing and I figured I'd change the spelling and give him a real name." He spelled the name for her.

She frowned. "I'm seeing his name differently."

"Like how?"

"I've always read anything I could get my hands on. One of the women who taught me to read loaned me an old book on Irish history. It had a story about a man named Ó Fearghail." She spelled it for him. "It means man of valor. I think that better describes your jaguar."

"Huh." Rory was quiet for a moment, then smiled. "He likes that."

His jaguar knew what they were talking about? She smiled, feeling a little connection to his jaguar.

He eased her to the ground and led her to where he'd taken his clothes off. With her help, he didn't look as bad as he would have if he hadn't healed.

The jackal shifters had incredible regeneration.

Once again, she'd felt Rory and Ferrell's energy, which seemed powerful.

Why was he not healing at least as fast as the jackals?

She brushed that off to ask, "Who was the wolf shifter?"

"Black River pack. We can't stay in this city long. They'll send a search team by tomorrow. It might take them a day to locate the body, but they will. When they do, they'll hunt for our scent. I don't think we can wait a week."

The most wonderful day she'd ever spent just crashed at the idea of leaving before she found Baatar.

He'd be at the mercy of the Black River pack once they caught her scent and tracked it to the grocery store bulletin board. If Mother Cadellus had joined up to help them, she'd have one of her people share something with Baatar's scent.

Had Siofra led the Black River pack straight to her brother?

CHAPTER 27

RORY HAD SIOFRA TUCKED CLOSE to him as the ferry arrived back in Portland just after four, which meant he had to figure out a place to stay soon.

He kept reliving Siofra being up in that tree on the island where he couldn't get to her with his busted-up body.

The Guardian had said he was the only one who could heal the problem with Ferrell. Rory had finally seen just what his boss had been talking about.

Siofra had done wonders to repair Ferrell's body, but his jaguar should have been able to fix a lame ankle on his own.

He couldn't expect her to be around to keep patching him up. He'd never put that on anyone.

But Rory understood what the Guardian had been saying. The time was coming when a major wound would be too much for even Siofra's healing energy.

What then? What if she was in danger again or Ferrell faced something more deadly than that wolf shifter?

Whatever Rory had done to his animal now put Siofra at risk in addition to Ferrell.

This had to be Rory's fault. His animal worked on a simple premise of living in the moment and fighting when called upon.

Rory looked inward. How was *he* living?

Not in the moment. Not in the past. And sure as hell not in the future.

Shit, he was fucked up beyond help. He didn't belong with humans or shifters. What had he been thinking to even consider a mate?

Siofra caught his hand once they walked off with the other passengers, pulling his thoughts from the dark place he'd gone. When she touched him, their energies hummed.

It was the craziest thing, but his body relaxed and Ferrell withdrew, but in a peaceful way.

As they neared the street, she asked, "Are we going to the hotel?"

"No. Not that one." He'd just punched the information into his phone for one of the cars for hire that drove visitors around cities these days. A cab driver might not want to meander.

When the small black sedan showed up, they climbed in and Rory asked him to drive through the college area, to do a general tour of Portland.

Next he gave Siofra a look and tilted his head at the driver then said, "This guy knows the city better than me."

She nodded and leaned forward, asking questions the driver answered.

While those two were busy chatting, Rory used his phone to arrange a new hotel, which he paid for electronically, then checked in. He sent a series of texts to one of the special numbers the Guardian provided.

A human the Guardian trusted would go to their current hotel with new luggage that had no shifter scent, break into the room, transfer their belongings to the clean luggage and take that to the new location, along with a different rental SUV. Before leaving, the human would spray a special mix of scents they kept on hand, which would override the human's scent. The spray's smell would disintegrate in an hour.

Once he had everything in place and the human had been given enough time to deliver his luggage, Rory said, "You know what, honey? I'm beat. Ready to go grab a shower?"

She said, "Yes, me too."

The driver swung around at the next street, drove a new route, then dropped them at their new hotel, which was only two miles from the grocery store.

They would not be walking tomorrow, though.

At the upscale hotel he'd chosen for its tighter security, Rory tipped the driver as generously as he did everyone else, and finally drew a deep breath when he closed the door to their new room behind Siofra.

She spun around. "How far are we from the grocery?"

"We're just as close as yesterday, but we'll grab a ride tomorrow to limit the time we're on the street where someone can scent us." He'd also make her tell him what Baatar would leave for a message, because he fully expected a Black River pack wolf to be waiting at that grocery. Siofra would be safe in their Expedition.

She had that worried look and he knew why.

He said, "I'll stay as long as I can, Siofra, but I'm telling you right now, I will not keep you here if the Black River pack shows up in force."

Her eyes looked ready to gush, but she nodded. "I understand. I will stay inside, whatever it takes to remain as long as possible."

That agreement should have surprised him, but it didn't. Siofra would be willing to keep a low profile and do anything else Rory asked for the hope of finding this Baatar.

He'd been holding back through the walk to the dock on the island, the ferry ride and the tour route through Portland, but he had to get his hands on her.

Striding forward, he said, "I need you." He was stalking her. She should have backed away.

Nope. She took a step and launched into his arms. He caught her and spun around, feeling his soul glide as he did. This had to be what heaven felt like.

"Take off your clothes," she demanded in a husky voice.

He walked to the bed and dropped her in the middle, then yanked his shirt off. He kept his eyes on her as he shed everything until it was just him.

Her gaze slid down his body to his dick. Well, there was that as well.

She kept her hungry eyes on his groin and fumbled with the snap and zipper on her jeans. He leaned over and yanked her jeans off and out of the way. The T-shirt came off next, leaving her in a bra and panties.

"I wish I had pretty underwear for you," she complained.

"Why? I'm just going to take it off. Men are simple creatures. Sure, we like to see frilly stuff sometimes, but only if it's coming off soon. No underwear compares to you naked."

Her eyes went soft. "You say the nicest things and make me feel pretty."

He dropped down over her with his arms on each side and her dangling legs between his thighs. "You are pretty. Why would you doubt it?"

"I was never around other women who had any more experience with things like clothes and makeup than I did. Cadells wouldn't give us makeup or anything special to wear, but I read about how women share tips. I wish I had that."

He wanted to give this woman everything. "We'll look into that when we go back."

She lowered her gaze and he knew her next words would be a lie. She said, "Sounds good. I can't wait."

What was she holding back from him?

Why did he give two shits right now when she was soft and sexy and ... his. All his right now.

He kissed her, not because he wanted to drive into her, which he did. No, he kissed her because just this simple touch gave him something special.

She had her hands on his neck again, holding him to her as if she feared he'd leave.

Hell no.

One of her hands moved down his neck to his chest. She had a fairy touch, so light and warm. He wanted to feel her hands everywhere and no more thinking.

She hooked her legs around his waist and lifted up, wiggling against his dick.

"Just remember," he muttered against her smiling lips, the vixen. "You started it."

Grinning, she moved her hips again and he almost came right then.

He stood up with her hooked to him and pushed his fingers inside the panties she still wore. She gasped at his touch.

He wanted to hear more, feel more. When he moved his finger around, she moaned and begged, "I'm close."

Then he pulled his finger away. That would be too quick.

She squeaked out, "Please."

Hell. That voice saying please would talk him off a cliff. He reached down and ripped the panties apart from each side.

"I don't have many of those."

"I'll get you new ones in whatever colors you want."

Her eyes darkened. "Then rip away." She eased her wet folds up and down him and he shuddered.

He gritted out, "On the bed or ... "

She had herself worked up to a raspy voice. "Or what?"

"Against the wall."

"I want number three," she said, breathless and rubbing him to the point of insanity.

He clenched his teeth when he held back his release and asked, "What's three?"

"The island restaurant. You said you'd bend me over ... "

That was more than he could take.

He turned and headed for the sofa facing the window. When he got there, he dropped her down and grabbed a fat pillow he plopped on the top of the sofa back.

Moving behind her, he lifted her just enough to place her stomach down on the pillow. She made a tiny sound.

"Change your mind, baby?"

"Hell no. Make me like this the best."

Like he needed a challenge? He moved behind her, spreading her legs gently with his more powerful ones. He ran his fingers over her soft bottom and down between her legs where she was wet and hot.

She whispered, "That. I want that."

He wanted her ready. He teased her until she begged for him to finish it. He could have kept her on the edge longer, but he was too close himself.

When he squatted down, he moved her legs further apart and used his tongue on her.

She arched and her legs shook, then she gave into the release that kept going until he pulled back. "You taste like the best dessert every created."

Her body had fallen limp over the sofa. She said, "More."

He stood and eased her back. She lifted up on her arms, back arched, breasts at the perfect spot.

Nudging the head of his dick into her warm opening, he reached around and caught both breasts.

Siofra made the most wonderful sound of pain and pleasure.

His hands massaged her breasts, bringing her nipples to hard beads as he pushed his cock in a little at a time.

Halfway home he pulled out.

"No," she cried.

If he hadn't been so focused on holding back, he'd have laughed. He knew that order and pushed deep inside her. She gripped the sofa with white knuckles, scaring him.

"Are you okay, Siofra?"

"Yes," she squeezed out. "I like you deep in me."

This woman could snap his control so easily it should scare him. He moved in and out, loving the feel of her. He teased between her legs until she was shaking again, close to coming.

As he picked up speed, he gave each hard nipple a pinch and shoved hard to push her over the edge.

She held onto the sofa, calling his name over and over.

He'd never forget this moment.

When her muscles relaxed around his cock, he gripped her hips, driving hard into her over and over until his body let go. He gave into the mind-blowing orgasm.

Mine. She is mine!

Energy rushed through him with his orgasm and she held on, moaning his name.

He lost all track of time and space. They might have been floating in another realm, one that was all theirs.

When the sparkle of stars cleared from his vision, he looked down at her arms flung over the edge of the sofa. His cock still hidden inside her and that beautiful ass perched for him to stroke. What a gorgeous sight.

Slipping an arm under her middle, he lifted her up and an aftershock ripped through him.

She let out a long hiss of air. "Oh, yes. That last little extra umph. I like it."

He liked her. More than liked her. *Mine.*

He wanted to keep her.

She was everything wonderful about the world and the future.

He wanted to share a future with her. He'd never even considered such a thing.

He'd never expected to have a future beyond the mating curse.

Siofra was a Cadell, but she could handle bonding with him without any doubt. Her power rivaled anything he'd ever felt.

If she had no power, he'd want her, but then he couldn't bond with her without his power killing her.

No one would harm her, not him, no one.

Then there was the Guardian and all his Gallize brothers. The idea of bonding with a Cadell wouldn't fly. That wouldn't stop him from being with Siofra, but he had some thinking to do.

No way to get his mind off anything but her while he was deep inside her. He lifted her off of him and laid her on the bed. She didn't move.

"Roll over, baby."

"No muscles left. You roll me."

Chuckling, he moved her enough to put her back to his front and spoon. He never spent this kind of time with women.

Spooning had its merits.

After a bit, she regained her strength and turned to face him. "I like you."

"I was just thinking that about you."

Her eyebrows lifted. "You were?"

"Yes." He waited to see what she'd say next since this was uncharted territory for him.

"That's nice. Makes me happy."

He wasn't sure if that meant anything more than happy at this moment, but he'd take it. When she said nothing else, he asked, "What're you thinking about?"

"Baatar. He would be angry with me."

"Because of me being a shifter?"

"Yes. I have never liked them, but he hates shifters. Really hates them."

Rory started to ask if it had anything to do with Cadells preaching how bad Gallize were, but he didn't want to address a topic he couldn't really be talking about.

Instead, he stuck with finding out more about this elusive Baatar who thought Siofra was going on the run with him.

Not happening. Rory asked, "Why does he hate shifters so much more than you do?"

Her eyes were drowsy soft and her voice sounded relaxed. "I shouldn't share this, but you are helping us and you fought the wolf who would have ruined everything. I trust you. I think Baatar would be your friend if he knew you like I do." She yawned.

She could use the sleep, but Rory felt he was close to learning something about Baatar that might be useful in finding him. "You were saying about Baatar?" he nudged.

She blinked her eyes open. "Oh, yes. Here's the deal. As I said, I trust *you*."

He swallowed at that admission spoken so fervently. "Thank you. I value that trust."

"You're welcome, but what I'm saying is that I'll tell you something about Baatar, because I want you to understand his issues, but you can't tell your team or that eagle man. I don't trust anyone but you. Okay?"

Rory normally would not agree to such a thing, because it was his duty to share everything with the Guardian and his team. But they'd never met someone like Siofra who grew up with the Cadells and he could not let this golden opportunity to learn more pass.

Besides, what could she possible say that he couldn't sit on for a while?

He said, "I understand and I appreciate your trust. I won't speak to my team or my boss about it unless you tell me I can."

"Okay." Her finger drew circles on his chest then paused to toy with the pale chest hairs that ran to his groin. She sighed again and said, "Baatar has been handed off his entire life, too, but he was sold every time from one Cadell group to another. Whenever they sold him, they would claim he was a tiger, so even now everyone is on him to shift. He would have shifted as a cub or an adolescent, like other shifters, if he were a tiger shifter. Why would they think he could do it as an adult if he hadn't as a child? Stupid Cadells and now the Black River pack probably believes it, too."

Rory had stopped breathing as she explained. He slowly took in a deep breath, trying to process what she'd just said.

Elianna, Justin's mate, had shared a vision of a Siberian tiger shifter, a Gallize like her husband, who she believed was in the northeast corner of the country. The Guardian had been shocked, later telling Justin, Cole and Rory that the only one he knew of should have died in an attack on a tiger shifter village the day he was born... twenty five years ago.

Could Baatar be a Gallize shifter who was going crazy because the Guardian had not called up his tiger?

Siofra said, "Okay, I told you a secret of mine. Tell me something special about your people."

Oh, hell, he couldn't do that. He thought for a minute, then realized what he could tell her without giving away too much. "The mate of one of my team members is pregnant and her eyes changed color."

"Really? I've never heard of that." She smiled and his heart thudded at making her happy.

Rory needed to find out one more thing on her camp brother. He kept his voice casual and asked, "How old is Baatar?"

"I always tease him that he's an old man at twenty-five." She laughed and shook her head.

Shit. If Baatar was *that* tiger, he was definitely losing his mind with a beast trapped inside of him.

Rory had to do something, but he couldn't break his word to Siofra. If he did, she'd never trust him again.

But neither could he risk Baatar making a run for it if he got suspicious when Rory showed up. He also owed it to the Guardian to not interrupt the search that his boss, Justin and Cole were on at the moment.

First, Rory had to figure out for sure if Baatar was the missing Gallize tiger.

CHAPTER 28

STRETCHED OUT WITH AN ARM behind his head and the rest of him as limp as his well-used dick, Rory ran a hand up and down Siofra's arm. They'd been lying here for ten minutes as he tried to figure out some plan on Baatar.

One that didn't involve destroying Siofra's trust by Rory contacting his boss.

In the other room, his phone dinged with a message.

Siofra announced, "I'm taking a shower. You stay here or I won't be able to walk tomorrow."

"Quitter."

Laughing, she climbed off the tall bed and fished what she needed out of her new suitcase. As she made her way to the bathroom and closed the door, he glanced at the time.

A few minutes past six. What would she want for dinner?

He went into the living room to where his pants were piled on the floor and dug out his phone.

A missed text message from Scarlett, the investigator.

With so little time to find Baatar and wanting to help Siofra, Rory had asked Scarlett to find out what she could about Baatar based upon Siofra's description. Scarlett had scowled, telling him his boss had asked her to search Vermont with no specific intel, just go look.

For that reason, getting any message from her was unexpected.

It would be nice if Scarlett found out Baatar was somewhere other than Portland so Rory could get Siofra out of the city. Her text just said to call, so he did.

"You found me," Scarlett said, not acknowledging her name.

"This is Rory. Do you have something on Baatar?"

"Oh. Didn't recognize your number. Maybe. There's a rumor that bounty hunters in Vermont captured someone who fits the description of a big guy with a beard, acting strange, not exactly human and with a load of power."

"Sounds like him."

Scarlett crushed his enthusiasm at finding Baatar quickly when she added, "He escaped, which is saying something considering he had to fight shifters."

"No kidding. He's that strong?"

"Could be or just an insane person with power, which makes him hard to combat. Sort of like a human on drugs walking into a hail of bullets and still standing. If this guy is Baatar and he gets cornered, you need to watch out. Sounds like he snaps and his power amps up."

Dammit. That did sound like the man Siofra hoped to have answer her bulletin board message.

Rory glanced at the still-shut bathroom door. He turned his back, keeping his voice down. "Have you had any luck with the tiger my boss is looking for?"

She didn't answer.

"I'm trying to help," he said encouragingly.

"Why do you want to know?"

The cooling system kicked on, making a bit of noise, then quieting down. With so little time to talk before Siofra came out, he ignored everything and pushed on.

He said, "I might have a lead for you on the tiger."

"Really?"

"Yes," he said. If Scarlett reported this to Rory's team and boss, that would be out of his control, thus allowing him to keep his word to Siofra. The boss needed a heads-up, but he could never face her and lie about calling this in.

He walked a tightrope of trying to do right by her and perform his duty. Before he said too much, he asked, "Have you been given any other directions on hunting the tiger beyond that first meeting?"

"No," Scarlett said, but qualified, "I do have a lead."

"Really? Great."

"Not so fast. I won't tell you a thing if you're going to call it in to your boss and screw all my hard work."

There went any hope he had of Scarlett informing the Guardian. She'd boxed him in as much as Siofra had, but he was either in or out on something like this.

He said, "Agreed. I think Baatar could be the tiger shifter we're hunting. If he is, we have to bring him in."

"Baatar as in Siofra's brother?"

"Yes."

"Huh. I've got a tip on a Sumatran tiger who shifts."

The Guardian had not mentioned that he searched specifically for a Siberian tiger shifter, probably to keep from limiting the information Scarlett would bring him.

Scarlett asked, "What makes you think Baatar could be a tiger shifter? When Siofra told me where she was going with you, she never mentioned her brother was a shifter."

Rory couldn't tell Scarlett too much, because Baatar could be a Gallize. He said, "I'm telling you more than I should right now. If he is the one we're after and you help me, I'll make sure you get full credit."

"What about Siofra? Does she know you think this?"

"Not yet. I don't want to say anything to her until I know more."

"Where are you two?"

"Portland, Maine. We're trying to make contact with Baatar. We got jumped by a Black River pack wolf yesterday."

"Are there more?"

"Maybe, but that one can tell no tales."

"Good," Scarlett said, making it clear how little she cared for that pack. "I'm west of you, just over the border in New Hampshire. The Sumatran tiger shifter was reported captured in Vermont as well, but the bounty hunters were on the move and heading to Maine. It's thought they're gathering exotics for a shifter auction. I'm heading over to Portland and should be in your area in two hours. Text me if you get anything new. I can be mobile fast."

"Will do if you'll do the same for me."

"I will. I give few people one chance. Don't screw it up."

Siofra's shower was still running.

Rory tossed his phone on the bed and opened the bathroom door to join her. A cloud of steam hit him.

He took a moment to enjoy the seductive look of her naked body with steam billowing around her as she washed her hair. Moving fast, he slipped in behind her and wrapped his arms around her. She tensed for a moment.

"It's me, baby. Who else are you expecting?"

She relaxed and patted his hand. "I was just deep in thought."

Truth.

"Let me give you something more relaxing to think about." He nuzzled her neck and kissed her shoulder.

"Maybe later. I'm a little sore and tired."

Lie. He stilled, wondering what was going on with her, but he had more to learn about this woman and would give her the time she needed. "That's absolutely fine. Let's get done and order some food."

"Yum. Can't wait."

Not the whole truth.

He shook it off, determined not to be the grouchy shifter who snarled about everything.

But when she moved out of his embrace and hurried out to dry off on her own, he had serious concerns that something was going on.

Rushing through his shower, he was out, dried off and dressed by the time she finished drying her snowy locks.

He lifted the in-room dining menu. If anything grabbed her attention, it was ordering food. "What do you want for dinner? Then we'll watch a movie." He didn't want her to think he only wanted to be between her legs.

Siofra meant more to him than a romp in the sack.

He shouldn't have let this happen, but in truth he didn't know that he could have stopped it once they met.

She said, "Whatever you decide for food is fine by me."

Closing the menu folder, he said, "What's going on? I've never been involved with a woman beyond one night of sleeping together, but I like being with you and I want to do this right. Please don't make me guess what's going on in your mind and don't hit me with 'fine' as your only answer."

Giving him a frosty glance, she said, "I told you I have a lot of things on my mind. Will Baatar get in touch with me before we have to leave? What will I do if he doesn't? What will happen if he does? I have to be prepared for every possibility. I've never been in a true relationship either, but you aren't looking for a mate and I can't stay beyond giving your boss everything he's requested."

Mine. He couldn't stop that from playing through his mind and feeling it in his soul. He would never push her to do something she didn't want, but ... she hadn't said she would not mate.

He'd have to wait until Baatar was safe and talk to her then. He'd tell her what she meant to him and explain that he had to fix the problem with his jaguar first, but he'd been wrong about not wanting a mate.

Maybe once he had her brother safe ... shit, her brother had to go to the Guardian if he was the tiger shifter.

There were so many hurdles that could block him from her.

Siofra said, "Just give me some time right now, okay? That's all I'm asking for."

He could do that, but it felt like she was pulling away and he didn't care for the panic he felt at that possibility.

He sucked at knowing what to say or do right now, but he gave it a shot because she needed to be reassured. "Sure. I know being in this hotel room is confining. Just relax and I bet you have a message waiting when the store opens."

She smiled and nodded, but her eyes were bleeding sadness.

Why?

CHAPTER 29

ℚ

HOW COULD RORY DO THIS to her?
    Siofra had finished her shower and now sat on the sofa, reading a magazine. The same sofa Rory had given her the orgasm of her life against an hour ago and left her thinking maybe, just maybe, there could be more between them.

After that, she'd obsessed about what she could say to Baatar to gain his support for her being with Rory. Her brother was a stubborn man, but he'd always been considerate and wanted to see her happy.

With Rory, she'd felt something that she'd never allowed herself to embrace. Hope. The kind of hope that was far more than running away to be free, but instead, standing and having something forever.

Then Rory went and ruined everything.

She'd started the water for her shower and had eased the door open to whisper something sexy at him ... when she heard him talking to someone about Baatar.

Rory had not told her that his boss was hunting a man thought to be a tiger shifter, but something she'd said had obviously convinced Rory that Baatar could be that person.

She'd listened until she couldn't any more.

He'd been talking to someone on his phone and said, "I think Baatar could be the tiger shifter my boss is hunting. If he is, we have to bring him in."

She'd been so shocked, she pulled the door shut and slumped to the floor, heart hurting. She'd trusted Rory with Baatar's secrets and he'd betrayed her trust by sharing that information not even half an hour later.

We have to bring him in.

Rory's words kept playing through her head. He intended to capture Baatar, the man she considered a brother.

Not while she had Baatar's back.

Rory had been staying away from her since they'd showered, which was easier in this large room with a sitting area, but still hard in a confined space. He'd had sports on the television for a bit, but when a knock sounded at the door, he turned it off.

He'd said nothing to her about the phone call, so he clearly intended to keep whatever his people were doing secret from her. She could understand their need to shield information, just as she'd had to do for survival, especially once she'd escaped.

But Rory knew how important it was for her to find her brother and ensure his freedom. She'd trusted Rory more than her brother and shared the one thing Baatar had said not to—that people expected him to shift into a tiger.

She'd never forgive herself for lowering her guard, but in her defense, she thought she'd finally found someone she could trust with all her secrets.

She considered confronting Rory, but hesitated when she had no idea how he would react. Would he take her back to his headquarters while his people hunted Baatar?

Not happening.

"Would you please put your hat on?" he asked, being so polite it made her teeth ache. She missed the natural Rory, but then again she'd been the one to push him as far away as she could.

She grabbed her hat and shoved her hair under it.

The door opened and a man chatted with Rory about where he wanted the meal. Next, the hotel server wheeled the cart through the room and placed covered food on the coffee table next to her.

Before the man left, she looked over her shoulder and said, "Thank you."

"Very welcome."

More conversation at the door, then it shut and everything turned deadly quiet again.

She was no good at being angry.

She'd never held a grudge or spent time avoiding people. If she had an issue at a camp, she tried to solve it so that everyone could get along. But those people had been captives like her who needed any friend they could find. They sometimes stole from each other, but that was easier to forgive since she'd never had anything she wouldn't give away.

Nothing had ever mattered more to her than freedom.

If Rory and his people captured Baatar, she'd lose her last hope for freedom. She could no longer trust Rory's group, not when they'd kept things from her.

Rory lifted a lid on a lobster dish that smelled incredible. He'd enjoyed watching her indulge in new food.

She could be angry and still eat. Sitting up, she took the plate he offered. "Thank you."

He muttered, "I've been demoted to service staff."

"You don't like me to be polite?" she asked and stared at her food to avoid looking at the hurt in his face. This was not her fault, dammit.

"Doesn't matter," he said, sitting down in a chair across from her to eat his meal.

Should she ask what he meant or ignore his comment? She picked at her lobster and finally gave up. "What doesn't matter?"

He finished chewing his food, took a drink of water and swallowed, then looked over at her. "You said you weren't staying. I just hadn't expected you to pull all the way back this way before we had to part."

How was it she felt like a jerk when he had betrayed her? But if she told him the truth, he'd screw up her plans. Instead she said, "We agreed this would be temporary."

Her heart hurt just saying that, but she wouldn't stay with a man she couldn't trust. Rory had kept his emotions bound up so tightly at first, that she regretted seeing the end of his opening up. He'd been so happy these past two days, and she had a feeling he'd never really been happy before.

Knowing she'd been the reason weighed on her now.

Her head hurt from trying to do the right thing.

Her first promise had been to Baatar. Rory had known that from the start of this trip. She hadn't changed her position, but he had, and intended to grab Baatar.

Taking a sip of her water, she put the glass down. "I'm sorry if I've misled you. That wasn't my intention."

"No problem. We all have a job to do and I'll do mine."

Hearing him confirm that he intended to do what his boss expected was all she needed to brush away her doubts. "Great. I would expect no less."

They finished eating during the brittle silence. Lobster had been her new favorite food until now. It sat like a rock in her stomach.

She'd gone through both magazines she'd found in the hotel room while Rory observed her, because she needed it to appear that she'd read everything available.

Once he'd called the hotel staff to remove the dishes and they were alone again, she got up, searching the room.

Being a cat, that was all it took to pique his curiosity. "What are you looking for?"

"Nothing," she mumbled.

"That's a lot of effort for nothing."

Giving him an exasperated sigh, she said, "I want more magazines. I've read everything and I'm trying to not inconvenience you, but I know you don't want me to leave the room."

He stood up and walked over to her.

She didn't move, unsure what he was going to do.

"Dammit," he murmured and pulled her against him. "All you have to do is ask me for anything and I'll do my best to give you what you want."

Her arms went around him as if that was their most natural position and her gaze got watery. "I know." She had a thousand more words to say, but if that dam broke loose she'd slip up and tell him how badly he'd hurt her with one phone call.

Giving her a tight hug, he released her and headed for the door, but turned back. "What do you want?"

"Anything on this northeastern area. It's really fascinating about life on the coast and in the cold up here."

"I'll find it and be back in a few minutes. Bolt the door behind me and please don't leave."

She walked over to him. "Where would I go?"

The expression on his face hid his thoughts from her. "That's what I worry about."

He stepped out and she set the deadbolt then heard him say, "Good girl."

She dropped her forehead against the door and sniffled. Everything about this was killing her, but now was not the time to cry.

Standing up, she hurried to the hotel phone and used the number she'd memorized.

When a woman on the other end said, "You found me," Siofra asked, "Is this Scarlett?"

"Yes. Siofra? Are you okay?"

No, she was not okay. Her heart had broken and her insides were shredding, but she said, "I'm fine, but I have a problem."

"What is it?"

"I need you to get me out of here."

CHAPTER 30

ℚ

RORY HELD SIOFRA AS SHE slept and wondered how long he'd be able to do this. The alarm he'd set on his phone to ensure they arrived at the grocery store on time had been wasted. He hadn't been able to break through her distant attitude until they went to bed, then she turned to him with a desperate look in her eyes.

One touch and everything keeping them apart went up in flames.

If sex was all she'd give him right now, he'd take it just to be close to her and allow her the time she needed to sort through whatever bothered her.

But he needed more than that from her.

He'd been alone a long time. Now, he didn't want to live alone and without her with him.

Pulling her closer, he hugged her back to his chest, loving the feel of her in his arms.

She mumbled something in gerbil language, making him smile. No one had ever pulled a smile from him the way she could with a look, a word or a laugh. She brought light into his dark existence.

Ferrell had never been this content.

Rory brushed his hand over her white hair. The one benefit of her pushing him away yesterday was that it had forced him to spend time thinking everything through.

Yes, she was a Cadell. Had to be with that tattoo and being raised in those camps. Sadly, it confirmed what the Guardian had first believed about her.

Her brother might be a Gallize shifter or he might only be

someone with an uncontrollable power. They'd cross that bridge once Rory got a chance to meet the guy.

He'd need Siofra's help convincing Baatar to at least meet his boss, but Rory couldn't imagine someone in Baatar's physical misery not welcoming help.

If he was a Gallize, the Guardian would know what to do.

The Guardian could call any of his shifters to him by putting the command out to the universe, but only if he'd first called up their animal.

Getting Siofra to trust him enough to convince Baatar to meet the Guardian? Yeah, that was another issue, but he'd find a way.

All those thoughts brought him to the most difficult one.

Should he even consider mating her when he might be dying? He would not take her to mate to cure him. He'd never put that burden on her shoulders, so if he wanted to mate he had to fix the problem with his jaguar.

But damn if he knew how.

She had trust issues and believed the Gallize were worse than the Cadells. He'd have to cross that minefield when he came to it.

But if she'd consider staying to be with him, she deserved a healthy mate.

When he'd reached that point in his analytical thinking, his heart took over and vanquished all doubt. They were a mismatched pair, but he wanted Siofra as his mate.

If she said yes and the Gallize couldn't accept a Cadell among them, he'd leave so that she wouldn't have to live under a cloud of suspicion the rest of her life.

Mate. More and more, the word echoing in his brain came from him and not his jaguar.

He did want to live.

He did want a mate, but only Siofra.

He'd damn well figure out how.

Bells chimed on his phone.

She jerked and pushed up. "What time is it?"

"Six. We're good. You can grab a shower and get dressed. It's already light outside. We have an hour to make a ten minute ride."

Stretching and yawning, she said, "Okay."

When she started to move, he pulled her back to him so he

could whisper, "I loved every minute with you last night. I love your touch and just being with you. We'll find Baatar, then I want to talk to you … about the future."

He held her as she took a couple of breaths before saying, "We'll talk."

With that lie, she got up and went to the bathroom, leaving his heart blown apart.

He'd just figured out that he wanted her forever. Fool that he was, he'd been assuming he could convince her to stay and give him a shot. Now? He had no idea what to think. He had to tread carefully here, or he could end up without his Gallize brothers *or* the mate he wanted.

Ferrell rumbled softly inside Rory. He sent an image of Siofra walking off into the sunset and his jaguar crying out in pain.

Give me a break, Ferrell. I'm trying to figure this out.

His jaguar sent back, Ó Fearghail.

Rory grumbled, ignoring his jaguar. He had a duty to keep Siofra safe and to determine if Baatar was indeed the missing Gallize tiger shifter.

Siofra stayed in the bathroom until she was fully dressed. He felt cheated that she hadn't come into the room to finish like every other time.

When he stood to take his spin in the shower, she came over to him and put her arms around him. That was all. She let go and moved over to the sofa to put her shoes on.

He jumped in the shower and finished in record time. Washing his face, he stared at a man who used to know how his life would play out, but that had changed.

He had changed. He wanted more time and to be with Siofra.

There were healers in other countries that might be able to tell him what to do about his jaguar dying.

Siofra had healed his body, but the connection to his jaguar still felt hollow.

Ferrell snarled in a panic. *Mate!*

What the hell was that all about?

Rory cocked his head and listened. Normally he could hear Siofra even if she was only turning pages in a magazine. It was too quiet on the other side of the door.

Hairs stood on his neck. Had someone found them?

He slowly opened the door and his stomach dropped.

Her scent remained, but she was gone.

"Fuck!" He hurried to pull on his jeans then raced over to grab a shirt and shoes. But his clothes were gone, as was his phone.

Screw it.

He found the keys to the new Expedition and his wallet he kept hidden, then ran out of the room. When the elevator didn't open immediately, he raced down eleven floors to the garage, but had to slow to human speed when he got there.

Hurrying through the parking garage, he reached the vehicle and found all four tires slashed.

A curse ripped out of him that should have blown out car windows. Everyone stopped pulling rolling luggage and walking through to stare.

He started to leave then paused. That was a shifter scent, one he knew. He inhaled again to be sure.

Scarlett?

She'd done this? Was she kidnapping Siofra?

No. He'd have smelled Scarlett's scent upstairs.

He grabbed his head and leaned back against the hood to think.

The only way Scarlett could have spoken to Siofra was if Siofra called the shifter. He'd bet money there was an outgoing call on his hotel statement.

Why had Siofra done this?

Because she'd intended to meet up with her brother and run all along.

That cut him to the bone.

When they talked last night, everything she'd said sounded so sincere. Yeah, he'd fallen for her. Loved her, dammit, and lost a few IQ points as it happened.

Had she pushed him away so that she could shower alone this morning and he'd have to wash second? That was so simple it was brilliant.

Looking at his watch, he had four minutes to reach the store. They'd planned well, but they'd underestimated him.

CHAPTER 31

Siofra walked quickly across the grocery store to the bulletin board with Scarlett on her heels. Only a few other shoppers had entered at seven when they unlocked the sliding glass doors.

"There it is," Siofra whispered as if shoppers would care about the cryptic message she'd just located on the pegboard.

Scarlett kept her back to Siofra, watching for any threat. "Do you have the location?"

"Yes. He will be there at ten." Siofra reached up, pulling the torn piece of paper off the board and ripping it into pieces.

"Where is it?"

Siofra whispered, "Fort Knox. Is that here in Maine?"

As she and Scarlett left the store, Siofra dropped the tiny pieces into a garbage can.

Scrolling on her phone, Scarlett said, "Yes, that fort is two hours north on the coast. We should make ten with no problem." She hurried them to her truck, which she'd parked at the edge of the lot for easy exit.

Siofra went through the motions, doing as Baatar had instructed, but her mind was somewhere else.

She should be elated over getting Baatar's message. Instead, guilt over leaving Rory to find the empty room with no clothes, no vehicle and not even a note ate at her.

That was behind her now. *Let it go.*

Baatar needed her. That was what mattered.

Rory had opened up a place in her heart where she stored every second she'd spent with him. She'd cherish that time one day when she'd gotten over how he'd disappointed her in the end.

She could forgive him. He was doing his duty and she was doing hers.

That eagle man expected loyalty from Rory and she owed hers to Baatar. She and Rory had never had a chance. She'd been foolish to think she could have a man like him and a normal life. She wanted to be furious with him, but Rory had only been doing his job.

Frowning, Scarlett said, "You probably don't know this, but Fort Knox is *literally* on the Maine coast. Pretty exposed."

"Baatar would not choose a place unless there were a lot of trees nearby for us to disappear easily. He'll expect me to get as close to that spot as I can, then wait so he can see who is with me before he comes out. We may have to sit for an hour until he feels sure no one is using me as bait."

"Good thinking. What are you going to do when you two meet?" Scarlett asked, driving her truck to the interstate. This was no late model truck, but one from the sixties and refurbished. Had Scarlett been the one who lovingly restored the red pickup?

"We're going to disappear. I'm the only one who can watch over Baatar," Siofra answered, mesmerized by the Cape Cod style homes she'd only seen in photographs. The real world was so much better.

"What's wrong with him?"

"I don't know," Siofra admitted. "Neither does he, but we both think it has to do with his power. He said he was strong and happy until he reached his twenties, then he started struggling physically and emotionally. He'd have moments where he wanted to pull himself inside out."

"Ugh. That sucks." Scarlett flipped on her blinker and moved smoothly onto the interstate. "What if he gets worse?"

"I don't know," Siofra admitted. She had no answer for that question. She'd asked herself that a hundred times, but until they were both free to hunt for help she'd just keep him as stable as she could.

"Do you think he's a tiger shifter?"

Scoffing with a dark laugh, Siofra mused, "Why does everyone want to explain his problems as being a shifter? He's twenty-five and he's never shifted into anything. Don't shifters change the first time as a kid? When did you first shift?"

Scarlett's profile turned serious. She answered the question in a roundabout way. "Most shifters go through their first change somewhere between one and five years old. I've heard of two who were late bloomers, shifting at eight and ten, but an adult? Nope. Can't say I've run across that."

"See? Makes no sense."

"Why did Rory think he might be the tiger I'm tracking for his boss?"

Siofra's brain stalled. "What? When did he tell you that?"

Glancing over at her, Scarlett said, "Before you two left Spartanburg, Rory asked me to dig around and let him know if I ran across any information that might lead to finding Baatar. I called him yesterday to tell him I had a tip. When he called me back, he said he thought Baatar might be the tiger his boss asked me to hunt."

"Wait. Why would Rory ask you to help find Baatar when we were on our way to meet up with Baatar?" Siofra had a sinking feeling about Scarlett's answer.

Keeping a steady speed, Scarlett shrugged. "He said something about you having a limited time to locate your brother and he'd pay out of his pocket for any information on Baatar if I'd put feelers out. I heard about a guy who could be your brother. Bounty hunters captured him in Vermont."

"When?"

"Doesn't matter, because he escaped and evidently is waiting for you at Fort Knox," Scarlett reminded her. "Now that we're not on a dead run, tell me why you think Rory is going to lock you up?"

"I thought ... " Siofra ran back through it all in her mind. She'd thought his phone call was about helping his people hunt Baatar. She'd called Scarlett and said she had to sneak away for any chance at gaining her freedom.

"You thought what?"

Siofra started to understand the sick feeling she'd been suffering. "I was in the shower when you called and I thought he was talking to his boss after he swore to me he would not tell his boss what I'd said about Baatar. I told Rory the Cadells all believe that Baatar can shift into a tiger, but he can't." She could hardly breathe. "I thought Rory was conspiring to capture Baatar and lock him up."

For the next few minutes, Scarlett wove around traffic until she had a clear lane again. "To be honest, if Baatar is the tiger shifter Rory's boss is hunting, then I'm supposed to bring him in. But from what you say, he can't be."

Sitting back, Siofra sank into a new level of misery.

She'd hurt Rory. She'd feared being locked up and losing any chance to find Baatar before everyone else did, but now she wished she'd risked her own freedom by confronting Rory over what she'd heard to get his side of that phone call. Years of being lied to and yanked around by men, shifters in particular, had colored her thinking. She'd jumped to the most obvious conclusion ... that Rory was going to betray Baatar and her by stealing their freedom.

Maybe it was a good thing nothing worked out between her and Rory.

He deserved a better woman than she was, but she still wanted to turn around and go back to beg his forgiveness. What must he be thinking right now? That she never actually cared?

Lies are stupid.

She'd just given him reason to believe that everything between them had been a lie when it had been anything but.

Siofra's gaze went to Scarlett's mobile phone. She started to ask to borrow it, but remembered that she and Scarlett had tossed Rory's phone to slow him down. He'd said it was a burner that couldn't be traced, so Scarlett had no new number for him.

Besides, Rory would demand they turn around and come back. She couldn't do that.

She'd find Baatar and get him safe, then she'd make good on her promise to share Cadell information with Rory's boss once that eagle man could not come for Baatar. She'd also tell Rory's boss that she'd tricked Scarlett and not to hold it against her.

Once she got all of that out of the way, she'd ask to speak to Rory so she could explain what happened.

But would he actually talk to her?

It took just over two hours of driving north to find the fort that spread over a wide-open spot with the ocean as a backdrop.

Just as she'd thought, a forest thick with trees bordered one side.

Scarlett parked and tossed her phone into her pocket. She paid for two tickets and led Siofra into the historic sight.

Most people were fascinated by the cannons and taking pictures with the ocean behind them. She and Scarlett were headed to the other side of the fort.

As soon as they had an opening, Siofra and Scarlett snuck off and wove their way through the musty interior of the fort structures. After a couple of tries and misses, they found a way to the outside of the fort where the rear faced the woods.

Siofra chose a place in the middle of the wall of cut gray stones to lean back against. "Now, we wait."

She felt eyes on her more than once, but did not try to locate Baatar. Instead, she spoke to Scarlett, asking her about what she did exactly.

"I help shifters, especially cat shifters. I normally wouldn't have gotten involved in your case, but the woman you helped with the little boy felt bad that bounty hunters captured you. She pleaded with me to make sure you were okay and told me ... "

"Told you what?"

"Shoot. I hadn't meant to say that, but it's in the past. She said she felt your energy, but didn't think you were a shifter. I'm on the board of a foundation which helps shifter females and their children, but I figured we could make room for someone who wasn't entirely human."

Siofra said, "Thank you for at least being open to helping me."

"You're welcome. Sure you'll be okay once you and your brother take off?"

"Yes," Siofra said, hoping it wasn't a lie. "Will things be a problem with Rory's boss for you helping me?"

"Hell, no. I'm my own person. They owe me right now. If they give me grief, I won't share any more intel with them."

At least that lightened Siofra's burdened heart.

"Is that him?" Scarlett whispered.

Siofra turned to see Baatar striding across the expanse of grass between them and the woods. She jumped away from the wall and ran to him.

He grabbed her and wrapped her in his big arms, swinging her around. Her brother was a giant.

"I'm so glad you're safe, Baatar."

"Happy to see you, too," he said. "Who is that?"

Pulling back, she twisted around to find Scarlett a few steps behind her.

"I'm Scarlett. I know who you are, but not *what* you are."

Baatar grumbled, "I am me. That is all you need to know."

Scarlett sniffed. "No, I think there's more to you than meets the eye."

"Then close eyes. We are done."

Siofra frowned during that exchange and told Baatar, "Be nice. Scarlett helped me reach you."

"Where is man I saw yesterday?"

"You saw Rory?"

"Saw this man hug you. Did he send you as trick to make me come out?"

"Oh, boy," Scarlett grumbled. "Paranoid much? No, he didn't set her up and neither did I. Siofra, I hope you have a good life. Baatar, best wishes on getting through life with that boulder on your shoulder."

He gave Scarlett a confused expression, looked at each shoulder, then back at her. "Hope you do not get lost with bad eyesight."

Siofra said, "Oh, good grief, you two." She told Scarlett, "I'll explain the boulder reference later. Thank you and be safe."

"Will do." Scarlett turned and walked away.

Siofra was ready to get out of the open, but Baatar kept staring at Scarlett so she pointed out, "Scarlett is a very nice person and very intelligent."

"I do not see. Talk too much." He turned with his arm around her shoulders. "We must go. I have no transportation."

"How'd you get here?"

"Ran." He headed them into the closest woods.

Shaking her head, Siofra said, "Lucky for you that Scarlett likes me and gave me a hundred dollars to help us out."

"What?"

"Yep, the woman you were rude to is the reason we will be able to pay someone for a ride and buy food. Feel bad now?"

"Always feel bad," he mumbled.

She stopped teasing and put her arm around his waist as they entered the cooler shade. "We're going to find someone to help you. I'm here now. Everything is going to be okay."

Something sharp stuck in her back.

Baatar jerked away and reached for his back. When he did, she could see a dart jabbed into his skin. Her legs turned to rubber and the woods around her blurred.

She heard a distorted voice order, "Hurry up and get them loaded."

CHAPTER 32

RORY STAYED IN THE WOODED area paralleling Highway 1 as it ran up the coast from Portland.

The scent he followed became more distinct out here without so many human smells to sort through. Breathing in a lung full of pine scent beat the city any day.

When he realized he had one chance of catching up with Siofra, he'd made the gamble to shift and give Ferrell his head. His jaguar had been behaving better lately and had a single-minded focus when it came to Siofra.

Ferrell's ability to scent and move at hyperspeed made it worth the risk of being spotted.

Someone would have to catch Rory's jaguar to figure out if he really *was* a jaguar. With Ferrell clocking over seventy miles an hour even with leaping obstacles, the odds were in his favor right now.

If he'd had the time, he'd have gotten another phone and tried to call Scarlett, but time was the one thing he couldn't spare. He'd made the decision to not to waste any of it when he'd reached the grocery store so close behind Siofra that her scent felt warm.

Besides, she'd made a conscious decision to help Siofra get away from him. That hurt.

He'd actually thought Scarlett was someone who could become a trusted friend of his people and the boss would eventually tell her the truth about Gallize shifters.

Not now. The Guardian would never trust her again.

Rory sure as hell wouldn't.

After finding the slit tires on his ride in the garage, he'd raced in human form to the grocery store, probably looking like a crazy jogger wearing jeans and no shoes.

Siofra and Scarlett had already been there.

But he picked up another scent as soon as he entered, of someone who had been at the bulletin board. A nonhuman scent, but not a shifter. He'd bet it belonged to Baatar.

That person had been here many hours ago, maybe last night.

He'd caught one more scent, which disturbed him the most.

A wolf shifter.

Rory had spun around and rushed out of the store, following all four scents across the parking lot. Scarlett and Siofra's had ended at a parking space, but the one he had tagged as Baatar's continued into the woods, turning north up the coast.

Just as the wolf shifter had right behind him.

Even with Ferrell's speed and agility, Rory's jaguar had to stop a couple of times to cross the road to follow the scent. That had meant pausing to wait for an opening where cars were far away and would mistake him for some local wild animal.

In a little over two hours, Ferrell ran through woods where Baatar's scent zigzagged back and forth until a large open space with an old fort came into view.

Rory told Ferrell to not leave the woods, but finish tracking the scent.

His jaguar reached a place where Siofra's scent entered the woods ... then four other shifter scents converged on Siofra and Baatar.

If not for being shifters, Rory might have thought the others had been there to help.

Ferrell roared and snarled. *Kill wolves!*

Yep. Two of those scents matched the wolf shifters who had escaped the Black River Pack compound that he and his team raided. The same pack that had captured Siofra.

But the other shifter scents were new.

He had no phone, no vehicle and no idea where they'd taken them.

But he knew who might.

CHAPTER 33

SCARLETT LOOKED AT THE UNKNOWN number on her mobile phone and debated answering since her stomach grumbled that noon meant food.

Sighing, she hit the button on her mobile. "Your dime."

"You better be able to find them," Rory warned.

Shit, she hated getting in the middle of domestic issues and Siofra had smelled heavily of Rory. Scarlett said, "Don't be pissy with me. Siofra called and told me you were going to lock her up. She begged me to help her find her brother."

"You left them at Fort Knox, right?"

How did he know that? "Why?"

"My jaguar ran the hundred-and-twenty-miles there and back."

She looked at her watch. Just after noon. Impressive, but she said, "You're lucky no one saw you."

"No. I'm not even a little bit lucky," Rory snapped. "We followed Baatar's scent from the grocery store. His trail stopped in the woods next to the fort where six shifters captured them. Two were Black River Pack wolves. I could also smell a chemical. They were drugged."

"*Fuck!*"

"Exactly. I called the office and—"

She yelled, "You said you wouldn't tell your boss about what I'm doing."

"Don't interrupt me again," he warned in a voice that threatened serious harm.

He didn't scare her but this guy sounded terrified for Siofra, so she let him finish.

"I called my people to say my burner phone had a problem—but *not* that it was tossed by you two—and that I needed your number. I asked what they knew about the tiger you were looking for and they said they suggested you search Vermont. The only two people I would trust to bring into this are out searching with my boss. If Baatar turns out to be a tiger shifter, we'd have to call in my boss just to keep everyone safe. I can't tell you more than that, but it would turn bloody in seconds. So that leaves you and me. We're going to find Siofra and Baatar."

She might have argued or just hung up on him, but she felt a level of responsibility for Siofra getting caught. Not Baatar. That asshole could suck hind tit.

Pounding the steering wheel of her truck, she said, "There's an auction happening somewhere in western Maine. That would be the first place I'd look. I'd planned to wait until it was over and I got word of someone buying the tiger to track him down without a crowd."

"Where are you?"

She gave him the general location since she was almost to New Hampshire.

"Since you trashed my ride, come and get me."

She gripped the phone so hard the plastic squealed from the pressure. No one ordered her around.

"Stop, dammit," Rory's voice yelled from the phone she'd pulled away from her ear. "You don't want to smash your phone any more than I want to crush everything in my way. We can't do this if we don't work together."

Easing her grip, she said, "Fine. I'll pick you up, but if you give me one more order I'm going to rip your balls off."

"You must be a joy to date."

"I don't date," she shouted. "Hard to do when men are such pricks. So pull your head out of your ass before I get to you."

"What the hell? Why would you say that shit?"

"Siofra's a nice woman. You must be a major jerk for her to run from you when I could smell your scent all over her. I'm coming to get you for *her*. Not for you. So don't screw up or I'll dump your ass on the side of the road."

He muttered a curse and said, "I'm in love with her. I will go through anyone and everyone to get her back and keep her safe."

Scarlett had no words for that, but told him, "See you in an hour."

She'd thought Tess had been crazy to mate a shifter, but that wolf would lay down his life for her, too. Tess had also told Scarlett about Justin, the bear mated to a woman named Eli. According to Tess, Justin would destroy the world for his mate.

This jaguar sounded like them.

She didn't know where these men came from, but she'd never met any males she'd trust to stand beside her.

CHAPTER 34

RORY CLENCHED HIS FIST FOR the hundredth time, impatient to get his hands around the neck of anyone harming Siofra. Had to be the worst Friday of his life and with the clock approaching eight in the evening it was still far from over.

Riding in the passenger seat didn't lower his blood pressure at all, especially since he'd rented this Mercedes, but Scarlett had made a solid point about being in character as much as possible. Her character in this dangerous game would be the driver.

Also, he hadn't wanted to waste time in a power struggle.

She could drive as long as she didn't lose time. So far she'd kept a steady pace of five miles over the speed limit. This had better work.

He would not lose Siofra.

"Cut it out," Scarlett snapped.

"What?" How could this woman find something wrong when he'd been quiet for most of the trip?

"Your anger is generating some nasty energy and it's crawling across my skin."

Sometimes his Gallize brethren would power up to the point it was irritating to one another, but that was because their energies were equally strong and battling for dominance.

Was Scarlett that powerful?

First he calmed down and felt his body relax, then he asked, "Just what are you?"

"Oh, I'll show you mine then you show me yours? Pass."

"What crawled up your ass and died?" Rory asked. "I'm trying to have a conversation with you and understand why my energy clashed with yours. I already told you I'm a jaguar. What's the big deal about your animal? You already said it's a cat."

He must have gotten through to her, because her stiff profile relaxed and she ran a hand through her thick hair in an agitated motion. "I'm a cougar."

"Not many of those around."

"Nope."

"You're powerful. Don't deny it, because I felt your energy rise in defense against mine."

"I'm strong enough for what I need to do. End of discussion."

That was fun for the ten seconds it took her to shut him down. What a loner, and crabby as hell.

Ferrell had been worked up around Scarlett at first, but he'd settled down during the ride. Now he sent Rory an image of Rory and Scarlett lying next to each other in a giant pea pod.

Wiseass.

Damn. Had he been just as difficult as Scarlett to be around before he met Siofra?

Ferrell sent him an image of a smut-black pot and kettle.

You're fucking hilarious, Rory grumbled telepathically.

But his jaguar was right. Rory kept seeing his life as before Siofra and after Siofra.

It still hurt that she'd run away from him, but not because he'd been mean in any way. He'd known all along that she could be a flight risk. He'd gotten confortable and assumed they were still on the same page.

He asked Scarlett, "Did Siofra really think I was going to lock her up?"

"In hindsight, I don't think so. She thought the night you talked to me on the phone that you were talking to your people about catching Baatar to take in. I think she assumed that would mean her being contained, too, which she clearly doesn't want."

"I wouldn't have done that."

Slicing a look of disbelief his way, she asked, "You mean if Baatar turns out to somehow be a tiger shifter that you have no plans to take him to your boss?"

He opened his mouth to explain his job, but Scarlett didn't care about his duty any more than Siofra had when it came to her brother. In truth, he did need to take Baatar to the Guardian if Siofra's brother turned out to be a tiger shifter, but the Guardian wouldn't lock him away.

The problem was that Rory would have to explain the Gallize to Scarlett and Siofra to convince them his intentions were honorable when it came to Baatar.

As for Siofra, Rory would allow no one to lock her up.

He said, "She was right and wrong. If Baatar is a tiger shifter, I would have to take him to headquarters. But my boss would not put him in a cage or misuse him. Baatar would be treated really well and given specialized training, then he could be free once he could control his beast."

"Why would your boss even think Baatar might be a tiger shifter?"

"We have a seer in our group. She told him."

Scarlett's eyebrow lifted at that. "Hmm. She a shifter, too?"

"Yep."

After another stretch of silence, Scarlett asked, "What kind of shifters are all of you?"

"What do you mean?"

"Now you're insulting me. I've felt a load of power over the years, but what you were generating earlier was substantial and not close to full strength. Then there's your boss. His power is off the charts when he's at rest."

She was right, but Rory couldn't talk about the Gallize. "I don't mean to insult you, but we both have our secrets. Ask my boss that question. He's the best one to answer it."

Nodding, she said, "You guys are like dealing with a bunch of shifters trained to be SEALs. A bunch of ghosts. I never knew you existed until I got to know Tess and then met Cole at that meeting. He's not cut out to be a pack member unless he takes the alpha role. That goes for you and the bear as well."

"You've pretty much summed us up. I'd tell you more if I could, but I can't. Let's work on our plan."

"Nothing to work on. My contacts will have everything in place for us to get inside the location and spend just long enough to survey everything. We locate Siofra and Baatar. You make an offer, like we talked about, then tell them you'll be back tomorrow for the auction. We'll know exactly what we have to do to break them out tonight by the time we leave."

She sounded too confident, just like he had on his first big mission. Everything looked good on paper, but the minute things went to shit he'd been glad Sammy had gone in with a backup plan.

Damn, he missed that big grizzly shifter.

Thinking about how the Black River pack had killed Sammy would only piss Rory off and flood this cab with energy again.

He said, "If it goes down like that, I'm thrilled, but we need to think of contingency plans."

"Like what?"

"Like we walk in and they don't buy our story, so they capture us too."

She pfft. "Not going to happen. They might get you, but they won't cage me."

Damn, he hated overconfidence, but from what he could tell she'd worked alone a long time. It might not be arrogance speaking so much as a deep survival instinct and the fear of losing her freedom.

Still, if she was his partner in this, they had to be on the same page.

Holding back his warning tone and going with a conversational one, he said, "I'm in agreement on not wanting to end up caged, but we have to get our signals straight now so there's no confusion if something does go fubar, don't you think?"

Flipping on her blinker, she turned off Highway 27 to take a back road that hadn't been resurfaced in a long time. The sedan bounced through the occasional rut and pothole as she delayed her answer.

Running her fingers over her hair again, she said, "I'm definitely in on rescuing them, but I am not allowing anyone to cage me. All the signals in the world will not change that."

Shit. He let it go.

He had his own contingency plan, though it had a few holes.

The deeper they drove into the backcountry of western Maine, the more Rory felt eyes on their car.

Could be his imagination or that sixth sense keeping him alert.

Scarlett's contacts were wolf shifter bounty hunters, of all things, a group she swore by. She said they ran down criminal humans, not shifters. For that reason, she'd developed a relationship with them where she paid them well to hunt for female shifters in trouble and feed her intel from the shifter communities.

Without that connection, they'd never have been able to find this auction site so quickly or be allowed to enter. Her bounty hunter allies had connections inside the auction system so he and Scarlett had to be careful not to blow their covers.

North of Saddleback Mountain, she slowed to watch for a tree with an X carved into it. Humans would have to be walking up closer to the tree to see it, but Rory spotted the mark right away.

"There it is, Scarlett."

She slowed all the way to a stop, keeping an eye on her rear-view mirror. "No one coming from either direction."

Rory jumped out and strode to the tree where he could see two paths carved by tires a little way in behind a fallen tree. He found the upper area of the downed tree and lifted it, then walked the tree up enough for her to drive under. Once she was inside, he lowered the trunk across the path again, then moved the tall brush back in place.

If they had to make a run for it with the car, this would be a problem.

Climbing back in, he lifted a pair of shooter's glasses with yellow lenses from the seat next to him and slid them into place. Scarlett had unloaded a treasure trove of useful items from hidden compartments in her truck before they left it at his last hotel and took off.

He pulled the black ball cap with a hockey logo onto his head. He and Scarlett had discussed the plan by phone while she'd driven to pick him up in Portland. They'd spent most of the afternoon acquiring anything they didn't have, such as the Mercedes sedan, needed to make an impression.

She'd told Rory he would play the part of a financially independent, but reclusive, shifter who bought exotic shifters. She had an identity already built for the recluse, and she'd used it with another man two years back, which gave it some depth and credibility. As for her, she'd enter as arm candy who attended auctions, representing the recluse.

Before Rory had hung up, she'd given him a list of clothing to have ready when she arrived.

He'd had a hell of a time finding the top she wore on short notice. He'd never shopped for women's clothing, but she looked the part in a sheer red top that could be see-through if she turned just right in the light. Tiny sequins covered the red material, catching any light when she moved.

The male shifters would probably be too focused on her prominent boobs to notice any sparkles.

She'd changed into a tight pair of silk shorts with bling along the sides, unbraided her hair and dropped her head down to brush the wavy mass. Pretty amazing when all those small braids turned into a full head of brunette hair. Gave her more of a wild and exotic look. The last things she'd put on had been a pair of fuck-me shoes, long, flashy earrings, and layers of fine chains. She'd finished it off with red lipstick.

He'd found a black sport coat and coordinating dress pants for his part, and wore a tie-dyed T-shirt beneath it.

From another box, she'd produced all sorts of jewelry and other accessories, including a wig neither of them needed. He'd had to take a second look at the Louis Moinet Magistralis watch, because someone had crafted a great reproduction.

The real Magistralis rose-gold watch had an actual piece of the moon in it from a lunar meteorite, just one of the reasons the price tag ran in the high six figures.

He'd complimented her on the prop, which caught her off guard, but he had to admit it was a brilliant touch. There were duplicates of this watch being sold alongside fake Rolexes on occasion, but this particular faux watch would pass a quick inspection.

Based on the history she'd built for Adalbert Wauters, Rory's new identity, he was a Dutch recluse who enjoyed unusual shifter auctions, but rarely came out of hiding. When he did, it made news in the underground world. That she'd actually represented the elusive Wauters in past auctions aided her credibility to enter any illegal auction.

She claimed to have never had anyone else show up in person as him, only rumors she carefully fed to the black market community, but there were always risks with this kind of undercover.

The time spent getting ready and renting the car would have put him over the edge, but they couldn't arrive before eight in the evening.

On the dot. If they were late, they wouldn't be met.

If they were more than five minutes early, they'd regret it. Simple rules.

When Scarlett drove up to a wide, deep gulley that could be crossed only by footbridge, Rory noted the second major obstacle to a fast escape.

Not being able to turn the car around would be obstacle number three.

The last hundred feet of the trail had been lined with fallen trees when the live ones were spaced too far apart to prevent going off the path.

The minute he stepped out of the car, he owned the role of Adalbert, complaining in a thick voice, "First you make me ride from Portland and bounce me down a cow path through the forest. Now I am expected to *walk* the rest of the way? I have been in some remote areas, but this is absolutely primitive."

Scarlett had been picking her way around the front. "You said you wanted in. I got you in. I didn't set the guidelines on how we arrive. Ask them about flying in by helicopter tomorrow."

He scowled at everything in general. "If they do not have the prize I am expecting, there will be no tomorrow."

Scarlett looked across the ravine. "Ready?"

"No. I am having second thoughts," he said and it wasn't far from the truth, but nothing would prevent him going to find out if Siofra was there.

"Are you kidding me? After all I went through to arrange this so you could come in person?"

"Are you so sure you can trust these shifters?"

She snapped, "I trust my contacts. They like the money I pay them. If they say it's safe, then it's safe. You should be worried about them trusting *you.*"

He searched the surrounding woods one last time and said, "Fine. We shall go. The bridge will probably fall apart before we reach the other side. I am not going to be happy if anything happens to this shirt after what I went through to gain it."

"I'll tie-dye you another one," she quipped, keeping her balance as she moved ahead of him across the narrow walkway.

He put his arms out as if he struggled to keep his balance. "Very funny. I would not pay nine thousand dollars for yours. A master created this one."

"I'd save you eight thousand, nine hundred and eighty-five dollars, Adalbert, and bet you that extra amount that ten people off the street couldn't tell the difference."

She'd win.

He'd taken a gold marker and scribbled a name at the bottom edge of the T-shirt he'd bought for fifteen dollars.

On the other side of the bridge, Scarlett hurried off and let out a loud sigh. "Glad that's done."

"Indeed." He stepped onto firm land and two shifters appeared from where they'd been hiding behind trees and brush.

Scarlett startled for real, as if she hadn't scented them.

Rory hadn't either.

He sniffed the air. Magic had been used.

Once they dropped the spell shielding their scents, the first shifter smelled like a bear and the other a fox.

Best to pay closest attention to the bear shifter talking.

"Mr. Wauters?"

Rory arranged a suspicious expression on his face. "Yes?"

"We're here to escort you and Vivi. My alpha apologizes for not suggesting you fly in, but his intense security is what will keep you and others safe when we move to the auction site tomorrow."

Shit, that meant this bunch would be on the move tonight. Rory said, "Apology accepted if you have adequate transportation."

"Yes, sir. If you'll follow me." The shifter led Rory and Scarlett through a path to a … helicopter.

Fuck.

They climbed in and were handed black bags, which Rory and Scarlett pulled over their heads. The chopper lifted off, flew for five minutes and landed, but Rory had no idea if they'd flown miles or in a circle to land close to where they were picked up.

With the bags in place, they were led to a Hummer and helped inside.

The same shifter said, "Apologies for the inconvenience, but we'll be there shortly."

The security these shifters set up would be tough to breach even if someone could find them.

Rory had to keep his head if they found Siofra and Baatar. He'd have to calmly observe them as captives, then walk out of the camp with Scarlett so Rory could call in a team to help him extract them.

The plan had one potential flaw.

Once he found Siofra, the idea of walking away without her in hand would be the most difficult thing he'd ever done.

He had every intention of sticking with their strategy for the sake of getting Siofra out safely, but he had serious doubts about Ferrell agreeing.

With their connection getting weaker every day, his jaguar could break loose on his own if he stopped listening to Rory.

CHAPTER 35

SIOFRA SLUMPED IN THE CORNER of her six-foot-wide by
six-foot-tall cage, which sat on a flatbed transport truck. Her
cage sat in the shade beneath branches covered in leaves, but the
whole encampment had an overcast look to it due to netting spread
across the open area.

They'd lit some gas lamps, which hung on limbs and gave off
enough light for a human to move around, but the shifters still
held the advantage with the place surrounded in darkness.

Sheets of plywood had been placed over the center of the area,
covering forty or fifty feet across. Tripoli must have done that to
prevent the large flatbed trailers parked on the wood from getting
stuck.

Way over on the opposite side of the plywood and trailers,
Baatar stood with chains stretched from his wrist cuffs to two trees.

Another chain circled his waist with the ends secured to the
same trees. Besides that, he wore a titanium collar around his neck.
What in the world did they think he was capable of to chain him
like a wild beast?

Oh, right. Everyone thought Baatar turned into a tiger.

He could hear her if she spoke, but he wouldn't want her saying
a word in front of these shifters.

Bounty hunter shifters had caught them both this time.

As if that hadn't been bad enough, Mad Dog Hector from that
Black River wolf pack had shown up an hour ago. She lost what
little hope she'd had at that point. He'd greeted Tripoli, the shifter
in charge of these bounty hunters, like an old friend.

Tripoli walked Hector to the left on the far side of the trailers.

The two solid walls at each end of her cage prevented her from seeing past the trailers, but she'd heard Tripoli talking about showing off the other exotics.

Meaning they thought Baatar was an exotic shifter.

Hector had returned with Tripoli to stand in front of Baatar. They discussed her brother as though he were a prize bull.

Hector's final words had chilled her blood. "I am prepared to top any bid for this one, but only if you can prove he shifts by the auction. I will pay a bonus if he is truly a Siberian tiger."

Hector left shortly after.

Now they expected Baatar to be a *Siberian* tiger as well? She worried more for her brother's safety than hers.

What would happen when Baatar did not shift?

How had Hector not caught her scent?

Not that she was complaining, but an alpha wolf shifter should have smelled her even though she'd flattened her body in the farthest corner of the cage when they'd passed.

Hector hadn't so much as paused.

Had Tripoli put her in a spelled cage that shielded her scent?

Did he really think someone was going to show up and rescue her?

Siofra dropped her head to her knees. She'd screwed up so badly by leaving Rory without a note. He would have no way to find her. Scarlett had said she was headed to Vermont after leaving the fort.

If Siofra had not tossed Rory's phone to slow him down, he'd have called Scarlett and possibly spoken to Siofra.

She lifted her head and banged it against the bars, disgusted with her knee-jerk reaction in the hotel room. Yes, she had every reason to doubt most men, but Rory had proven to be nothing like other men or shifters, excluding Baatar.

Rory had been trying to help Siofra when he asked Scarlett to put out feelers for Baatar.

Everything jumbled in her mind, but Siofra knew one thing for sure. If she had confronted Rory and asked him about the phone call, she might not be sitting in a cage and Baatar might not be chained like an animal.

If she ever saw Rory again, she'd apologize. If he gave her the chance, she'd prove she could stop judging him by other men.

The sound of that big Hummer coming back stirred activity. Tripoli's men had delivered Hector in it earlier.

Groaning, she got up on her toes again to see who Tripoli would show off Baatar to this time.

The shifter driving and the one riding shotgun got out and opened the rear doors.

They hadn't done that for Hector. Who could be so important?

Siofra's jaw dropped when Scarlett and Rory got out of the sport utility looking like a pair of lost celebrities. What were they doing?

She had no idea, but her heart did a happy dance at the sight of Rory and she felt a spiral of hope.

That lasted only until she started worrying about Rory and Scarlett being captured, or worse.

When Tripoli walked up to the couple, Scarlett introduced herself as Vivi of New York.

Tripoli said, "Your reputation precedes you. Our mutual friend speaks highly of your ability to represent your clients at auctions. As I told you, I don't allow that at my auctions. I am not Christie's to accept anonymous bidding."

Siofra had read about the famous auction house where wealthy investors sent representatives to bid on expensive collector items, not people.

Unlike the woman Siofra had spent a two-hour ride with to find Baatar, Scarlett now carried herself with the air of someone who bathed in money. "I'll be honest with you, Tripoli. I suggested Adalbert pass on this auction. He's been a client for a long time and is not meant for this … environment."

Rory, aka Adalbert, had been busy studying the ground around him as if dirt might jump on his pants.

Siofra could not believe this version of Rory, but clearly Tripoli did, because he said, "That would have been disappointing."

Scarlett continued, "Had I been able to satisfy his newest request for a specific exotic, I would not be here. But I am and so is he." She turned to Rory, who appeared to pay no attention to the conversation. "Adalbert."

His lifted his head. "Yes."

"I'd like to introduce Tripoli, the collector I told you about."

"Hello, Tripoli." Rory's voice held no emotion. "If you have what you claim, I will consider attending the auction." He brushed his clothes as if dust had dared to settle on him and added, "But I prefer to arrive by helicopter next time, as you clearly have a landing spot."

Tripoli said, "That is not possible. My auctions have the highest security. Even my men do not know the location until we arrive and no one is given coordinates to use for flying."

Rory turned to Scarlett. "You should have known all of this, Vivi. I pay you to know these things and not waste my time."

Scarlett gave him a dramatic sigh. "Give Tripoli a chance to show you what he has, Adalbert. I told you his rules. You said you were willing to attend in person for this particular tiger. I've searched everywhere for the past three years and have never found one until now. If you like what you see, perhaps Tripoli will allow me and your *money* to attend the auction."

Rory looked at her with a smile. "Brilliant idea. That is why you are my number one representative."

"I should be your *only* rep." She glared at him.

"In time. All things in time."

"Three years is enough time, Adalbert," Scarlett groused.

Tripoli cleared his throat and interrupted. "Are you ready to review the exotics?"

Rory ignored Scarlett and turned to Tripoli. "First, do you or do you not have a Siberian tiger?"

That shut up Tripoli, who glanced over at Baatar then back at Rory. "I definitely have a Sumatran tiger and—"

"I said Siberian."

Huffing in an irritated way, Tripoli said, "I wish to show you the Sumatran first and I do plan to offer a Siberian. Every exotic I have is of great value. Tomorrow's event will not be a pick and choose auction, but a winner takes all."

"I could have reviewed everything else before arriving," Rory said, sending Scarlett a sharp look.

Scarlett shrugged. "Tripoli allows no filming or I'd have delivered videos in person, as usual. Tripoli runs this operation. He calls the shots."

That vote of support made Tripoli happy.

Rory gave her a peeved look then turned to Tripoli. "Is the Sumatran solid, no mental issues?"

"He's fine and fierce in battle. He has never lost a fight with any shifter."

Nodding, Rory said in a cocky tone, "I can do something with that one, but I'm most interested in a Siberian."

"There is no guarantee you will end up with any of these animals," Tripoli said with smug confidence. Rory had pissed him off.

Siofra wished she could tell Rory that Hector had been here and planned to win the bid. Or would Hector return with a force of Black River pack shifters to raid this place and take what he wanted? What about Mother Cadellus? Was she in league with Hector, or a different division of that wolf pack?

Rory gave Tripoli a dismissive look. "No one can outbid me if I see something meant to be mine."

Tripoli's eyes lit with greed, having heard almost the same thing from Hector. The bounty hunter appeared close to having an orgasm. "I will have your Siberian for tomorrow."

Looking extremely interested, Rory asked in a hushed voice, "But you absolutely have one?"

Tripoli nodded.

Rory had paid no attention to Baatar, but they'd never met. Scarlett would know Siofra's brother, but she'd not even glanced his way either.

"Very well, the Siberian will be mine," Rory claimed with no more emotion than saying he would buy a loaf of bread. He suggested, "You could save yourself the trouble of moving the Siberian and Sumatran to a new location if you gave a demonstration right now and named a price."

Vivi sucked in a short breath. "Adalbert! He can't do that. What if he'd sold the tiger to another client before you arrived? You'd be pissed! Tripoli would never risk his reputation by such a move."

"She is quite correct, Adalbert," Tripoli said, sounding pleased to have Vivi on his side. "You will have an opportunity to bid tomorrow."

"Vivi," Rory said.

She asked, "What?"

"I am not speaking to you, but clarifying that you—Vivi—will bid in my place. This has been an exhausting trip. I care nothing for the battle, only the spoils of victory. You are my general for tomorrow."

If Siofra had no idea who Rory and Scarlett were, she'd be sold on his act. He depicted an eccentric lunatic too well.

What if Tripoli had accepted his offer to buy the shifters outright?

Scarlett seemed to know these people, which bothered Siofra on one level but not enough to question a potential rescue.

Turning to Baatar, Tripoli waved a hand at him. "This is the Siberian tiger."

Rory studied Baatar as one would a slab of beef hanging in a cooler. "Can he shift in those chains?"

"No. The ones around his neck and waist are titanium. If the chains did not cut him in half when his massive tiger belly came to the forefront, the cuff at his neck would behead him."

"Hmm. A sound way to keep your cattle." Rory started toward Baatar, but Tripoli stepped in front of him. "Do not step over the rocks circling him."

Backing up, Rory looked down. "You have put a spell around him?"

"Yes. Scents attract other animals and unwanted shifters."

"I see. I wondered why I could not scent him. Do you have a video of him shifting?"

"No."

"Why not?"

Tripoli said, "He has no alpha to force the change, but I have an incentive. I wish to use it only one time and that will be tomorrow."

Baatar's eyes had not moved from staring straight ahead, but they shifted slightly to Siofra. She needed no other confirmation that she would be the incentive.

Rory clarified, "You are *sure* he will shift at the auction?"

"Of course."

Appearing satisfied with that explanation, Rory told Tripoli, "Very well. I would like to see the Sumatran."

Two shifters blocked the path on the far side of the trailers, so

Tripoli led Rory and Scarlett toward Siofra, bringing them close to her cage.

She sat still, curious to see if Rory or Scarlett would notice her.

Scarlett glanced up and dismissed her as if Siofra didn't exist, but when Rory's gaze lifted to hers, they were furious.

He stared at her too long and Tripoli must have sensed something. The bounty hunter turned and asked, "Do you know this one?"

Siofra heard the whip of suspicion in his voice and froze.

Rory huffed. "No. Is she a shifter? There is no scent here."

"Unfortunately no. She was caught much as crabs are trapped in nets intended for fish," Tripoli replied. "I planned to unload her at a different time, but if you wish I will give you a price for this one now."

Rory abruptly said, "Not interested.

She knew he was playing a role and told her heart not to listen, but the words cut.

What if he truly didn't care anymore? Had he only come out of duty to his boss and his fury was about the trouble she'd caused him?

She sat back hard, feeling more alone than ever.

Not for long.

Her female ghost, who showed up occasionally and never spoke, appeared opposite her in the cage. She'd been young when she died if her thirtyish appearance was accurate. She had blond hair held back by a wide cloth band, pale eyes and a pretty mouth. She seemed comfortable sitting there in her usual jeans and T-shirt professing *Live. Love. Laugh.* worn loosely over them and no jewelry, plus always barefoot.

Siofra had given up asking what the ghost wanted after never receiving a reply in her head. Now, she stared at the woman, glad for even translucent company.

The woman had a nice smile. She'd probably been a mental case when she lived, unable to speak, but she always smiled at Siofra as if sincerely happy to see her.

Only a loon would be happy to see Siofra here.

The woman positioned her arms as if she held a make-believe baby, then moved her arms back and forth. She cooed to the non-existent child while looking at Siofra expectantly.

Siofra sighed and kept her voice soft. "I don't know what happened to your baby, if that's what you're asking."

The woman grimaced and shook her head then pointed at Siofra.

A rogue wind blew Siofra's hair back. "Hey, be careful with that finger if it's loaded."

Rolling her eyes, the woman slapped her forehead.

Siofra had never seen this one attempt to communicate even this much. The last time she'd seen her, the woman had held her feet to the ground while Dyson attacked Siofra, then stopped Siofra from running away when the little Toto dog approached on the side of the road.

Checking to each side that no one was near, Siofra said, "Maybe you should try writing in the sand. I'm not good at guessing games."

At the sound of Rory, Scarlett and Tripoli approaching from the direction they'd walked, her ghost vanished. Tripoli sounded exuberant, as if he mentally counted his gold.

Loud talking from the path the Hummer used to travel through the woods drew Siofra's attention to what she considered the entrance.

Four men emerged from the trees. The same ones that had captured her and Baatar. Probably all shifters.

One of them had been pumped up with so much steroid, or whatever shifters used, that his arms wouldn't lie flat on the sides of his body. She could only imagine what kind of monster he hid inside of him.

Because of that creep and the way he'd leered at her, she'd been glad to be shoved in a cage.

Everything had been rocking along quietly until that bruiser walked up to Tripoli, Scarlett and Rory.

He inhaled, expanding his wide chest as if he planned to blow a house down on his exhale.

That would have been so much better than him pointing at Scarlett and shouting, "You're the shifter that brought the caged woman to this guy." He swung his dark gaze to Rory. "And *you* stink of that bitch's scent."

Steroid Guy pointed at Siofra.

CHAPTER 36

R ORY'S SKIN TURNED COLD AS ice during the seconds
that no one spoke after the wolf shifter's accusation.

He and Scarlett were so fucking busted and he had no way to
get to Siofra.

Ferrell banged and snarled to be released. He sent bloody images of body parts tossed everywhere and howled, *Mate.*

Tripoli rounded on Scarlett. "You have one chance to explain
yourself."

This was what Rory meant when he said they'd needed a contingency plan. He'd put a safety valve in place, but Justin and Cole
weren't expected to check in with headquarters until this evening
and maybe not until morning. When he'd called in to inform the
Guardian his trip with Siofra would take him to Maine, Vic had
informed Rory that the Guardian, Cole and Justin were gone,
saying only that they'd be checking in.

Had his people gotten a lead like Scarlett had on the tiger? If
so, his boss would be spending evenings in eagle form while Justin
and Cole covered the ground.

It wasn't even close to nine yet. Rory's backup plan wouldn't
activate until much later tonight after he and Scarlett had left. He
hadn't expected to be unmasked during their initial meeting.

Now he had two issues. One was the netting overhead, which
would make locating this spot difficult even during the day. The
second problem involved time. There was no way he and Scarlett
could hold this bunch off for long.

Scarlett, to her credit, kept her cool.

Rory couldn't even hear her heart rate pick up when it normally would have for someone facing a riled Tripoli.

Growling with undisguised contempt, Scarlett sent a menacing glare to Rory. "Sorry, Adalbert. I didn't make this mess, you did." Turning back to Tripoli, Scarlett pointed to Siofra's cage. "That bitch wormed her way into Adalbert's mansion, working as part of the human domestic staff. She *acted* human, but she's not. Adalbert didn't realize until he'd banged her a few times."

"Eight, to be specific and it was all in *one* night," Rory interjected, sounding like what he'd think an egomaniac would say.

Pinching the bridge of her nose, Scarlett groused, "I can't account for his lack of taste in bed partners, Tripoli, but I can attest to his swift action in calling me to remove her."

Rory crossed his arms and stood calmly as fear for Siofra and Scarlett clogged his throat. He would not save his and Scarlett's ass at the cost of Siofra's. And maybe her brother's, but that bastard was the reason they'd captured her.

Hand on hip, Scarlett continued explaining, "I told her if she went quietly, I'd give her enough money to never come back. That's when she drops a new bomb on me. Says her brother was on the run from SCIS. Unbelievable." Scarlett shot Rory another loaded glare, which he ignored. Undeterred, Scarlet said, "His play toy then begged me to take her to her brother. At this point, I wanted to strangle everyone involved, but the idea of putting a lot of distance between her and us was appealing."

Giving her a dismissive roll of his eyes, Rory said, "These things happen."

She shook her head and with a disgusted voice told Tripoli, "I took her way the fuck up the coast of Maine. Idiot that I am to do Adalbert's bidding, I even drove her there in a piece-of-shit truck I borrowed from a friend to avoid being seen with her. I am not on the SCIS radar and I want to keep it that way." She turned to Rory. "If you ever ask me to do anything like that again, I will not be your number *anything* rep. Told you it was stupid to screw domestic staff."

He gave her an unconcerned look. "I was bored. She was entertaining."

"Nothing is entertaining enough for this shit. You're fucking with my business reputation. I do have other clients."

"None who pay as much as I," he quipped and the conversation ended.

Tripoli had followed the back and forth conversation, saying nothing.

Rory had a bad feeling about the bounty hunter's silence. He turned to Tripoli and admitted, "When I saw her in the cage, I was shocked. I had no idea how Rose ended up here. If I had admitted knowing her when you asked, it would have complicated our business. Nothing interferes with my business. I thought she was gone and she never told me she was related to a shifter. Now that I think about it, I am incensed I did not find the man she was caught with before you did, if he *is* the Siberian." He looked at Tripoli with a raised eyebrow, as though association with Siofra had lowered Baatar's value in his eyes.

Scarlett frowned. "Rose? Her name is Gilda. Where did you get Rose?"

Rory hoped the yellow glasses allowed him to appear embarrassed. "That was my pet name for her. She reminded me of a rose petal that opened into a flower."

Scarlett made a repulsed sound.

Tripoli must have heard enough and he wasn't looking like any of it had sold him. He glanced at the shifters standing around then back to Rory. "We have a problem. While I can accept your explanation, you have undermined my trust. I do not deal with those I do not trust."

Shit. Rory had counted five shifters, including Tripoli, but excluding his caged exotics. Now four more had arrived, and he'd scented those at the woods near the fort where Siofra and Baatar were snatched.

Two were definitely Black River pack shifters. One looked like he'd been juicing on the pack's special brew. Rory didn't like the way that bastard kept eyeing Siofra, either.

The Black River pack was either working with Tripoli or those wolves were here covertly.

Rory would bet on the latter and that the pack planned to raid the auction tomorrow. That would be the perfect opportunity for the Black River pack to capture all the exotics, plus every shifter who showed up or stood around as guards.

He'd give Tripoli the edge if not for the possibility that Cadells would be involved. It depended on whether Mother Cadellus had anything to do with this division of the deadly wolf pack.

Rory changed his earlier lighthearted tone to one that belonged to a man who possessed a dangerous animal. "I can appreciate your concern, Tripoli. Like Vivi, I also have a reputation to maintain and absolutely do not want her barred from any future auctions because I made a bad choice in bedmates. How do we make this right?"

Tripoli's eyes twinkled with a thought that thrilled his black heart. "There is only one way to right this wrong. I will need a show of good faith to reinstate my trust."

Now Rory had to be careful not to allow *his* heart rate to jump. That sounded like they had a potential out. "I am listening."

"One of you will battle an exotic while the other one waits as my ... guest."

Everyone standing in the area knew that this was not a suggestion, but the only way out of this place alive. Rory pinched the bridge of his nose as if considering the offer. While he did, he risked a quick look at Siofra, who looked terrified.

Scarlett's heart rate jumped.

Shit. Before she could fall on any misplaced sword, Rory said, "I accept."

Siofra gasped and it warmed his heart that she would still care what happened to him.

Scarlett cut her eyes at Rory, lips parted in surprise.

Rory gave a casual lift of his shoulder. "This is my fault, Vivi. I knew what I was doing when I got involved with Rose. You did as I asked and I regret having put you in this position. I will take care of this myself. It is not as though my animal has never battled."

Scarlett looked worried and he didn't think she was acting.

All the men laughed, which made sense after Rory had acted like some pampered pussy.

Ferrell continued to bang at Rory's insides. Rory sent his jaguar a silent message. *Wait until I tell you it's time.*

For that, he got more snarling and one word. *Mate.*

Yes, they had to save Siofra.

Mate. Mate. Mate. The word bounced against the inside of his brain.

Ferrell had never repeated words like that. Would Rory be able to manage his beast?

Tripoli lifted a hand and flicked it in a signal to get his men moving.

Two shifters came forward to stand next to Rory.

"Open the hole," Tripoli ordered.

Shifters ran to pull trailers off the plywood and shove them into the edge of the woods.

While they did that, Rory met Siofra's gaze and hoped she could see how much he cared for her in spite of the glasses. He gave her a tiny lift of his lips on one side.

Tears ran down her face.

In a matter of minutes, the shifter team had removed the wood, exposing a twenty-foot-deep hole crudely cut in the shape of a circle of about fifty feet in diameter. A ramp from ground level went down to a substantial gate, the only access point.

The entire area, top, bottom and sides, had been constructed of titanium.

Fuck me.

He now understood Tripoli demanding super security to keep this location hidden.

Rory told Ferrell telepathically, *All we have to do is win this battle. We'll probably face the Sumatran. Tigers are bastards to beat, but we can do it if we work together.*

Ferrell didn't show any sign of listening. He hadn't ceased furiously pounding Rory's insides.

His jaguar had better be the invincible animal he constantly claimed to be.

Tripoli said, "Escort our guest to the hole." Before Rory took a step, Tripoli said, "Adalbert, if you do not survive, I will send both women in next."

Rory jumped on the train to Crazyville with his jaguar at hearing that.

He would kill everything they threw at him to keep Siofra and Scarlett safe.

These beasts would not touch those two women.

Ferrell roared his agreement.

Before walking down the ramp, Rory paused to take off his clothes so he could shift immediately. If not, the predator Tripoli sent in to fight him might be shifted already, putting Rory at a huge disadvantage.

He would shift only if his opponent did. His jaguar was too ready to kill everyone here for Siofra, which would be nothing more than murder.

Naked, Rory marched down to the ramp and caught a last sight of Scarlett standing between two shifters. Her face had lost some of its flush of color, but she stood strong even after hearing Tripoli's last words.

The titanium lock clanged as one of Tripoli's guards opened it. He pulled the gate back for Rory to enter.

One step inside this pit and Rory's skin crawled with the sense of being imprisoned, because this was nothing more than one giant cage. It would be small once another shifter entered and the battle started.

He crossed the space and put his back to the wall opposite the gate, preparing for whatever Tripoli threw at him. He hated to kill a shifter without reason, but he would not fail two women depending on him. He would also not hold his jaguar back to be trounced by that crazed Sumatran he'd seen.

In human form, that tiger shifter had ripped a chunk of hair from his own scalp and laughed while he held the bloody piece. Tripoli had lied about the Sumatran having no mental issues. Rory had no reason to believe Tripoli had told the truth about he and Scarlett leaving alive, even if he won this battle.

Tripoli stepped around to stand at the edge of the hole on Siofra's side, blocking Rory's view of her. Prick.

Siofra's scream pierced Rory's ears. He stretched his neck until he could see her.

She was on her knees pleading, "*Nooooo. Please don't do this.*"

His heart pounded madly.

Chains clanged.

Four men escorted his opponent down the ramp. They unlocked the cuffs and unchained him, pulling the neck cuff off last once Tripoli's captive was inside the hole.

The gate slammed shut and the lock clicked.

His opponent sniffed the air and roared, "You smell of my sister. I will rip you apart."

Rory had to fight Baatar.

CHAPTER 37

 ɑ

SIOFRA GRIPPED THE BARS OF her cage, her entire body shaking.

Rory was a powerful shifter. He'd kill Baatar.

She'd seen his monstrous jaguar. Rory already believed Baatar was a tiger shifter, but her brother couldn't make the impossible happen.

A low growl rumbled behind her. She flipped around to find the over-muscled shifter smiling at her. His eyes glowed more animal than human and saliva dripped from his lips.

He lifted a ring with three keys to show her.

His leering smile got broader.

Siofra looked around. Tripoli and the other shifters were yelling for blood. Tripoli kept shouting, "Shift, you bastards!"

No help there.

But at least Rory was not shifting. He had too much honor to attack a man in human form with his jaguar.

Tripoli shouted, "Bring the Sumatran."

No. That tiger would kill Rory *and* Baatar, unless Rory shifted. Even so, once the tiger ripped into Rory's jaguar, the wounds would not heal.

Scarlett had been moving slowly to this side of the hole, which brought her closer to Siofra's cage. Her guard appeared eager to close in on the action, and wasn't paying attention.

The cage door key jingled behind Siofra.

From the left where Tripoli had been showing off more exotics, two shifters led a man with was cocoa-bean dark skin and eyes that would be beautiful if not for the insanity shimmering in them. His face began distorting as he was led down the ramp. He let out a roar, letting everyone know what was about to be unleashed in the below-ground arena.

Scarlett's gaze slashed to Siofra's and widened.

Siofra shook her head. Her new friend could not do anything.

The door to Siofra's cage creaked as it opened.

CHAPTER 38

ODGING BAATAR, RORY MOVED AROUND the titani-
um-barred enclosure, heaving deep breaths. Even in human
form, Siofra's adopted brother would have crushed a non-Gallize
shifter by now.

If Baatar turned out to be a Gallize, it would explain the load
of power Rory could tell the guy struggled to handle. It also explained the crazed look in Baatar's eyes. That power and a tiger he
couldn't release were tearing him apart.

Rory struggled to keep Ferrell locked inside with his beast just
as crazed over Siofra being caged.

Tripoli kept screaming for Rory to shift.

Ferrell roared for the same thing.

Baatar ignored it all, determined to destroy Rory.

When Rory couldn't imagine anything worse, he heard a new
roar at the gate.

The Sumatran tiger shifter had been brought to the party and
that bastard had already begun shifting in spite of a titanium cuff
around his neck.

Muscles bulged around the cuff.

Baatar spared a glance at the tiger, but didn't back off a step.

Shit. Now Rory had to protect Baatar while defending himself.
He called up his jaguar. Ferrell's need to get out rushed the shift.
His muscles tensed and twisted.

From the corner of his eye, he saw Baatar forget about the tiger
as soon as he realized Rory was changing, the most vulnerable
moment for a shifter.

But as Baatar swung a huge fist, the strike landed on the shoulder of Rory's jaguar. Ferrell swung around and snapped at Baatar's head, backing him off.

Rory told Ferrell, *Don't kill the man. He is our mate's brother.*

Ferrell needed a target right fucking now. Rory gave him one. *Protect Siofra's brother from the tiger.*

The guard shoved the insane shifter into the hole and locked the cage as a massive Sumatran tiger clawed its way out of the man.

Baatar watched both of them and chose to run at Ferrell even though the tiger had not fully changed, damn him.

Ferrell leaped out of the way of Baatar's charge and slammed the almost-shifted tiger into the wall of bars. Rory's animal had never killed a shifter or animal when it was defenseless, but Ferrell believed everyone here was a threat to Siofra.

His jaguar was spot-on and Rory would leave him off the leash as long as he didn't harm Baatar.

Tripoli shouted, "Only the last one standing walks out."

As if Rory would pay attention to that lunatic right now?

Even if Rory walked out of here, Tripoli would claim a greater prize than any in his inventory. He wouldn't know he had a Gallize, but he'd be happy to have captured the elusive Adalbert Wauters and his animal revealed.

He'd auction Rory to the highest bidder.

That would happen only if Rory didn't take him apart first.

Ferrell roared and sent a string of constant words to Rory. *Kill wolf. Kill tiger. Kill fox. Save Mate.* Then more crazy mangled sounds.

Those cheering above them were safe only as long as the cage held Ferrell. His jaguar snarled and stalked around, taking in the threats.

The tiger roared to life and lunged at Ferrell, who met him midair. Teeth and claws gnashed. Pain ripped through Rory, but his jaguar never backed away.

Ferrell didn't know the meaning of quit.

At least Baatar had moved to the side and watched, no doubt waiting to let the two cats tear each other apart, which would benefit him.

Tripoli's men shouted and pumped their fists when the tiger took Rory's jaguar to the ground.

Not Tripoli. He was furious, screaming for Baatar to shift.

Vicious clawing and jaws ripping at bodies went on for a minute then the tiger gouged Ferrell's shoulder. Rory's jaguar laid on his side, breathing hard, and tried to get up, but the jaguar's wounds were seeping blood. Not healing.

Ferrell had inflicted plenty of damage on the tiger, too. Blood ran into its eyes. The tiger shook his head as if trying to clear its vision and reorient.

Not for long. With Ferrell still able to bite and claw, but not on his feet yet, the tiger turned to Baatar and roared at the easy opponent.

It could have been an overload of adrenaline or just the need to protect someone who mattered to their mate, but when the tiger headed for Baatar, Ferrell leaped up and landed on top of the tiger.

The cage door opened and a shifter Rory had not seen entered. He had a head of bushy blond hair and angry, orange-brown eyes.

The tiger struggled to get Ferrell off its back and snapped huge jaws at his jaguar, claiming Rory's attention.

Ferrell caught the tiger across the back of its neck and held on, but he'd need the underside for any hope of ripping out muscle.

A new thundering roar unlike any Rory had heard from a shifter filled the air as the tiger rolled hard to his back to unload Ferrell. The move worked.

Rory's jaguar barely escaped his stomach being clawed open when the tiger whipped around to face the new threat.

Fucking Tripoli had sent a lion in.

Rory's jaguar looked up at Tripoli, who grinned. The bounty hunter said, "Everyone shifts ... or dies."

CHAPTER 39

S IOFRA PRESSED HER BACK AGAINST the bars.

The steroid shifter with her cage door open laughed, enjoying her terror. He said, "Come here, dinner."

She begged for the energy that had stopped the jackal from raping her to come forward.

Nothing, not even a tingle hummed in her body.

Shouting erupted behind her. She looked over her shoulder to see Scarlett in the grip of her guard. Her friend must have tried to run to Siofra's aid.

Tripoli noticed and shouted, "Toss her in the cage with the other one."

Scarlett's face froze in panic, but she recovered as her guard latched onto her arm, dragging her to the cage. Scarlett could shift. Why didn't she?

The sound of wild animals in a frenzy poured from the hole. Were Rory and Baatar still alive? Either of them?

She couldn't help anyone from here.

Facing the shifter leaning into the opening with his hand extended to grab her, Siofra shoved her legs to the side, anything to stay out of his reach.

"Move, fucker," Scarlett's guard ordered as he dragged her up to the cage.

Monster guy yanked his arm out of the cage and whipped around. He growled a demonic sound. "Mine. Back off."

Siofra took in Scarlett's face, where the eyes of an animal glowed. She was close to changing, but holding back. Why?

Now that Siofra thought about it, if Scarlett shifted she'd either face all the guards, who would also shift, or Tripoli might throw her into the hole.

Rubbing her hands together, Siofra pleaded with the universe to help her.

The female ghost returned.

Siofra shouted, "Not now."

Everyone looked at her for a second, then the men returned to arguing.

The ghost glared at Siofra. Great. She didn't have enough to do without feeling guilty for yelling at some uninvited spirit?

Energy tingled in Siofra's hands. She stared at them. Not the mother lode she'd had before, but more than nothing.

The guard holding Scarlett said, "Fuck it. I'm not fighting your hairy ass."

Siofra hoped this did not turn into the worst idea of her short life. She launched herself at the monster shifter while he was distracted.

Time slowed as if the world had a malfunctioning axis.

A lion roared.

Tripoli and his men cheered the fight.

At the same moment Siofra went airborne, Scarlett shoved her guard at the monster shifter. Siofra hit her target, taking him down with the other guard.

Scarlett followed her guard down, punching his throat over and over. He gagged twice and his body went limp.

The monster shifter had begun changing. He struck at Scarlett with a clawed paw, raking the sharp tips down her arm.

"Shit!" Scarlett grabbed her arm. Her head warped.

Siofra wrapped her hands around the monster's neck, which was too big for her fingers to meet. She forced what energy she had into him.

The huge paw of the partially shifted monster froze in midair. His eyes bulged and he made strangled sounds.

Holding her injured arm, Scarlett sat back on her knees. She spoke in a low hiss. "Run, Siofra. You're the most vulnerable of us."

"I have to save Rory and Baatar," Siofra answered, just as quietly, but her words were terse and unyielding.

Scarlett gave her a hard look. "Both of them will want you to be safe. We came in here to rescue you. Don't ruin a great rescue by sacrificing yourself like an idiot."

"You do realize I just took down this shifter?"

Scarlett paused and stared at both shifters. "What'd you do?"

"I don't know. I have a power of some sort. It kills and heals. I wish I could say I ruled it, but it rules me. Give me a chance to help the guys."

Lifting up to look through the cage first, Scarlett squeezed her arm, which had stopped bleeding profusely. She said, "They're all watching the battle, but someone will smell my blood before I can get it fully healed." Coming back to face Siofra, she said, "I'll distract them, then it's all you. I hope like hell you have a plan and you don't die or I'll have an army of apex predators after me."

Not wasting a second to ask who Scarlett referenced, Siofra stood. Adrenaline and power rushed through her. Her heart held a boxing match in her chest.

She had no real plan, but she nodded and said, "Thank you. Be safe."

Standing, Scarlett yanked her shirt off as she kicked her feet free of the shoes. She said, "I won't make it back any time soon to help."

"I understand, but don't get caught."

"Not once I shift." She shimmied out of the tight shorts and the change that had been threatening to take hold happened fast. Scarlett shifted into a magnificent cougar, huge and sleek, except for the scar across its back.

Moving around to stand between the fighting pit and the Hummer, her cougar gave a deep-throated growl of challenge.

Siofra waited to see how the distraction would play out.

Tripoli shouted at his men, "*Fuck! Get her!*"

The guard standing near the gate to the hole rushed up the ramp to Tripoli, handed off a key, then joined the other guards already changing.

Scarlett's cougar took off, getting a head start at a dead run.

Once the shifters raced from the area, Siofra had to act. She went around the back of the truck holding her cage and ran as hard as she could toward Tripoli.

She caught his arms and felt energy push into him as he

wrenched around. She snatched her hands back, because he started shaking, then stilled.

The key fell from his hand. She snatched it up and ran to the ramp, falling down in her need to reach the lock. Jumping up, she looked inside the barred enclosure in horror.

Blood covered Rory's jaguar. Too much to even see the wounds. He fought a huge lion.

Baatar had slashes across his body, but he slammed a fist into the jaws of the tiger.

She had to get Rory and Baatar out of there or they would die.

Shaking like a leaf in a storm, she jabbed the key in the lock, but got yanked back and tossed around to hit the upper part of the ramp. Pain burned across her skin and blood ran down her arm where she'd been cut by claws.

Tripoli stood over her with fangs in his distorted jaws. His eyes glowed with madness.

He would kill her.

She shoved to her feet and he came at her.

Dodging his claws as they reached for her face, she grabbed his arms and screamed as energy surged through her.

She had the advantage of standing uphill from him on the ramp. He stumbled back and back. She went with him, clutching his arms, too terrified to let go.

His back hit the gate.

He shuddered over and over, but she'd let go last time and now faced his wrath.

His eyes bulged. One eye exploded from the socket. Blood poured from his mouth.

Everything blurred for Siofra until she couldn't see anything.

She must have blacked out.

The sound of roaring and Baatar shouting woke her. She blinked and stared into the dead eye of Tripoli. Scrambling back from the gruesome image, her vision cleared and she snapped back to reality.

She had to shove Tripoli out of the way and open the gate.

Pushing to her shaky legs, she dragged Tripoli's heavy body aside and reached for where she'd left the key. "*No, no, no!*"

The key, lock and surrounding metal had melted into one lump of sludge. Her power had destroyed their only way out.

She would lose Baatar and Rory.

A screeching sound in the sky echoed seconds before the silhouette of a massive bird flew above the canopy. Claws shredded an opening a truck could drive through, then a huge eagle dove straight down.

It would crash into titanium bars.

At the last moment, the eagle flared its wings, spun around in a circle and landed at the edge of the hole. She doubted a natural bird could have made that maneuver.

As it shifted, Rory's boss with the eagle eyes took its place, fully dressed in a suit.

Siofra had never seen a shifter with the ability to manifest clothes like that. Rory's boss must have some kind of crazy power or maybe even magic. She yelled at him, "The lock and key are ruined. I can't open it. Rory's jaguar is bleeding out. Do something."

"Not even I can break titanium."

CHAPTER 40

SIOFRA WOULD NOT LOSE THE men she loved. Furious that Rory's boss had not been the rescue she'd hoped for, she shouted, "Rory and Baatar can't survive this."

Rory's boss looked to her. "The one in human form is Baatar?"

"Yes."

"What is his entire name?"

Was he serious? Would that make a difference? "Gan Baatar." Then she corrected it and said, "Ganbattar, all one word. Do something. They're going to die!"

"No, they aren't." The eagle shifter put his hand down on the titanium bar and power sizzled at his touch.

She said, "What are you doing?"

"Opening a small hole in the magic."

"How is that going to help?"

"Watch." He raised his voice and the power in it expanded, shaking the trees and raising chill bumps on her arms. "Ganbaatar, I am your Guardian. By the power granted me by Vercane, the Gallizenae druidess of the Gallize, I command your tiger to come forth now and show itself."

Siofra felt sick.

Everyone was insane.

But as she frantically searched for Baatar and found him, Baatar shoved away from the Sumatran tiger.

Her brother's body arched backward in a painful way. He fell on the ground. His fisted hands unfolded and claws extended. He yelled in pain as bones broke and muscle reconfigured.

She stared. He was *shifting*?

The Sumatran tiger roared over and over, then dropped its head and went for Baatar.

Siofra screamed, "*Baatarrrr!*"

ᘓ

Rory's telepathic plea for Gallize aid had been answered.

The Guardian had found them. He'd heard the Guardian's order and felt the eagle shifter's power rush into the hole, but had ignored everything except the lion he'd been battling. His jaguar's body had been beaten and slashed, with no healing.

Then he heard Siofra's scream just as Ferrell rallied to land a vicious slash across the lion's face, sending the beast backing up.

Ferrell jerked around as the Sumatran tiger leaped at Baatar, who was in the middle of a shift.

What the fuck?

But Ferrell didn't hesitate to lunge across Baatar, taking the hit from the tiger that sent the jaguar rolling over and over.

Pushing to stand on wobbly legs, Rory realized this would be the last moment with his jaguar and he was slammed with deep remorse for losing this animal.

He regretted having never embraced his jaguar and accepted life as a shifter, because his animal stood here prepared to die to protect their mate and her brother. Ferrell did this, even knowing Rory had been willing to give up their lives.

But Rory had changed his mind and wanted a life with Siofra.

He'd clearly changed it too late and would now loose Ferrell as well as Siofra.

How wrong could he have been? He hadn't chosen to be a shifter, but other people didn't choose their lives, either. Many had the good sense to not waste time wishing things had been different.

He would not die without letting Ferrell know the one thing Rory had owed his jaguar their entire life.

He whispered to his jaguar, *Let's make this last stand together as one. I am sorry for all the years I looked toward death, waiting for the mating curse to show up. I was wrong. If I had a chance to do it again, I would show you how important you are to me and how very glad I feel right this minute to be a shifter. To be one with you. You are better than I ever deserved and while I may not deserve Siofra as a mate, you sure as hell did. Let's kick some ass and save her brother.*

A strange energy rushed through Rory unlike any he'd ever felt, but he had no time to think on it as the lion came for him.

Ferrell moved fast, getting between Baatar who still labored with the change and the two beasts after blood.

His jaguar fought with renewed energy, but his hind legs were badly damaged. Blood ran through his eyes from barely escaping the lion jaws, and his chest had been sliced open by the tiger.

Rory's jaguar tried to stand his ground, fighting both the tiger and lion until the lion stepped back and circled around, allowing his jaguar to expend the last of his strength to battle the tiger. Ferrell held his own, then slashed the Sumatran's throat once, twice, then ripped it apart.

The tiger collapsed.

One down.

But the damn lion had been in here the least amount of time and had wisely conserved his energy for the final attack. Rising in the air with huge lion paws slashing, he roared like the king of the jungle he was, but Rory's jaguar still had fight in him.

Dropping to all fours, the lion seemed to grin, taking one step forward at a time, enjoying the hunt.

Ferrell showed no fear, but he was being pushed back to where Baatar's straining body made painful sounds.

Rory still recalled his first time shifting. The Guardian had him in a quiet place where he talked Rory through the shift.

For Baatar to change the first time without knowing he was even a shifter would be bad enough. Doing it while fighting in a cage and crazed from holding that animal in so long? Rory couldn't imagine the pain Baatar suffered.

Ferrell stumbled and Rory couldn't see through his jaguar's eyes. Ferrell blinked, but blood loss had his jaguar fighting to remain lucid.

Wide jaws opened, coming at his jaguar.

CHAPTER 41

SIOFRA COULDN'T TAKE ANY MORE of watching Baatar struggle to change and Rory being shredded. She'd rushed around the circle to his boss. "Do something. Rory can't hold two animals off forever."

His boss's eagle eyes were disturbed. Veins stood out on his head from strain. "I have done the only thing that might save them until Justin arrives to cut the titanium."

From the opening in the netting above, a black turkey vulture flew in like a bomb being dropped and hit the ground hard. It shook its head and managed to stand.

Now this?

Dead eyes stared at Siofra. It's beak opened and the voice of Mother Cadellus called out, "Where is my tiger? You should know that Hector tried to deceive me when he found out where Baatar had gone. He has paid with his life."

Siofra couldn't dredge up any sympathy at that news.

She didn't get a chance to respond to the bird.

Rory's boss had watched the vulture with deadly intent and said, "He is not yours, Cadellus. He belongs to me."

The vulture turned and if a bird could sneer, this one did. "No. We raised him. You cannot just claim him, not unless you are ready to hand over one of yours. Do not dare to think I will stand by while you take one of mine."

"Leave now, before you give me reason to hunt you."

"Yes, come to me, mighty eagle guardian. I wish for that day."

"Only a fool would wish for what I would do to anyone, especially a Cadell who dares to touch those who belong to me."

She started screeching and the eagle guy pointed a finger at the vulture, which exploded into a fine dust.

It drifted to the ground.

Lesson learned. Never doubt that eagle shifter's power.

Siofra asked, "Will she be back?"

"If she does, I will disperse her creature again. If she had Cadells nearby, they would have been here by now."

A new Hummer burst through the woods from an entirely different direction than the one Tripoli's guard's had been taking. Rory's friend jumped out.

His boss boomed at the bear shifter, "Justin, cut the cage door open. It's titanium."

"I'm on it." Justin rushed to drag a tank and torch from the truck to the gate.

Siofra asked, "Will it take long to cut through?"

"No. That torch burns faster through titanium than steel," eagle man said.

When Justin raced past her, Siofra followed him around the cage. From the top of the ramp, the scene inside couldn't get any worse.

The jaguar shouldn't be standing. His legs and body had brutal injuries with blood everywhere. How could he even see through so much blood on his face?

She had no idea, but his jaguar lunged for a final takedown on the tiger, ripping its throat apart. She'd feel encouraged if not for the way the lion waited patiently, not wasting energy yet.

Justin shouted, "The torch isn't cutting fast enough."

She ran down to see what he was talking about. Smoke billowed into her face. She swatted it away until she could see the problem.

The torch would flare against the metal then dim, struggling to burn. Had to be the spell Tripoli used to protect his secret fighting arena.

Rory's jaguar stumbled under a vicious attack from the lion. Justin shouted, "Stand up, Rory. Get up."

But Rory had defended Baatar longer than any one animal should have been able to do against two huge beasts and survive.

A deafening sound exploded from where Baatar had been

struggling.

She couldn't believe her eyes.

Baatar really was a tiger?

Not just any tiger, but a giant Siberian tiger, which leaped over the fallen jaguar and smashed into the lion. What followed was an unbelievable battle with throaty snarling, clawing and biting. Two giants fighting to the death.

Rory's jaguar had battled the lion first, giving Baatar's tiger a hand up in the fight. Baatar's tiger moved with lightning-fast strikes born of raging energy.

It didn't take long to finish off the lion.

The tiger lifted his big head, roaring over and over in triumph.

Then he lowered it and swung toward Rory's jaguar with the same menacing snarl Baatar's tiger had turned on the lion.

Justin moved to cutting the bars. It wouldn't be fast enough.

CHAPTER 42

RORY PRAISED FERRELL. *YOU FOUGHT well, better than well. You did the impossible and battled both of those beasts. I'm proud of you, proud of all you've done even before today.*

He wanted to ask Ferrell for forgiveness, but he didn't deserve redemption after all the years he'd let his jaguar down.

Hindsight sucked, because it played out in the rearview mirror of life where nothing could be changed.

Had things been different, he'd have enjoyed the previous seven years with Ferrell and maybe even a lifetime with a mate.

Ferrell growled painfully low and pushed out, *Love. Forgive.*

Hearing two words, *those* two words, broke Rory. *Love my jaguar, too, Ferrell. If we get out of here and I never have a mate, I will still try my best to keep you alive.*

That's when something special rolled over Rory. He could feel a stronger connection than he'd ever had with his jaguar.

Their bond, which had been missing all this time.

The titanium hole turned very quiet.

Ferrell had been lying on his side. He lifted his head to find the Siberian tiger Baatar had shifted into standing over a defeated lion. Good. Siofra would have her brother and she would help him adjust to being a shifter.

She had a heart so big she could love anyone who earned it.

The tiger roared and put his head down, heading for Rory's jaguar.

Well, fuck. He hadn't expected this.

It would kill Siofra to watch her brother rip Rory's jaguar to pieces.

The Guardian's voice came into Rory's head. *I have tried to reach Baatar, but he's caught in the chaos of his first shift under stress. He probably thinks my voice is just another crazy voice in his head. I can't use my power to stop him. They've spelled the titanium cage. It would take a while to break the spell.*

Rory had never heard his boss sound so upset. He told his boss, *I understand, sir. Thank you for coming. I won't hold this against Baatar. Please tell Siofra that and keep her safe.*

His boss did not offer false hope of surviving this, which Rory appreciated. If anything could be done, it was happening. The Guardian said, *I failed you and your jaguar. I should have known sooner what was happening. I am sorry.*

Not your fault, boss. It's all on me. Then Rory realized he could talk to Baatar. He drew on all the strength he had left to send a telepathic message. *Baatar, I am your friend. You smelled Siofra on me, because I love her.*

The tiger stopped and shook his head as if something clung to him. Then he focused on Rory again.

If that didn't work, nothing would.

The gate clanged and Siofra shouted, "Stop, Baatar," she pleaded. "Don't kill the jaguar. He's mine. *He. Is. Mine!*"

Justin stood next to her, doing his best to cut through titanium bars, because the lock had somehow melted.

Baatar snarled at Siofra as if she understood tiger talk and kept coming toward Rory.

Ferrell struggled to his feet, prepared to meet Baatar standing, but Rory knew without a doubt his jaguar would not harm Siofra's brother. Rory did the only thing he could with thoughts of sparing his jaguar and Baatar.

Ferrell shouldn't have to face this.

Not this time. Rory had to return to his human form and hope Baatar had the Gallize sense of honor built into his animal form, and would not attack a shifter in the middle of a change.

Rory began changing, but it was so slow he had doubts about making it all the way as the tiger moved toward him.

CHAPTER 43

S IOFRA YELLED, "*HURRY!*"
    Justin growled. "I am hurrying." He'd moved from trying to cut the lock her energy had melted and fused to cutting the individual bars.

His boss called out, "Baatar, it is time to change back."

The tiger made no such move.

Siofra asked, "Why doesn't his command work?"

Struggling with the torch, Justin said, "He didn't order him. He only suggested he change. We're normally allowed the time we need to call up the change ourselves. Baatar is lost in his own mind right now. He can't hear the Guardian, who I'm sure has been talking in Baatar's head, trying to help him gain control. If the Guardian forces another immediate change, Baatar may never gain control and would have to be put down. But if Baatar attacks Rory, the Guardian will force his change."

A fourth bar fell away, making a small, box-size opening.

When Justin moved to cut another bar to widen the gap, Siofra put her hands together and dove through the small space. Jagged edges snagged her skin and tore her clothes.

Justin yelled at her, but Siofra was the only one small enough to fit through the opening and get in the hole right now.

Waiting another ten seconds could be too late.

She ran over to stand in front of Rory's jaguar, which struggled to change back to Rory's human body.

Baatar's tiger had been going for the defenseless jaguar, but pulled up short in front of Siofra. He growled and roared at her, slapping a paw against the ground.

She crossed her arms. "You are not a murderer, Baatar. The lion and tiger wanted to kill both of you, but Rory, this jaguar, stood strong to protect you. You will regret killing him for the rest of your life and you will have to go through me to get to him."

The tiger roared, swinging his big head back and forth, the frustrated sound heart wrenching. He pawed at his head, raking the skin with a sharp claw.

Blood ran freely. He shook his head, then lifted it and roared some more.

Siofra hoped he was beginning to understand.

He took another step forward.

Nope, no one home.

Her brother would hate himself forever once he came back to his human form and realized what he had done. He was confused and angry, too gone in this form to know what was happening.

Rory grunted and his body still made sickening noises as he changed far too slowly.

Baatar's tiger opened his jaws wide and she prepared to have her head snapped off.

A powerful arm grabbed her and swung Siofra to the side. Rory cursed at Baatar. "You would kill your own sister?"

Siofra said, "Put me down. I don't think he'll attack me, but he may think you're stealing me."

"No. You're mine. He might as well get used to it right now."

Thickheaded men would be the death of her. Even so, her heart thrilled that Rory still cared so much. "How about we all stay alive and discuss that later?"

Rory hugged her with his least-damaged arm. "He has to change on his own and right now. If he doesn't, my boss will force him and—"

"I know. I heard that if your boss has to do it, Baatar will die."

"Right." Rory said, "I'll put you down. You run back to the gate." He hugged her and whispered, "I love you. If he kills me, don't blame him. He's out of his mind right now."

"No."

"Don't fucking start that."

She looked up at him. "Don't curse at me."

All of a sudden the backside of a big tiger paw slapped Rory across his head.

They both turned to find Baatar's tiger right in front of them.

In a softer voice and with tears in her eyes, she said, "Baatar, I know you hear me. Come back to me."

Insane eyes stared straight ahead.

Eagle man said, "Back away, Rory. I will call up his change."

Rory said, "Please, don't, sir. I won't let him harm Siofra and she knows what will happen if you do it."

Siofra said, "Please, brother. I need you to come back."

The mighty beast dropped his head and shook hard, then began twisting and falling to the ground. In moments, Baatar's naked body lay there.

Siofra slapped her hand over her eyes. "Ew, yuck. I don't need to see that."

Rory pulled her around and kissed her head. She cupped his neck and held on tight.

When he dropped his forehead to hers, he said, "You scared ten lives off me."

"You scared twenty off me."

Baatar's human voice said, "You both make me crazy. Put her down."

Rory sighed and said, "Turn around, Baatar. Your sister doesn't want to see your junk."

"What is junk?"

Justin yelled, "Your balls or your dick, dumbass. Hang on." In thirty seconds, a pair of gray warm-up pants fell into the hole.

Siofra watched Rory's eyes cut to the side. She asked, "Is he decent?"

"Yes." Rory put her down and a pair of warm-ups hit him against his head. "Very funny, Justin."

"It was that or wait until you're out for the boss to clothe you. There's a spell preventing his magic getting past the titanium."

Siofra ran to Baatar, who picked her up, hugging her. He sounded humiliated when he said, "I am shifter, sister."

"I know." She smiled. "But there's good news. I find that I like some shifters."

Baatar's dark daze went to Rory. "You will find someone better."

She wiggled out of his arms and stepped back. "No. I want him."

Baatar said, "He is like me. Not like other shifters. Ha. I see by confusion in your face he did not tell you. You should know what he is before claiming him."

She swung her face to Rory, realizing Baatar had a point. She loved Rory, but she'd heard everything eagle man had said. Did she know all there was to know about the man she'd fallen for?

CHAPTER 44

ORY'S HEART THUMPED PAINFULLY. THAT look on
Siofra's face worried him.

Our mate. Ferrell sent Rory a picture of Siofra with a ring on
her hand. Then he sent a picture of Siofra smoothing her hand
over the jaguar's clean coat.

Then he sent a picture of Rory and Siofra kissing.

The last image was of Siofra with a rounded middle.

Rory cupped his forehead, pleading with Ferrell to cut it out
before he got a migraine.

The images stopped immediately.

Maybe things would improve between them now.

But his jaguar did not understand that Siofra could not get
pregnant. He silently told Ferrell, *Please give me a minute to talk to
Siofra.*

Yes. Happy mate. Happy mate. Happy mate.

Why had Rory complained about Ferrell's limited communication before? His jaguar wouldn't shut up now.

Justin hooted as he finished cutting the titanium. "Got it. You
can all leave now."

Rory glanced over to see the gate open with chopped bars
sticking out along the edges.

The Guardian appeared behind Justin.

That man could move like lightning.

Justin asked, "What about the spell?"

The Guardian said, "It appears the magic had been fed into the
structure and cutting through enough bars destroyed the circuit."

Justin stepped into the cage and then to the side, allowing room for the Guardian, who strode over to stand between everyone. He said, "Siofra, would you please give us a moment."

Baatar clamped his hand on her arm. "No."

Rory snarled and started for them.

The Guardian lifted a hand and everyone stopped.

Even Justin.

"*Now*, you can leave, Siofra. Please wait above," the Guardian said.

She looked to Rory, who couldn't even wink at her. With a last glance at Baatar, who could not move either, she shook her head and walked out of the hole.

Once she was gone, the Guardian released Rory and Baatar.

Baatar raised his fist and shook it at the Guardian. "You will not—"

The fist turned around and stopped short of Baatar's nose. He looked at it cross-eyed for a moment then glanced at the Guardian, who had established his position.

When Baatar's arm fell to his side, he lifted it up and looked at his hand, closing and opening his fingers, then gave up and crossed his arms. "I am slave to no one."

Rory said, "Give me a fucking break. We're not slaves."

The Guardian arched an eyebrow at his language.

"Sorry, sir."

Nodding acceptance of the apology, the Guardian turned to Baatar. "You will be no one's slave. You are correct in thinking we are not like other shifters. We are an elite group of apex predators, to which you belong. You are exceptionally powerful, just as Rory is or he would not have been able to battle a tiger and a lion while protecting you."

Baatar's eyebrows lowered sharply at hearing Rory had protected him. He stared at the ground as if trying to recall everything. When his gaze lifted to Rory, he said, "I remember jaguar standing before I am tiger."

"That's right."

"Why would you do that? You do not know me."

"First of all, we don't attack a human form or a shifter in the middle of change. We're so powerful it would be like a man killing a child. That's murder. Secondly, I knew you were Siofra's brother, at least she considers you one. Why do you think I didn't shift when it was just the two of us in here at first? I would have fought you as long as I could in human form. If it had come down to you or me, I would not have taken the only family Siofra has and leave her alone."

The Guardian said, "I know this is all strange for you, Baatar, but we are a close-knit group. My Gallize take care of each other."

"Gallize? What is Gallize?" He shook his head. "Just make me not shifter again."

Instead of the Guardian explaining how that was not going to happen, Rory's boss asked, "Were you happy before you changed into a tiger, Baatar?"

Siofra's brother didn't answer.

"You had to be suffering," the Guardian continued. "It's amazing you survived as long as you did without changing. I follow all the Gallize shifters from birth. I went to the village where you were born and thought you were dead along with the others who were attacked. No one laid claim to that assault. Now, I believe it may have been Cadells who wanted you merely as a tiger shifter, which your mother and father were. You were born a twin, because one died with your family. That is why I did not know you survived or I would have brought you to me by the time you reached twenty."

"You know my mother?"

"I knew of her. I do not interfere with the raising of children. Gallize shifters become adults before I send our people to bring them to me. When that happens, I explain as much as the future shifter is willing to hear, then I call up the animal. Like Justin who opened this cage, you are a rare Gallize born into a shifter family."

Rory looked over to find Justin had gone back up top. Poor Justin had suffered as a child born into a bear clan but unable to shift with the rest of them. He'd been chided and humiliated growing up.

He'd had the last laugh. His massive grizzly could take on any bear in that clan now.

Hard to say who had had it better since Baatar had lived an equally difficult life. Maybe worse.

Baatar swallowed hard and asked, "Why was family killed?"

The Guardian explained, "Unfortunately, when I sent someone to begin watching over you at birth, he arrived to find the small village raided and everyone dead. I went myself and discovered a tiny infant still in the birth canal. I doubt Cadells ever knew you were a Gallize, but came to poach a rare tiger shifter as he was born. I will help you uncover more about your family, but I know of none who survived."

Damn, Rory had been crushed by the loss of his brother, but he still had family even if he didn't see them.

Maintaining a soothing tone, the Guardian said, "You must learn how to manage your tiger as well as your shifts. I have a place for you to spend time doing that, where you will harm no one. You will have miles of open range to roam and time to work much of this out on your own. If you do, you'll be stronger for it. The sooner you gain control and prove to me you possess this control, the sooner you'll be able to enjoy the freedom you deserve."

That sounded like the Guardian had another place similar to Wyoming, where Adrian still resided while he battled to lock down control of his wolf.

Baatar asked, "What if I do not want to do this?"

"Then I will keep you with me until you can gain control," the Guardian said, his tone making it clear there would be no ifs, ands or buts.

That brought a deep frown from Baatar.

Rory didn't blame him. He carried the highest respect for the Guardian, but he believed it was easier for a new Gallize to figure things out around his peers.

Their Guardian had no peers since the female Guardian had been missing for centuries.

Baatar let out a weary sigh, one that said he'd fought his body for a long time. "At least I do not feel too many things in my head now. Only this ... animal."

"That sounds like a good start. Why don't we get out of here and talk some more?" The Guardian made that request and walked out of the hole.

It took a moment, but Baatar left as well.

When Rory reached topside, he inhaled a breath of blessed

free air.

Baatar had been two steps ahead, but he turned quickly and pointed a finger at Rory. "Stay away from Siofra. She is innocent. Not shifter. No reason to be around shifters."

Rory considered his words and felt a pang of remorse at wanting her to stay with him when Baatar might be right, but then he pushed that away and said, "That's Siofra's decision, not yours or mine."

Without turning, the Guardian said, "Baatar, follow me. I'd like to see you."

The desire to refuse the Guardian was written across Baatar's angry face, but his feet turned and he started walking. He looked over his shoulder at Rory, who grinned at the bastard.

No Gallize could resist a direct order.

That tiger had a tough future ahead of him if he fought the Guardian every step of the way, but Rory's boss had a vested interest in the tiger shifter. In fact, it had been clear that his boss carried a heavy emotional burden from not having gotten to Baatar as an infant.

Siofra stood by one of the two Hummers now present, talking to Scarlett, who wore a T-shirt and jeans. Had she shifted? He'd missed a lot while in the hole.

He stared for a minute, heart in his chest. She'd stood her ground and told Baatar that Rory was hers. He started to call to Siofra, but she looked over at him.

Instead of smiling or waving, she returned to her intense conversation with Scarlett.

His heart dropped further and further until he'd be kicking it any minute when he took a step.

CHAPTER 45

"THANKS FOR EXPLAINING THE TATTOO," Siofra said. Baatar had to accept being a shifter and she had to accept ...

She couldn't think on that right now, because she had a more pressing concern. "When you were telling me about the program you have for female shifters and their young, you said you helped women in need, right?" Siofra asked Scarlett. She hated how her voice sounded shaky, but she'd just looked in the mirror to clean up while she had a moment and her heart almost stopped at what she saw.

Scarlett said, "Sure. Why?"

"What if, uh, I'm the one in need?"

Scarlett gave her an assessing look. "I'm not discounting you, but I don't understand the problem."

Leaning close, Siofra whispered, "Take a look at my eyes."

Scarlett opened hers wide and raised her eyebrows. "I'm looking." Then she lost the silly look and said, "Oh, shit. Your eyes. The right one is now—"

Siofra shushed her. "Not so loud." But at least now Scarlett realized Siofra's two eyes had swapped colors. Someone not paying attention would miss it, but once everything settled down, Justin, Rory and the eagle man would know.

Scarlett mouthed, "I saw a change something like that in Tess's eyes."

"Is she mated to one of Rory's shifter buddies?"

"Yes and she admitted the eye color change was because she's pregnant. Are you, too?"

Keeping watch out for Baatar and Rory, who were both across the open area and busy bitching at each other, Siofra said, "I don't know for sure, but I think so."

"Oh, shit."

"You have no idea," Siofra said. "I can't carry a baby. The Cadells stuck three in me and my body rejected every one, killing the embryos." It hurt to swallow past her thick throat. Siofra said, "I need some time. I don't want to tell Rory, make him feel responsible and forced to make a decision based on this. I will probably lose the baby ... soon. That way I can wait until he decides about his future and we can figure out whether I'm in it."

"I can find a place to put you up, but you might want to keep this from Baatar, too," Scarlett suggested.

"My sister keeps nothing from me," Baatar said, walking up. "What is going on?"

Siofra jumped.

Scarlett scowled. "Don't sneak up on her. This is none of your business. We're having a private conversation so back the hell up."

He crossed his arms. "No. You leave."

"Please, Ganbaatar," Siofra said, using his full name as she did when he got overbearing.

"No. You tell me anything. I am brother."

Taking a step toward him, Scarlett said, "That does not give you the right to interfere with Siofra's private conversations, *Gan*."

"Yes, it does. Name is Ganbaatar," he said.

Siofra rolled her eyes at that. He never used his whole name.

Scarlett and Baatar were locked in a glaring match.

"E-*nough*," Siofra said, pushing them apart. "Thank you, Scarlett. I'll get in touch with you later."

Scarlett's face softened when she turned to Siofra. She pulled out a card. "You said you memorized my number, but take this in case you forget it. You can call it any time, day or night." Tossing a disgusted look at Baatar, Scarlett added, "Call me as soon as you have a moment *alone*. I can help you go wherever you want."

Undeterred by Scarlett's last dig, Baatar said, "Siofra will not be alone. She has me."

Scarlett had started walking off, but turned back. "I'm not seeing that as a positive at the moment, *Gan*."

She continued on until she reached Justin, who told Scarlett, "Cole said SCIS is looking for you, but Tess covered and said you were on a case for her."

"His mate is a good woman. I'll check in with SCIS once I get out of here and grab a shower."

Siofra warned Baatar, who had been watching Scarlett, "Don't be mean to my friends."

Looking puzzled, he said, "You did not hear her? She is with SCIS. They hunt shifters. We don't associate with her kind."

"Evidently we do, because Scarlett is my friend. You should be thanking her. She did bring me to you. Without her and Rory risking their lives to come for us, you would be auctioned off and probably tortured to make you a tiger, which clearly would not have happened. I would be sold to someone. Did you forget about them coming here voluntarily?"

His big shoulders moved up and down with a heavy breath. "I had bad time in head while chained."

Siofra filled him in quickly, right down to Scarlett racing out of the camp to draw all the shifters away except Tripoli. She finished by saying, "Not only did she pull them out, but backtracked and dealt with each one alone."

"I owe apology." Admitting that clearly pained him.

It didn't stop Siofra from taunting him. "Hope you enjoy the taste of shoe leather, brother."

"I do not eat shoe."

"It means uh... you have to eat crow, admit you were wrong."

"Oh. I will wait for this meal."

When Siofra looked over at where Rory stood with his boss and Justin, Baatar turned to see what took her attention. He said, "You must make smart choice, sister."

"I know. I'm working on it." She'd had a moment of thrill when she saw her eyes had switched colors and knew in her heart she was pregnant.

Then reality hit her between those very same eyes.

Rory had said he loved her, but he had yet to say he wanted to mate and she was bound to lose this baby as she had the others.

CHAPTER 46

W HILE RORY STOOD WITH THE Guardian and Justin, he
waited for Siofra to come to him. He didn't know where
they stood. She'd looked unsure when Baatar had called Rory out
for keeping his identity secret, but she would understand.

His mate was intelligent.

Being a Gallize could not be a deal breaker for her taking a
mate, not when Baatar was one also.

Rory covered his eyes with his hand. He could not keep thinking of her as his mate when he'd never given her reason to think
he *wanted* a mate.

She put a hand up in Baatar's face and walked around the other
side of the Hummer.

Too far. She was too far away.

Rory couldn't hear the Guardian or Justin. The farther Siofra
went, the more his link to her shrank.

Baatar followed her around.

Rory interrupted Justin who had been talking quietly with the
Guardian. "Where are Baatar and Siofra going?"

The Guardian and Justin could take that as Rory just being curious about the newest Gallize member of the team, but one look
at his boss told Rory he had fooled no one.

Justin said, "We were just talking about Baatar. If you had listened, you would have heard the Guardian say he wants to take
Baatar to Wyoming and introduce him to Adrian."

"What?" Rory searched their faces. "Put a crazy tiger with
Adrian's insane wolf?"

Justin held his hands up. "I'm not in charge. I voiced my opinion and was overridden."

The Guardian angled his head in his birdlike way. "Are you questioning my decision, Rory?"

"No, sir. Never. I just ... we want Adrian back."

"As do I. It may do Adrian good to be responsible for someone other than himself."

Great logic unless the next time someone showed up in Wyoming there was either a wolf or tiger hide stretched across the partially rebuilt cabin Adrian had burned to the ground.

Rory gave up trying to be subtle. "What about Siofra? Where is she going?"

Justin said, "I don't know, but when I was putting the tank back in the truck I heard Scarlett tell Siofra she could help her go wherever she wanted."

Scarlett was not taking his mate anywhere.

His jaguar growled to go after Siofra and the sound was more longing than angry.

Standing here with her out of sight was more than Rory could take. He walked away.

Justin called, "Rory? We're not done yet."

Without looking back, Rory said, "I'm done."

The Guardian literally appeared in front of him. He didn't teleport, but that man moved fast. "Where are you going, Rory?"

"I need to see Siofra, sir." Rory tried to step around his boss, but with a lift of his hand the Guardian put up an invisible wall.

Rory growled, which was stupid when the Guardian could close his throat. Speaking through clenched teeth, Rory said, "Please get out of my way, sir."

"Not until we have finished speaking."

Dammit. He stepped back in front of his boss as a show of respect. "What do want to talk about, sir?"

"Your reason for going after Siofra."

The muscles in Rory's jaws flinched with grinding his teeth. "I want to make her my mate, but I would like to ask her first before I announce it."

Sighing, the Guardian said, "You must be whole to do that or you'll damage your jaguar even more."

"My jaguar and I are now one," Rory said, proud of that statement. He pulled up his shirt tail and held his other arm wide, exposing where under the crusted blood were signs his body was mending on its own, and quickly. In fact, quicker than he'd ever healed even in the early days of being a shifter.

The Guardian asked, "You're saying you and your jaguar did that and not Siofra?"

"Correct, sir. I'm happy to be a shifter and proud of my jaguar. It's hard to explain, but I now realize I've hated myself for a long time. That's changed. I like being alive and having a future. It took me almost losing my jaguar to realize how much I cared about him. I've been fortunate he's been there for me so long. Now, I'll be there for him, too."

The Guardian nodded. "Well done. Not everyone could have done that."

"Thank you, sir. I want everything life has to offer for as long as I can live it."

"That makes me very happy, Rory."

"Now I need to talk to the woman I want to mate."

"While I am quite pleased to see you and your animal joined as one, I have a new concern," the Guardian said. "We may not be human, but we are men of honor. I am not sure you have considered what it would mean for a Cadell woman to take a Gallize mate, if Siofra is Cadell, as I suspect."

"She is. I saw the tattoo confirming it. She may have their mark, but Siofra's not *really* a Cadell," Rory argued. He would not categorize her with his hated enemy.

"But I am, Rory."

Rory and the Guardian turned to find Siofra standing there, eyes downcast. "I'm half Cadell, at least. I talked to Scarlett about it and she said she'd help me find out the truth. I know my father was Cadell, because Scarlett explained how the fathers mark their daughters."

"Scarlett knew this?" the Guardian asked, just as surprised as Rory. Clearly, the Guardian had more to learn about their new intel resource.

"Yes," Siofra confirmed. "That explains my father, but my mother ... I don't know. He said she abandoned us."

Rory asked, "Do you know if you have an older sibling?" Sure, she was Cadell, but he'd never known a Cadell born with so much power to be overlooked by that group. It probably happened because Siofra's power didn't surface when she was younger.

Her lips moved into a frown. "Not sure why you'd want to know that, but I recall my father saying my mother took my brother and left. He would have been older than me."

Rory checked the Guardian's face to see understanding dawn there.

Sounding heartbroken and still unable to meet his gaze, Siofra said, "I'm sorry I didn't trust you, Rory, and give you a chance to explain about your phone call with Scarlett. I am going to do my best to let go of my past and judge people around me based on their actions, not someone else's. Now you know everything about me. I don't fit into anyone's world. Thank you for saving Baatar." She turned to walk away.

Rory pushed against the Guardian's invisible wall to find it gone. He rushed after her with his emotions tangled into knots.

Cadell or not, Rory knew the only thing he had to know and that was how much he needed Siofra. Not as healer, but as his mate. He called out, "Don't go, Siofra."

She turned back and rubbed her forehead. "Why?"

He walked over and stopped short of reaching for her. Damn difficult, but he wouldn't hold her unless she gave him an indication she wanted to be held. He had to find the words and not screw this up. "First, I want you to know that my jaguar and I are bonded like never before. We're able to heal."

Her face lit up, but she still wouldn't look at him. "That's wonderful, Rory."

He smiled. "That means I don't need a healer."

Her face fell, but she recovered. "Hey, really good news."

"I'm glad you think so, but there's one thing I need above all else."

"What?"

"A mate."

Her lip quivered a second. "Thought you said you never wanted a mate."

What had he done so wrong that she wouldn't even look at him right now? "I did say that before I figured out a lot of things, like the fact that I no longer hate being a shifter. I had to be whole before I could ask anyone to share a life with me. I want someone to stand by my side and build a home with me. Someone who calls me on my shit and makes me laugh when no one else can. Someone I can take care of in return. Someone who loves my jaguar. Only one woman can fill that role and it's you. I want you as my mate ... if you'll have me. My jaguar loves you and I love you, Siofra, more than I've ever loved anyone, including my family."

Tears spilled from her eyes.

His jaguar had settled down and Rory could feel his animal purring.

She might deserve better than a surly jaguar shifter, but Rory wanted a chance to show her he could be a loving mate.

He wanted everything with her.

"You still want me even though I screwed up?"

"Are you kidding?" he whispered. "I've screwed up almost everything for half of my life. Baby, you're the best thing that's ever happened to me and my jaguar."

Her throat moved with a hard swallow. She held back her tears and pointed out, "You don't want children, but I do."

Giving her a wobbly smile, he said, "That's another thing. I want them, but only with you. I know you can't have any. We'll adopt. Nothing will stop us from having a family."

Now the tears poured. "I love you, too, Rory, but I am a Cadell. We both know it now."

"Does it bother you that I'm a Gallize?" he asked with a load of worry. Could that be deal breaker for her?

"No, of course not. I'm the one with the bad blood. Scarlett told me the truth about them. They're horrible people and I was born one."

He wondered how Scarlett knew so much about the Cadells, but that question was for another day. Right now, he needed Siofra to know just how he felt. "Your blood is beautiful. You're not like the Cadells who have tried to extinguish us for generations. Plus, you're now our new secret weapon who can coach us on what they do. You're not less, but so much more. Your energy is powerful enough to bond with mine and I'm not sure the run-of-the-mill Cadell could even do that. I want you forever, Siofra. Will you accept me as your mate?"

She finally raised her watery gaze to his, gripped the hands he held out to her, and stepped up to him. "Yes. I accept you as my mate."

Power spun up between the two of them and shot out from where they stood. Bright light flooded overhead, exploded and sparkled down around them.

Rory could feel her energy bind to his and flood his body in a way unlike his Gallize power alone, even more powerfully than when he'd joined fully with Ferrell.

Her face glowed and she gasped. "That was incredible."

She'd taken his energy in to bind with hers. She leaned up and kissed him. This was no mere happy kiss, but one of a forever union.

The kiss continued until the sound of cheering broke through.

Rory recalled cheering for Cole when he'd witnessed Cole and Tess bonding, but he'd had no idea just how magical it had been for two souls to unite as one.

Baatar strode up. "Siofra? Are you sure?"

"Very. I love Rory."

Grumbling a moment, Baatar sent Rory a menacing look and warned, "You had better never hurt her."

Siofra glowered at him. "Way to ruin a great moment. Go away, brother, or I will make you regret those words. Go stand with your *other* brothers."

Baatar scowled harder and stomped away.

Turning back to Rory, Siofra said, "Did you mean it about the children?"

Now Rory groused, "Do you think I'd lie to you, especially about that? I know you think you're infertile, but we're bonded now. That might make a difference. I'm ready to prove everyone wrong," he said in a husky voice. "In fact, we can start working on making a baby as soon as we get alone."

Nibbling on her lip, she whispered, "Too late. We might have one on the way."

"Really?" Then he squinted at her and noticed what he'd missed earlier.. "Your eyes changed colors."

"Yes," she squeaked. "Sure you aren't angry?"

"Hell no! I'm amazed and in the best way. Wait, did our bonding hurt the baby?"

"No. It's hard to explain, but I can feel the bubble of a small new life energy inside me." Her eyes overflowed again. "I never felt that the other times. No guarantees, but I hope this one survives."

"I hope so, too. Best fucking Friday ever." He lifted her and kissed her again, then turned to his brothers, which now included Baatar. "Meet my new mate, Siofra."

They applauded and yelled again.

Baatar stood off to the side, arms crossed, undecided.

Then Rory added, "Oh, and we're expecting."

"No shit?" Justin shouted. Then he groaned. "I'm gonna catch hell from Eli. I want time off, boss."

The Guardian wore a grand smile. "You will have time to catch up, Justin."

All that chatter brought Baatar out of his stormy mood. He unfolded his arms and started for them.

Scarlett came rushing up to Siofra. "Are you sure you want to do this, because I could help you?"

Rory's arm tightened around Siofra, who laughed and told Scarlett, "This is exactly what I want, more than anything. He is the father I want for my children."

Baatar stepped up and ordered Scarlett, "Leave sister alone. Do not ruin special moment."

Siofra rolled her eyes.

Scarlett wheeled around on him. "Don't try to tell me what to do, tiger. I've been a shifter longer than you, so you don't scare me."

Rory complained, "If you two aren't going to congratulate us, then please move on."

Baatar dismissed Scarlett and hugged Siofra. He told her, "I will make best uncle ever." He looked over at Rory. "You had better be best father ever."

Siofra said, "Stop threatening my mate."

Rory laughed. When she gave him an arched eyebrow, he said, "Never thought I'd be so happy to be mated. Baatar just needs some time to acclimate to all of us."

The Guardian walked up and everyone backed away from

Rory and Siofra as if an invisible arm had pushed them a few steps.

Baatar gave the Guardian a wide berth.

Yep, that tiger shifter had a few things to learn about the Gallize and their boss.

Addressing Siofra first, the Guardian said, "I have observed many unions over the years. Your power is quite special."

She smiled. "Thank you. I'm just glad it was strong enough to bond with Rory and happy you all seem to be accepting."

Gifting her with a smile that could belong to a doting father, the boss said, "There is no doubt you were powerful enough. I believe you just may be a Gallize female."

A hush fell over the crowd.

Rory swallowed. "Truly, Guardian?"

"It is possible. That explosion of power between the two of you was as genuine as any I've seen. We don't know who her mother was, but we may find out." Speaking to them both, he said, "Knowing that you are mated and expecting a child are the greatest gifts I could wish for two people who love each other. Welcome to the Gallize family, Siofra."

CHAPTER 47

Ꮋ

SCARLETT HEADED TO THE BOUNTY hunters' Hummer, which she'd take back to the Mercedes sedan she hoped was still there.

So Rory and his friends were Gallize, enemies of the Cadells. This whole trip had produced lots of significant intel.

She must have gained a new level of respect. The Guardian, aka the powerful eagle shifter, had shared his title and invited her back to become acquainted with all of the Gallize in the southeast.

He wanted to introduce her as being an ally of the Gallize.

That new status would come in handy with the cases she took on.

But right now, she needed to get to the phone she hadn't brought with her for fear of it being taken or damaged. When Rory said it was his best Friday ever, she'd panicked a little. She never went more than a day without checking at midnight eastern time for a particular message, and prayed she'd find none tonight.

"You."

She stopped at the arrogantly spoken word, when she should ignore the irritating tiger shifter. Turning around, she crossed her arms and upped her don't-fuck-with-me look in case her negative body pose didn't get through his thick head.

Wild dark hair fell around his head and his face sported a dark beard. If she didn't know him to be an asshole, she might think he was sexy.

She'd met plenty of sexy jerks in her time. "You? Is that how you address everyone?"

He came to a stop too close. The man had no sense of personal space. "No."

"Really? Why did you use it with me?"

"Because you are you." After dropping that illogical nonsense on her, he changed the topic. "Sister says you help her."

"Yep."

"She said you help us."

"Yep." She could have said she only did her part and that everyone had to step up to win today. She could have even said he had fought well.

But she didn't.

Jerks didn't need any additional ego stroking. They did the backstroke better than any Olympian.

"I owe debt. Tell me what to do. I pay debt."

He felt beholden to her? Oh, this was rich.

She considered the things she could make him do like paint her toenails or wash her clothes ... but in truth that would be a poor way to accept his offer.

Acting like a bitch would only lower her to his level.

She didn't like to give a jerk the benefit of the doubt, but this one was Siofra's brother and Scarlett was now an ally of the Gallize. She knew where to find him.

Also, nothing better than an open-ended IOU in her pocket.

He waited silently.

Running a hand through her hair, she said, "I'll keep that in mind and let you know if there's anything you can do for me."

His eyes darkened and his mouth curved into a wolfish smile.

Her body reacted to the hungry ogle.

Damn tiger and stupid body getting aroused over *him*.

Then he sucked in a breath and his nostrils flared. The bastard knew the effect he'd had on her.

She'd nip this right now. "On second thought, don't hold your breath waiting to hear from me. If our lives never cross paths again, mine will be better for it."

She left him with his mouth open. Confused him, did she?

Score.

By the time he figured that out, she'd be gone. Her achy body could just calm the hell down. Nothing would ever convince her to trust a damned tiger shifter.

Not again.

CHAPTER 48

Three days later in Virginia

SIOFRA HELD HER HAND OUT the open window of Rory's Expedition as he drove them through gorgeous Virginia country. Air flowed through her fingers. Rory kept the windows down when it was pretty like today, because he understood how she couldn't get enough fresh air.

It smelled of freedom and happiness. She took in everything on the drive and mused, "Richmond is beautiful. Do you miss it?"

"Sometimes."

Rory would be a work in progress, same as she was. He did his best to open up, but the trip to his hometown had been her idea.

She could tell he didn't want to go, but he'd do anything for her as she would for him. What she hoped to do for him this afternoon was bring closure so he could heal parts neither Siofra nor his jaguar could heal for him.

Chilly air rushed across her neck. Not from the open window and not the normal kind. Siofra glanced around.

The female ghost she could never speak to, who had appeared in the bounty hunter's cage, now rode with them, cross-legged in the backseat. Same jeans and *Live. Love. Laugh.* T-shirt on. Her hair band had not changed, nor had her bare feet

Siofra had explained to Rory about seeing ghosts and sometimes communicating with them. Instead of looking at her as if she were crazy, as she'd feared, he'd called it a gift and thought it was cool. He said it made her even more special. But she hadn't mentioned the ones that hung around regularly like this one, and she didn't want to bring it up now. Rory had plenty to think about right now without alerting him to unexpected company.

For the first time, two things happened that shocked Siofra. The translucent woman smiled, and she spoke in Siofra's head.

I felt your power, Siofra, when you joined with your mate.

Siofra glanced at Rory to be sure he hadn't noticed anything, but he was deep in his own mind, wrestling with painful memories.

Siofra tried communicating with the woman mentally. *Why have you never spoken before now?*

I did, but you couldn't hear me. Your Cadell energy interfered, but your Gallize power has now risen to the surface and is dominant.

Siofra considered that this woman knew so much about her and asked, *Who are you?*

I'm your mother.

Hot tears hit Siofra's eyes, and she blinked hard, taking a few breaths to fight them back. She flashed back to this woman rocking an invisible baby in the cage at the auction, then pointing at Siofra. Well, duh. No wonder this ghost had seemed so frustrated. She'd been trying to tell Siofra even then.

Siofra's head swirled with questions, but one popped out. *That means you have to be Gallize, right? But why did you ever get involved with a Cadell?*

I did not know I carried Gallize blood when I joined with your father. My father pushed me on him to get rid of me and I was so young I did as I was told. Your father gave our first born, my son, to the Cadells while I was pregnant with you. I never let him near my body again.

You didn't want me?

Of course I wanted you, her mother quickly said. *I did not want him to give another child to the Cadells. He was excited about a female. At that point, I realized it was for all the wrong reasons.*

Siofra realized something. *You didn't abandon me, did you?*

No. I tried to run with you. He found me and … beat me badly. I didn't recover.

That miserable dog.

Rory turned to her. "What's wrong? I can feel that you're upset."

Life with a shifter would make keeping secrets tough. Siofra wanted to share all her secrets with Rory, but she'd spent the last three days getting him to Virginia. She would have plenty of time to share this with him.

She smiled and drew a calming breath. "I'm not upset, honey, just excited about our future and still anxious about the baby."

He gifted her with one of his smiles and pulled her close enough to kiss her without losing sight of the road.

She patted his arm and he went back to driving and frowning again.

I must leave, Siofra, her mother said.

Why? Siofra was careful to keep her breathing even and not alert Rory again.

Over the years, I would force myself to take some form when I could so I could find you. I have fought against going to the light for too long. I did not want to leave you alone, but you are safe now. More than that, you are powerful and have a good man. I am proud of you.

Siofra fought the tears that wanted to roll. Rory was too close to their destination. Smiling when her heart broke for the woman who had loved her, Siofra said, *Thank you for being my mother, my personal guardian, and for giving me life. I will miss you.*

It was my honor. I will miss you, too, but your baby girl will have my light blue eyes.

Siofra almost gasped and silently asked, *My baby will live for sure?*

Yes.

What is your first name? Siofra asked as her mother's image began to become more see-through.

Devany. I must go. I will always love you, my baby girl.

It took everything she had to not react. As Siofra watched, her mother faded until a tiny light sparked and vanished. Her heart broke a little.

Rory looked around. "Did you feel anything?"

"Like what?" Siofra asked, concerned that he'd freak out. She needed time to process this for herself and could wait until after this trip.

"Ah, it was nothing. Forget I asked."

Happy to do that, she sat back and thought on all the times she'd wondered about her mother. She mulled over the times she'd seen her mother's ghost and smiled to herself.

Then she sat up and kept watch. They were close to their destination. Time would come soon for her to share with him about her mother and that she had a name for their little girl. Devany. Once Siofra had a chance to tell him all about her mother's spirit and this meeting, and he knew where the name came from, she had no doubt her mate would be thrilled.

Her heart felt lighter. That's what closure should do for a person. She felt giddy with the knowledge their child would live, because she believed her mother. The baby had already lived for three days, longer than any of the Cadell attempts.

She hoped she was right in pushing Rory to find his own closure, because he was turning into the cemetery where his brother had been buried. Rory had not made it to the funeral and still felt guilty for not being there for his kid brother.

Once they parked, he took her hand and led her around as he searched for the marker.

When they found it, she noted, "Fresh flowers. Someone else has been here."

Rory's voice was thick with emotion. "My mom probably."

She wanted to make this easy for him, but buried feelings of guilt were never easy. "Tell me about Tyler."

"He was a good student, strong athlete and out to save the world."

"Sounds like someone you'd want for a brother or son."

Rory didn't reply at first, then said, "He was the best of us three boys. I had issues. I didn't realize until later they were early warnings of what Baatar ended up dealing with, but that doesn't excuse letting Tyler and my family down."

If she could not get Rory to forgive himself, this wound would stay with him forever.

While she struggled with a new question to move the conversation in the right direction, she felt energy form next to her in a chilly cloud.

A young man who favored Rory stood there. Could that be his brother?

He looked barely twenty. His gaze moved to Siofra. He asked, *Can you hear me?*

Yes. She asked, *Are you Tyler?*

He nodded, staring over at Rory. *I wait here every day for Rory. I didn't think he would come and I'd eventually disappear. I am so sorry for what I did to him.*

Siofra couldn't believe this. She had to figure out how to relieve both of them of their guilt.

She said to his brother, *Rory doesn't blame you for anything.*

Rory's hand reached for hers and she wondered if he could feel his brother. He squeezed her hand.

His brother said, *I know. Rory blames himself for me. I heard my family talking about it.*

She needed to do something. She asked the brother, *Would it be okay if I told him you were here?*

Tyler leaned forward to look harder at Rory. *What if he runs away?*

She said, *He won't go anywhere without me and I'll stay.*

Okay. His brother straightened.

Squeezing Rory's hand, she said, "Babe?"

"Yes."

"Uhm, your brother wants to tell you something."

Rory let go and jumped away. "What? Where is he?"

"Right next to me, big bad scary shifter."

"Shh! He doesn't know."

His brother said, *Yes, I do.*

She repeated that.

Rory stared at the headstone then at Siofra. "How could he know?"

"Does it matter?" she asked, wanting to stay on topic.

His brother said, *Tell him an older man with strange eyes, almost like eagle eyes, comes sometimes to talk. He can't hear me, but he tells me how you are and the many great things you've done.*

Softening her voice, she said, "Sounds like the Guardian has been visiting here to talk, but he can't hear Tyler."

Rory's mouth gaped open.

She explained, "Tyler feels guilty about what happened."

"Why? I'm the one that screwed up," Rory complained in a savage voice. "I'm the one who left him to attend a shifter meeting alone."

Tyler told her, *Ask him if I had died five years later in a car wreck, would that have been his fault, too?*

She passed along the question.

Rory didn't respond.

His brother said, *Exactly. I'm sorry I died, but it was going to happen at some point no matter what. I followed my heart and did what I believed in, which had nothing to do with Rory being here or not. I wanted to learn more about shifters. A shifter murderer killed me along with others that night. Tell him he might be glad to know they were captured and put down. I didn't die because of a shifter and Rory is not evil because he's a shifter.* Looking over at Rory, Tyler spoke as if Rory could hear him. *You're a good man, Rory. You should stop punishing yourself and start living your life. You should visit our family, too.*

She related it all word for word.

Rory shook his head and told his brother, "Our parents will never accept me again after I missed your funeral."

Tyler said, *Give them a chance. You might be surprised at what they're willing to open their minds and hearts to for the sake of not losing another son. Don't make them lose two.*

Rory physically staggered when she said those last five words. It hurt to say the words, but he needed to hear them, and based on what Tyler said, Siofra worried there might not be another chance for these two to fix this.

She'd talked a lot in the last three days to Rory about his family, leading up to asking him for this trip. Once he got used to the topic, he admitted he recalled his mother begging him to come home more often, but his mind had been in chaos.

Rory stomped around a moment, then he squatted down and cried. He'd probably never allowed himself to mourn his brother. She dropped to kneel beside him and put an arm around her mate.

When the worst of it had passed, she pulled a tissue from her purse, because the baby was already triggering her own occasional waterworks.

Rory wiped his eyes and stood, pulling her up and to his side. He cupped her cheek. "Thank you."

"You're welcome, but I think your brother is waiting for you to speak to him again."

Wiping his face and eyes with his palm, Rory stared at the marker since he couldn't see his brother. "I still wish I had stuck around and at least talked to you, Tyler, but I was too embarrassed. I'd become a shifter and had seen how dangerous this world was for humans. I got angry about you exposing yourself to something I couldn't run away from."

His brother asked, *Does Rory like being a shifter?*

She would not answer for Rory so she put the question to him.

He hugged Siofra close. "I do now, bro. Took me a long time to accept it and I almost destroyed my animal in the process, but my savior showed up in time." He kissed her head.

That started a flow of Siofra repeating his brother's words and Rory answering in a relaxed way as if she wasn't even present.

Tyler asked, *What is your animal?*

"A jaguar," Rory said, pride filling his voice.

Wow, I'd love to see it, Tyler said.

Rory chuckled. "Can't do it right now."

What about later? Will you come back and show me?

Pausing, Rory had a thoughtful look. "Sure, I can do that, but ... don't you want to like, cross over?" Those words had clearly been tough for Rory to get out.

His brother admitted, *At some point, but I want to enjoy this a bit more before that. I miss you.*

In a choked up voice, Rory said, "I miss you, too, bro. You have no idea."

When Siofra noticed Tyler's ethereal form wavering in and out, she suggested they come back tomorrow and talk some more. Tyler thanked her for bringing Rory, which touched her.

As Rory walked her back to their ride, he said, "That was ... pretty special."

"Special enough to go see your family?"

"Yes, but not today or tomorrow. Soon though."

That was good enough for her. Now that her energy had bonded to Rory's, she could feel the difference. The dark places were shrinking and the lighter ones were filling in the holes.

Her mate would be a content man, a happy shifter and a good father.

THE END

THANKS FOR READING STALKING HIS MATE. The next League of Gallize Shifters book is **SCENT OF A MATE**. Keep up with all of Dianna's releases by joining her private newsletter list at AuthorDiannaLove.com.

Order any of Dianna's print books (signed!) and preorder upcoming releases (shipped early!) from
www.**DiannaLoveSignedBooks**.com

THANK YOU FOR READING MY new League of Gallize Shifters series. I hope you enjoyed it and would appreciate a review wherever you buy books.

Would you like to order a SIGNED copy of this book, or any of Dianna's print books?

Now you can, plus you can preorder future print books, which are shipped two weeks ahead of the e-book release.

www.**DiannaLoveSignedBooks**.com

To be notified first about any news and special deals, sign up for Dianna's occasional newsletter at
www.AuthorDiannaLove.com

**GRAY WOLF MATE,
MATING A GRIZZLY
and
STALKING HIS MATE
are available now in e-book and print
(order it 'signed and personalized' at
www.DiannaLoveSignedBooks.com).**

All of these books are stand alones, so you can read them in any order. If you'd like to be notified of each future release, just join my Private Reader Community newsletter list on **www. AuthorDiannaLove.com**. I DO NOT share anyone's information. I hate to have mine shared. All I do is send you occasional news and give you special deals and extra content.

LEAGUE OF GALLIZE SHIFTERS
Gray Wolf Mate
Mating A Grizzly
Stalking His Mate
Scent Of A Mate

Order any of Dianna's print books (signed!) and preorder
upcoming releases (shipped early!) from
www.DiannaLoveSignedBooks.com

Dianna writes the
**BELADOR URBAN FANTASY SERIES and the
SLYE TEMP ROMANTIC THRILLER SERIES
(completed for those who want to binge read!).**

⌀

Keep watch for more BELADOR books and her new
LEAGUE OF GALLIZE SHIFTERS coming out soon.

Book 1: Blood Trinity
Book 2: Alterant
Book 3: The Curse
Book 4: Rise Of The Gryphon
Book 5: Demon Storm
Book 6: Witchlock
Book 7: Rogue Belador
Book 8: Dragon King Of Treoir
Book 9: Belador Cosaint
Book 10: Treoir Dragon Hoard
Tristan's Escape: A Belador Novella

Order SIGNED Print Books at
DiannaLoveSignedBooks.com

★To keep up with all of Dianna's releases: sign up for her newsletter on her website.

⌀

**THE COMPLETE SLYE TEMP
ROMANTIC SUSPENSE SERIES**
Prequel: Last Chance To Run (free for limited time)
Book 1: Nowhere Safe
Book 2: Honeymoon To Die For
Book 3: Kiss The Enemy

Book 4: Deceptive Treasures
Book 5: Stolen Vengeance
Book 6: Fatal Promise

For Young Adult Fans...
the explosive sci-fi/fantasy **RED MOON TRILOGY** by
USA Today bestseller Micah Caida
(collaboration of *New York Times* Bestseller Dianna Love and
USA Today bestseller Mary Buckham).

Book 1: Time Trap (ebook free for limited time)
Book 2: Time Return
Book 3: Time Lock

To buy books and read more excerpts, go to
http://www.MicahCaida.com

A WORD FROM DIANNA...

THANK YOU FOR READING STALKING HIS MATE and to all the readers who have written wonderful notes about my new League of Gallize Shifters series. I appreciate your feedback so much! And, yes, I do have more books planned.

As always, thank you to Karl, my rock and world. He handles many things so I can write like a madwoman.

A special thank you to Jennifer Cazares, Stacey Krug and Sherry Arnold for being very early super readers who catch a number of small things missed by all of us even after multiple editing passes.

I want to send a huge THANK YOU to my Super Team peeps who read early versions for review – you rock!!

I appreciate Cassondra's sharp eyes and input, plus all the encouraging notes. Thank you to Judy Carney, who is always ready to help and with a smile on her face. Thanks to Joyce Ann McLaughlin, Kimber Mirabella and Sharon Livingston for being wonderful early readers, too.

Sending a shout out to Candi Fox and Leiha Mann, who support me in so many ways.

The amazing Kim Killion creates all of my covers and Jennifer Litteken saves my butt all the time with great formatting. Much appreciation to both of you.

Hugs and love to Karen Marie Moning, a wonderful and talented woman I think of as more than a friend.

Thank you to my peeps on the Dianna Love Reader Group on Facebook.

I love coming out to visit with you.

Dianna

AUTHOR'S BIO

a

NEW YORK TIMES BESTSELLER DIANNA Love once dangled over a hundred feet in the air to create unusual marketing projects for Fortune 500 companies. She now writes high-octane romantic thrillers, young adult and urban fantasy. Fans of the bestselling Belador urban fantasy series will be thrilled to know more books are coming after Treoir Dragon Hoard, plus Dianna has launched a new paranormal romance series – League of Gallize Shifters. Her sexy Slye Temp romantic thriller series wrapped up with Gage and Sabrina's book–Fatal Promise–but Dianna has plans for HAMR BROTHERHOOD, a spinoff romantic suspense series coming soon. Look for her books in print, e-book and audio (most series). On the rare occasions Dianna is out of her writing cave, she tours the country on her BMW motorcycle searching for new story locations. Dianna lives in the Atlanta, GA area with her husband, who is a motorcycle instructor, and with a tank full of unruly saltwater critters.

Visit her website at Dianna Love or Join her Dianna Love Reader Community (group page) on Facebook and get in on the fun!

Printed in Great Britain
by Amazon

77567598R00200